Whisper Who Dares

Terence Strong

CORONET BOOKS
Hodder and Stoughton

Copyright © Terence Strong 1982

The right of Terence Strong to be identified as the Author of the Work
has been asserted by him in accordance with the Copyright, Designs
and Patents Act 1988.

First published in Great Britain in 1982 by Hodder and Stoughton
A division of Hodder Headline PLC
as a Coronet Paperback

30 29 28 27 26 25 24 23 22

British Library C.I.P.

Strong, Terry
  Whisper who dares.–
  (Coronet Books)
  I. Title
  823′914[F]   PR6069.T

ISBN 0 340 27908 7

Printed and bound in Great Britain by
Mackays of Chatham PLC, Chatham, Kent

Hodder and Stoughton
A division of Hodder Headline PLC
338 Euston Road
London NW1 3BH

Whisper Who Dares

Ducane rolled sideways as the sheet of steel sliced into the earth where he had lain.

Another automatic weapon added to the firepower coming from the car, and Ducane peered through the long grass to see the nun firing a stubby sub-machine gun that had been concealed in the folds of her habit. The front seat passenger fired again at Ducane's position, then swung his gun around to the Land Rover.

'Run, you bloody fool,' he yelled at the nun. 'I'll give you cover! Get down the road while I keep 'em busy!'

Having seen the fate of the other Provo gunman, the nun hesitated for a second. Then as though deciding it was the only chance, fired a final burst from the hip in the Land Rover's direction. Gathering up her habit, she turned, scrambled onto the road, and began running hard towards Eire . . .

'Alive!' Ducane bawled. 'I want him alive!'

Also by Terence Strong

The Fifth Hostage*
Conflict of Lions*
Dragonplague*
The Last Mountain*
Sons of Heaven*
This Angry Land*
Stalking Horse*
The Tick Tock Man
White Viper
Rogue Element

available from Coronet

About the author

Terence Strong, the author of eleven bestselling thrillers, is renowed for his detailed and authoritative research. A freelance journalist and writer, he has a keen interest in international and political and military affairs, and special forces in particular.

You are welcome to visit the Terence Strong Web Page at: http://www.twbooks.co.uk/authors/tstrong.html

AUTHOR'S NOTE

In May 1980 the men of Britain's crack Special Air Service Regiment blasted their way into the world's headlines. For fifteen brief minutes, during the dramatic ending of the Iranian Embassy siege in London, the veil of secrecy had parted to give just a rare glimpse of the shadowy figures whose origins can be traced to the North African deserts of the Second World War.

Yet it may come as a surprise to those who do not know, that the troops of the SAS are not supermen. Most are only average marksmen. Except for the squadron that recruits largely from the Regiments of the Guards, they tend not to be tall. Physically they are more likely to be of average height and wiry, but with an immense capacity for endurance. Many are older than people might imagine. But, most importantly, they are trained to a pitch that the layman cannot even conceive. And they are trained to *think*.

Of course, the soldiers in this book are necessarily fictitious, but their reactions to events and methods of operation are accurate enough.

Actions and dialogue attributed to PIRA members believed to have made up the Army Council in 1976 are, naturally, purely imaginary. However, every care has been taken to draw the characters, their relationships, and attitudes realistically, but inevitably there is some artistic licence.

Although this book concentrates on military and intelligence operations at the time, the reader should bear in mind that, however sickening PIRA tactics have been, the Army Council itself *believes* in the historical and human rights causes for which it fights. And, as such, has proved itself to be a resilient enemy.

Unlike the Princes Gate raid, most exploits of the SAS generally go untold. Actions by the regiment in Malaya, Borneo, Aden and Oman have been reported. More sensitive operations, such as those in Vietnam, have been refuted by political sleight of tongue.

But, with a regimental motto, and a living philosophy like 'Who Dares Wins', it is hardly surprising that other missions have been of an even more 'deniable' classification. And that means exactly what it says.

So have events like those that are described in this book ever taken place? Have SAS hit-teams ever struck illegally at PIRA terrorist camps in the Irish Republic?
Of course not. They wouldn't dare.

Terence Strong
London 1981

For Princess,
and the man from Arcadia,
but especially the lads
of the British
Army and those
long-suffering
Ulsterfolk who
have steadfastly
refused to accept
violence as any
sort of solution.

PROLOGUE

Still there was no sign of them.

In twenty minutes the soldier hadn't moved a muscle. From his concealed position, in the small hillside meadow overlooking the winding tarmac lane, the scene looked deceptively peaceful. The pale, late summer sun was sinking. Its rays scattered low under the trees in the thick, roadside hedgerow to dapple the greenery with spots of gold.

Its surprising warmth seeped through the material of the soldier's camouflage smock. He felt a trickle of sweat gather along his spine. Still he did not stir. Only his eyes, hidden behind the brown faceveil, moved ceaselessly.

There were three other members of the captain's Sabre team hidden in the 'bandit country' of South Armagh.

Just a few yards to his left a bee worked its way around a cluster of buttercups, its sound clearly audible in the absolute stillness. He grinned to himself with satisfaction. Even at that moment the bee was hovering a few inches in front of Corporal John Turnbull's face, totally unaware of his presence.

Below the captain, but some fifty yards to his right, he knew Sergeant Forbes waited in the three-quarter ton Land Rover. But for the moment it remained concealed, backed into the hedgerow and completely disguised by the green and black paint and drapes of camouflage netting. The specially-modified vehicle, with a reinforced chassis, Hotspur armour and smoke dischargers, had lost its bizarre desert camouflage colour that had earned its famous 'Pink Panther' nickname.

Back along the hedgerow to the left the lane disappeared from view beyond a thicket of blackthorn trees.

It was here that the fourth and last member of the captain's team waited. Young Tom Perrot, a soft-spoken trooper from south Dorset, perched amid the purple sloe fruit of the lower branches, oblivious of any physical discomfort. He had only joined Captain Jack Ducane's team two months earlier and it was providing the most excitement, and the biggest test, of his twenty-four years to date.

Already Ducane was pleased with the way he was shaping up, confident to post him as lookout for the car that Intelligence had predicted would approach.

The captain spoke quietly into the mike of the VHF Pye Pocketfone clipped to the front of his smock. "Anything to report, Tom?"

"Not a dicky bird, boss." Young Tom's voice was distorted with static in his earpiece.

"Okay. Don't nod off."

"Boss?" Tom was too earnest to appreciate the legpull.

"Keep your eyes peeled. They'll show soon."

Of course Int. was always getting it wrong; that was the name of the game. You win some, you lose some. In the end you just hoped to win more than you lost. But this time they had seemed pretty confident.

They had been after Cochran for two years now, ever since he'd made a daring escape from Long Kesh, leaving the authorities with a lot of egg on their face. It had been a skilful, professionally-executed job, of which the inmates of wartime Colditz would have been proud. Indeed it was a far cry from the early attempts by the Provos to dig themselves out of the prison. They'd actually tunnelled the wrong way into the centre of the camp. That story had spread ad nauseam through the British Army with the speed of a forest fire. It had provided light relief amongst the troops for weeks afterwards.

But times had changed now, Ducane reflected. As the Army had tightened its grip and picked off its adversaries one by one, the PIRA, losing its widespread support, found itself with a small nucleus of hardened and experienced active service units. The concrete jungles of the deprived urban areas had weeded out the weaklings and idiots. It had been the survival of the fittest, and those survivors now had a wealth of experience and knowledge on which to draw.

More recently PIRA activity had shifted to the border counties, particularly Armagh which was a stronghold of Republican support. Having been eased out of the city areas, the PIRA were fighting hard to maintain their command of the hilly farmland where hundreds of narrow roads and lanes provided their 'lifeline' with the south. In this rugged and uncompromising territory, entire battalions of regular troops might be swallowed up without gaining any semblance of control. Save recalling the Rhine Army, the only practical way to secure the country was by the use of small groups of men, highly-trained in anti-guerilla warfare and able to survive independently for weeks on end. Working themselves into the background countryside, and into the minds of the enemy.

The Prime Minister's announcement in January of that year that men of 22 Special Air Service Regiment were moving into Armagh to put an end to the wave of sectarian killings meant little to Captain Jack Ducane and his team. They had been operating there regularly for months and, previously to that, largely on undercover assignments in Belfast and Londonderry.

The Provos, too, knew they were there, but that was their misfortune. Now the world knew that an entire SAS Sabre Squadron was moving into the area, and Ducane could not deny he enjoyed the squeal of anguish that came from the Republicans at the very mention of the regimental name.

In fact the PIRA became the victims of their own propaganda machine. For, in fact, in the very early days of the latest troubles, SAS operations had been far from successful as new techniques and lessons were learned. Despite this fact, horror stories, generated by the Provos, had the effect of striking terror into their own active service units in Armagh. The sectarian killings stopped almost overnight without the SAS teams needing to do a thing about it.

However the 'thinking bayonets' had set themselves a

target of their own. Armed with five years of hard-earned experience in Ulster, they determined to go for the ten Provo leaders in Armagh. Although Ducane did not know it then, the SAS were to capture four of them and send the other six fleeing over the border before the year was out.

Now it should be the slippery Mr Cochran's turn. That would no doubt delight the RUC. The men from the Royal Ulster Constabulary were very anxious for a chat with that gentleman about the carefully-orchestrated execution of so many of their number. Not even dignified, properly-conducted firing squads following some form of perfunctory trial. Just a hail of bullets in the belly as the victim answered his front door. A merciless butchery that frequently left wives and young children splattered in the entrails of their husbands and fathers if they happened to be standing too close.

Ducane swallowed hard. Unfortunately Mr Cochran was believed to be a current member of the PIRA Army Council itself. A real VIP who was wanted for questioning. Well, they would have him, but the other two, thought to be travelling with Cochran, would have to behave themselves. They were known murderers and they would have only one chance. Otherwise, Ducane had decided, their time had just run out.

His eyes ran over the length of the Mark 5 Sterling submachine gun in his hands, its stout barrel camouflaged with strips of green and brown cloth. A second reversed magazine clip was taped end-on to the first for a quick 'wrist-flip' reload. Sixty-eight 9mm rounds. This could be martyr time.

If they showed.

And if they did, the first thing they would see would be Big Dave Forbes manning the heavy GPMG mounted on the Land Rover that would completely block the road.

Suddenly Ducane frowned and looked up.

Five hundred feet up the Eagle patrol clattered over the deserted South Armagh landscape. At the controls of the

4

old Wessex 2 helicopter, Flight Lieutenant George Seiv-wright felt irritable.

The unremitting glare of sunlight and the warm lager he'd had before take-off had combined to start a headache throbbing beneath the bulbous, white plastic helmet. The bulky armour chest-plate was restricting and uncomfortable.

And he didn't like the Royals' chalk commander who sat below him in the cramped fuselage with his stick of fifteen troopers.

"*I said let's go over the route,*" Major Simmond's voice repeated on the intercom.

"You sure, Major? We're supposed to await the call-sign," Seivwright reminded him testily.

He could sense the displeasure in the Royals officer's words. "*If this is a wild goose-chase, the sooner we find out the better.*"

Seivwright couldn't be bothered to argue. This was a brown job op. anyway. As far as he understood it, they should still have been on the ground until they heard from the SAS men manning the ambush. Obviously the major had his own ideas.

"Dave, get onto Blue Leader and tell him to sod off." Ducane was furious. "Is he trying to blow the whole thing?"

"*Okay, Jacko,*" crackled the sergeant's reply. "*Guess old Simmonds wants in on the action.*"

"We all know that. Get on with it."

There was a pause while the sergeant began to contact the Eagle patrol on the Land Rover's UHF radio.

Suddenly Ducane's earpiece was alive. It was Young Tom's voice, talking rapidly with hardly suppressed excitement. "*We've got something, boss. A motor-cycle.*"

Ducane frowned. Int. had said it would be a car. Was this a farmworker returning home from the fields? Or was he riding point for Cochran's car, inspecting the route?

"Forget Blue Leader, Dave," he snapped. "Stand by."

"Now we have a car!" Young Tom's voice was euphoric.

That's better, thought Ducane, he *is* riding scout.

"And another car! In close succession. The cyclist's seen the chopper. He's slowing and looking around."

Shit! Was Young Tom mistaken? Panicking even? Ducane dismissed the thought. He may be young and relatively inexperienced, but Perrot was as cool and calm as they come. Perhaps Int. had got it wrong after all, and his team were waiting to carve up a convoy of luckless civilians.

That's it. Convoy. Sweat had collected on Ducane's forehead and was trickling down the side of his nose into his eyes. He squeezed them hard shut and blinked rapidly. His raised pulse receded. Of course, that was it. He glanced at the watch on his left arm: 1735. Over an hour later than estimated.

It was explained now. He remembered the briefing two weeks earlier, when they'd been warned of the recent new ploy used by some PIRA gangs to distract the increasing attention from themselves. Rather than drive furtively down quiet roads in conspicuous single-file, they would slip in behind an innocent vehicle, or preferably a line of vehicles, using them as cover, especially in deserted areas. That was why they were behind schedule; waiting for a casual passerby. The motor-cyclist could be civilian, or a new innovation on the technique. The Provos were getting desperate lately. Ducane wondered if the others recalled the warning. A dead, innocent civilian was worth hundreds of column inches in propaganda to the Provisionals.

The clear sound of the high-revving Honda motor-cycle crackled through the quiet afternoon air, from beyond the blackthorns.

Ducane said into the mike: "Watch it, lads, there could be a decoy in this lot. Okay, Dave, MOVE IT!"

Immediately the powerful, super-charged V4 engine coughed angrily to life. The heavy-duty 16inch tyres spat earth as the Land Rover leapt forward. Sergeant Forbes slammed on the anchors with the vehicle blocking the lane. Heaving on the handbrake and shoving the gear into first, he threw himself at the GPMG mounted on the passenger's side.

Ducane kept his eyes on the copse of blackthorn. Now Young Tom would be down near the telegraph pole at the roadside. An hour before he had wrapped six coils of white Cordtex cable around its base. The small knot would ensure the pole came down straight across the lane.

As he came suddenly into view, the teenager on the motor-cycle was so busy watching the hovering Wessex 2 that he didn't notice the Land Rover blocking his path. The large, red crash helmet looked incongruous on the thin body as it swivelled back to face the road. He saw the sergeant manning the GPMG fifty yards ahead and grabbed at the brakes. The rear wheels tried to overtake the front. Caught off balance, he hit the tarmac in agonising, slow motion.

"Evel bloody Knievel," murmured Turnbull as he glanced at Ducane. The captain nodded.

The corporal sprang forward, through the spindly hedgerow and onto the road. Before the youth had orientated himself, Plasticuffs had been snapped over his wrists. Despite his diminutive stature, Turnbull had no difficulty in physically hoisting the dazed, gangling body into the roadside shrubbery. As usual the soldier remained immaculate and unruffled in spite of his sudden exertion.

The first car came round the bend at speed. It was a blue Cortina 3, and was followed closely by a battered grey Humber.

Ducane squinted hard. There appeared to be three men in the Cortina. The two seated in the front looked middle-aged.

The earpiece crackled. It was Tom. *"Looks like Cochran's in the first, boss. Just two women and an old bloke in the second."*

"Hear that, lads," Ducane said. "Let's go!"

With a squeal of brakes the Cortina slewed across the road. It brushed the hedge for a few feet before it halted twenty yards in front of the Land Rover. The middle-aged woman driving the Humber had slower reactions, over-spun her steering-wheel and clipped the rear of the Cortina before stopping. There was a bright tinkling of plastic, glass and chrome as the offside light mounting shattered.

"HALT OR WE FIRE!" Forbes' voice boomed over the Land Rover's bullhorn. He waved a Yellow Card emphatically. "THIS IS A BRITISH ARMY VEHICLE CHECK! GET OUT OF YOUR CARS SLOWLY! HANDS ON YOUR HEADS, PLEASE!"

The doors of the Cortina swung open.

"KEEP IT SLOW! USE THE RIGHT-HAND DOORS ONLY."

Ducane joined Turnbull at the roadside.

Gingerly the three men, all dressed in mud-splattered rubber boots, and typical farmer's clothes, stepped out onto the tarmac.

The SAS captain threw a glance at the second car. The elderly man in the passenger seat looked startled as he spoke to the woman driver who wore a silk headscarf. The nun in the rear seat was leaning forward, asking something of her relatives who were obviously treating her to an outing.

It was the nun's thick, horn-rimmed glasses that Ducane remembered from the identification photo sheets at the Tac HQ briefing session.

Turnbull said: "None of these, boss!"

Before Ducane could reply, the Humber's engine roared. The gears grated in protest as the woman threw it into reverse and stamped on the accelerator. The whine of the straining prop-shaft was ear-splitting.

Simultaneously Young Tom struck the Fuzee match and lit the fuse cable to the telegraph pole. As he hurled himself away, the explosion tore through the timber. The pole hit the road three seconds before the rear wheels of the Humber crunched into it.

Ducane grabbed the first of the farmers by the arm. "Down!"

Turnbull pushed the other two tight against the car's bodywork as the Humber was forced back into first gear and leapt towards them like an attacking bull.

The GPMG burst into a throaty roar, its shells biting chunks out of the tarmac in front of the speeding car.

Forbes' intention was to hit the wheels in order to avoid damaging the Provo VIP. But a fast approaching vehicle, going under his elevation of fire, and restricted by the nearness of the Cortina passengers and his colleagues, was a hopeless target.

Trapped against the side of the Cortina, Ducane and Turnbull were unable even to bring their weapons to bear before the Humber veered suddenly to the right, through the hedge shrubbery and climbed into the meadow, swinging around the Land Rover. In a cloud of exhaust, flying stones and clods of earth, it swerved left, bouncing back onto the lane. The body pan bottomed noisily. Feverishly the driver corrected the steering and punched the accelerator. The engine squealed as a fresh burst of power set the rear axle spinning. Gathering speed the Humber fishtailed on the greasy tarmac.

The precaution of placing the Lazy Tongs vehicle-trap across the road had been Turnbull's idea.

As the Humber's front tyres disintegrated, the driver was caught totally by surprise. Under a mesh of grass trimmings and manure, the concertina of alloy spikes was unrecognisable.

Out of control, the Humber ploughed into the left-hand hedgerow and mounted the embankment, lurched to a halt, and tilted sideways. Like a helpless metal beetle, it slid back down the slope and rocked to a standstill.

For a moment a heavy silence fell over the valley as the noise reverberated away across the hills of Armagh. Dust and gunsmoke hung in the still air. The Cortina passengers climbed nervously to their feet, gawking in amazement as Ducane and Turnbull raced towards the Land Rover.

Forbes swung the GPMG round to line it up on the crashed Humber, using the body of the vehicle for cover.

Again he yelled into the bullhorn: "STAND STILL! I AM READY TO FIRE!" Turnbull dropped down beside him, peering over the seats through the doorless front section. Meanwhile Ducane sped past him, up onto the meadow. He threw himself into a clump of long grass overlooking the Humber.

9

The driver's door of the car suddenly fell open and the middle-aged woman emerged, the headscarf having slipped to reveal cropped ginger hair. Using the open door as a shield, she aimed a hand pistol quickly at Forbes and fired twice in rapid succession. As the sergeant ducked instinctively, the woman sprang back, racing down the lane towards the border, taking long, ungainly strides.

Ducane grated his teeth and fired a short burst at the centre of her back. As if carried by a terrific wind, the force of shells thudding into her carried her forward. Arms and legs spread in supplication, she pitched headfirst into the road. A pair of blue Y-fronts showed above the muscular white legs.

Now Ducane's position was known. A rain of automatic fire broke from the Humber's passenger seat, the roar of the assault rifle mixing with an almost musical tinkling of glass. Swiftly Ducane rolled sideways as the sheet of steel sliced into the earth where he had lain.

Another automatic weapon added to the firepower coming from the car, and Ducane peered through the long grass to see the nun firing a stubby sub-machine gun that had been concealed in the folds of her habit. The front seat passenger fired again at Ducane's position, then swung his gun around to the Land Rover.

"Run, you bloody fool," he yelled at the nun. "I'll give you cover! Get down the road while I keep 'em busy!"

Having seen the fate of the other Provo gunman, the nun hesitated for a second. Then, as though deciding it was the only chance, fired a final burst from the hip in the Land Rover's direction. Gathering up her habit, she turned, scrambled onto the road, and began running hard towards Eire.

Still cowering in the front seat, the passenger turned his attention to Ducane, attempting to fire up the gradient of the embankment. Forbes' GPMG and Turnbull's Sterling exploded into action from the Land Rover. The Humber disintegrated under a furious hail of fire as twenty or more high-velocity shells hammered into the metalwork, tearing it apart. Two shells hit just below the man's neck and, with a macabre theatrical movement, the severed head dropped neatly out of the open window. A fountain of crimson liquid hit the inside roof of the car, driven by the force of the man's last few heartbeats.

Ducane quickly stood up and scanned the lane to the border. The nun had gone.

Sheer terror had given her an unexpected burst of energy. Some two hundred yards away, realising the danger of staying on the tarmac, she had crossed the shrubbery and was pacing fast up into the meadow.

Ducane lowered his Sterling and signalled Forbes not to fire. At that range his sub-machine gun would be inaccurate and the sergeant's GPMG just pure overkill.

He cursed silently. Major Simmonds would love this.

Glancing the other way Ducane saw young Tom Perrot sprinting up across the meadow from his forward position in the blackthorns. The SAS captain recognised the high-velocity rifle he was carrying. A 7·62mm sniper rifle with a telescopic sight.

"Alive!" Ducane bawled. "I want him alive!"

Immediately Young Tom slid to a halt on his knees in the grass, his rifle held level and steady.

Another whipcrack joined the dying echo of gunfire. The single bullet slammed into the nun's habit around the knees, spinning the body round like a corkscrew, the sub-machine gun tossed aside in a spasm of agony.

Ducane scrambled up the slope to where Young Tom still knelt. "Well done, lad. I just hope you've not killed him."

"I don't think so, boss."

Ducane nodded. "Go back to the copse and keep away any civilian traffic until we've cleared up this mess."

Shouldering his rifle, Young Tom turned and made his way back down to the lane. Sergeant Forbes joined Ducane and together they approached the groaning body of the nun. She was roughly pulled to her feet and frog-marched back down to the lane.

One of the Cortina passengers stepped forward, his initial shock now giving way to anger. "Who the hell are you and your friends?"

Ducane pulled away his faceveil. "British Army, sir. I'm sorry if you've been inconvenienced."

The man blinked as he scanned the soldier's camouflage smock in vain for an insignia of regiment or rank. "You're not from the Ulster Defence Force or some such? You've no badges."

Ducane shook his head. "That's right, sir. We're on special duties."

"Bloody killers!" interrupted one of the other passengers. "Murdering innocent women and nuns." There were no doubts where his loyalties lay.

"Oh, yes," Forbes said. "Our nun." He stepped forward and, grabbing the moaning figure by the scruff of the habit, hauled it roughly to its feet. He pulled away the hood and stared at the grimacing face of a middle-aged man with a day's growth of stubble on his chin. Cold blue eyes glared back at him through the cracked lenses of a pair of heavy horn-rimmed spectacles.

"Pleased to meet you, Sister Cochran," Ducane said.

"Bloody hell!" gasped the farmer.

Ducane nodded. "And you, gentlemen, nearly shared their fate. They were using you as cover. How long had they been behind you?"

"Hey, he's right!" said the third passenger, a small man in an ill-fitting tweed jacket. "They came off a side road about five miles back. Didn't seem to want to pass us."

"No, Sister Cochran wouldn't want to do that," Ducane said. "If anyone was going to get shot, they intended it would be you ..."

"Oh, come on ..." the farmer began.

Ducane laughed at his astonishment. "I won't tell you how close it came to working. Now, what about the kid on the bike?"

"The one in front?" the farmer asked. "Oh, he turned up about the same time. Just joy-riding. I think he's local. Seen him working in Claranagh."

"What'll you do to him?" the man in the tweed jacket demanded.

"Nothing much," Ducane replied. "Just have him put

away for a bit ... for his own protection as much as anything." He turned to Forbes. "You'd better call down the chopper, Dave, before old Simmonds gives himself a coronary."

As the sergeant moved away to the Land Rover, the farmer asked: "What about us? Are we free to go?"

"I expect Major Simmonds would like a word with you. To get your side of the picture and that sort of thing. After that I'm sure you'll be at perfect liberty to go about your business. But you must promise me you won't breathe a word to anyone about this operation."

Meanwhile Turnbull had secured Cochran's hands, one from the rear and one from the front, held beneath his crotch with a pair of Plasticuffs.

"That should give Houdini something to think about," the corporal muttered with satisfaction.

There was no need for Forbes to radio the Eagle patrol.

The Wessex 2 swung fast across the tree tops to hover over a flat area of the meadow. It swaggered drunkenly downward until the large wheels hit the ground with a jolt. Everyone turned away until the blades slowed and the whirlwind began to subside.

Already the detachment of bare-headed Royals had doubled out towards the lane, dropping to their knees with weapons at the ready, in a wide semi-circle. After a few moments the helicopter rotors came to a stop. Finally Major Simmonds stepped down from the hatch and picked his way carefully through the grass.

He paused at the centre of the line formed by his detachment. The sun glinted on the Polaroid sunglasses beneath the deep peak of his cap. He surveyed the carnage with disdain.

Forbes gave Cochran a friendly push that sent him sprawling uncomfortably alongside the motor-cyclist by the roadside. "Two fresh, plucked chickens, trussed and delivered to order, Major."

Simmonds ignored him and snapped orders briefly to his men. Two troopers shouldered their SLRs and advanced on the wrecked Humber. Carefully they picked their way through the debris and tangled mess of glass and metal until they found the headless body. The younger man retched violently at the unexpected sight. The other, a veteran of twenty-one, patiently helped his mate to one side and began a routine check of the car's contents.

Having talked to the men from the Cortina and sent his own troops to seal off the road, away from the scene of the ambush, Major Simmonds walked purposefully towards Ducane, his hands behind his back.

"Well, Captain, I hope you are satisfied?" He didn't look at the SAS officer as he spoke, but past him at some indefinable spot in the middle-distance. His voice was crisp and clipped with traces of a public school accent.

"I hope *you* are, Major," Ducane returned evenly. "You were supposed to wait at Cornoonagh Hill until we called. Not until you *thought* it was time. With your chopper flying over the area we rather lost the element of surprise. It put my men at serious risk."

Major Simmonds' eyes darted quickly away from the middle-distance and he looked at him coldly. The gaunt cheeks and tight-lipped mouth added several years to the age he shared with Ducane: they were both thirty.

"For someone *at risk* you seem to have conducted your butchery with your usual efficiency," he said sharply.

"You've got two prisoners and the corpses of two men you've been chasing for three years." He indicated the two shapeless polythene body-bags now neatly stacked at the side of the road.

"We are not Americans, Ducane. We don't have to keep our body counts up to please the computer statistics." He pulled off his Polaroid glasses. "You just couldn't bear to follow my advice and man a full VCP. A show of totally superior force. Those Provos would soon have seen the sense."

Ducane looked at the fresh-faced young man clearing the road under the direction of a bored sergeant. "And perhaps the Provos wouldn't have seen sense. They didn't exactly wave the white flag at us. We've lost enough young

14

lads over here, Major. They joined an army designed to fight other armies, and fighting terrorists is not second nature to them." He jerked his thumb at the Cortina. "We were nearly fooled by that decoy ... if your lads had been involved ..." He looked Simmonds straight in the eye. "Do you think Cochran would be alive now?"

The major paled visibly. "Don't be facetious with me, Captain! I don't see how we could have made a *bigger* mess. You don't yet have a completely free rein in Armagh. And we managed well enough before your barbarians arrived on the scene." He glanced pointedly at the wreck of the Humber. "You are seconded to us for your special skills in surveillance and ambush techniques—not to act as your own judge, jury and executioner."

Ducane swung the strap of the Sterling over his shoulder. "Major, when the Micks are armed with battalions of T62 tanks, armoured carriers and artillery, I'll be begging for the help of your chaps. Because *that's* your business. Until that time, I'll act in the way I'm trained, qualified and authorised to do. And that is to capture and if necessary kill Provo thugs. Just learn to accept that our way there's less chance of adding more of the few troops we've got left in the British Army to the VSIL." He looked straight in the major's eyes, now shaded beneath the deep rim of his cap. "And if you don't like it, complain to your CO. He, at least, understands the difference between your job and ours."

Simmonds smarted. In the past month he'd had three men on the Very Seriously Injured List and one DD— Discharged Dead. He said acidly: "There'll be a full account of this conversation in my debriefing, Ducane."

"And in mine, Major. So be sure you've got it right." He glanced at Forbes by his side. "And a witness for verification."

He turned sharply, leaving the major facing the grinning SAS sergeant. Simmonds looked quickly around. Not one of the Royals was within earshot.

Still grinning to himself, Forbes joined the others at the Land Rover.

Ducane slapped Corporal Turnbull on the back. "Your idea of using the Lazy Tongs was excellent, John."

Young Tom, flushed with the confidence of a successful mission, added, "Specially covering it in all that dung and mud, Corp!"

As they climbed into the vehicle, Forbes said: "Forgot it was your idea, Johnny old lad. Bravo." He added pointedly: "I suppose you'd better have the privilege of cleaning that crap of it then, eh?"

Turnbull couldn't suppress a smile. "With mates like you, Dave, who needs the IRA?" He got to work scraping with his knife.

Now free to go, the three Cortina passengers watched as the Land Rover was finally loaded up, and began edging its way through the wreckage being cleared by the Royals. One or two of the younger troopers gave the occupants a friendly wave or admiring thumbs-up sign.

"*Special duties* be damned," the farmer said. "To be sure them was the SAS."

"Ruthless bastards," muttered one of his companions.

"Yes, I'll be thinkin' I wouldn't care t'get on t' wrong side of them."

"So what y' smilin' at then, Dominic?"

"Oh, nothin' t' be sure," the farmer replied. "I was just thinkin' them was the same lads that sorted out Rommel's lot in North Africa. In the last war."

"They're still vicious bastards."

The farmer nodded in agreement. But as he walked across to the Cortina, he subconsciously pulled in his stomach. Although he was still only five feet five tall, he could have sworn he had grown a few inches more.

Part One

THE
MASTER'S MEN

CHAPTER 1

The passengers of the blue Cortina kept their collective promise of silence for six days. Finally, it was the farmer who could contain his urgent desire to gossip no longer. He had been content to keep the news from his wife, who would certainly have dismissed the matter as imagination and exaggeration, but his weekly trip to the local was to prove too much of a temptation.

By twelve-thirty the pub had filled with lunchtime drinkers.

A low, white-walled building, its small windows keep the plain plastered rooms cool on the hottest days. But this day the late August sun was chilled by a brisk north-easterly and the proprietors Shelagh and Patrick Brady lit the fire in the large flagstone hearth for the first time since the previous spring.

Early drinkers were standing with their backs to the fire or seated in the warm pools of sunlight by the windows. As more arrived the general drowsy hubbub of voices increased and the air thickened with the smell of tobacco smoke, warm bread and stout.

As with many isolated rural communities the pub forms the focal point of the community, providing a welcome break for the farmworkers who have usually been up since before dawn. Already plates heavy with pie and chips and warm, fresh bread were passing steadily across the counter.

"Hey, Shelagh, ye're forgettin' me brown sauce again!" It was the voice of the farmer, known to all as Dominic, who owned the blue Cortina.

Shelagh Brady waved at him to be patient and finished pulling a pint of mild and bitter for Jim O'Nions, a grizzled middle-aged Republican who ran a freelance delivery service for many of the numerous smallholdings in the area. With him was a man she knew only as Malone. She'd seen him several times in the company of Jim O'Nions. Judging by the state of his overalls and fingernails he was a mechanic of some sort. She turned her attention back to Dominic. The man would cheerfully complain about anything and everything if it meant the chance of a free pint in compensation.

"Now I *am* sorry," she said forcefully. "But even the best establishments run out of something sometimes ..."

Dominic washed down the pie with a heavy swill of stout from a straight glass. He wiped his mouth with the back of his hand and belched lightly. Already he'd decided on a new tack. "Now listen, Shelagh, how'd you like to hear a little first-hand gossip?" He paused for effect. "Like a British Army secret operation I saw meself with me own eyes just last week ..."

But Shelagh wasn't falling that easily. "Where was this then?"

He jerked a thumb vaguely over his shoulder. "Back there a pace. Not far from the old copper mine at Tully-donnell. We were caught up in this ambush. Me and Pete, and me cowman."

"Aw, get away," Shelagh said. "To be sure even I heard about that, t'was just a roadcheck. They caught that Drummond boy from Claranagh."

Dominic looked about with a conspiratorial air, then beckoned Shelagh to lean closer—as much to get a better view of her bosom as to keep his conversation secret. "I tell you it was an ambush. We were nearly at that wood at O'Donnell's place, where the road narrows in the valley by the meadow. There's this Army Jeep blocking the road an' suddenly the car behind us blows up."

Shelagh was still disbelieving. "A Provo mine?"

"Bah, Provo mine be damned! The car tried to go round t' road block, didn't it? 'Twas the Army t' be sure. Suddenly these great big Brit lads appeared from nowhere."

"How big?"

"Bloody great giants they was," enthused the farmer.

"Go on!"

Dominic banged his fist on the bar to emphasise the point. "None of 'em under six foot if them was an inch."

Shelagh's husband, absently drying glasses, overheard. "Were they regular squaddies then, Dominic?"

Dominic looked suddenly hurt, and thrust his empty glass towards Shelagh. "Look, Pat, I'm no tittle-tattle. I was sworn to secrecy."

"Who by?" Pat demanded.

The farmer waved his hand vaguely. "By these big fellas, of course. Told me not to discuss it with no one, didn't they?"

Satisfied it was Farmer Dominic's vivid imagination at work, Pat said in triumph, "If it's so secret, why are you telling us about it?" And he moved away to pull a pint for a new arrival.

Shelagh had ignored Dominic's empty glass, unconvinced it was worth a free pint of stout for the farmer to finish his story.

It was Jim O'Nions who spoke. "So then, Dominic, who were these supermen then?"

The farmer jumped, unaware that the deliveryman had overheard him, and no less reassured by the gap-toothed grin. Everyone had heard the rumour that the crusty old soak had connections with the Provos.

"W-ell, I-I don't know, Jim," the farmer stuttered. "I just know they was big fellas with no markings on them. Secret assignment they said."

"I know," said O'Nions, and shoved the farmer's glass towards Shelagh. "Top that up for my friend, love, will you."

Malone was standing close to O'Nions, peering over his shoulder. He was a short wiry man in his mid-thirties, with thick black hair, sideburns and bushy eyebrows which met above his nose. His dark eyes were bright and fierce.

Quickly the farmer shifted his gaze back to O'Nions' more than friendly smile. "W-ell, they shot up this car behind us, see. Then some of the passengers tried to get away."

"What people was these then?"

The beer was thrust in his hand. He looked down at it. Perhaps things weren't so bad. Suddenly he felt more relaxed, warming slightly to the subject. "Well, a bloke and this nun and woman . . ."

O'Nions frowned.

"Ah, but they *weren't*, see," the farmer added quickly. "They was men dressed up, see? They had guns, too. Modern automatic things. Didn't do them much good though. These soldiers appeared out of nowhere and blew 'em to bits. Well two of 'em, anyway."

Malone spoke for the first time. His voice sounded hostile. "Which two?"

"The one dressed as a woman. And the other passenger. He was a nasty mess."

"And the nun?" O'Nions demanded.

"Just wounded, I think. They trussed him up like a chicken."

Malone's dark eyes flashed sideways at O'Nions. "Cochran."

"That's what one soldier called the nun," Dominic confirmed, eager to please. "*Sister* Cochran! I think it was a joke."

"A pretty sick one," Malone replied. The smile vanished from the farmer's face. "Looks like the SAS buggers got him."

At that moment the door opened. The man who emerged to the tinkle of a bell was tall and slim with well-groomed fair hair. Compared with the other customers, his appearance was almost aristocratic: sharply pressed cavalry twill trousers and tweed jacket with a nugget-coloured silk cravat, carefully knotted and tucked neatly into a shirt of small pattern check.

"And the top of the mornin' to you, folks!" he called out as he approached the bar.

"Morning, sir," returned Shelagh. "Usual, is it?"

The young man nodded, leaning casually against the bar on his elbow.

"Hi, Dominic. Nice day."

O'Nions and Malone exchanged glances and glared at the newcomer with undisguised hostility.

"It was nice 'til you marched in," O'Nions grunted.

"M-Mornin', Mr Harrington," Dominic said. He was unsure how much he should say in front of the two Republicans.

Harrington's blue eyes flashed quickly, sizing up the situation. He grinned warmly at O'Nions. "Come on, Jim, you're not your usual friendly self today. Let me get you a drink, you miserable old devil."

Malone interrupted sharply. "We don't drink with the likes of you and yours."

Harrington ignored the outburst. He put some loose change on the counter in exchange for the double whiskey and soda. "Thanks my little colleen," he said to Shelagh.

He studied the dark haired man called Malone carefully. "Who's your friend, Jim? I don't think I know him."

"Malone," O'Nions answered.

"Just Malone?"

Malone leaned forward. "To you, soldier boy, it's just Malone!" He almost spat the words.

Harrington's eyes twinkled mischievously. "Well, Mr Malone, I'm sorry you won't be joining us for a drink. But O'Nions and I usually crack a bottle together, don't we, Jim?"

"Course, he does," chimed in Shelagh, laughing. "And usually more than one!"

The blood rushed to O'Nions cheeks. His eyes darted from Shelagh to Harrington to Malone in quick succession. He realised Harrington was too sharp for him to combat. Silently he cursed Shelagh for her damned jocularity.

He said quickly: "Not today, Mr Harrington, if you don't mind. Er, I'm with my friend."

"Come on," Malone snapped. Together they found a small table in the corner and began their conversation with Dominic in hushed earnest.

Cochran had been held for a week by the security forces without any official announcement being made. Before the day was out Malone would make sure Sinn Fein had the confirmation of the man's recapture. You could never be too sure what pressures might be applied to get Cochran to talk whilst no one knew he was back in custody. Cochran's whole new network could be in jeopardy until he was back in a general prison, safe amongst his compatriots. Malone would make sure the story hit the press that evening to embarrass the authorities into making an announcement. Allegations of torture and interrogation would be made. A further chat with the farmer, too, could result in some good anti-English propaganda about the SS-style terror tactics of the British Army.

"Sorry, there's no pie left, Mr Harrington." Shelagh's voice distracted Lieutenant Harrington's thoughts from the two Republicans. "Will a Scotch egg be all right? There's some hot peas and potatoes."

"That'll be fine, thanks." He sipped on the whiskey. "Tell me, has Roisin been in yet?"

"No, love, not yet," Shelagh replied and disappeared into the kitchen.

Dominic, who had now returned thankfully to his place at the bar, inclined his head in the direction of O'Nions and Malone. "Sorry, about those two, Mr Harrington. I don't usually pass the time o' day with that sort."

Harrington grinned and gave him a friendly tap on the arm. "Don't you worry about me, Dominic. Or them for that matter. You mix with who you like. It's a free country."

Dominic swallowed some beer. "Not if those two bastards had their way, I bet. They hate the British Army, even more than most round here. You ought to know they're no friends of mine!"

Harrington laughed easily. "Dominic, I seem to remember you spend most lunchtimes telling me how much better it would be if the Army went home. Leave Ulster to itself to sort things out, that's what you always say."

"That's as maybe. But last week I decided perhaps your lot was right." He swallowed the dregs of his beer. "Perhaps we do need some protection. We're getting so many shootings around here no one's safe. Intimidation is wide-

23

spread and bleddy indiscriminate. And as for mines, t'be sure there's so many in the roads round here, it's not safe for my cows to go out alone." He chuckled at his own humour.

"How many cattle have you lost due to mines, then?"

Dominic looked dubious. "Well, none actually. But there's still enough around and accidents can happen."

Harrington grimaced. "Not with command-controlled mines. And that's what the Provos are using."

The farmer jerked his thumb towards O'Nions. "Half the time silly buggers like him are drunk as newts. 'E couldn't tell one o' your armoured Pigs from one o' my cows!"

Harrington laughed, the warmth of the whiskey and the Irishman's friendly manner reaching him. "You can smile," Dominic said, irritated that the soldier couldn't tell when he was being serious. "It might be *your* Jeep blown up one day."

"True."

"Well, then. I reckon the less bombs and mines and guns around here, the best it is for all of us."

Shelagh brought in Harrington's meal. "And you think we need the protection of these supermen do you, Dominic?" she asked.

He nodded soberly. "Well, I admit, I was impressed." He turned back to Harrington. "I was just tellin' her about the ambush I saw last week down near the old copper mine. Carved up a carload of Provos good'n'proper those SAS lads did."

"How d'you know they were SAS?" Harrington asked. "Don't tell me they told you?"

"No. But you could tell they was different. Very quiet— and polite for English—but, y'know, sort of mean lookin'."

Harrington smiled. "Some lads in the Pay Corps can look pretty mean at times."

"You know what I mean!" replied the farmer. "I was in North Africa in Hitler's war and I saw some of the Long Range Desert Group fellas. Had that same mean look. Cool and mean."

Lieutenant Charles Harrington-Corbett continued his conversation with the farmer and the two other passengers from the Cortina who came into the pub later. He encouraged their imaginative tales about the SAS troops they had encountered the previous week. He carefully dropped in a few random suggestions that would add fuel to the fire of local gossip. Soon the farmer and his friends were considering themselves experts on SAS operations, but had they ever stopped to recall where these ideas originated, they would find it difficult to remember Harrington's casual remarks and innuendoes. Their imagination fired, the farm men actually began to believe that even while they were drinking the SAS had infiltrated a PIRA Chiefs of Staff meeting in Dundalk. They had laid electronic monitoring devices throughout Armagh, and every public house was bugged. *That* one caused particular concern!

But of more immediate importance Harrington had learned that the story of Cochran's recapture was now in circulation, and that an announcement would have to be made promptly to short-circuit any propaganda plans the PIRA may be making.

He did not, of course, mention that it was he who had set up the ambush.

Meanwhile he implanted the idea that Cochran may have sung his head off to save his hide and that two major cells in Belfast were about to be rounded up. That could soon lead to a quietening of operations in the city for a few weeks. And a few inter-PIRA murders with any luck, as the members became nervous and suspicious of each other.

Behind his back Harrington was known as 'Lord Charles', an affectionate reference to the famous ventriloquist's dummy. It was a name earned by his cultured accent, which was softened with an attractive Irish brogue —and the fact that he frequented so many pubs.

Until the early 1970s he had served full-time in the Royal Artillery, commanding a battery of obsolete 5·5inch guns. It was then that Ministry of Defence officials, anxiously scouring the records for officers and men who could possibly offer something to the intelligence effort in Ulster, had discovered the Irish connections of his wealthy Cumberland family. Harrington had spent much of his childhood in Armagh with two aged aunts, and still paid them regular visits several times a year during his leave.

After a couple of discreet interviews, the Ministry had been amazed at the number of friends and contacts he had in the heart of County Armagh, despite the fact he was a known Army officer.

On the understanding that he should have complete discretion as to the information he passed on, Harrington accepted the assignment as Liaison Officer to the local battalion commander. He underwent an intensive course in unarmed combat and signalling techniques at the Special Air Service Regiment headquarters in Hereford, before being sent to stay with his aunts, with the cover-story that he had been invalided out of the Army following an accident. He also made it well-known that his sympathies were with Official Sinn Fein. His support for the breakaway hardline Provisionals would have been too much of a volte-face for anyone to swallow.

The ploy had worked beautifully, largely due to Harrington's background. He found the job much easier than he had expected and had thoroughly enjoyed meeting his old friends and making new ones. Whilst gathering snippets of information, he had launched his own vigorous campaign to win over the 'hearts and minds' of the locals and he had met with some considerable success. He was frequently critical of the Army's actions in Ulster, but balanced this with well-reasoned arguments for their reluctant presence. Only one attempt had been made on his life. But the two gunmen who had rammed his car and opened fire with automatic weapons had been forced into panic-stricken retreat, when he fired back. Being in civilian clothes they had made the dangerous assumption that he was unarmed. That same night they had been arrested in an RUC swoop.

Harrington had known them since he was sixteen.

*

Now he was interested to learn more about Malone. The man had been seen in O'Nions company several times in the past, but in recent days they had seemed inseparable. O'Nions was a known Republican sympathiser, but Harrington has considered him so inept, as to be best given a full rein. So far this had paid off. By keeping in close contact with him and plying him with liquor, Harrington had managed to pinpoint three particularly dangerous gunmen in the last eighteen months. Malone's presence suggested something new in the air although, to his knowledge, the security forces had nothing concrete on the man to date, except that he came from Londonderry and was an out-of-work mechanic and a Catholic.

But as he finished his meal, Shelagh Brady mentioned something to him that had caused Harrington considerable personal concern. She said she thought that Malone was a friend of the McGuires. And that had a very sobering effect. Harrington had actually come into the Brady's pub early that lunchtime hoping to talk to Roisin McGuire. The daughter of a local farmer, who had been killed by an Army patrol in 1969 when he was caught planting a bomb, Harrington had known her since she was eight. Unlike her wild brother Sean, she held no bitterness for the incident and plainly failed to comprehend or care about the complexities of Irish politics or religious bigotry. He had met her again soon after his current assignment had begun, and found himself quickly and profoundly attracted to her. At the age of eighteen, some ten years younger than himself, she seemed to Harrington to represent all that was good about the country and its people.

Roisin was bright and intelligent with a superb sense of humour which she delivered with a deliciously lilting accent. She was goodlooking, too. In recent months, when he had lain in his bed at his aunts' house trying to sleep, he had found his restless mind turning more and more frequently to thoughts of the young Irish girl. He had taken her out several times, to dances and the cinema. On each occasion she had displayed an uncanny, but welcome, knack of being able to dispel all his fears about the precarious existence he was living in Armagh. They would talk for long, precious hours.

Her wide dark eyes and girlish laughter had enchanted him completely, and yet he felt a strange reverence and purity towards her that was alien to him. The first few times he asked her out, it had been to gain some background information, particularly about her brother Sean. Their meetings had continued, Harrington scarcely realising that he no longer needed a reason to see her. In fact his CO had noticed it first, making some dry, but not unkindly remark. For the first time he had realised that this girl, so many years his junior, had quietly worked her way deep into his system. When the CO chided him, he was at first resentful and then overwhelmed by his own sense of private anguish at the thought of reducing the frequency of their meetings.

Although during that earlier period he had never indulged in more than a light and gentlemanly kiss, he felt he had known her more deeply than if they had lived together for years. Yet, as the awareness of his feelings for her slowly crystallised, he also began to fear the urge to accelerate their relationship. What, he asked himself, if he found after all, that there was simply nothing there?

For Roisin, so open and happy in his company, had never led him to believe there was a promise of more than a casual, occasionally flirtatious, relationship. She had responded to his kisses spontaneously, but never with eagerness or passion.

Two weeks earlier, Harrington had decided to win her over into his adult world. He had attempted to show her some of the glitter and romance that lay beyond rural Armagh. He decided that, by swirling her into a new and sophisticated environment, he might be able to discover how she really felt. Persuade her that in the great world outside things were different. For days and nights before he imagined how it would be. He went over the dialogue a hundred times in his mind until he could visualise the entire scene in the minutest detail.

He had picked up Roisin early from the farmhouse,

where she lived alone since her father had died and her brother had left for the north. They set off for one of the quiet Belfast suburbs that had been left relatively unmarked by the troubles. The afternoon sun had scattered its glow into the car, setting off Roisin's simple white dress in contrast against the neat black pageboy haircut. An inexpensive silver chain and crucifix glistened around her throat. Her perfume had filled the car, rich and heady. As he glanced sideways, her upturned nose and the slight pout of her lips gave an impression of sophistication, almost arrogance. Harrington had never seen her made up so fully nor so immaculately. Even her hair, usually such a soft muddle, was faultless.

He felt fraudulent. Trying to impress her with a fat wallet. Trying to buy her favours. No better than the local teenage casanovas, who boasted of their feats for the Provos in the hope of some bodily reward.

But, despite his fears, it had turned out to be a delightful evening at the little bistro that was sandwiched in a row of bomb-damaged shops. They had spoken little, but danced a lot. Their mood was quiet, but strangely intense. Words didn't seem necessary.

When they were about to leave, Roisin turned to him. "Don't expect too much of me, Charlie."

They had walked slowly back to the car through slogan-daubed streets, the pavements streaked with rain from an earlier shower. They said nothing, not wishing to disturb the unusual quiet of the warm, moist night. Afraid to break the spell.

Neither had they spoken as the homeward drive began. They had been travelling for some minutes through a wood, with a three-quarter moon shedding its silvered light across the landscape, when he pulled off the road. She showed no surprise that he had stopped. Indeed she seemed to have been expecting it.

As they made love, he knew he would remember the words she had whispered in his ear. "I need you. I need you more than you realise." And then she had cried out, involuntarily.

Later, still cradling her in his arms, he brushed aside the wisps of hair that clung to her damp forehead. Her tear-filled eyes looked up at him, and she smiled. She looked very young.

He said: "There, I didn't expect too much of you, did I?"

Her eyes closed, content; the smile still on her lips.

Memories of that night warmed Harrington as he chatted absently to the farmer in the Brady's pub. Since that time both he and Roisin had become very busy, their conversation snatched during brief encounters at the pub. Developments over Cochran had kept him fully occupied, and Roisin's heavy workload at the farm meant they had not been able to be alone. Neither had mentioned the night in the car, but Harrington was sure it had cemented the growing bond between them.

He had decided he must see her, explain how he felt and persuade her to leave the farm. Leave it all to Sean if necessary, should he not be prepared to sell. Within a month Harrington could complete the assignment for which he had volunteered; he had done more than his fair share and he knew the CO would back his decision. After eighteen months in the field he had a considerable amount of R and R due to him. If Roisin would only agree, they could marry and set up home on the mainland. A small place, perhaps near Larkhill or Lulworth.

He'd talked it over with Jacko. The tall SAS captain was a good friend and Harrington valued his experience and advice. If Jack Ducane said he should take his chances in life as and when they presented themselves, then he would do. The captain had once met Roisin briefly and said he liked her. It could have been politeness, but at the time he sounded as though he meant it. He'd certainly meant it when he agreed to be Best Man—missions permitting. But he had added that he thought the plans were a bit premature until Roisin had agreed.

Harrington knew she would.

It was gone two when Roisin eventually arrived, evidently straight from the farm, wearing tight jeans and a white roll-neck sweater. She glanced quickly around the crowded bar, her eyes lighting up when she saw him. As she made her way over, he excused himself from Dominic and the others.

After buying her a small lager he took her to a window seat, overlooking the narrow country road. They sat down and he found himself grinning at her fixedly.

"Well," she said, amused. "Cheers, Lord Charles!" Her eyes twinkled mischievously at him over her glass.

He laughed. It was the first time she'd ever used the locals' nickname for him.

"I'm sorry I've been so busy," he said. "I feel I've hardly seen you since that night."

"Sssh!" Her eyes were wide with mock warning. "You'll ruin my reputation, your lordship."

"Still, I'm sorry." He was too anxious to respond to her light-hearted mood.

She indicated the clock above the bar. "I'm sorry it's no better today. A cow got herself caught in the wire this morning, and old Terry doesn't exactly rush around with activity when I'm in charge."

"Your brother's still not back then?"

Her smile dropped. "No, not yet." She sipped her drink. "But it might not be long now."

He reached across the table, placing his hand over hers. "When he's back, I'd like us to make some plans."

Her eyes clouded. "What sort of plans?"

He grinned. "I thought maybe it was about time Lord Charles took himself a lady."

Again she put the glass to her lips, peering at him over its rim thoughtfully.

Finally she said, "Would I be thinking that was some sort of marriage proposal?"

"You would indeed."

"Are you mad?"

"I think not. What do you say?"

She smiled hesitantly. "Thank you, I suppose."

"Not if you don't mean it."

"It's a surprise to be sure."

He squeezed her hand tightly. "But a nice one?"

She leaned forward, whispering: "I'm not pregnant, you know."

"A pity," he said. Too loudly for Roisin's liking.

"You know Sean won't like it."

The conversation was starting to veer in the expected direction. Firmly Harrington said: "I'm not asking your brother."

"He'd still be furious. There's no knowing what he'd say. Or do."

"There's not much he could do. And he couldn't say much more."

Roisin said: "He hates you, or so he says."

"He's always been pleasant enough," returned Harrington.

She smiled. "He tolerates you, Charlie, that's all. And then only to your face. After you've gone he calls you a bastard Brit spy."

"He knows I'm convalescing," Harrington replied evenly.

"For too long, as far as Sean's concerned". Her voice was muffled by the glass as she put it to her lips: "And I didn't find any scars the other night in the car ..."

"You were drunk."

"*Thank* you!"

Again he squeezed her hand. "You still haven't said yes."

She looked at him seriously. "Have you really thought it out, Charlie? I'm eighteen, just. I'm Catholic and I come from a staunch Republican family. By comparison you're an *old man* and, if you're not a spy, you certainly can't deny you were an officer in the British Army. If you don't see any obstacles there, then you're losing your brains as well as your hair."

He said defensively: "If you come to England with me, all our problems are solved."

"England!" She said it so loudly that several heads in the pub turned. In a far corner Malone and O'Nions glowered across the smoke-filled room at them.

"Until the troubles die down," he added soothingly.

The clear skin of her forehead furrowed and she leaned across the table until her eyes were a few inches from his. "Don't you know what Ireland means to me? Sean and all my relatives. The farm, my friends, my whole life. I may only be eighteen, Charlie, but I'm not an idiot. I know where my life is; where my roots are. They're here. In Armagh. And, as for the troubles, if you think they'll ever die down, you're a bigger fool than Sean says you are."

He said, "I love you, Roisin."

She drew back, looking at him, her head shaking gently in disbelief. "Oh, Christ," she said quietly, turning her head away.

He caught her hand again. "Roisin, I love you and I need you ... You mean more to me than Ireland itself."

She looked back at him, her head still shaking, but the dimpled clefts deepening as she started to smile. "Sean's right. You're a fool Charlie. But a lovable one. And I'm just as mad because I'm just Irish and perverse enough to agree to marry you." She seemed to find it difficult to believe her own words. "What do you suggest?"

Harrington breathed a silent sigh of relief. "Look, in a month I'll be able to return to the mainland. Well, two months at the outside. Obviously it'll take a while to tidy things up. And, of course, to break the news to my aunts. Anyway time for Sean to get used to the idea."

"Selling the farm, do you mean?" She looked hurt.

"That would be up to you, but not necessarily. I've as many friends here as in England, I'd be pleased for you to keep the family farm. It would be nice to visit often. Even settle back here eventually."

"I don't know ..."

"Of course, Sean would have to spend more time at the farm."

She looked at him thoughtfully, her eyes brightening. "That's true. He'd have to stop ... gallavanting around the way he does."

33

"You could be doing him the biggest favour ever ..."

"What do you mean?"

"Just that it would be best for him if he kept out of trouble."

"You know a lot about him, don't you?"

"Yes, I'm afraid I do, Roisin."

She watched him thoughtfully, his words confirming what she already knew in her heart. "So Sean was right about you." It was a statement.

Harrington nodded.

"And you've been protecting him for me?"

"Just a bit," he conceded. "But my powers are very limited. If he gets careless and they get conclusive evidence of his activities, anything I say would be overruled."

She nodded towards the throng of customers around them. "You're doing this work because you think it will help these people, aren't you, Charlie?"

"That belief eases my conscience. But it *is* my belief, however incorrect. Violence begets violence. As a soldier I know that's true. I couldn't inform on good people I've known all my life. But I'd still rather it was me, who knows them all well, than some professional, cold-blooded Intelligence plant to whom they mean nothing."

"I believe you," she said quietly.

He looked up as he saw Malone pushing his way through the crowd towards them, followed by O'Nions.

The dark man stood above them, and, ignoring Harrington, addressed himself to the girl. "If your brother could see you now, he'd throw a fit. Fraternisin' with this English scum is lowerin' yourself to his level, you stupid little slut."

Harrington went to rise, but Roisin's hand restrained him. The Irishman met his gaze, then, gathering the saliva in his mouth, he spat squarely onto the table between them. "An' you fuck off back to where you came from, soldier boy!"

Malone turned on his heel and continued towards the door. A silence had fallen over the pub, conversation dying away; all eyes turned to the small window seat.

O'Nions shrugged his shoulders in a gesture of hopelessness at the couple, then scurried after the other man. The door closed noisily as the latch crashed home. Voices started again, one or two at first, then others. The sudden hubbub of rumour and speculation rose rapidly.

"I'm sorry," Harrington said, wiping aside the mess on the table with a paper serviette.

Roisin shook her head, her face quite pale and bloodless.

"Let's not talk about things here anymore," he said. "Meet me tonight. We'll go somewhere quiet and talk things over."

She said quickly: "No, it can't be tonight."

"Oh? Even if I come to you?"

She looked flustered. "No, it's impossible. I've an uncle staying over."

"For a holiday?"

"No, no, just tonight. It would not be a good idea for you to call. To tell the truth he's a bit, well, a bit anti-English, if you know what I mean ..."

Harrington nodded, understanding: "Yes, I know. Who is it, your Uncle Pat?"

"Oh, you don't know him. He's called William ... Uncle William."

"I see. From Belfast?"

"No, Derry." Her eyes flashed. "What is this, Charlie? An inquisition?"

Harrington forced a smile. "No, sweetheart, I'm just concerned about you."

She said: "Look, tomorrow would be fine. Can you collect me from the farm at eight?"

"Sure," he replied. "We'll go somewhere less public and talk. Perhaps you can also tell me something about Malone?"

Her eyes flashed again. "Perhaps. I don't know much. He's just a friend of Sean's ... I'm sorry to say."

Harrington pulled aside the curtain to be sure O'Nions' car had gone and Malone with it. Finishing their drinks he and Roisin stepped out into the watery sunlight, the breeze chill but refreshing after the pub. She reached up and kissed him lightly on the lips.

35

She said seriously: "I did ask you not to expect too much of me. Please remember."

He smiled. "I will."

As he watched her climb into the battered grey Mini estate he thought back over her words with increasing anxiety. Roisin obviously did not appreciate the extent and complexities of the Army's computerised intelligence network in Ulster. Nor did she fully appreciate his own intimate knowledge of her background and her family.

There was no Uncle William in her family. Nor was there any close family friend who might reasonably assume such an affectionate nickname.

Harrington waved as she reversed into the road, changed gear, and accelerated away in the direction of the farm.

There was, however, a 'Willy' Joe McNally, a PIRA IED (Illegal Explosive Device) expert who had been a resident in Long Kesh at Her Majesty's pleasure, until he had managed to moonlight four months ago. Recently his name had been closely associated with a certain Sean McGuire.

CHAPTER 2

Some sixty miles to the south of the Brady's pub and at the same time as Harrington watched Roisin McGuire drive away, another Mini was pulling up outside one of the tidy semi-detached houses in a quiet backstreet of Sutton, a seaside resort a short distance from the centre of Dublin. The car was a later model than its counterpart in the north and its red paintwork gleamed immaculately, bearing witness to the many hours of work which its driver had lavished on it.

The interior of the car was also spotless and a scent of lavender lingered after the latest application of polish to the black leatherette upholstery. Its excellent condition did not reflect the natural inclination of its driver, who would prefer to spend his free time drinking heavily in the Dublin bars. It was the car's passenger who insisted that everything in his life was well-ordered and efficient. That included his chauffeur, who was not asked to face much in the way of danger or hardship in order to earn his £20 a week.

As the nearside door swung open and the passenger emerged, the man reading the *Irish Times* in the van parked opposite nodded gently without looking up. His radio was tuned to the police frequency and the nod meant that the coast was clear.

Martin McGuiness felt his shoulders relax involuntarily beneath his smart white military-cut raincoat. Pausing for a moment he looked up at the drawn curtains on the top floor of the house. A distinct breeze was in the air and it ruffled through his neatly-trimmed, thick light brown hair, but failed to displace it. His fresh complexion belied his thirty-five years, and his mouth, with a slightly receding lower lip, had an almost girlish pout about it. But any impression of femininity or weakness was more than countered by the alert and deep-set blue eyes. Tucking the sealskin document case beneath his left arm, he walked briskly through the open gate and up to the front door.

After a brief and cautious exchange with the man who opened the door—just enough to allow his squint eyes to examine the new arrival—McGuiness was ushered in to wait in the parlour. Outside, the red Mini pulled away, the driver heading towards a bar in town where he knew he could indulge himself to excess.

Upstairs in the front bedroom, where the blinds had been drawn to conceal the proceedings from inquisitive eyes, an extraordinary meeting of the PIRA Army Council was in full session. The normal bedroom furniture had been removed to another room and a polished teak G-Plan dining table extended to its full length to accommodate the five men. A dim light was cast by a standard lamp in the corner. Although no one smoked on the insistence of the chairman the atmosphere in the small room was unpleasantly stuffy.

Billy McKee felt his eyelids getting heavier as he listened to the gruff monotony of the speaker's voice. As officer commanding Belfast it was his job to chair the meeting, but he nevertheless had to allow the 'old guard' to have their say, regardless of their predictable views and reactions. Always, when Joseph B. O'Hagan began, McKee felt an inexorable weariness creep over him as he listened to the Quartermaster drone on in his abrasive mumble, florid cheeks quivering as he paused in his stumbling dialogue. It was as though he was defying anyone to challenge his operations in organising arms and explosives for the entire movement. Few did, even when his suspected inefficiency became just too much to ignore. Aware that he was no public speaker JB would place his fists on the table edge and glare at his fellow members, his chin jutting in defiance, occasionally running a stubby hand nervously through his grizzled grey hair. His old friend Seamus Twomey, who was Chief of Staff, rescued him as usual by subtly steering the conversation to another topic.

But today McKee was in no mood to tolerate JB's defensive ramblings. He felt tired and irritable after his long journey from Belfast to attend the emergency meeting, and he was aware of a dull ache beginning over his eyes.

"I'm sorry to interrupt you, Quartermaster," he said quietly, using the accepted and correct form of military address, "but I feel that your predictions of munitions delivery dates are not of immediate relevance to the matter under discussion."

"But, I ..."

McKee smiled reassuringly. "I think I speak for everyone when I say we are most pleased with your efforts in keeping us fully-equipped and supplied."

"Oh, I see, well ..." JB blustered. Never at ease with such fluent speakers, he suddenly realised he had the opportunity to let someone else defend him from the chairman's uncompromising interrogation. "Oh, well, thank you."

Joe Cahill, Adjutant General in charge of discipline, allowed himself an audible chuckle as he relaxed back in his chair and casually examined his fingernails. This earned him a disapproving glance from McKee, who had not failed to note the gradual change that had affected Cahill over the years. He now appeared less concerned with the Council's affairs, happy to wallow in the glory of his own reputation and adopt the attitude of an elder statesman, watching activities with the bemused look of a man apart from mundane everyday operations.

However the man seated beside Cahill welcomed the light relief. As the man with special responsibilities for border activities, Eamon Doherty, was pleased about anything that would take the pressure off him. For it was over his area of operations that this emergency meeting had been called. Not by him, but by Martin McGuiness.

At thirty-nine Doherty was the youngest man on the Council, the others being in their fifties, but he had been quickly accepted into the hierarchy when his hard-line policies and ex-paratrooper's experience had been seen to be working. Despite his long, unkempt curly hair, which was a constant source of irritation to the other Council members, he had earned considerable respect. His policies of land-mining roads and setting booby traps in Armagh had been especially successful and had kept the British Army's head down for some time. Now, just because of some temporary setbacks, McGuiness was trying to interfere in his usual know-it-all manner, calmly persuading McKee to convene an emergency meeting as though some monumental catastrophe was about to befall them.

"With respect, Mr Chairman, I believe the Quartermaster's account of how we're overcoming the problems of getting arms over the border intact is very relevant." It was Seamus Twomey's voice, forceful and highly-pitched, inevitably coming to JB's defence.

McKee looked across at the slight figure in the crumpled suit as he leaned forward earnestly, his eyes wide and bright through the tortoise shell spectacles. His scalp glistened with perspiration where the lank hair had receded.

"Do you now, Chief of Staff?" Billy McKee asked, his voice flat to underscore his sarcasm.

"Yes, sir, I do. Young Doherty is doing a grand job down in Armagh, and before we consider what is going wrong, it's as well to get things in perspective and examine where they are going right!"

McKee waited patiently for the outburst to subside. "Thank you for your valued opinion, Chief of Staff. However we have not called this meeting to praise the splendid works of the Quartermaster. Nor Doherty's prowess at blowing the legs off of Brit soldiers at which he is past-master. This meeting has been called to discuss what is going wrong. What is *not* going right.

"If I wanted to discuss our successful past operations I would hire a country club on the west coast where we could spend the weekend fishing, reminiscing and congratulating ourselves!"

Seamus Twomey blinked rapidly. Then he leaned back in his chair, loosening his collar.

McKee continued: "It may have escaped your notice

that there are two empty seats. Cochran left Londonderry a week ago for a meeting with me in Dundalk. He never arrived. He was last seen in Mr Doherty's border territory. Now either he was blown up by one of Mr Doherty's mines, or else his disappearance has something to do with the matter for discussion on today's agenda."

"If it was one of my mines I'd know about it," Doherty interjected emphatically.

"Stow it," Cahill hissed, recognising that McKee was losing patience.

He was too late to stop the chairman's retort: "I should hope you would, Mr Doherty, or else you wouldn't be sitting in your present privileged position. But we also expect you to know about it when someone as important as an Army Council member disappears into thin air *on your patch*."

"There's been rumours about SAS snatch squads, but nothing concrete," Doherty replied fiercely, realising immediately he'd made a mistake.

McKee eyed him coldly, content to savour the moment before he tore the man apart: "Of course there's nothing concrete. Of course there are only rumours. If they wanted us to know about it they'd have sent in an armoured battalion of Guards to get Cochran!"

"And there's Willy Joe McNally," grunted JB pointedly, pleased to see the arrogant youngster being put through McKee's mincer.

"Oh, c'm on," Cahill said. "I know Willy's been under great pressure in Belfast just recently with the Army undercover teams, but that's hardly Doherty's fault. His territory's along the border, not Lower Falls. Besides I shut a couple of loose mouths last week, and they were causing half the trouble."

The point had not been lost on Billy McKee, who was himself commanding officer of Belfast. He cleared his throat before speaking. "The Adjutant General is quite correct, of course. Willy McNally's problems have nothing to do with Mr Doherty just because he has the most dealings with SAS groups ..." He paused deliberately, implying that Mr Doherty should make it his business, "and it's unfortunate that he, too, has been unable to join us. At least he hasn't got lost on Mr Doherty's patch and, as he'll be crossing the border tomorrow, it's an ideal opportunity for Mr Doherty to prove just how good his security arrangements are."

"He'll be okay," Doherty insisted. "I'll stake my life on it."

"Your knee-caps anyway," chuckled Twomey.

"That's enough, Chief of Staff. Sufficient to say I've a meeting with McNally in Dundalk the day after tomorrow and I expect him to keep the appointment." And he added with thinly disguised contempt: "That's assuming he doesn't find some little harlot to distract him on the way."

The conversation was interrupted by a knock on the door, followed by an irritating creak of unoiled hinges as the man with the squint peered in.

He addressed himself to no one in particular: "Beggin' yer pardon, gentlemen. But the Chief of Northern Command is waitin' in the parlour." The military tone he was expected to adopt embarrassed him.

Billy McKee sat upright. "Good, good. Show him up immediately." At last, he thought, we might get some original thought and action.

Martin McGuiness was a man McKee liked. On more than one occasion he had turned down an offer to join the Army Council, preferring to keep contact with the three Provisional IRA Brigades, Derry, Belfast and Mid-Ulster, so Council members could learn what was happening before they read it on the front page of the *Belfast Telegraph*.

Although only thirty-five, McGuiness had quickly established some reliable lines of communication with the PIRA, even from the old hands who liked to go their own way, seizing opportunities as and when they presented themselves, with little co-ordinated pre-planning. Recently McGuiness had been installed as Chief of Northern Command, a newly created post, which was as impressive as it sounded. In effect he had become the chief liaison link between the Brigades and the Army Council. In that time things had improved still further, with McGuiness frequently more in touch with operations in Belfast than McKee himself.

However McGuiness' smart appearance and sardonic manner had not earned him much respect from Seamus Twomey, who saw his position as Chief of Staff severely undermined, and had endeared him even less to Eamon Doherty, who had at one time been the up-and-coming star of the Council.

All eyes watched as McGuiness saluted stiffly and, placing his raincoat carefully on the hook behind the door, took the seat at the opposite end of the table to McKee. Opening the sealskin document case, he spread a thin sheath of neatly-typed papers before him.

"My apologies for lateness, Mr Chairman," he began crisply, "but the urgency of this meeting necessitated gathering some up-to-the-minute facts which delayed me."

McKee waved the words aside expansively. "Forget it, Chief, there is no great loss in twenty minutes. It's better we are in full possession of the facts. You requested the meeting, so would you care to begin?"

"Thank you, sir," returned McGuiness. He hunched over his papers slightly, his penetrating eyes glancing up at the members around the table. "To begin gentlemen. It is my humble but well-informed belief that the Provisional Irish Republican Army is facing the most dangerous, and potentially fatal, challenge of the past eight years. With temporary setbacks we have always held our own in all the Brigade areas, particularly the inner Provo strongholds. Many of us have served time, but most have continued to give of our best when released, our methods improving with experience. Our ceasefires and other political manoeuvrings have all served their military purpose, and we have given the Brit Army a good run for their taxpayers' money.

"But, whereas a few years ago we could have counted out active numbers in Belfast alone in many hundreds, now we'd be pushed to call on two hundred in the whole of

43

Ulster. And the majority of them are not particularly competent. The rest have been eroded by arrests, murders by the Brits, injuries and plain disillusion. As the Adjutant General will no doubt testify, disciplinary action has never been so widespread, nor so severe."

Joe Cahill nodded soberly.

"But even this we can cope with," McGuiness continued. "Indeed we are coping with it. I for one am trying to make up for low numbers with better training, planning and co-ordination. Brit Intelligence has penetrated very deeply and, in our inner circles, Special Air Service agents in particular have caused us great problems. But our own security and counter-measures are proving successful with the smaller numbers in our ranks.

"Because we have always had freedom of movement, most particularly across the border, vital supplies from Europe and the United States, Libya and the Soviet bloc have continued unabated. Recently the quality of weapons has improved significantly."

JB grinned broadly and his eyes flickered around at the sober faces of the others around the table. No one was noticing him.

"But since Wilson moved in the SAS, even Armagh and other border districts are in danger of slipping from our control. Our life-lines with the outside world have been virtually severed, affecting movement of men and materials alike."

Eamon Doherty sat up from his lethargic slump. "Excuse me, Chief, but that is something of an exaggeration. We've had setbacks, but all that eyewash by Wilson was just a big propaganda scare. He's worse than Goebbels!" He added pointedly: "We all know they were active months before the public announcement about reinforcements."

"Exactly!" McGuiness exclaimed. "They've had plenty of time to get established; get the lie of the land; permeate throughout the fabric of society in Armagh. They've been biding their time, Mr Doherty, and we've been too blind to see it. Now it suits them, they are putting on the squeeze and I think it's starting to hurt us."

"Rubbish," Doherty growled.

McGuiness' eyes flickered coldly across to the representative from Tipperary. "Mr Doherty, a few weeks ago I sent my own man, a Mr Malone, into your territory to do a little independent investigation. I have a copy of his report here."

Doherty couldn't believe his ears. "Like bloody Christ you have!"

"Mr Doherty, be silent!" Billy McKee snapped. A deeply religious man in his own way, he could tolerate profanity even less than he could accept smoking, drinking or promiscuity.

Doherty looked wild-eyed and helpless as he glanced around at the sombre row of faces. "This upstart poking his nose into my affairs ..."

"Keep cool," warned Cahill out of the corner of his mouth.

McKee leaned forward. "This is the affair of *all* of us. The future of Ireland is in the hands of the people in this room, and we are *all* deeply concerned about the future of our beloved country. With an all-consuming passion! Calling The Christ or our Holy Mother in vain will not help. But possibly the Chief's unorthodoxy will. Please proceed, Mr McGuiness."

"Mr Chairman, my man reports that there are at least sixteen Special Air Service detachments operating in and around south Armagh."

"We know that!" spat Doherty.

McGuiness ignored him. "Also the Brits have some intelligence officers who have been successfully tapping our lines of communication for the past two years. They know what we're about to do before we think of it ourselves. One even spends much of his time buying one of Doherty's men drinks in return for a constant flow of vital information. He's even going around with the sister of one of Willy McNally's top henchmen! But that just indicates the scope of their operation. The really hard pill to swallow is their activities in the past six weeks."

He consulted the list before him. "Five safe houses raided and a total of 150lb of explosives taken, plus two dozen rifles, including the latest American Armalites. Twenty people arrested. Six active service unit members shot dead whilst crossing the border at night. Two wounded and three in custody. Those men are like phantoms. They'll wait in a hedgerow for days on end, without hot food or obvious communication with the outside world. Just waiting their opportunity to pounce. And, as we well know, SAS techniques are starting to be employed by regular Brit battalions. So much for Wilson's eyewash!"

He stopped as the words sunk into the deathly silence.

McKee turned to Seamus Twomey. "How much of this do we know about?"

The Chief of Staff shrugged. "Mr Doherty's reported a couple of these incidents to me."

McGuiness said: "I've a full list of names and details here, Mr Chairman."

"Let me see," demanded Doherty.

McGuiness gave him a copy. "Mr Doherty no doubt hasn't reported in full, because he just doesn't *know*. After all, that is why I suggested my role. So that our right hand would know what the left is doing."

JB grunted. "It's still a pretty bad show. It's his patch the Chief's talking about."

McKee asked: "Is there anything else, Chief?"

"Yes, Mr Chairman," McGuiness replied, happy to play his trump card. "Just over a week ago a kid called Drummond was picked up."

He saw Doherty blanch visibly.

"Drummond was outrider for Cochran on his border crossing."

"No!" gasped Twomey.

"Any news of Cochran?" McKee demanded.

McGuiness shook his head. "I'm afraid not, sir. But I've got my ear to the ground. We'll be informed as soon as there is news."

McKee shook his head slowly. "I hope so, Chief, I hope so. And I hope Willy McNally has better luck when he crosses the border tomorrow ... at this rate I'll be the only one left on the Council."

McGuiness coughed lightly. "Actually, sir, I've taken some precautions. I feel that we could be in the middle of a concentrated SAS campaign against suspected Council members. So I'm sending my man Malone in with Mr Doherty's men to assist in the crossing. They'll pick him up at a safe-house and escort him over. He's a good man."

Doherty had slumped back in his chair, his head in his hands, too defeated to reply.

"In view of this report," breathed McKee, "I think you have acted wisely. No reflection on Mr Doherty who has done well in the past. But the more precautions we take at this crucial time the better."

Everyone, including Doherty, nodded in agreement. For a moment there seemed nothing anyone could add, and it was the timely arrival of a tray of tea and digestive biscuits that broke the awkward silence.

As the squint-eyed man left the room, McKee said: "I assume Chief, that you have had some thoughts about coping with this menace."

McGuiness took a long time stirring his tea before looking up. "As you might imagine, Mr Chairman, I have also received strong representations from Gerry Adams and other fellow GHQ staff to take decisive action. I have been thinking about it hard for the past few days. And I believe there is a solution. The question is whether we are strong enough to put it into effect . . ."

He paused just long enough to let all the Council members know that he was about to say something of deep significance. The older men leaned forward to catch the quietly-spoken words.

"Of all the countries in the world, Britain has always enjoyed more success than any other in combating guerillas and terrorists—as we know to our cost. In Aden, Malaya, Kenya, Borneo . . . always they have won. And always the Special Air Service has played a key role. Small groups of highly-trained men fighting the terrorists at their own game. Even now SAS men are hired out to Oman and have virtually wiped out the rebel resistance in a war we scarcely hear about."

"What is the point you are making?" Seamus Twomey asked, peering over the top of his spectacles.

"Just this, sir. In their role against us, the SAS are acting like guerillas, thinking like guerillas. To all intents and purposes they are more like terrorists than we are."

"So?" pushed Twomey. The use of the word *terrorist* irritated him.

McGuiness smiled gently. "I am suggesting that we set a thief to catch a thief, so to speak."

"Ugh? What 'you talkin' about?" demanded JB, the importance of McGuiness' words lost on him.

Seamus Twomey's eyes burned fiercely through his spectacle lenses. "You mean deliberately hunt the hunters?"

Cahill let out a long, slow whistle.

"It could be done, by using the right men," McGuiness said firmly. "Against regular Brit units and the SAS themselves when possible."

"Our lads couldn't." Twomey said with feeling.

"But some ex-SAS men could," returned McGuiness.

Suddenly the air became charged with expectation. Thin, uncertain smiles began to spread across the faces around the table. Even Doherty was leaning forward, his chin resting thoughtfully on his folded arms.

McGuiness said: "I think Mr Doherty appreciates what I'm saying."

"I think we all do," McKee said, ignoring JB's puzzled expression.

"Not ex-SAS men." It was Doherty who spoke.

"Why not?" Twomey asked, warming to the idea. "They're always on the lookout for mercenary jobs. We've seen 'em, queuing up to get shot in Angola. Or bodyguards. They're always advertising themselves as bodyguards for some piddling head of state in darkest Africa or somewhere."

"Not ex-SAS," Doherty repeated.

Cahill said: "That chap Bank or Banks. The one who did all the recruiting for the FNLA. He'd be able to get hold of them."

"I've met Banks," Doherty said. "He didn't know who

48

I was, but I soon got the picture. Maybe he's only in it for the money, but I think he'd shop us rather than help us. He's trying to get himself a respectable reputation and he won't do that with the Brit Government if he gets mixed up with us."

All eyes had turned to the ex-paratrooper.

He sat up and looked at the Council members. "And I suspect he's something of a cock-eyed patriot. For that same reason we'd get short change from any ex-SAS men, unless we picked up some screwball. Their selection and training ensure they're never likely to be trusted with us. Nor fighting their own kind; even their old mates. All those who've joined us in the past turned out to be touts."

Cahill nodded vehemently.

McGuiness didn't like the way Doherty was steering them; he couldn't be sure that the man from Tipperary approved of his plan. "It's worth a try," he repeated emphatically. "After all, I'm suggesting they train the cream of our men, not fight themselves."

"It's *not* worth a try," sneered Doherty. "All of us here know their sort. Don't forget we're still talking about *my* territory and *my* sphere of operations." No one countered his statement, so he continued thoughtfully. "The Chief's concept is good. It could just work. But it won't be cheap and it's a sphere of operations that'll be new to our men in the field. So let's not make light of it. If we can't use ex-SAS men, we must look for some alternative. Foreigners without any personal, nationalist or patriotic hang-ups."

"Ex-Foreign Legionaires," Cahill suggested.

Doherty said: "I was thinking more of some Green Berets from Stateside. The ones who operated in Vietnam."

Twomey raised his hands in despair. "We can't afford the canned beer, artillery and air force to support them."

Doherty allowed himself a smile. "I'm talking about Green Berets, sir. The Special Forces who were conducting a private war in 'Nam long before the club-footed Marines splashed ashore. You won't find better, meaner bastards."

McGuiness smiled, relieved.

McKee said: "JB, you spend a lot of time in the States, don't you? Come across anyone?"

At last JB had caught up with the conversation. Although still unsure exactly what it all meant, he said gruffly: "I've come across several in the arms sales business. I remember one in particular." He chuckled hoarsely at the memory. "He was a mean devil all right. Left the Army some time ago and is trying to carve a new career for himself in international arms. Mercenary work and all. Catholic. Irish mother, in fact. There was this man we met when I was with him. Tried to sell the American short on stolen grenades. As he was walking away, the American discovered what he'd done. Threw a knife at him from thirty paces. Straight in the jugular. Didn't know what hit him. That was the cheapest arms deal we ever got. In fact I've a man in New York due to see the American next week."

"Good," McKee said. "In that case I propose that we put a proposition to this American chap to train some of our best men to fight in Armagh. Beat the Brits at their own game. And let's see what he has to offer."

Twomey raised his right arm. "Seconded."

As all hands were raised, Billy McKee announced: "Motion carried!" He scribbled a note on the paper before him.

There was a knock on the door and the squint-eyed man entered carrying an envelope. He handed it to McGuiness.

He read it quickly. "Gentlemen, I've just had a communiqué from my man Malone."

All eyes turned to the young PIRA commander.

"He reports Cochran was wounded and captured last week in an SAS ambush. The two men with him were both killed."

At the head of the table, McKee crossed himself. He looked up. "The sooner we contact this American the better. What's his name JB?"

"Er ... McClatcher. That's right. Captain Earl Lee McClatcher."

CHAPTER 3

Harrington and Captain Jack Ducane came back together from the briefing-room at Bessbrook. Their boots cracked in unison on the worn lino floor of the dingy corridor, its windows long since boarded up as a precaution against a surprise attack by the Provisionals. The two men provided a sharp contrast: the Artillery Regiment officer dressed in a smart pair of barrack trousers and a jersey, complete with deep-peaked cap and brass-buckled stable belt; the Special Air Service captain in a baggy camouflage smock, the material streaked with a disruptive pattern in shades of black, green and brown. It gave the appearance of adding pounds to his already powerful build, and the fawn beret with its winged dagger badge emphasised his height.

They could have been mistaken for brothers, but the older man's features were tanned and weather-beaten from years spent in the open air, often under a tropical sun; his fair hair slightly longer than was usual for a service cut.

Harrington was saying: "I'm sorry it's all in such a rush, Jacko, but I only got wind of it myself at lunchtime."

Ducane grinned reassuringly: "That's okay, Charlie, I'm only sorry it's happened like this. It's not going to be any picnic for you with Roisin at risk."

Harrington nodded soberly. "That's why I asked if your mob could have a chance to go in first. I know you'll take care of her. I hope you don't mind?"

"It's pushing the Best Man's duties a bit far, but I don't mind. And I'm sure the lads will be pleased you chose 'em." Ducane added: "I think the CO was right to turn down your request to come along."

Harrington shrugged. "I suppose so."

Ducane laughed. "You don't seem too convinced. But

51

you and your two left feet might slow us down. Besides the bride wouldn't thank us if you went and got a vital bit shot off, now would she?"

Harrington halted at the door to the SAS team's billet. He started to speak, then paused, unsure how much to say. Ducane sensed there was something troubling the younger man, something that must have been fairly important for him to hesitate about sharing it.

Ducane put a hand to the other man's shoulder: "What is it, Charlie? C'mon, spit it out. The worse they can do is have you shot for it."

Harrington forced a smile. "Have you got a cigarette?"

"Yes, sure." Ducane rummaged in one of the enormous pockets in his smock, pulled out a battered packet of Players and gave one to Harrington. He took one himself and lit them with a black plastic lighter. He noticed the man's hand was trembling. Only just, but there was a definite tremble.

Lord Charles, my lad, thought Ducane, you are starting to crack. Hardly noticeable yet, but it will get worse. In your line-of-business, once it begins that faint hairline fracture just gets wider and wider until it swallows you up whole. The tension of living a half-true lie for months on end was enormous, hoping all the time the little jig-saw pieces are always joining up to present the right picture to the enemy. But what enemy? The hands that belonged to those friendly smiling faces were quite capable of holding a gun. A knock at the door one morning. The milkman for his money? Or one of those friendly smiling faces you know so well leering down the dark snout of a sub-machine gun? Sudden death, splattered all over the walls, soaking the carpet. It happened; all the time it happened. Switch on the car. Click! No ignition. Just one-fifth of a second to know what's coming next. Just one-fifth of a second to remember that for the first time you forgot to check under the chassis. But an eternity in which to regret. Phoof! No, Lord Charles, my lad, you're well off out of it. Stop pretending you're a Mick. Forget your great-grandfather owned half of Ulster. Remember the country lanes back home, where you can drive knowing full well that the cow-pat in the middle of the road doesn't conceal a landmine that will blow your legs and your balls off. Get out now, Lord Charles, before it gets to you. Before you make the one mistake they're all waiting for.

Harrington inhaled deeply. "Jacko, I didn't tell the CO everything."

Ducane frowned, wondering what was coming next.

"It's about Roisin. She didn't tell me about William McNally."

"But you said ..."

"I know what I said," Harrington replied evenly. He paused, watching the blue smoke curl away from his cigarette. At last he added: "But she didn't tell me deliberately. It just sort of slipped out. I said I wanted to see her tonight and she gave me some cock 'n' bull story about some uncle staying over tonight. I know her background well enough to know it was a pack of lies. Knowing her brother's connections and knowing the heat's been on McNally in Belfast, her use of his name made sense."

"No wonder you Int. boys are always screwing things up."

Harrington pulled a half-hearted grin. "It's more than we usually have to go on, believe me. No, I'm sure it's William McNally. But you can see I couldn't tell the CO I found out by accident."

Ducane studied the end of his cigarette. "I'm not so sure."

"If I told him that, she'd be in the can as well. Locked away for two or three years at least for knowingly harbour-ing a terrorist. A possible member of the PIRA Army Council at that."

Ducane said flatly: "You've set me up nicely, Charlie."

Harrington shook his head. "There's no problem. The CO thinks she informed to help me, and no one else in Int. knows different. When you get there, you arrest him and leave her. No one's to know any different. Christ, Jacko, she's only a kid."

Ducane nodded. "Sure, Charlie, she's only a kid. And

they were only kids who used to lure the squaddies in Belfast to make-believe parties, so their Provo boyfriends could butcher them. Like lambs to the bloody slaughter. And it was pretty teenage kids who used to dish out ham sandwiches to grateful soldiers—filled with crushed glass."

"For God's sake!" Harrington snapped. "Roisin's not like that. Dammit, you know, you met her."

Ducane eyed him steadily. "I met a nice big-eyed bit of crumpet just out of a gymslip for five minutes in a dark corner of a pub, Charlie. For all I know she could have been bloody Moira Drumm's daughter."

Harrington turned on his heel. "If that's your sodding attitude stuff it . . ."

The grip of Ducane's large hand restrained him. "I'm sorry, Charlie, but you've got to admit there is a danger."

Harrington looked at him coldly. "I've known Roisin since she was eight. She's just not like that. What she's doing she's doing for her brother Sean, I'm sure of that."

"I just wish she'd volunteered the information. But thanks for telling me anyway."

Harrington said: "How could she admit to me she helps her brother? But I think this'll be the last time she does anything for Sean." He added: "She's agreed to marry me, Jacko. She wants to talk it over with her brother when he gets back."

Ducane smiled, although he found little amusement in the situation. It was not beyond the bounds of possibility that the girl was trying to set Charles Harrington up for an execution squad. Drop a juicy morsel to get him intrigued and . . . But it would be him and the rest of his Sabre team who walked into it. There was always that possibility. At least he was grateful that Harrington had the courage to confess what had really happened. On reflection he was not sure he wouldn't have done the same had their positions been reversed.

"Okay, Charlie, let's look on the bright side. I'm sure you're right. Let's go and give my merry men the briefing." He paused with his fingers on the doorhandle. "I won't mention anything you said. We'll just make sure they appreciate that it could be tricky."

"Thanks," Harrington said.

Ducane's men looked up as the two entered the cramped makeshift billet. Virtually no daylight penetrated the small, mesh-covered window high on the outside wall. It looked onto a bank of stacked sandbags. A single fluorescent tube flickered its hesitating glow around the plain tobacco-stained walls, there being no way to determine the original colour of the gloss paintwork. A double utility bunk ran the length of each side wall, but only one was occupied.

As junior member of the team Tom Perrot was relegated to the lower left-hand bunk, which caught the full blast of the chill draught that whistled under the badly-hung door. It also guarded the large mousehole in the corner, and it was Young Tom's job to keep the upper hand against the wiley rodent intruders. 'Big Bert' still eluded them, as he had eluded the previous occupiers. No one had ever seen him, but everyone accepted his existence. Nor was the possibility ever raised of blocking the hole; it never entered anyone's mind. While it was there it was a chal-lenge, a constant topic of conversation, amusement and, occasionally, unseen company.

Having freshly baited the traps under his bunk, Young Tom had settled down on it to compose a letter home to his widowed mother in Poole. He never mentioned 'Big Bert' to her; she would only worry.

Sergeant Forbes had been sitting at the table that ran between the bunks, with his back to the door. Dressed in camouflage trousers and an open-necked khaki shirt, he had sat hunched over a back copy of *Penthouse* studying one particular picture of a girl from Barnsley for a full five minutes. He had planned to catch up with his Russian studies, but had soon got bored, casting the text book aside. Forbes held a curious, intense affection for the woman in the centre spread. Only Ducane had guessed the reason for Big Dave's morbid fascination with the girl. They had been friends a long time and he had known Dave's estranged wife, Elaine, well. She was no great beauty; but she had come from Barnsley.

Also at the table Corporal John Turnbull had stripped down his 9mm Sterling 'smudge' gun and laid out each separate part on a sheet of newspaper. Carefully he cleaned each piece of metal until it gleamed, then lovingly re-oiled them. Despite the messy nature of the work, there was scarcely a trace of oil on his fingers. Even in his camouflage smock, hardly a becoming item of bespoke tailoring, he managed to look immaculate. It was with something approaching awe, although thickly disguised with sarcasm, that he had earned the name 'Action Man', being always turned out with the newness and freshness of the popular plastic dolls. His slight build and slim five foot seven frame did nothing to lessen the overall effect.

But should anyone ever mistake the taciturn Liverpudlian's appearance as a sign of weakness they would be in for a rude awakening. The bewildering array of precision-engineered gun parts spread before him would become deadly and fully-loaded in seconds, as his hands flew to re-assemble the weapon with dazzling and dexterous speed.

Turnbull was a loner, introverted, and his degree of independence and self-containment was his own personal measure of success. He never allowed this private driving force to form a barrier between his colleagues. If he had, it would be impossible to work within the Special Air Service, where total trust, reliance and compatibility within a Sabre team is of paramount importance. He knew that he would never find the action he craved nor the independence he enjoyed outside the regiment, or at least not on the right side of the law. So he was prepared to relent, to allow himself to tolerate the others, and to be tolerated himself. If ever the others became mildly irritated with him during mundane daily routine, any rancour would quickly dissipate in combat. Turnbull would be there, in the thick of it, covering a suddenly exposed flank, appearing from nowhere in the nick of time, thinking the enemy's thoughts before they had themselves, with a knack that was singularly uncanny and greatly appreciated by the team.

He was not unhappy with his 'Action Man' tag, secretly cherishing the respect that went behind it, confident that he could match himself against any other man in the team. In his own mind he knew that he could outwit and outfight each one.

There was a sudden shuffling movement as Ducane and Harrington entered.

"Okay, at ease, lads," Ducane said with a wave of his hand. "Let's keep it informal. Lieutenant Harrington has chosen us for a very special mission to rescue a distressed damsel."

"That sounds promising, boss!" Forbes' leered, folding his magazine and flicking it deftly on top of the pile. Young Tom drew his legs off the bunk, and climbed to his feet, brushing the spilled cigarette ash from his ribbed Army sweater. A sudden series of clicks and clunks came from Turnbull's side of the table as he went through his popular routine of re-assembling the Sterling.

Harrington gazed in amazement as the rows of metal parts took shape with lightning speed.

Ducane said: "Thirty-five seconds, Turnbull. You're getting old."

"Afraid you're right, boss." He looked across at the liaison officer as he cleared the newspaper, and added pointedly: "Still, I expect they'd still have me in the RA."

Harrington smiled, uncertainly. He still found it difficult to accept the ordered informality of the SAS teams. He found it hard to imagine the officers, NCOs and men of his own Royal Artillery sharing quarters like this except under the direst circumstance, and even then not without voluminous protest. "Our standards are pretty high, Corporal," he ventured.

"Bah!" Forbes retorted cheerfully. "If you had men like old 'Action Man' here you could make do with one man per battery! I bet Turnbull could strip and clean a 175mm howitzer in five minutes flat."

"No," replied Turnbull evenly. "I'd need ten at least."

Ducane spread a large scale military survey map across the table, then sat casually on the edge.

He began slipping quickly into the standard briefing format. "Taking part in tonight's jaunt will be ourselves, Johnny Fraser's Sabre team and B Platoon of the Royals. The op. will take place at the McGuire farm. We're all familiar with the area; we've done many a Farmer's Daughter there ..."

For once the jokey Army slang for surveillance of remote homesteads brought an instant smile to the row of solemn faces. Everyone remembered Roisin, and Forbes laughed aloud. He remembered how young and fresh she'd looked, and how he'd hogged the IWS Starlight nightsight every summer evening when she'd been preparing for bed. From their vantange point on the hill, his line of sight had carried in over the net curtains that covered the lower half of the window. He recalled her slender, pale body as she crossed the room and the cutting remarks from Turnbull as he had tried to focus his concentration. It was, he had decided, one of his perks and, anyway, no one really believed he saw all the sights he claimed. It made a change, he reflected, from the other less pleasant sights in Ulster.

Young Tom, too, remembered the girl. It had been he who had told them all when he first saw her undress one evening. He had watched, fascinated, for a full three minutes before he recovered from his good fortune and called out to the others in a hoarse whisper. It was a move he'd instantly regretted. Forbes had immediately taken over, his eye glued to the viewer. After that the sergeant had adopted the late evening watch as his own.

Ducane jabbed a finger at the map. "As you know, the farm's land runs to about seven acres, situated between two roads. Access is from the north, off the Drumbally–Glasdrumman road by a rough chalk track, the farm building itself set back about three hundred yards, surrounded by a cluster of trees. To the south the farm is bordered by a lane which leads to three border crossing points. However, travelling overland from the McGuire farm, the border is just over a mile away.

The team members nodded as they recalled the layout of the terrain surrounding the hilly border smallholding.

"As for Enemy Forces," Ducane continued, "Int. anticipates a small group of Provos, exact strength unknown. But probably they'll be fairly competent as they're acting as escort for a VIP travelling south."

Forbes let out a long, low whistle. "Not another Council member?"

"Getting embarrassing, isn't it?" Ducane replied with a grin. "This time it's the elusive Mr Willy McNally, late of the Lazy K."

"That little shit?" Forbes asked incredulously. This was unbelievable good fortune. "The one who's been causing the latest rumpus in Belfast?"

Ducane nodded. "Since he got out of Long Kesh he's been giving Felix a pretty bad time." They had all heard of the rash of vicious, booby-trapped bombs that had claimed the lives of two men from an Explosive Ordnance Disposal section. It had been so bad that 'Top Cat' himself, the Chief Ammunition Technical Officer of HQ Northern Ireland with the rank of lieutenant-colonel, had personally taken over supervision of the spate of McNally bombs until the defusing problems had been overcome.

For his part, rumour had it that McNally had been promoted from the PIRA General Headquarters Staff to the ruling Army Council itself.

"It'll be our operation," Ducane explained. "We don't want the slightest risk of alerting the escort party. But Johnny Fraser's mob will be deployed to the south between the farm and the border just in case we miss them, or they decide not to stop at the farm."

He allowed himself a slight smile. "Now for the bad news. I'm afraid the main part of the operation will fall to the Royals, who'll be waiting in two or three Wessex 2s to the east. It seems like our friend, Major Simmonds, has persuaded his CO that we might damage the goods." A spontaneous groan went up from the men around the table. "And, of course, guess who'll be leading them .. ?"

"Bloody gong-hunter," Forbes said.

Ducane ignored the muttering and went on to the part they were all waiting for, details of the mission itself. "Tonight Int. are expecting McNally's party to visit the McGuire farm on a run south. We've been closing in on him in Belfast, putting on the squeeze ... in fact he just escaped a raid on a safe-house a couple of days ago by a whisker.

"With the pressure on our patch at the moment, we don't think they'll chance using a car. Especially after our escapade with Cochran last week. So they'll probably come on foot. Overland by night.

"Personally I expect he'll do the journey in two short hops. At the moment he's probably in or around Creggan. That would allow him to slip southward along the Creggan River valley, veering uphill to the east. And that would keep him clear of most roads and farmhouses until he reaches the McGuire farm.

"Our job is simply to pull out the youngster Roisin, quick, and let Major Simmonds sweep in and collect the VIP ..."

"And a bloody gong!" added Forbes with feeling.

Ducane held up his hand as the look of incredulity swept over the men's faces at the fact they were being ordered to risk their collective neck to save a Republican sympathiser—however pretty she might be. The captain continued briskly, ignoring Harrington's obvious embarrassment and the bursting curiosity of the team.

It was twenty minutes before everything had been covered from timing and routes to the objective, rendezvous points, observation duties, action on arrival, signals to be used and passwords. Finally they synchronised watches.

Ducane raised his eyebrows. "Any questions?"

As he expected, all three soldiers began at once. Forbes scowled at the other two. "I'm sure I don't have to remind you, gentlemen ..."

Turnbull, straight-faced, bowed stiffly from the waist. "Of course, after you, Sergeant."

Forbes sniffed, turned away, and fixed Harrington with a penetrating stare. "This girl has been under observation for months. Her brother's a guaranteed bona fide Provo. We're goin' to pull her out because Int.'s been playin' Chinese Whispers again, and has been offered something on a plate. To a lowly NCO that sounds mighty suspect. Can I ask you how reliable is the information we're acting on?"

Seeing Harrington hesitate, Ducane answered. "The information is likely to be correct as it comes from Roisin McGuire of the McGuire farm."

Turnbull frowned. "What's so reliable about that? It's under regular surveillance as a Provo safe-house. It's a Republican family of long standing."

"I know that," Ducane said evenly. "But what *you* don't know is that our liaison officer here has been courting Roisin McGuire for some time. Now obviously it's difficult for her to shop her own brother, but she's given the lieutenant the nod that McNally's passing south."

His face reddening, Harrington watched the frozen expressions of disbelief as the words sank in. An uneasy silence fell over the billet.

Forbes broke it first. "You crafty old sod, Charlie!"

"Sergeant," Ducane chided.

The big man ignored him, climbing to his feet and grasping Harrington's hand in a rigorous shake. "No wonder we're beating the Provos hollow with crafty old buggers like you working for us! Stone-a-crows, I can hardly believe it! You ol' cradle-snatcher!"

Young Tom gritted his teeth. First Forbes with his coarse and vulgar comments about the girl, and now Lord Charles had been chatting her up, flirting with her, no doubt dripping with his usual oozy syrup and his public school accent. The bugger could charm his way into anyone's knickers, he'd heard. And this girl, virtually the only one he'd known in Northern Ireland—albeit through hours of long-distance surveillance—had to be the one Harrington chose to slop over. The liaison officer must be at least ten years her senior, decided Young Tom angrily.

Not for the first time he cursed his own ineptitude with the girls he had known. How many times had his inhibitions tied his well-rehearsed phrases into tongue-knotting nonsense? Even when he had gone on leave to Bournemouth after joining the Parachute Regiment, resplendent in his new uniform that brought admiring glances from many girls, he had failed dismally to fire the sparks of youthful lust in any of them. His old mates had assumed his success and he had done nothing to delude them.

"No congratulations for Lieutenant Harrington then, Tom?" Ducane's words jarred him from his seething thoughts.

"Ah, sorry, sir, I was daydreaming." He hesitated, aware that all eyes were on him. "Yes, of course. I wish them all the ... er ... all the best. Sir."

Forbes chuckled. "I think Young Tom fancies the young lady himself, boss."

Perrot's anger swelled instantly. "Piss off, Sarge, for Chrissakes."

Ducane ignored the outburst, aware that the big sergeant had hit a raw spot. He glanced across to John Turnbull, who sat attentively, also without comment. He disapproves too, thought Ducane, and I don't know that I blame him. Different reasons from Young Tom, no doubt, but more valid. It didn't take an expert to work out that this assignment could backfire into a nasty mess.

Ducane said: "Miss McGuire's agreed to marry Lieutenant Harrington shortly, and no doubt he plans to whisk her away somewhere out of harm's way. But for tonight we face a tight situation. She'll be hosting McNally for her brother, and we'll have to get her out without the little lady getting hurt."

"Couldn't she slip out before we go in?" Turnbull asked.

Harrington felt a renewed rush of blood to his cheeks as he answered. "Unfortunately, I couldn't discuss a plan of action with her. There was a danger of us being overheard at the time."

Turnbull nodded, but he didn't look very convinced. "How long is he stopping at the farm?" he asked quietly.

Harrington shrugged. "I've no idea. He may be planning to rest up all tomorrow and travel on again at night. He may just stop for an hour or two and continue. Or he may brazen it out and just walk out at dawn and mingle with the farmworkers. It wouldn't be difficult to just drive over the border in a tractor from there."

There was a cutting edge to Turnbull's voice: "Your young lady didn't tell you too much then, did she?"

Harrington flushed. "Enough for us to go on."

"Couldn't we or the Royals just nab him as he leaves the farm, whenever that is?" Forbes suggested. "That way the McGuire girl wouldn't get in the line of fire. Safer."

Harrington shook his head. "It's a nice idea, Sergeant, but once you know the rat's in the trap, you don't give him a snowball's chance of getting away. You'd have to guarantee an undetected approach and remain in close proximity to the farm until whatever time he decides to leave. If they've got armed pickets out, or look-outs, you couldn't guarantee that. No, you'll have to go in and stay in."

"I'd rather get Miss McGuire out sooner than later," stated Young Tom emphatically.

"I don't remember anyone asking you, trooper," hissed Forbes.

"He's entitled to his opinion," Ducane said sharply. "And anyway we are not given much choice in the matter. We monitor the enemy's arrival, move in, neutralise any sentries and spring young Roisin. We then send the signal which is the sign for Major Simmonds to bring in the flying cavalry . . ."

"Oh, Christ," groaned Forbes.

Ducane continued: "He reasons that they can't afford to let McNally slip through the net—or get himself shot." Broad smiles spread all round. "He reckons that a sudden heli-borne assault with split-second timing would ensure overwhelming odds, especially as we've already picked off the look-outs. McNally would have no real choice but to give himself up. I know we all think we'd do a better job, perhaps with Johnny Fraser's Sabre team, but unfortunately Simmonds' got the CO's ear. At least he didn't have it all his own way. Originally our Major wanted to handle the whole op. himself.''

Harrington said: "If it wasn't for Roisin, he may have a point. Obviously I'm concerned they could use her as a hostage, if he's given half a chance.''

Forbes lit a cigarette and studied the charred match with deep concentration. It was going to be a tricky operation sneaking the girl out; the odds didn't look good. The others looked decidedly glum.

It was rare to see Forbes in such a contemplative mood. He enjoyed projecting his naturally wild and earthy personality, switching, when it suited him, to play the traditional role of the unthinking and unreasonable Army sergeant. Nothing could have been further from the truth. Although he had little regard for authority in general, particularly the bureaucratic type, he never questioned the authority or traditions of the Regiment.

When not on duty he took a delight in hitting the bottle hard—not a common trait in SAS soldiers—but had never been known to lose the slightest grip on himself or control of any situation, however difficult. At times his larger than life image had caused a couple of his squadron commanders to raise an eyebrow. But every routine 16PF psychology test had shown him not to be harbouring any unstable or psychotic characteristics deep within his personality.

The truth was that Forbes was a natural born warrior. It was like a primeval instinct, a driving force. And he had been drawn naturally into the one regiment that was always at war, even in peacetime, however remote or small the conflict may be. Meanwhile his determined love of life and ruthless disregard of orthodoxy had lost him his wife and prevented any quick promotion.

Ducane was adding: "Of course, it may be necessary to use a little artistic licence. We'll play it Simmonds' way, but the action on objective may have to be played by ear. The lieutenant knows which is Roisin's room, so we'll pay her a call first. Any problems and, for safety's sake, Major Simmonds may have to wait for his hour of triumph."

"That's the ticket," murmured a smiling Forbes.

John Turnbull's expression remained deadpan. He did not regard Ducane as an ideal commander, prone to act on instinct and intuition when prior brainwork may have made many tasks less arduous. This seemed to Turnbull to be a typical example. Luckily the captain's animal senses usually proved correct; if they hadn't the team wouldn't have survived so long in Armagh.

Although promotion didn't count for too much in the SAS, as an individual's rank was inevitably lower than it would have been in an orthodox regiment, Jack Ducane was overdue for a majority. He had never been able, or perhaps wanted, to shed fully the vestiges of his working-class background. Turnbull suspected that this could be part of the reason, despite the fact that 'The Professionals' were supposed to be a classless family nowadays. Of course, it may be something to do with the rumour that his paper-work wasn't up to scratch. Or his long friendship with that renegade Sergeant Forbes. Perhaps it was a combination of all of these.

If you screw this one, thought Turnbull bitterly, it will be another rung kicked out of your promotional ladder, Captain Jack Ducane. Just make sure I don't get tarred with the same brush.

CHAPTER 4

"I think I've found another one," Forbes said.

They had been dropped an hour earlier from the Makrolon-armoured Land Rover which had roared down the unmade road at great speed, until it reached the sharp bend. There the road dipped out of sight of the surrounding countryside, hidden by tall hedges on both sides. As the driver hit the brakes with force, Ducane and Young Tom leapt out through the tailgate.

Together they had landed at a crouch in the dusty track, sprinting for cover in the shrubbery. The Land Rover had slewed wildly in its skid, the heavy-duty tyres spinning for a grip in the loose stones and chalk. Forbes and Turnbull emerged from the choking cloud as the vehicle sped forward again, out of the dip and around the next bend. Briskly they had followed the first two into the hedge.

Even to a PIRA observer, hidden in the surrounding countryside, the sight of the madcap Army driver racing down one of the labyrinth of twisting roads would attract no special interest, provided he kept moving at speed. It was a well-rehearsed procedure, and gave far less indication of an active Army presence than the menacing clatter of a helicopter. And, surprisingly enough, it held little danger. The speed at which the vehicle travelled down the winding roads made it virtually impossible for a 'snipe' to hold it in the cross-hairs for more than a split second. Similarly it would have taken superhuman reflexes to catch it with a controlled landmine. Even an instant contact-fuse would be unlikely to explode before the vehicle had passed completely over it.

Simultaneously, a mile to the south, four men of Johnny Fraser's Sabre team detached themselves one by one from a trudging platoon of Royals and slipped quietly into a roadside ditch. Even the soldiers with them didn't realise they had gone.

Meanwhile Ducane's team had found the narrow drainage ditch that stretched up the steep hill until, at the rim, it overlooked the McGuire farm. It was through this sodden trench, overhung with gorse and bramble bushes, that the four men had crawled. It took twenty minutes to reach the site of their old observation lair.

At that point a cluster of trees grew on both sides of the ditch and the low shrubbery thickened considerably. A few minutes careful hunting in the undergrowth located the rough trestle that they had built earlier to provide a dry platform over the ditch, without disturbing the waterflow. It was from the edge of these trees that Forbes suddenly announced he could see something.

Ducane, his face smeared with camouflage cream, wriggled across the trestle to where the sergeant held the Starlight scope. He took it, adjusting the focus marginally.

Despite the low cloud, the weird semi-negative green of the surrounding countryside was as clear as daylight through the viewer. In order to operate, the image-intensifying process required just the merest trace of light, which was magnified through a series of lenses and electronic circuits. Only in the rare situation of absolute absence of light was it ineffective. Normally starlight or moonshine was a luxury.

After a few moments Ducane said: "You're right. A slight movement below the old elm tree. A clump of grass swaying. Different direction to the rest."

"Out of tune with nature," Forbes mused.

"Nice job he's made though," Ducane replied. "Must have been a devil to spot. Professional."

Forbes chuckled quietly. "Not really. Silly sod couldn't resist a drag a moment ago. Like a little glow worm."

It was a joke they could all share. They had long since learned to give up smoking at a moment's notice for months on end, especially when up against trained jungle fighters. They had learned from the Gurkhas' survival rulebook that said even chewing gum, traces of soap, toothpaste or hair dressing would betray a soldier's presence to an expert enemy.

"Whatever he did to catch your eagle eye, it looks like we've found three sentries. Shame. Four would have made a nice round number. I just hope we haven't missed one."

"Where're the other two?"

"Turnbull spotted the one on the approach road to the farm. I located one guarding the south road. Charlie was probably right. Yours would have a good view towards the river valley in the west. Keep your eyes peeled for the VIP's arrival."

"How about knocking off the pickets now?"

Ducane shook his head. "He may be expecting a recognition signal. Or a pre-arranged meeting. We'll wait until he's in the box before we shut the lid."

There wasn't long to wait. By 2300 hours the night had become inky black, the damp ground mist thickening as the air became chiller, reducing the nightsight's range of visibility to scarcely two hundred yards. The faint breeze shifted the cleaving vapours, mesmerising, forming and dissolving shapes until the backs of Ducane's eyes ached with strain.

Forbes had closed in on his quarry, snaking forward on his belly. Working his way along a shallow indentation in the rough pasture, he had found himself within fifty yards of the picket. Above and behind him. With his scope he could see some distance across the field that fell towards the valley.

Earlier, Turnbull had edged around the eastern flank of the farm, probing the numerous hay bales and stacks for any sign of the fourth sentry who would have closed the square. He had found nothing and had crept on until he was hidden beneath the hedge that ran alongside the main Drumbally-Glasdrumman road. A hundred yards away he distinguished the shadowy outline of the picket on the approach road to the farm, concealed beneath a bush. An M60 glinted dully in the headlight glow whenever a car passed by on the road.

Back at the lair a voice crackled on Ducane's Pocketfone. "*Some business*." It was the signal from Forbes that someone was approaching.

Quickly Ducane tried to focus through the mist to where he knew the sentry was waiting. Everything seemed indefinable through the drifting shroud. Then he swept down the crest, below the lookout point, to where the descent to the river valley began. He peered hard through the scope until his eyes began to water. Still nothing. Backward sweep. Pause. No movement from the sentry.

"Time?" he hissed.

"2320, boss," came Young Tom's reply.

'And there's no movement from the farm?"

"No, boss."

"The young lady hasn't gone to bed, then?"

"Hard to tell. She drew all the curtains tonight. The only lights appear to be downstairs. Won't please the sergeant much."

Ducane grunted, engrossed as he scanned back over the crest. The mist coiled and twisted in a sudden gust of wind. Forming new shapes, then dissolving. A dark patch began to take form, solidifying, refusing to be blown.

"Ah!" Ducane breathed. It was a figure all right. No doubt about it. A man, stooped, waiting, cautious. Very dark, no tell-tale flashes of pale flesh. He was down now, leaning on one elbow, peering over the crest, down towards the lighted windows of the farm.

Another movement, wraith-like. A second figure joined the first. The movements were more alert, the face less-well hidden. Nervous, jerky. This could be McNally.

A pin-prick of light stabbed briefly up to the slope towards the old elm trees.

Probably an old Army surplus signal-lamp, Ducane decided. Waiting for the answering flash from the sentry? There it was. Green. One quick spot in the darkness. You could have missed it if you weren't expecting it. A brief pause and the two dark figures moved forward. The first beckoned to the other to keep low as he slithered over the crest and down towards the farm. Feeling safe in the swathes of cloying mist, they made no more attempt to follow the contours of the land for cover. They strode forward now in a half-hearted crouch in the direction of the haloed patches of light. If they had taken even rudimentary precautions, reflected Ducane, they might never have been spotted.

He took the scope from his eye and handed it to Young Tom. "Keep track of them," he said, "and let me know if you see your girlfriend."

He caught the gleam of white teeth in the darkness.

After an hour the lower lights of the farmhouse were extinguished. For a moment the only illumination came from some glow deep within the building, probably the hallway or stairs. Then one bedroom light came on, the girl's bedroom, followed closely by a second at the side of the house. Ducane judged that to be the guest-room Harrington had predicted would be used. Shortly afterwards all the lights went out. No sign of movement came from the farm.

It had previously been decided to wait for an hour before closing-in. The only exception was to have been in the unlikely event of McNally moving over the border immediately. Had that been the plan, Ducane reasoned, it was unlikely he would have bothered to stop at the McGuire farm at all.

After the build-up of tension the long wait, until the occupants of the farm were asleep, came as an unwelcome anticlimax. Although it was still only late August, the wind had developed a chilling edge and carried with it the first traces of rain. The mist had cleared from the high ground, leaving behind only patches clutching to sheltered gulleys and depressions. Moisture from the damp air collected in the leaves around the lair. Icy drips had an uncanny knack of finding exposed flesh. A runway trickle at the wrist, and always the neck. Like a cold, slow worm down the back.

It was 0100 hours. Ducane breathed a sigh of relief. He was glad of the opportunity to flex the muscles of his legs and arms, which had stiffened during the tense period of inactivity. He pressed the transmitter button on the Pocketfone.

"Activate," he said quietly and switched off.

To the east Forbes would begin to move down the fifty yards of slope towards the old elm tree where the sentry was probably fighting off fatigue.

By the Drumbally–Glasdrumman road, Turnbull would be inching his way along the drainage ditch in the shadow of the wall towards the approach road.

Only minutes before Young Tom had slid silently out of the lair, in the opposite direction to the farm, south to where the third sentry guarded the lanes that wound towards Eire.

It was time. Ducane strapped the Sterling sub-machine gun across his back. Considered little more than a toy by some, the weapon was still popular for close-quarters combat in confined spaces. Its low-velocity 9mm rounds tended to stay in the victim and not continue on to cause accidents. Silently he eased himself out of the thicket, moving through the grass in a leopard crawl, belly and rump low, using knees and elbows for propulsion. There was little need to worry about leaving spoor trails of flattened grass this night, but old habits died hard.

He hugged the edge of the ditch for five minutes until he reached the low wall of local stone that divided two fields. It dipped slowly down to the farm, and here progress was quicker. His outline was concealed by the uncemented, interlocking rocks; the only danger of detection would come from a sudden, careless movement. There would be no stray reflections from the SAS man's equipment.

At 0130 hours he arrived at the end of the wall, where it butted a large wooden machine-shed, which stood a hundred yards behind the farmhouse. The breeze now beginning to gust was heavy with the smell of wet straw and manure. It carried the sound of cackling chickens from somewhere on the far side of the building. Above him one of the several elm trees which encircled the yard rustled its leaves and sprinkled down moisture in heavy droplets.

He heard no other sound, and moved quietly along the

wall of the machine-shed, his back pressed hard against the creosoted planking. From the outer edge he could see clearly across the yard. The farm's one ancient tractor had mashed the spongy ground into a complex series of criss-crossed patterns, the deep gouges filled with rainwater. To the left of him, set back between the machine-shed and the rear of the house, he could distinguish the high dark shape of the open-fronted barn. Within, the paler shades of stacked straw bales were just discernible.

To reach Roisin's bedroom at the rear, Ducane had already decided he would scale the low outhouse, and gain access by the window that had, on earlier occasions, provided Sergeant Forbes with such entertainment.

But tonight no light came from it.

Between his position beside the machine-shed and the barn ran a worn wooden fence, in front of which stood a stone cattle trough. From the barn, Ducane decided, he would not only be able to make the dash to the farm outhouse with safety, but he would also get a clear view of the window to McNally's room.

Crouching on all fours, he began to wriggle across the narrow gap to the fence, the smells of the yard thick in his nostrils. He paused at the first upright post. Nothing stirred. He continued, easing his way through the long grass at the edge of the yard, the lower plank of the fence rubbing his shoulder. At the water trough he stopped suddenly.

What was it? His ears listened to the faint howl of the quickening wind and the rustling of the trees. There was nothing else. Even the chickens were quiet. He peered round the side of the trough at the silent house. Still nothing.

Then, as he glanced over his shoulder, he saw what some sixth sense had told him. A dewy bead of moisture glittered in the air by his feet, suspended. Carefully, without moving the angle of his boots more than a fraction, he twisted around into a sitting position. He leaned forward and inspected the thin strand of nylon wire on which the moisture had collected. Even a few inches from his face it

72

was scarcely visible. Cautiously he located it with his fingers, tracing it down to where it had caught around his left boot, trapped in the deep tread of the rubber sole.

Maintaining the tension with his right hand, he traced the wire with his left. Up and over the top of the trough.

Christ, he thought, it's a booby-trap. He felt the heavy sweat break out on his forehead, and the unpleasant surge of heat along his body.

Keeping his feet exactly where they were, he hoisted himself onto one arm and peered into the trough. Two empty tin cans were poised precariously on the rim of a galvanised bucket. One more half-inch and the wire would have toppled the cans into it with a clatter that would have woken the dead.

He breathed an audible sigh of relief. Just a warning system. Primitive but effective. Gingerly he lifted the two cans from the edge of the bucket until he felt the wire slacken around his foot. He placed them on the grass, and sat with his back to the trough, breathing in the cool night air deeply.

Wake the bloody dead, he repeated to himself, turning the words over in his mind, examining each one. No, that wasn't it! Tin cans in a bucket wouldn't wake the dead. Probably not even a sleeping man. It would probably alert a dog, but they had gone over that one at the briefing. Roisin McGuire didn't have a dog.

But the noise would be sufficient to warn a look look-out —even whilst he tried to keep himself awake as his body temperature dropped to its lowest point around four in the morning. Even at that vulnerable hour he couldn't fail to hear the cans.

The man who had travelled with McNally. Perhaps not professional, but one who obviously knew a few tricks, and who was evidently responsible for his charge's unmolested arrival.

For five full minutes Ducane scanned the farmhouse, until he was sure there was no window from which an unknown face could be watching; no shadow that concealed a tell-tale flicker of movement.

Time was running out. Having disposed of the pickets, the others would be stealthily closing in on the buildings, making their way to the barn. The captain shifted his gaze, scanning the bales of straw that were now clearly visible, stacked to the roof. Nothing. Just some discarded shovels and forks, rusted with age. An earth-encrusted trailer with a wheel missing, tilted at a careless angle. A ladder reaching up to the small crane-hoist platform. A black plastic water-butt.

A ladder.

He squinted at the dark mass towering above him where the roof formed its apex. A few feet below it was a deeper shadow, marking the entrance to the hoist platform. Black as black.

A glow came suddenly from the window of McNally's room. Not the main light, probably a bedside lamp. Enough to cast the faintest smear of light through the thick curtains to illuminate the front of the barn. For a brief second Ducane caught the outline shape of the crouched figure in the entrance to the hoist platform, and the blur of flesh as the head turned towards the window. Then it drew back into deeper shadow.

Crafty bastard. Ducane's lips formed round the silent words.

Quickly he opened one of his belt pouches and lifted out a coil of fishing tackle. Deftly he tied it round the lid of one can, which he then suspended from the bottom of the bucket. He wanted a slight noise, but not enough to disturb anyone inside the house.

Carefully playing out the line, he left the shelter of the water trough. Continuing his slow crawl beneath the remaining length of fence, he found himself in the lee of the barn. He climbed to his feet, tugging gently at the line that ran back to the trough until it became taut.

He pulled it once, hard. The crack of metal sounded like a clash of swords to his ears, but it was short and sharp enough to have been well-muted by the wind. He ran his hand down his right leg until his fingers found the handle of the heavy US Marines K-Bar fighting knife. It shouldn't be needed, but he released the retainer just in case as he listened to the faint movement above him.

Seconds passed by like hours until he heard the creaking of the ladder under weight. Soft-soled shoes. The merest crackle of dry hay underfoot as the look-out reached the ground.

Another endless wait before the dark shape appeared from the edge of the barn a few feet before him. A smell of cologne reached him, faint but discernible.

One step, two, muscles moving fast like well-greased pistons, fluid, culminating in a rush of determined, vicious movement. Just like the manual.

The left hand swept around from the back. The forearm lashed tight back into the man's mouth and nose, smothering both before a snort or gasp could be expelled. The straight edge of the captain's right hand hit the back of the neck with the force power of a 28lb sledgehammer. As it did so the left hand jerked sharply backwards. The bone gave a distinctly audible snap.

This close to the objective there must be no chance of a prisoner raising the alarm, even if he was thoroughly bound and gagged. There was no safe alternative to the sentry's accidental fall from the barn.

Ducane stepped slowly back, allowing the man's feet to trail, and dragged him unceremoniously behind the wall of the barn. It took him a few moments to regain his breath as he crouched in the shadow, heaving down lungfuls of cool, pure air. The rain was refreshing against his face.

He looked down at the crumpled body before him and rubbed his bruised right hand before closing the lids of the corpse's wide, accusing eyes. Oddly, the man had not let go his double-handed grip on the rifle he had been holding across his chest. With difficulty Ducane wrenched it free. He released the magazine clip and tossed it into the night; the rifle he stuffed between two straw bales.

Something odd.

He was aware of a presence behind him. He spun quickly, pitching to one side as he did so, to throw off the aim and to allow him to reach his knife as he fell. It was in his hand before he hit the ground.

Forbes grinned widely, shaking his head in mockery. He then nodded in the direction of the main road, and Ducane turned to see Turnbull emerging from the hedge on the other side of the barn.

The three men stood for a moment, saying nothing, just studying the wall of the farmhouse. Young Tom hadn't yet turned up, but they all welcomed the moment of relaxation before proceeding with the next stage of the operation.

It had been decided that Ducane would first get to the girl's room and get her out using a rope from the window. Meanwhile Forbes would scale the drainpipe that ran vertically a few feet to the right of McNally's window. There he could wait in case things went wrong. If Roisin wasn't where she was expected to be, Turnbull and Young Tom would force an entry downstairs, check for any unexpected residents, then proceed to the upper floor to McNally's door. If Roisin had still not been located they would break in. As they did so Forbes would smash the window and roll in a paralysing stun-grenade. They nodded in agreement to one another. There was no need for a change of plan.

Young Tom emerged suddenly, ashen-faced, pointing to where he had tripped over the concealed body of the lookout. His eyes were wild, his skullcap gone and his hair awry. A vivid red patch marked his cheek through the sticky grease of the camouflage cream.

Growing pains, as Dave Forbes would describe such combat injuries gained by young recruits.

Without further communication Forbes and Ducane began their separate climbs. Although the captain's ascent appeared easiest, the outhouse brickwork was mildewed and crumbling, so that some of the retaining brackets of the downpipe and guttering pulled free with a trickle of mortar. Testing his weight, he finally found a point strong enough to take his twelve stone bulk. His boots pushing against the sill of a lower window, he sprung upwards. Straightening his arms with a jolt, he swung his left foot onto the guttering. The slates were loose, and slippery with moss and rain. It was with some difficulty that he finally found his balance. He began to crawl up to the ridge tiles, his body flush to the roof, his face pressed against the streaming slates. Once astride the ridge, it was an easy task to propel himself along to the window ledge of Roisin's bedroom.

The curtains were closed. The nursery pattern seemed absurdly incongruous in the circumstances. No light came from beyond them, and the sash-cord frame was slightly ajar at the bottom.

It was important that he reached her before she had a chance to awaken with a cry of alarm. Once more he was thankful that Harrington had come clean and not pretended that Roisin was expecting their nocturnal visit.

Carefully he pushed upwards against the frame. After a moment's resistance, it began to move, screeching slowly on its cords.

No movement came from within. There was a smell of perfume. Quickly he slipped the Sterling sub-machine gun from his shoulder, and, grasping it about the trigger guard in his right hand, swung softly through the curtains onto the carpet.

He landed in a crouch, so as not to provide a silhouette against the window frame.

A gentle light shed from somewhere beyond the hall, casting an aurora around the bedroom through the small window above the door. Swiftly his eyes went round the room. Dressing-table littered with bottles, fancy and coloured; a pack of tissues; hairbrush. Cheap whitewood wardrobe, stuffed to overflowing; a white cotton dress hanging on the outside. A chair, hand-painted white, draped with discarded jeans and a pink candlewick dressing-gown. The bed, tousled, empty.

Ducane frowned. From his crouched position, he shuffled over to the bed. The blankets and sheets had been pulled back carelessly. He placed his hand on the lower sheet. It was cold.

He spoke quickly into the Pocketfone. "Abandon A. Activate B." Standing up he moved across to the door, twisted the handle and allowed it to drift open under its own weight. The landing was lit from the small window over the door to the spare room. Farther on there were three more doors to rooms at the front of the house. A worn carpet muffled the creaking boards as he crossed. The first of the three doors opened into the main bedroom. It smelled of camphor and must. Obviously it had not been used since Roisin McGuire's father had died. The second door opened into Sean's room; that, too, was empty. The third opened onto an antiquated lavatory.

Ducane returned to the landing, now concentrating on the door to the room where McNally was surely lying. He became aware of faint, muffled sounds of movement and a female voice. Just distinguishable. Small, moaning sounds.

A cold, spider-like sensation went down his spine, and he felt perspiration break out above his upper lip. His mouth felt suddenly very dry.

Turnbull appeared at the top of the stairs, followed closely by Young Tom. Both looked curious at finding the captain outside McNally's room.

Ducane nodded urgently at the door, holding two fingers towards them. He saw the shock register on Perrot's face, but Turnbull's expression was more of a complacent I-told-you-so.

Ducane pointed two fingers in a gunning motion at the ceiling. If they used the usual six inches above the heads of the target whilst the hostage was grabbed, they were likely to blow Forbes straight off the outside window ledge. The others nodded, laid their Sterlings within easy reach, and swung the secondary weapons from their shoulders: two short-barrelled Remington pump-action shot-guns with special skeleton frame butts.

The team were about to go into one of many Close Quarter Battle (CQB) routines that they had practised endlessly at the Pontrilas training centre, ten miles to the south-west of the SAS Bradbury Lines barracks. Countless permutations of hostage rescues were tried with straw dummies, human beings and live bullets. They knew this bedroom layout from Harrington and detailed contingency plans had been prepared and memorised.

Without a word the two men moved to positions either side of the door, each shot-gun trained on one of the hinges. The locks, which might have additional bolts, were ignored.

Ducane hissed into the Pocketfone. "Here we go, Dave!"

The hammers came down on the solid shot cartridges with a double roar that shattered the stillness of the farmhouse. Ducane's booted foot crashed into the dismembered timber. Swiftly he followed through, diving to the left. He threw his weight backwards, pinning the toppling door to the inner wall with a shuddering jolt.

Simultaneously a series of spitting explosions came from behind as Turnbull pumped in another burst from his shot-gun.

Plaster burst apart with a dull crunching thud as the shot-holes studded the ceiling. A cloud of white dust and debris showered down onto the bed where McNally hunched over the girl.

There came a violent crack and snap of glass as the window caved in behind the curtain. Ducane and Turnbull averted their eyes as Forbes tossed in one of his 'flash-bangs'. The stun-grenade detonated with a roar, a paralysing tonal screech that hit the middle ear, and the room was filled with a blinding dazzle. Even through the noise the girl's shrill and startled scream couldn't be mistaken.

Stunned for ten vital seconds, McNally left it too late to reach for the automatic on the floor by the bed. As he heaved himself off Roisin and flung himself out, his outstretched hand scrabbled for the weapon. Forbes' large booted foot landed on his fingers. He shrieked to the distinct sound of cracking bones.

Turnbull leapt forward, jabbing the barrel of the Sterling sub-machine gun between the proffered naked buttocks. "One more move, McNally, and you've lost your hollihocks!" he hissed.

The man was scarcely in a position to argue, merely replying with a string of obscenities through teeth clenched in agony.

Roisin McGuire had slid quickly out of the sheets and cowered in the corner, panting heavily. Her eyes were wide with fear and bewilderment.

"Keep her covered!" snapped Turnbull. He was taking no chances.

Young Tom stood by the door, his mouth loose, staring at her pale nakedness, his eyes mesmerised by her small, dark nipples and the triangle of pubic hair she tried to cover with her hands.

Slowly the young soldier lifted his Sterling, then let it fall again. "She's not armed, Corp," he said quietly.

In the lull that fell over the room Forbes, too, noticed the girl, running his eyes appreciatively over her young body. Then he noticed the bright livid bruising around her breasts and thighs. He looked down at the sprawled naked figure at his feet, addressing himself to the near-bald head. "You fuckin' rapist," he snarled. "No better than a soddin' child molester."

His boot came down again, this time on McNally's uninjured hand with which he was attempting to support himself. The howl echoed around the room as he twisted involuntarily, his legs slipping from the bed to join the rest of his body in an ungainly heap on the floor.

"That's enough, Sergeant!" Ducane said sharply.

He turned back to the girl who was now visibly trembling, tears beginning to stream down her cheeks. He said: "It's okay, love, we're friends of Lieutenant Harrington. He's sent us to look after you."

For a second her mouth dropped in disbelief. With her ears still ringing and spots still swimming before her eyes, she hadn't even realised they were soldiers, friendly or otherwise. As sudden relief flooded through her, she began to sob. She stumbled thankfully towards Ducane, burying her head in the chest of his camouflage smock.

"Now what have you got that I haven't?" muttered Forbes.

Ducane put a consoling arm around the girl's slim shoulders. He could feel the warmth of her skin beneath his fingers, as she tried to control her involuntary trembling.

He glanced round, aware of his cheeks reddening.

"Don't just stand there gawking, trooper!" he addressed himself to Young Tom. "Get the young lady some clothes. Then take her downstairs and make her some char."

"Oh, er, yes, boss," Perrot began, shaken from his thoughts. He picked up the nylon nightdress lying by his feet and took a hesitating step towards her. "Er, it's all right now, miss. If you'd like to come with me."

Ducane said, impatiently: "Well, put it on her then."

Young Tom nodded. Gently he draped the nightdress over her shoulders. He brought his hands away, leaving greasy, dark marks from the camouflage cream.

"I'm-er-sorry about the mess, miss." She nodded, stepping back from Ducane, sniffing hard to staunch the tears. She hugged the nightdress around her, allowing Young Tom to guide her towards the door.

Beside the bed, the naked McNally had regained some of his composure, now in a sitting position, his hands tucked under his arms in a vain effort to subdue the pain.

"Little bitch didn't need rapin'," he snarled. "Bloody askin' for it, she was ..."

Forbes knee hit him in the back of the head. "Didn't ask for your comments, you stupid Mick!"

Ducane pulled the Plasticuffs from his pocket—a pointed gift from Major Simmonds—and tossed them on the bed. "Put those on him, Sergeant. Then put some trousers on him and cover up that horrible sight."

Five minutes later he went down to the lower floor. It had been converted into one main split-level parlour area, the stairs leading directly to the kitchen at the rear. There was a shallow step down to the lower front area which was poorly carpeted and furnished with worn chintzy armchairs.

Roisin was sitting on the small sofa, wearing the candlewick dressing-gown from her bedroom, hunched over a mug of tea. Young Tom sat beside her, looking concerned. The conversation seemed limited.

Ducane nodded towards the front door. "Keep an eye outside, will you?"

"If you say so, boss," replied Perrot, reluctantly picking up his Sterling.

Ducane sat in the chair facing Roisin. When Young Tom had gone out the door he said: "How are you now?"

She looked up at him, fondling the mug. There was comfort in its warmth. "I'm all right, thank you," she murmured, then glanced quickly down again. "I'm sorry— I don't know who you are?"

"Ducane, Miss McGuire, Captain Ducane."

She looked up, surprised. "Jacko?"

He smiled. "We met before once."

Roisin nodded. Her eyes, red-rimmed, had a distant look about them. "Yes, I remember. A long while ago. But Charles has mentioned you several times since."

Ducane forced a smile. He paused, searching for the right words. "Look, this business upstairs." She studied the mug in her hands intently, saying nothing. "McNally raped you. That means that we must call in the police now. You understand that?"

Her head shook very slowly. Her hair, Ducane noticed, was very soft, very pretty.

"No ... I don't want that, Captain."

He reached out his hand, squeezed her wrist reassuringly. He felt her stiffen. "Look, it may be best. If anything happened you should prefer charges. It can't make things much worse for McNally, and we'll see to it that you don't suffer any more humiliation."

She repeated: "I don't want that."

"You're a Catholic?"

Roisin nodded. "I don't use anything," she whispered.

Ducane said: "Then you know there is a danger?"

She said nothing, sipping at the mug of tea. Ducane watched her, trying to read her mind. At last he said: "You heard what McNally said upstairs? That you were a willing party?"

Roisin swallowed and he saw she was trying to hold back more tears.

"I think it's important to know the truth," he said. "If for no other reason, Charles should know the truth."

She averted her eyes, her words coming out in short, painful gasps as she attempted to restrain the sobs. "It was difficult. He told me that Sean was dead. He was killed this morning in Belfast, by your people ... by the Army ..." She sniffed deeply, staring vacantly at the old fireplace. "... I was so upset ... McNally comforted me ... I couldn't help it, I started to think about Charles and all his questions ... I felt sure he was responsible for Sean getting killed ... after what he promised ... knowing Sean was already dead ..."

Ducane said: "I'm sure that's not true."

"... McNally ... you know, hugged me ... friendly, telling me not to cry ... that he'd see I was all right ... I didn't know what to do ... He started, well, kissing and touching me ... oh God!" The torture forced its way through her teeth in a gasp, and her shoulders shook as the flood of tears began.

"So you didn't resist?"

She tried to regain her composure. "... I suppose not ... I don't know ... I struggled, but he was so strong ... I was confused and crying ... and then, well, I started to feel what I felt with Charles. I'm sorry, I mustn't say that ..."

"Does it help?"

She looked at him, and he noticed the clearness and colour of her eyes. "Do you believe me, it does? ... Just before ... just before you broke into the room ... it was almost like being with Charles ... in the dark ..."

"Shut your eyes and think of England! God, it makes me sick!"

It was Turnbull, standing at the foot of the stairs.

Ducane turned round. "Enough said, Corporal! Please make yourself scarce for a few minutes."

Turnbull continued towards them. "It's damned obvious she's a Provo. Little bitch. We're just being set up. It sticks out a mile. Can't you see that?" he demanded.

"Corporal, get out of here, or I'll have you busted, so help me!"

Turnbull stopped. "Yes, boss!" Turning on his heel, he

went out through the kitchen door, crashing it behind him so hard that the window panes rattled.

Ducane turned back to Roisin. "I'm sorry about that. I hope you understand?"

She smiled thinly. "I suppose so. And I hope Charles will understand that I don't think I'll be able to marry him ... not now."

"He might understand, but I doubt it. I should think he'd do his utmost to persuade you. He talks of no one else. And from what you tell me, what McNally did was as close to rape as makes no difference."

"You don't understand, do you?" she challenged. "If I prefer a charge of rape, it doesn't alter *anything*. I know what happened. How I felt; what I did. And you think I can go through with everything now *knowing* the real truth? God, just what sort of friend are you!"

Ducane said firmly: "If there's a chance you two could be happy, could make it work, then I think its worth the risk."

She hesitated. "I can't believe you're a romantic."

"I try to believe there's good in people."

She drank some more of the tea. "I'll think about it, Captain."

"I have to call up a chopper now. Once that happens everything starts getting official."

"I understand," she said. "You must realise that Charles has meant a lot to me. If I still marry him, it must be ... well, honest. That's important to me. I'd have to tell him the truth. What I need is time. Just to think things over, get them in perspective."

"So no charges against McNally?"

She shook her head.

Ducane said: "By the way, Roisin, I'm sorry to hear about your brother." He was aware there was little sympathy in his voice.

"So am I."

The front door suddenly burst open as though struck by a tornado, and Young Tom came rushing in at a run, skidding on the carpet.

84

"Car approaching, boss! Just turned off the main road!"

"Oh, my God!" Roisin gasped. "I'd clean forgotten!"

"What?" Ducane demanded.

"It went clear out of my mind." She looked frightened. "It must be the border escort. They were coming for McNally at two."

Leaping to his feet, Ducane swung the Sterling butt at the overhead lamp. It shattered instantly, plunging the lower floor into darkness. A clatter of heavy footsteps came from the stairs as Forbes rushed down, leaping the bottom five steps.

"What's the commotion?"

"A carload of Provos for McNally," Ducane replied. "Where the hell's Turnbull? Never mind. Is our guest secured?"

Forbes chuckled. "Yep, I've secured him to the lavatory. He's got a comfortable enough seat."

"Get Roisin into the corner, quick!" He shouted at Perrot. "Make sure she keeps her head down." As he spoke the beam of the headlamps swung into the farmyard, playing its light across the windows.

Ducane beckoned Forbes and they crossed to the windows in a crouching run, peering out to see the doors of the car open rapidly and three men emerge. One reached back inside to kill the lights and, for a moment, they stood watching. Waiting.

"Playing cautious," Forbes observed. "Perhaps they're waiting for a recognition signal. All clear."

Ducane grunted. "We'll go for their legs. There could be a VIP amongst that lot."

The running footsteps from outside were quite distinct as the gunmen turned to face the panting figure of a fourth man. Breathless, he had started talking excitedly, jabbing a finger down the approach road.

"He's been looking for the sentry," Forbes said.

"And found Turnbull's handiwork by the look of it."

As though in confirmation, weapons started appearing from their concealment under the men's raincoats. One of them, evidently the leader, waved his arms, indicating to

85

two of them to go around the sides of the farmhouse.

"Quick!" Ducane hissed. "Get 'em while they're together."

In unison the soldiers punched gun barrels through the window-glass and opened up in a staccato thunder of fire.

A sheet of stabbing lead scythed low across the four men as they began to disperse. Three of them had their legs cut from under them, with a force that threw them down like nine pins. There came a tell-tale twang and whine as shells ricochetted over the car behind them. Immediately there was a tremendous rushing noise and roar as petrol ignited in a blinding flash of flame and smoke.

Glass crackled and tinkled as the front windows of the farm collapsed under the force of the explosion, icicles of glass whistling across the room.

"Outside!" Ducane yelled. Together he and Forbes leapt through the shattered front windows, firing a hail of bullets over the heads of the three men sprawled on the ground. Two of them had been hit in the legs, a third was lying petrified and shocked, his hair scorched and singed from the blast of the explosion. Their weapons were kicked away from their reach as the soldiers threw themselves onto the men.

"Behind you!" It was Turnbull.

Both soldiers threw themselves to one side as a rattling burst of fire from the fourth Provo cut through the air, narrowly missing the sprawled gunmen.

A muzzle flash from the trees sent the fourth man scurrying for a door at the side of the farmhouse. As he disappeared inside it, a returning blast of gunfire from Turnbull lanced into the brickwork, blowing out a cloud of masonry.

"There goes bloody 'Action Man' again," Forbes chuckled.

Ducane said: "C'mon, let's get these guys inside before their mate damages them!"

As if hearing him, the fourth gunman loosed off another round from the cover of the cellar door. A spurt of wet mud was kicked up just beside them. Hurriedly they bundled the injured and shaken men in through the farm-house door.

Firing from the hip, Turnbull broke from his cover in the bushes and sprinted across the yard until the gunman's angle of fire caused the bullets to bounce off the corner of the building in a spray of brickdust.

"Is there another entrance to the cellar?" Ducane asked Roisin.

"Only the outside door," she replied nervously. "But there's a coal hatch and ramp out the back."

Turnbull nodded. "Okay, I'll deal with our friend." He slid a fresh clip of cartridges in the Sterling and moved across the parlour and out through the kitchen door.

As Ducane and Forbes ushered the gunmen towards the centre of the room, Young Tom helped Roisin to her feet, brushing the dust, wood and glass splinters from her dressing-gown.

"Holy Mother," she breathed. "This is one night I won't forget in a hurry!" She looked out at the wrecked car, still flaming fitfully despite the drizzle. "Is Charlie one of your people?"

"Sort of, miss," Perrot replied.

The girl switched on the corner standard lamp and looked at the three gunmen sitting on the edge of the split-level floor. They looked distinctly uncomfortable, hands resting awkwardly on their heads.

"Do you know any of these men, Roisin?" Ducane asked.

"Two of them. The one with the wounded leg is called O'Nions. He's a delivery man. And the other one, who isn't hurt, is a friend of his called Malone."

O'Nions glowered up at her, his usually watery eyes hard with hatred. "So they was right about you 'n' your boy-friend, you double-crossing little bitch!"

"Tut-tut," Forbes said gently, and smashed him in the cheek with the butt of the Sterling.

Roisin looked quickly at Ducane. "Does he have to do things like that, Captain Ducane?"

"Sergeant."

"Yes, sir."

"Don't do things like that."

"No, sir."

It was at that moment that all hell broke loose.

It was difficult to tell which came first, the swirling roar of the helicopter as it swooped low over the roof of the farmhouse, or the sudden shattering of glass panes and woodwork as shells whined through the front door and windows, twanging around the walls in a deadly game of pinball.

Perrot pushed Roisin roughly to the floor, throwing himself over her body, as the withering spray of fire poured in. Everywhere plaster was cracking and exploding in tiny puffballs of dust as the walls punctured. Glass and china burst in a hundred jagged fragments. Furniture just collapsed all around them as though some powerful poltergeist was at work. Picture frames spun, propelled from the walls, smashing on the floor or in mid-air, adding to the debris flying in all directions.

Ducane hit the floor with speed, but not before he felt a searing pain in his left arm that almost wrenched it from the socket. The fire thundered on, tearing the front of the building apart with such ferocity that the brickwork around the shattered windows and door was starting to crumble away in a cloud of choking dust.

"Christ, it must be the entire sodding Provo army!" swore Forbes, his face pressed close to the carpet.

Ducane didn't reply. Trying to keep flat, he was attempting to pull the field-dressing pack from his smock to staunch the flow of blood.

"You okay?" Forbes hissed, wriggling across to him.

Another belt of shells sliced into the room, this time at a deeper angle, right across the centre of the room where the prisoners had crouched for protection. A piercing scream came from Jim O'Nions as his body appeared to explode from internal combustion, pitching him into the air like a rag doll. A bloody fore-arm flew into the hearth, clattering amongst the pile of fallen horse-brasses, and the remainder of his pulped body sprawled over his already dead companion.

"Roisin's hit!" Young Tom yelled above the furious row.

Suddenly the window in the kitchen door burst apart under a fresh hail of fire from the rear, hurling great slithers of glass through the air like giant transparent razor blades. Half a dozen lengths thudded into the back of the sofa to the sound of ripping fabric. Outside voices were heard.

"Oh, God," Ducane groaned, finally managing to get a bandage around his arm with Forbes' help. "It's bloody Simmonds and the 7th Cavalry!"

"Jesus wept!" Forbes cursed, picking up his sub-machine gun.

As suddenly as it started, the firing ceased. The silence was deafening, disturbed only by the low murmur of the girl's voice. Forbes glanced around the wrecked room littered with prone bodies, fallen masonry and dismembered furniture. It just couldn't be the same place he'd seen earlier.

"How's Roisin?" Ducane asked, worming his way across to where Young Tom had her head cradled in his lap. He was dabbing her torn cheek with cotton-wool.

"It was glass, boss. A chunk the size of a bread-knife. Caught her ear as well. Tore it a bit."

Ducane shook his head at the bloody mess. It undoubtedly looked worse than it was. She'd have a handsome three-inch scar. Her ear looked quite bad, but with luck she wouldn't lose it—provided the surgeon could operate fast enough. Luckily she was in a state of semi-consciousness.

"NOW HEAR THIS! NOW HEAR THIS!" There was no mistaking Major Simmonds' clipped voice, even through the distortion of the helicopter's Skyshout megaphone. "THIS IS THE ARMY! YOU ARE COMPLETELY SURROUNDED! COME OUT WITH YOUR HANDS UP AND YOU WILL NOT GET HURT! I REPEAT ..."

"Silly fucking sod," said Forbes.

Ducane looked around the room at the bodies of O'Nions and the other man.

"Trouble!" he said. "Malone's gone!"

"I'll check upstairs," Forbes said, moving swiftly.

He was back in a few moments. McNally was still safely secured. There was no sign of Malone.

"He must have got out the back before Simmonds' men got round there," Ducane said.

"I'll get after him," Forbes offered.

Ducane shook his head. "Simmonds has got himself enough casualties for one night. We'd better wave the white flag before he calls up the artillery. Besides, Johnny Fraser might pick him up."

"How's the arm, boss?" Young Tom asked.

"Bloody painful, what do you think?" Ducane returned unkindly, making his way towards the door that now hung in shreds at a curious angle, secured only by the upper hinge.

Outside, behind the stabbing glare of the helicopter's Nitesun searchlamps, the vague shapes appeared to be looming closer.

The SAS men stopped, to be joined by Turnbull who emerged from the cellar door. They waited until they saw the familiar striding gait of Major Simmonds coming towards them. He paused, bewildered, and glanced at the front of the house.

His voice was edged with uncertainty. "Looks like we arrived in the nick of time."

"Something like that," Ducane replied, shielding his eyes. "And put those damned fairy lights out, will you!"

"Corporal, lights!" Simmonds barked.

Two more Nitesuns flickered on.

"Off, you idiot!"

Forbes smirked visibly.

Ducane said: "Listen, Batman, you and your boy wonders have just killed two Provos being held for questioning, allowed another to escape, injured a female inform-ant, and nearly blown off the arm of an SAS captain!"

"What?" His face remained gaunt, the eyes invisible behind the peaked cap.

Ducane held up his arm with difficulty. "This, you Sand-hurst burk, is an arm. It belongs to me. And it's got a bloody hole in it!"

"Watch your tongue, Captain!"

"And who the hell told you to come in?" Ducane demanded.

Simmonds looked beyond them to the farmhouse. "You were a long time, Captain. Too long. Then we saw the explosion. Obviously the car. I realised you were in trouble." He turned sharply back to the SAS officer. "But evidently not as much trouble as you're going to be in. I was there when the CO issued his orders. You were to get the girl, then call me in. Not try and handle the whole thing single-handed!"

With his free hand Ducane pulled a cigarette pack from his top pocket, extracting one with his teeth. "Things don't always work out as planned, Major. You were told to wait for a signal."

A trooper, overawed by the significance of events and the furious row, stepped forward to light Ducane's cigarette— much to Simmonds' irritation.

"We'll see about this, Captain."

"You're damned right we will, Major Simmonds. Meanwhile I suggest you warn Captain Fraser to look out for our lost prisoner trying to cross the border. Name of Malone. Short, dark, mid-thirties, dark green windcheater. Hope you can get *that* right!"

The major glared at Ducane as he repeated the message tersely through clenched teeth to the radio operator behind him.

At that moment a Land Rover emerged at speed from the approach road, skidding to a noisy halt in the mud. The door was flung open, and Harrington climbed out.

"Are you all right?" he asked Ducane. Then, without waiting for a reply, he added: "Where's Roisin?"

In answer to his question the girl appeared at the front door, helped by a stocky lance-corporal from the Royals. She was walking unsteadily, holding a big wad of lint to her face. For a moment she glanced up, directly at Harrington. Her eyes seemed to look straight through him. Without pausing, she walked on.

Ducane restrained his arm. "Leave her, Charlie. She'll have a scar on her cheek, that's all. But she needs time to think things over."

More bodies were being extracted from the building: the

man Turnbull had killed in the cellar; O'Nions; the other man.

"Christ!" breathed Harrington, bewildered. "This is my fault."

Turnbull said: "Yes, it is." Emphatic.

Major Simmonds pounced on the words. "What do you mean?"

Turnbull, shouldering his weapon, looked close into Simmonds' face. "I don't believe you'd ever understand, Major." He walked away.

Simmonds shook his head. "Someone's responsible for this mess."

"Never mind," Ducane replied. "I'm sure you can talk your way out of it. Console yourself with a booby prize. McNally's upstairs. Unharmed."

"Alone?"

"Where he is, Major, there's only room for one."

CHAPTER 5

Each person was frisked thoroughly before being allowed into the upstairs room.

As usual Billy McKee sat at the head of the table. Both Seamus Twomey, Chief of Staff, and Eamon Doherty, the ex-paratrooper who had special responsibility for border activities, had drawn up chairs on either side of him.

Adjutant General, the infamous Joe Cahill, and Quartermaster J. B. O'Hagan flanked the table, close to their colleagues.

The remaining seats at the table were empty except for one, where Martin McGuiness sat patiently. As usual he was immaculately dressed. The dark blazer and trousers of pale blue check were set off by a crisp white shirt and a nondescript club tie.

Only McGuiness stood when the squint-eyed man showed in the two big Americans. The others remained seated with photocopies of the report spread before them, studying the new arrivals cautiously.

Earl Lee McClatcher stood six foot three in his white doeskin moccasins and the excellent cut of the grey Italian mohair suit served to emphasise his upright bearing and barrel chest. A gold crucifix glistened in the mass of curly brown hair that showed at the open neck of the blue denim shirt.

He was square-jawed and clean-shaven. The scrub of his clipped brown hair was only fractionally longer than the bristles that were beginning to appear on the full jowls. It had been a long journey across the Atlantic. His sunburnt skin showed up the pale grey-blue eyes, lined with the tiny crowsfeet of a man who had spent many years under a tropical sun.

Winston Loveday was only fractionally taller, his equally muscular frame dressed in a lightweight cream suit over a bright Hawaiian shirt. He was slightly longer-faced than McClatcher, his Negroid features disfigured by a broken nose. His eyes, arrogant and watchful, seemed to glow bright and menacing out of the surrounding mahogany skin.

"I trust you had a good trip, gentlemen?" McKee said.

McClatcher nodded. "It was okay," he answered dismissively. He jerked a thumb towards the squint-eyed man who remained by the door, and kept his right hand concealed in the front of his jacket. "Before we get rollin', perhaps you'd like to get rid of yer guard dog."

McKee eyed him for a moment, then grasped his hands together under his chin, his elbows on the table.

In his quiet drawl he said: "Captain McClatcher, you must understand that we have to be very careful in our position. Only our most trusted and loyal members can come to this room without the presence of an armed guard. We've lost two of our number in just the past two weeks."

"I read the papers," McClatcher replied.

McKee spoke softly. "Then you will understand. Now if you'd care to take a seat?"

Loveday and McClatcher exchanged glances. The Negro made a sudden darting movement towards the guard.

"BOO!"

The squint-eyed man jumped at the unexpected lunge, then, realising he was the subject of ridicule, shuffled his feet uneasily, trying to ignore the big black face grinning at him.

"Cool it, Winston," McClatcher said, taking his place beside Martin McGuiness.

"Just a li'le fun, Cap'n," laughed Loveday, sitting down heavily.

The members of the Army Council looked at one another apprehensively.

"I'm sure we'll all get along," McGuiness began. He wasn't at all sure this was a good start. McKee was a conservative man and proud of his achievements. He had

94

little time for anyone who attempted to belittle his organisation.

"Let's get on with the business in hand," Billy McKee said, opening the report before him. "Firstly, gentlemen, may I thank you for your prompt action in preparing this document. I trust you were given all the assistance you required?"

McClatcher inclined his head. "Mr McGuiness gave us a full briefin'. I don't 'collect he overlooked anything."

"No?" queried McKee.

McClatcher screwed up his eyes, an icy glare directed at the Council chairman. "I've no changes to make now."

Billy McKee sat back, resting his elbows on the arms of his chair, his fingers interlaced across his chest. "Well, gentlemen, we have had time to study your proposals. Not a lot of time, but enough ... And, well, we find them ..." He paused, staring at the ceiling as he searched for the right words. "... Well, to be quite frank, we find them, shall we say, a bit ... well, a bit airy-fairy. A bit pie in the sky."

"I think he means a loada crap," Loveday translated affably.

McKee continued. "Let's say misguided. I realise you are both experienced men, but you don't have the close knowledge and expertise of our particular situation. Nor an understanding of our organisation. You suggest the training up of a number of our best men to—er—Green Beret standards, as you put it. And to put them into the field, not only against ordinary troops, but particularly against the SAS groups. Lurin' them into killing zones with mines and ambush situations as though this were an extension of your Vietnam war. Well, gentlemen this isn't the Far East. And our men are not regular soldiers. They are ordinary, patriotic and brave men who have little formal instruction and only a few weapons with which to fight the Brits and their entire modern army for their cause of freedom and justice."

"Wowee!" burst Loveday. "Man, that's some speech!"

McClatcher ignored his companion. "Listen, McKee, as

far as I'm concerned your Micks are a lot of brainless morons who ain't got the guts to face an enemy in the eyes. Their only claim to bravery is throwing a bomb fulla nuts and bolts into bars to blow the legs and arms off innocent civilians. You ever seen a teenage chick hobblin' about on knee-stumps? Bet yer sweet ass you ain't. But I sure as hell have, and I assure you it ain't a pretty sight! Shootin' limey troops in the back is the nearest your Micks get to seein' the whites of their eyes, but then they ain't been too good at that lately, have they?

"Well, I'm gonna suggest you change all that. Put some spunk and some backbone into the best of those jerks you've got. An' do a bit of real soldierin'! 'Cos at the rate you're goin' there ain't gonna be no civilians left when you liberate Ulster!"

"Attaman!" whooped Loveday.

A stunned silence fell over the table. The knuckles of McKee's hands showed white, his lips thinned in an effort to control his rising fury. Injuries and maimings were never discussed in front of Billy McKee. He'd pray religiously every day for the souls of those his organisation had destroyed, but never once did he allow himself to dwell on the purgatory he had left those scarred broken men and women to struggle through for the rest of their years. They, he considered, were the lucky ones. They had survived.

Anxious to heal the rift, Twomey said quickly: "From what I've heard, McClatcher, your lot haven't got a record to boast about. In Vietnam."

"Say, what is this!" snarled the American. "We trying to see who can boast the most cripples? 'Cos if we are, buddy, I can tell you *we'll* win hands down. I'm not proud of it, but we were fightin' a real war and if we killed or injured innocent gooks it's 'cos we couldn't always tell the difference! Unlike the Vietcong I understand the British Army can still afford uniforms."

"It's not that simple ..." Twomey began, defensively.

McKee cut in: "Forget it, Chief. These two are just trying to provoke us. Look, McClatcher, I don't pretend

96

to like you or your friend, and I don't appreciate your offensive tone. I find it particularly distasteful, if not irrelevant. There are always, as you are aware, casualties in war. We all recognise that. In particular, you've put forward ideas for dealing with the Special Air Service Regiment that are ridiculous in the extreme. You've charged us a lot of money for doing it, and the cost of putting it into operation is ... well, astronomical. Absurd in fact."

McClatcher allowed himself a wry smile. "What's the price of success, Mr McKee? What value do you put on the effective elimination of the SAS teams in Ulster within a year?"

"They'd only be replaced," Cahill observed absently.

"Only with difficulty," McClatcher replied. "Each SAS man is worth a hundred times a normal soldier—in fighting value and trainin' time. You can't buy experience. There *are* only five squadrons of eighty men in the regular SAS Regiment. That's only around four hundred troopers in total. My plans will get rid of fifty men before next year's out. The Army will be forced to change its techniques. The SAS will be discredited and you'll have your old freedom back to cross the border when and where you please."

"With what guarantee?" Twomey snorted.

Loveday said lyrically: "We judge ourselves by what we feel capable of doing, while others judge us by what we've already done."

"What?" JB asked.

McClatcher smiled. "A saying by your Longfellow. Adopted by us at Nha Trang. With your propaganda machine goin' full blast, I guess you'll persuade the limeys to pull out when we get you results like that. If not the entire Army, at least the SAS guys."

"If it could be done," Cahill conceded, "I reckon we'd stand a good chance of that happening."

"But at what price?" Twomey demanded, peering over his spectacles. "A million dollars?"

"Exactly," smiled McClatcher. "Then you agree with

the price we put on success in this little backwater war of yours."

Eamon Doherty had been listening, mesmerised by the self-assurance of these two men. He had never met anyone quite like them, even when he served in the Parachute Regiment. With a hundred men like them, what couldn't he achieve? Even with ten.

He ran his hand roughly through his unruly mop of hair. "Look, just spell out again for us exactly how you'd do it. Not all that Yankee jargon in this report. In your own words."

Loveday smiled. They were winning through.

"First," McClatcher said. "You get me your best men. The very best, mind. None of ya backslidin' cowboys. From what Martin here tells me of your resources, I doubt if that means more than fifty. We'll take 'em away to a new camp down here in Eire. Somewhere nice an' private. Then Loveday an' me are given a free hand—a complete free hand—to knock tha crap out of 'em an' build 'em back into real soldiers. We'll equip 'em with the best kit money can buy. You know better'n anyone who the SAS is likely to be watchin', if you get my meanin'. So we can then set up our killin' zones an' watch'm walk straight into it. Like flies into a spider's web."

"But a million dollars!" harped JB, still wondering where he was supposed to get the money from.

Loveday said: "Man, you ain't seen one o' our killin' zones. We have access to sensors and radars that'll pin-point every movement 'dem bastards make! We'll know where they are; but they sure as hell won't know we're right behind 'em. And, man, that sorta technology takes bread. Big bread."

McClatcher added: "Since I left the Army, Mr McKee, I've been buildin' up my own li'le business. It's goin' well an' I intend to keep it that way. If me an' Loveday here have to put our lives on the line, then the sky's the limit. I ain't gonna die bust."

Anxious to keep to positive aspects of the proposals, McGuiness asked respectfully: "How are you able to guarantee they'll oblige you by moving into your killing zones?"

"Our killing zones will be fully mobile. If they don't come to us, we will go to them."

"You'd do this in Ulster?" Doherty asked.

"Why not? Once your Micks know what the hell they're doin', and we can be sure they know how to melt away into the landscape. Don't forget, we know everyone the Army should be keepin' an eye on. That'll give yer lads a head start, d'ya see?"

Doherty chuckled. You had to hand it to these two characters. They had the gall of the very devil.

McKee was shocked, but tried hard to keep the surprise out of his voice: "You'll actually try and ambush the ambushers, so to speak? Sort of hunt the hunters?"

"Got it in one."

"I don't believe our men could do it," Twomey said emphatically. "And I don't believe the Army, particularly the SAS, would let them get away with it."

"That," McClatcher said with a hint of triumph, "is why you are losing this goddamn war. You don't *know* your enemy."

"You'd need detailed knowledge of SAS operations. Top secret, classified stuff," McGuiness prompted.

"We'll set 'em up," laughed Loveday.

McClatcher nodded. "We don't know the details yet, but give us a few weeks and access to your intelligence sources. We'll suss out a way. It's just a game. Give us time and we'll find the way. Martin here will help."

McKee shook his head slowly. "It's all very well, but I'm not convinced. And certainly a million dollars for a year's work, even taking into account the electronic gadgets you talk about, is much too much. We just don't have the funding . . ." He added with a soft smile: "After all, as you said, we must judge you by what you've done. Not what you think you can do."

Loveday glanced at McClatcher. The captain kept his steely eyes firmly fixed on McKee. "Tell you what. We'll make the initial contract for six months. It'll make things more difficult, but we'll have made a good start on trainin' by then. Enough for you to see how things are goin'. Then you can cancel if you want."

"That's still half-a-million dollars," JB muttered, almost to himself.

McKee said firmly: "I'd want more than that, McClatcher. In six months I'd want to see the first bodies of dead SAS men."

Loveday whooped again: "Man, you drive a mean bargain!"

"You'll get 'em," McClatcher promised flatly. For half-a-million dollars he'd promise the entire British Army. "Fifty per cent up front, the remainder paid into my Liechtenstein account. Martin has the details."

Twomey scratched his head. This would mean a couple of big bank raids and fast. Unless Gadaffi could be persuaded to sign a cheque. But not dear old Boris; he added too many strings.

"Resolution proposed," McKee said.

"Seconded," Cahill murmured. At least this meeting was less boring than most.

"Passed," McKee confirmed, scribbling on his pad.

"Out of interest," Doherty asked, "just what qualifications do you guys have to carry out this operation?"

Martin McGuiness flashed an angry glance at Doherty, but relaxed when he saw the American grin expansively.

"Well, I'll tell you. Me and my ex-sergeant here, Winston, joined the Special Forces in Stateside when Kennedy raised the numbers from 2,000 to 5,000 men in the early sixties. Between 1962 and 1965 we ran our own private party in 'Nam before the 'legs'—GIs to you— arrived an' the whole damn' shootin'-match went sour. Mind you, before we landed it was a mess, too. The Viet Cong had the Diem government by the shorts. At Ap Bac just 200 Charlies wiped out over 2,000 of Diem's regulars. It looked like curtains.

"Well, we pulled together a ragtail army of some 40,000 Yards. They were non-Vietnamese tribesmen. Rhade Steing, Jarai, Churu and others who were happy to fight for a few bucks. Unlike the South Vietnamese who were better at runnin'. Well, we trained those jungle-monkeys so damn good they even put the fear of Christ into us!"

Loveday chuckled. "They sure as damnation did, an' we was livin' there right in with 'em. We ate Yard food, lived in Yard huts and had Yard tail! Wowee! Some broads them Yard broads. Still, they could scare us too, all right. Got the VC back where they belonged in no time. They was haulin' ass as fast as they could." He jammed his thumb down demonstratively.

"Then Kennedy got done," McClatcher said, "an' things were never quite so good. When Johnson sent in the 'legs' it all started to change. We still went over the border into VC country, Cambodia and Laos, but not with the same freedom as previous. Winston was with me with Detachment B–57, an' we had a ball."

Loveday flashed the silver talisman around his neck at the men around the table: "My ol' padre gimme this!" It read: *Kill a Commie for Christ.*

Only Doherty smiled.

"Then I went back to Fort Bragg," McClatcher continued, "an' studied in political warfare and psychological operations. When I returned to 'Nam it had all changed. The 'legs' were established by that time and the US Air Force paid our Yards better money to guard their bases. It was a downhill run."

"In them days," Loveday interrupted in a tone verging on heart-felt nostalgia, "we had guys from the top units 'round the Western world workin' with us on special trainin'. Foreign Legionnaires who'd previously served in 'Nam; SAS guys brushing up on jungle trainin'; German commandoes; Aussies ..."

"You've actually worked with the Special Air Service?" It was Cahill.

"Sure," Loveday said. "Did a lota ops. with 'em. Real gentlemen compared to some. Yep, real gents!"

McClatcher cursed. By the impressed faces around him that should have been his trump card. Still, half-a-million bucks was enough to be getting along with.

"Right," McKee said. "I think we can thank the captain and his friend, and leave them to liaise with Mr McGuiness. We'll call for you at your hotel tomorrow morning."

McClatcher climbed to his feet and threw a perfunctory salute. "'Till tomorrow, Mr McKee."

As they moved towards the door, McClatcher quickly reached out and grabbed the arm the squint-eyed man still kept under his jacket. His fist was like a steel vice, gripping the guard's forearm with such power, that the man was unable to pull the gun from his waist band holster.

"Now watchya gonna do, baby?" Loveday leered.

"Lesson Number One," McClatcher said. "If you're a bodyguard don't let every jerk in the neighbourhood know where you keep yer shooter."

As he released his grip the man grabbed his tortured wrist with his free hand and massaged it as though his life depended on it.

McClatcher shook his head sadly and left the room.

"Ciao!" Loveday said, grinning.

Outside they strode together along the pavement in the direction of Dublin centre, impervious to the chill snap in the air.

"You crafty motherfucker," Loveday said out of the corner of his mouth. "A cool half-million, man! And all that crap about his useless Micks. Dunno how you got away with it, goddamn you."

McClatcher tapped the side of his nose, grinning faintly. "Psychology, man, psychology. Get 'em on the defensive, then strike 'em where they ain't expectin' it. In the bread basket!"

"That's all very well," Loveday said, "but we still gotta earn that bread. Where'd hell we goin' t' find out 'bout the limey military?" And he added: "Less, o'course, you got contacts."

McClatcher was still feeling elated and allowed himself a tight, smug grin. "C'mon, Winston, you know me better'n that. I've gotten contacts everywhere." He tugged an airmail envelope from his inside jacket pocket and waved it. "From a friend in London town. He's been makin' enquiries through two private outfits called Saladin and KMS. They hire out ex-SAS men on consultancy work, security, bodyguards for VIPs, etc. They've a pretty open door to members serving in the regiment. I asked him to look up a name for me. You'll remember it. Ducane."

"Come again?"

"Ducane. Jacko. D-U-C-A-N-E."

"So?"

"Ducane. Captain Ducane."

The Negro shrugged.

McClatcher clamped the sergeant affably on the arm. "You can do better'n that, yer dumb nigger ... Ducane. Jack Ducane. Don't it mean nothin' to you?"

Loveday frowned, thinking back over the countless British officers he'd met through the years. "Hell, Earl, the name rings bells, but I can't place no Cap'n—*Ducane*, you say?"

McClatcher raised his eyes in despair, but he was in no mood to be angry. "Well, you must sure as hell remember his wife, Pat. A tall blonde broad back in Hong Kong about six years back."

"Hey, wait a minute ..."

"That party," McClatcher prompted. "The game of strip poker with that crowd of limeys. Ducane's wife dancin' ..."

"Wowee!" Loveday beamed. "Yeah, sure, Earl, I've got it. Never forget a pretty li'le ass like that. Jacko Ducane. Jees, I'd forgotten his name. Shit, I oughta remember, we did a mission with him an' a coupla others. A big guy with a dumb broad of a wife an' ..."

"Just 'cos she declined yer favourite card game!"

Loveday stared at the wall. "Yeah, Elaine ... I remember. Cold little bitch. But a nice frame. Married to the big guy. FORBES! That was it." He nodded to himself. "Forbes 'n' Jacko Ducane. Forbes was just a ranker then, an' Ducane a second lieutenant."

McClatcher waved the envelope again. "Well now,

Ducane's a captain, but Forbes ain't moved up far. An' those two bastards were the ones that pulled in that big fish in the Army Council."

Loveday whistled softly. "Well, can yer beat that for coincidence!"

McClatcher returned the envelope to his pocket. "I couldn't have hoped for a better break! I've been rackin' my goddamn brains to find a way into the SAS." He plucked a cigar from his top pocket, unwrapping the cellophane expertly with one hand. "It'll guarantee us an early success an' persuade those tight-assed jerks on the Council to renew the contract! Man, we could be made."

Loveday stared thoughtfully ahead. "An' you reckon ol' Jacko Ducane will tell you all about it?"

The American paused to strike a match and drew deeply on the cigar. "Hell, no, Ducane an' I, well, there ain't no love lost between us. But I got an idea how we might work somethin'."

Loveday looked sideways at him, his eyes wide. "You plannin' t' pay him a visit?"

"Well, I sure as hell ain't gonna ask him to Dublin!"

"Have yer got his address?"

"Nope, but that ain't gonna take a lifetime to find." He studied the glowing end of the cigar. "Might even persuade Jacko himself to come lookin' fer us. Hey, that ain't such a dumb idea!"

"Yer mean spring it on Jacko. Christ, man, that ain't very comradely!"

McClatcher laughed. "Nope, Winston, to be serious, I had more in mind that li'le wife o' his. If my memory serves me right, she had a bit of a weakness for both of us."

Loveday read his mind like a reflex reaction. "You thinkin' of maybe compromisin' the young lady?" He sniggered. "Gee, she sure was a frisky one all right. I reckon not much persuadin' fer her t'come to the boil!"

They both laughed, recalling the wild party they had had with some local Chinese girls and the British service-men and their wives before they had left for Vietnam.

It was a long time ago, but the memories had remained vivid.

"That's a wicked trick, Earl," Loveday giggled.

"You goin' soft in yer old age, nigger. Listen, I owe that bastard. Remember that village. We knew fer sure it was fulla VC, but Jacko—stupid limey shit—had t'go'n give 'em a chance first. Nearly cost me my Yard scout through that!"

"He didn't wanna blast the Gook women 'n' kids!"

"Since when did that worry us? An' we survived!"

Loveday shrugged. He could never quite share McClatcher's callous disregard for accidental casualties. The question of race was never one they discussed together, but the Negro was conscious that his own sensitivity at the needless killing of Vietnamese civilians may have been that his own skin wasn't white. McClatcher's one concern had been surviving, but surviving with the biggest bodycount he could muster. Loveday had seen the captain line up women and children and drop them with a sub-machine gun burst, one by one, until he got the information he sought. It was effective all right, but it also earned him the official request for his resignation. No one had been able to prove anything, and everyone respected McClatcher too much to offer any evidence. His methods were cruel, but no crueller than the rest of the war. After a while you became immune to the atrocities and debauchery, and were just thankful to stay alive. And McClatcher was an expert at keeping his men alive.

By contrast, Loveday remembered the British SAS trooper handing round sweets to the village children and doling out scarce medical supplies to those who were sick. McClatcher had been convinced that, as soon as his patrol passed on, they would have been used by the VCs they were hunting. Once Ducane had let a captured VC political officer put his case to the villagers without interruption; and then given the other side of the story. The Gooks just couldn't believe their eyes and ears. As one old man had said, no one had ever bothered to explain things from the American point of view. The VC's propaganda had just gone unchecked, with no one ever challenging the facts or political half-truths of convenience. They were a simple people in the village and Loveday had often wondered whether Ducane had made an impression on them. Perhaps he had, because two months later the village was decimated by the VC.

Loveday had decided that there were just too many hearts and minds to be won in Indo-China. And not enough time. So he had decided to stay close to Mc-Clatcher, gradually adopting the other man's attitudes and a layer of armoured skin that was impervious to the senseless waste of human life he saw around him. As far as he was concerned McClatcher meant life. His life. And although his blind belief in the big American's methods was shaken from time to time, he never allowed himself seriously to consider the moral issues. There were enough hippy jerks Stateside to do that for him.

His respect for McClatcher grew and did not diminish even over the resignation incident. Many of McClatcher's ex-colleagues in the Special Forces had disowned him. Out of genuine disgust, or because it caused them to focus more sharply on their own dubious deeds, Loveday could never be sure.

But his loyalty had not gone unrewarded. In civilian life Earl Lee McClatcher had gone about carving a new career with the same ruthlessness and uncanny instinct for self-survival as he had in Vietnam. He made the transition from the jungles of Indo-China to the concrete jungle of the big cities with consummate ease.

McClatcher was a survivor and, whilst he was, Winston Loveday had no intention of parting company with him.

"Yes," McClatcher muttered, the cigar butt clenched between his teeth. "Captain Jacko Ducane will do nicely, thank you." He quickened his pace. "C'mon, nigger, let's hit Dublin an' see if we can't find ourselves some classy Irish ass!"

"Daddy! Daddy!"
It seemed as though his head had only just hit the sack.

He tried squeezing out the excited call by burying his head in the pillow. But already he was aware of the dull thud at the back of his neck. Remembered coming home late. Breaking open the bottles of red wine. Eating the spicey casserole that had been kept for him in the oven. The sweet feel of Trish as he'd buried the violence and hatred inside her. The pure, cleansing rush of ecstasy that had washed it all away, removing the tarnish and bloodstains of his tour-of-duty. Life had begun to sparkle again. The plunging into the stiff warmth of starched sheets. Smothered in the welcoming warmth of the bed as deep sleep enveloped him. Peaceful, free of the recent violence flashing through his dreams. The faint smell of lavendar.

"Daddy! Daddy!" Sarah's voice came again. A tiny hand touched his arm.

Ducane cranked open one eye and looked out from the crushed pillow. Four years old with long brown hair and her mother's turned-up nose. A replica in miniature with the same inquisitive blue eyes and stubborn pout when she was angry or confused. Fiddling with the hem of her cotton nightdress, and a one-eyed Paddington Bear at her feet.

Seeing him stir, she stood still, gazing curiously.

"Hi," he said, his voice muffled by the pillow.

"Hallo!" she said suddenly. Then silence. They were both friends and strangers.

"How's my little angel, then?"

Her eyes looked cautious, gauging his mood. They twinkled before she said, provoking: "You didn't come and see me last night when you came home."

He smiled. "Oh, yes I did. But who fell asleep waiting for me?"

"No!"

"When I came up to see you, you were fast asleep." He propped himself up on one arm. "Snoring."

"I don't snore!"

"You were last night."

She laughed suddenly, giggling. "Like Mummy!"

Ducane chuckled. "Yep. Just like Mummy."

"Is Mummy snoring now?"

"I don't know. Go and see."

Sarah rushed quickly around the bottom of the bed in a series of little jumps. She peered closely at the mass of bubble-curls protruding from the sheet beside him.

"Are you snoring, Mummy?" Loudly.

He felt Trish stir, rubbing her long legs against his.

"Hey, come on, you'd better not disturb her. What's the time?"

"Three and a half."

"Three-thirty? Never!" He peered at the clock on the bedside table.

"Six-thirty, silly. Half past six. You don't believe in wasting the day, do you, young lady?"

Trish rolled onto her back and propped herself up on her elbows. The sheet slid from her bare shoulders, a cascade of ringlets falling over her half-closed eyes.

"What time is it?" she mumbled.

"Three and a half!" cried Sarah defiantly.

Trish tossed her hair from her face, peering at Ducane with those brilliant violet eyes that could see little without the gigantic gold-rimmed glasses she wore.

"Hey," she said. "There's a *man* in my bed!"

"It's *Daddy*!" shrieked Sarah, bouncing on the foot of the bed.

Trish laughed. "Why, so it is. Hello husband." She reached up and kissed him on the tip of his nose.

"Hello, wife," he replied, studying her face as though seeing it for the first time. She had high cheek bones which had kept her skin tight and youthful, speckled with faint freckles around her nose. Only the finely-etched lines around her eyes suggested that she had reached thirty and was not several years younger. Her eyes, large and long-lashed, blinked back at him, and a smile played at her lips. He couldn't resist them, kissing her hard and full, recapturing precious moments from the previous night.

Sarah watched, bored but curious.

He caught her stare from the corner of his eye.

"What about my other favourite girl?" he asked. "Don't I get a kiss from her?"

Sarah giggled. "No!"

He pulled a hurt expression. "Now you've broken my heart. What will Paddy think of you?"

She looked down at the toy bear she was holding by the leg. With a sudden movement she started crawling over the eiderdown, half-bouncing over Trish's body, then his. "Paddy says all right!" she said.

Straddling his stomach, she leaned forward and looked into his eyes closely, just as Trish had done. She pouted her lips, her cheeks puffed in an effort to suppress a laugh, her eyes twinkling mischievously. She shut her eyes, tight, and plonked a large, wet and noisy kiss on his mouth.

"Hello, Daddy!" Too excited to sound like Trish.

Playing the game, he replied: "Hello, daughter." Her eyes gleamed with delight as he gave the right answer, and she began to ride up and down like a jockey, laughing.

"Hey, careful of Daddy's arm," Trish warned.

Sarah stopped and studied the bandage around his arm. She pulled a face. "What's that?"

"I hurt myself," Ducane said.

"Does it hurt?"

"A bit. 'Specially when you jump on it."

She looked at it more closely, noticing the tiny brown patches where blood had seeped through.

"Were you shot with a gun, Daddy?"

"Only by accident."

Sarah looked thoughtful for a moment. "Did you shoot anyone?"

Feeling him tense, Trish interrupted quickly. "Do you think Daddy has brought you a present?"

Sarah looked around at the Army-issue brown-checked suitcases in the corner of the room, over which Ducane's uniform had been strewn, and then back at her father. "Have you brought Paddy a present, Daddy?"

He frowned. He hadn't thought of that one. "It's for you," and added: "But it's also a friend for Paddy. Why don't you have a look in the big case. It's open."

Trish chided: "Oh, Jack, you shouldn't. She'll have things all over the place!"

"That's all right." Sarah was already off, her foot accidentally delivering a glancing blow to his bandaged arm as she turned, his injury already forgotten. She slid down the bedcovers and scampered across to start her exploration.

Trish snuggled up to him, her cool arm around his waist, her ringlets under his chin, tickling. Softly she kissed the hairs on his chest.

"How long do they say the arm will take?" she asked.

He shrugged. "A few weeks. I'll be stationed back at Hereford on training while I recover."

She turned her eyes up at him. "I hope you're not starting to get careless, Jack. Sarah and I can't afford to lose you. And certainly not to a silly twit like that Major Simmonds."

"He was just doing his best, I suppose. 'Thought he ought to rescue us."

"Huh!" She ran her hand over his chest, scratching lightly with her fingernails. "He was quick enough to try and get you into trouble afterwards."

Ducane smiled. "That was just to ease his conscience. The Royals' CO was hardly likely to complain with two Provo Council members in the bag within two weeks. And obviously there was no sympathy from our squadron commander."

"Then why wasn't old Simmonds reprimanded? Or transferred or something?"

He lifted his bandaged arm. "As I was coming back with this anyway, it was a case of letting sleeping dogs lie. The whisper has it Simmonds will be transferred after a respectable time has passed. I think the Royals' CO has had enough of him anyway."

Trish sighed. "So you think you'll go back again?"

"I can't find it!" It was Sarah.

Ducane said: "It's not over yet, love. My team's working well together, and we know our patch well now. That makes it safer."

"Yes, so I see!" She added quietly: "It just all seems to get more dangerous. Bloodier and more murderous."

Ducane was defensive. "They're just thugs and villains whatever their political motives. Not worth the time of day."

"But what with McNally and—what was the other's name—Cochran. Well, I'd have thought you'd done enough. 'Specially now you've been wounded."

"I tell you too much, Trish."

"I like to know what goes on. You know I don't blab to anyone. Besides, Ireland isn't like a threat to national security. Closer to home. You don't tell me much about Russia, do you?"

"There's not much to tell." He hugged her closely with his good arm. "You still know more than is good for you."

She pulled away suddenly from him, the sheet slipping from her small, round breasts. "I'm not a child, Jack," she said defiantly. "Of course, I like to know what's going on. At least an outline. Think how it feels for me at home all the time, having no idea where you are or what's happening to you. Then every now and again you come back on sick leave. It *is* worrying, and damned difficult to cope with at times. If I know something of what happens, I feel I can at least share part of your life while we're apart."

"You pout beautifully, Trish."

Disarmed, she smiled at her own anger. "It can be trying for the folk back at home too, you know?"

"I know." He eased her gently towards him, feeling the soft weight of her breasts against his side.

"I found it!" came Sarah's triumphant cry.

She brought the brown paper package over to the bed, and began the laborious task of unwrapping the layers of paper and sticky tape. Eventually, after several minutes of exasperated grunts and cries, she succeeded in extracting the national doll in its perspex box.

"It's a colleen," he said. "From Ireland. A country girl."

She thrust it towards her bear.

"Paddy likes her," she said emphatically.

"What do you say to Daddy, Sarah?" Trish asked.

The little girl looked round suddenly. A beaming smile. "I love you!"

CHAPTER 6

The Old Man looked out of the window across the wet tarmac drill square to the lines of almost leafless trees and the rows of one-storey black barrack buildings that lay beyond. Winter was on its way, a stiff south-westerly wind driving a fine drizzle of rain before it, filling the neatly trimmed lanes between the huts with large puddles. As usual the Bradbury Lines camp at Hereford was near deserted. A specially-equipped SAS Land Rover, on a brake test after maintenance, drove past the clock-tower below which were listed the names of the men of the Special Air Service who had lost their lives in action.

Considering the extent and hazardous nature of their operations, there were very few. It was a testament to their thorough recruitment techniques and the ruthless, imaginative training. It was a record the Old Man was determined to maintain with an almost evangelical dedication.

Actually, 'Old Man' was a misnomer for the colonel, whose active career since he had joined the Irish Rangers as a newly-commissioned officer in 1951 had earned him an OBE and MC in recognition of his services to the military. He had fought with the SAS between 1955 and 1960 in the counter-insurgency campaigns of Malaya and Cyprus. He had won the Military Cross in 1960 whilst fighting in Oman with the SAS to assist the Sultan crush the left-wing rebels. After pushing a pen in Berlin he returned to the SAS as a squadron commander in the Borneo and Saudi Arabia actions. Again he left the regiment, until recently, when he had rejoined to lead it.

He reflected that the business in the Middle East was almost over. For the time being at least. But there remained the grisly Ulster theatre, and that was plenty to be getting on with. That and the almost regular request for aid from Western governments everytime an aircraft was hi-jacked. Still, it allowed them to keep their hand in. Better than that spell a few years back in the late sixties when they had virtually to become a mercenary force in order to see the whites of anyone's eyes.

It was strange to reflect that life had become more interesting under the Labour Government, even if the rest of the Armed Forces had suffered. But it always amused him when each successive Prime Minister discovered the SAS. Everyone would be surprised at the scope of their operations, and the depth of the 'services' they offered. It was obvious they were impressed, but always they attempted to give the appearance that they were quite aware such things went on. They weren't, of course. It must be the same for others whose activities went generally unknown. It was quite an eye-opener to a newly-empowered politician to learn the full extent of things that went on in the military and the murky world of the intelligence services. The extent of the underground defence complexes in central London; the secret regional headquarters in case of nuclear war or invasion; the massive UK 'listening' operation which allows intelligence gatherers to listen to radio conversations between tank commanders on the other side of the Soviet border; the submarine missions to Soviet ports, and, of course, the gentlemen in the sand-coloured berets.

It was obvious that each new Prime Minister would think hard about the outfit and toy for weeks with all the possibilities of this new-found instrument of power. Although liaison was provided by the brigadier in the Ministry of Defence, responsible for both regular and territorial regiments, it usually wasn't long before premiers arranged to meet the CO of 22 Regiment. Sometimes quite a close relationship was forged. At first tentative questions would be asked. What could we do if this ... What could we do if that ... All hypothetical, of course. And always the surprise, quickly concealed, when the Old Man didn't offer a hundred reasons why not. Unlike the Chiefs of Staff, who could more or less be counted on to be negative and obstructive when a PM asked for their help.

But it was always different with the Old Man and his predecessors. Never say no. Ideas would be modified all right, radically sometimes, but always he would be back with counter-proposals. Better suggestions. Professional confidant to Prime Ministers and would-be emperors on matters most secret.

It was a position he always enjoyed, and one that was the envy of the entire British Army, not least the Chiefs of Staff themselves. Obviously protocol was always followed. They would always be asked their opinion, of course, but they would be aware that not many days previously the Old Man had been invited for a round of golf, a spot of supper, or an informal luncheon.

In the Officers' Mess there would be heavy odds laid against the time it would take a newly-elected premier to test their mettle. Chiefs of Staff usually got used to it, learned the tricks, and suggested the 'cloak-and-dagger brigade' before the Prime Minister did himself. You had to keep ahead in the game somehow ...

A sharp knock on the door disturbed his concentration. It was the stocky orderly who stepped in smartly, his boots cracking loudly to attention on the worn linoleum floor. The Old Man wished he wouldn't do it, after all, this wasn't Catterick.

"Captain Ducane, SAH!"

The Old Man turned from his window to the paper-littered desk as the tall captain strode in and saluted, his movements correct but somehow casual. That's better, he mused, not too much pomp. Just the right degree of respect.

"Ah, Ducane, do take a seat."

"Thank you, sir." As the orderly closed the door the two men sat down. The Old Man pushed the battered gold and onyx cigarette box across the table-top. Although each eighty man squadron was commanded by a major, the colonel took the trouble to talk to every one of his troops from time to time. He could actually remember most of their names.

"Smoke?" While Ducane lit one of the hand-made pure Virginians, he waved his old pipe in one hand, a lighter in the other. "I'll try not to smoke you out, Captain."

Ducane relaxed. Always the same joke. Always the same informality. Despite their super-troop status, the Old Man was all too aware of their fallibility. He knew that they tended to be forthright and suspicious by nature, but often anxious and even shy. As always there followed the polite questions, quietly probing, reconnoitring the situation, pin-pointing problems and flaws, ready for the important thrust. Never quite what it seemed, and, just below the surface, the edge of the voice like a glimpse of cold steel. The razored foil in the velvet scabbard.

You bastard, Ducane thought affectionately, which way will you play it this time? Whatever, you'll have me on the defensive in no time, but I respect you for it. All the lads respect you for it. Can't hide anything from the Old Man, he'll find it out, find your weak spot, unearth your most private fear. Just as well. A chain is as strong as its weakest link and all that. And when you're moulding a group of individual men into a single living, breathing cell to fight, cut-off, behind enemy lines, you can't risk discovering the crack after you've arrived. And the men thank you for that, Ducane mused. That was just one of the thousand reasons they were always eager to go to hell for you.

You'd let them, too, you old sod, but for you it's always got to be hell *and back*. Any fool can get there; it takes one of the Master's mob to get home again.

"Arm all right now?" he asked through the clouds of smoke as he puffed the pipe alight.

Ducane lifted the arm slightly. 'Well on the mend, thanks, Colonel."

"Good, good. I expect you enjoyed that bit of R and R you had? You earned it."

"It was nice to get home."

The Old Man smiled, the waxed grey moustache flicking

upward. "And how's the missus? And the little girl? What's her name, Sarah?"

"Fine thanks, sir."

"Coping okay? What with inflation and all that. 'Getting a bit much lately. 'Had to sell my second Bentley last week, don't you know!" Joke.

"I won't pretend it's not difficult, sir. We're managing."

The Old Man nodded, understanding. "What with damn' Pay Codes and whatnot the Services don't seem to be keeping up with the great world outside. 'Can't live on patriotism alone, can we!"

You old bugger, Ducane thought. I swear to God you've been listening to conversations between Trish and I.

The colonel made another attempt to get his pipe going. "You've done well in Armagh. Two VIPs in the bag. Pity it got a bit bloody. Be an improvement if things could be tidied up a bit. I appreciate accidents happen, but I could do with fewer corpses. Gives fuel to the old Provisional propaganda machine, y'know." He paused. "Oh, at your discretion, *of course*. You and Sergeant Forbes have over fourteen years service between you, so I can't afford to have you take chances. Even so, a little less blood-letting wouldn't go amiss. Still, you're pleased the way the team's shaping up?"

"Yes, sir. Trooper Perrot's going to be a credit to the regiment. A bit sensitive, but he's learning fast."

The Old Man rubbed his eyebrow with the stem of his pipe. "Yes, I gather he got in a bit of a tangle with a Provo. Still, there's only one way to get real combat experience. And what about the corporal? Turnbull?"

Ducane's eyes darted with suspicion before he could check them; it was unlikely the eagle eyes across the table had missed it.

"He's very good, sir."

"Mmm," he nodded sagely. "Very much his own man, wouldn't you say?"

"Yes," Ducane conceded. "But he works well in the team. He'll go places in time, I'm sure of that."

"You can make a change if you like, Ducane. We've got

a dozen good men experienced in Armagh. There would be no problem." The very pale green eyes held his gaze.

Ducane shook his head. "No, Colonel, I'm happy for him to stick as long as he wants to."

"He's good to have around?" Opening parry.

"Yes, sir, he is."

"Re-assuring?" Thrust.

"Yes, sir, he's independent-minded, but reliable as a rock. Whatever he may think, he doesn't go off on his own. He's a team worker."

"Bright, of course." A statement. Not giving up.

"He's intelligent. A good planner. Thinks things out."

"Lacks a bit of the old animal cunning, perhaps?" Second thrust.

Ducane half-smiled. "We don't always see eye-to-eye, sir. But I think we make a good team. Sort of complementary."

"Good. So no change then?" Satisfied.

"No, sir."

The colonel leaned forward. "You're aware Sergeant Forbes is in the cooler today?" Not satisfied, after all.

"Yes, sir."

"Tried to visit his girlfriend in the nurses' hostel last night and got himself caught. Bad show."

"Sir?"

"Getting caught."

"Yes. Unlike the sergeant, sir."

The Old Man nodded. "Like you, Ducane, he's not getting any younger for this caper. Unlike you, the boozing has taken its toll over the years. You might look forward to another ten years at least before getting desk-bound. Forbes may not be so lucky." He leaned back in his chair. "And there's not a desk job in creation that could suit him."

"I know, sir."

"Have a word, Ducane. A friendly word. Get him to mend his ways—or at least modify them. I don't want to have him Returned To Unit. But if he's over the hill, then I can't keep him on."

"I'll speak to him, sir. I think he's a bit depressed about his home life. Or lack of it. He hasn't really got over his wife leaving him."

The Old Man prodded at the bowl of his pipe with a steel letter-opener. "Strain tellin', eh?"

Ducane said quickly: "Not on operations, sir. That keeps his mind occupied. It's just at times like this when we're on training cadre duty . . ."

The colonel interrupted. "Talking of your current cadre, Ducane, it brings me to the immediate point of my asking you to see me." He rummaged about in the mess of papers before extracting a memorandum. "Oh, yes. Now it appears that we're in the bad books of Warwickshire's Chief Constable. Seems a bunch of your lads have got a bit carried away. Held up a branch of Barclays Bank. Scared the life out of the damn' cashiers and got away with £20,000. Phoned up the police afterwards and said it was all part of an exercise. *Deep Throat* or something?"

Ducane grinned. "The idea was to see how far they could go. Behind enemy lines, that is. I've already written to the Chief Constable and the bank, sir, to apologise. My letter must have crossed in the post. The money's been fully accounted for."

"Mmm, should think so too. Anyway, since when has Warwickshire been behind enemy lines?"

"Just for the exercise, sir. They landed on the Yorkshire coast by submarine and were heading for Manchester, code-name 'Red City'."

"For Moscow?"

"Yes, sir. Well there was a car-chase with local police and they had to abandon some of their gear, including the money to pay the underground movement of Red Land. Rather than abandon the mission, they decided to go to the bank."

"This story is getting worse, Ducane!" The interested sparkle in the green eyes belied the harsh tone of his voice.

"It's all in the report in your tray, sir. I'm very sorry about the bank. And the police-chase. The men have been severely reprimanded. It won't happen again."

"Damn' pleased to hear it. You'll get us a bad name."
He paused, giving up the idea of getting his pipe alight
without emptying the bowl completely and starting again.
As he worked he said: "Seems to me the sooner we get
you and Sergeant Forbes back to Ulster the better. At
least the police over there seem to appreciate your efforts
more than they do here. Now, what about that arm of
yours? How long does it need to mend properly? A couple
of weeks?"

Ducane said: "I finish with the training cadre in a week,
sir. And the arm feels all right now."

The Old Man re-stuffed the bowl with burnt tobacco,
thumbing in a fresh layer on top. "Fine, fine! Now I've
had a word with your Squadron Commander at Bessbrook
and he's persuaded the Royals' CO to get rid of that gun-
happy major of his, you'll be pleased to know. I'm sure
they'd appreciate your help. Got a few problems at the
moment. Seems like one of our liaison lads has got himself
mixed up with a local lass. That's bad for business, so I
need to pull him out as soon as possible. Perhaps your
team can give him a hand in getting all the loose ends
sewn up until we get a replacement?"

"Desk-work, sir?"

The Old Man succeeded in lighting the pipe, filling the
office with obnoxious thick smoke. "Desk-work's good for
the soul, Ducane. Stuff that promotion's made of. Besides,
it'll just be for a few weeks. Then we'll set you loose
again. Been a lot of speculative talk amongst the men
recently about the possibility of some of our chaps losing
their way over the border. Wanderin' into Dundalk and
Sligo. Know about it, do you?" Absently.

"I've heard the talk, sir. To hit the IRA training
camps."

"Quite so. A bit of a dodgy wicket that. The balls could
bounce a bit, if you see what I mean? Ours, too, if things
went wrong."

"Could work, sir. It would certainly upset the Provo's
apple-cart."

"Mmm." Thoughtful. "Could also set back Anglo–Irish

relations a hundred years, wouldn't you say?"

"Only if someone was caught, sir."

"A big *if*, Ducane. Of course, the PM would never entertain such an idea. Nevertheless, I gather that in some quarters people are a bit cheesed off with feeding tit-bits to the Irish Government and finding nothing's done about it."

Ducane raised his eyebrows. That *was* a turn-up for the book. It was something Forbes had been promoting loudly for some time. Perhaps the idea hadn't landed on stoney ground after all. Over the border. In and out before they knew what hit them. You scheming old bastard, Colonel, you mean you're toying with the idea, and probably promoting it gently to the PM. Come to think of it, I heard you went to London last week for a dinner party.

The Old Man waved aside the pungent cloud that engulfed him. "Not that anything will come of it, but if it does, I'd consider your team as part of the operation. No promises, of course, but bear it in mind. Providing of course, you can persuade your sergeant to cool things off. That includes the booze."

Ducane grinned broadly. "That's the biggest incentive I could give him, sir."

The Old Man nodded. "Right, well, that'll be all, Ducane. Got to get back to me paperwork. Find out what I've done with the In-Tray."

Ducane climbed to his feet, saluted, and turned towards the door.

"Oh, Captain!"

"Yes, sir?"

"Did those men of yours reach Red City?"

"Yes, sir."

A twinkle came into the pale green eyes. "Carry on, Captain."

It was a filthy night.

By the time Ducane reached the small cluster of vehicles on the top of the hill, visibility had been cut to a few yards by the rain that slanted out of the low, black sky like stair-rods. As he climbed out of the Land Rover there was not even a light to be seen in the inky void he knew to be the Brecon Hills.

He found Forbes in the cab of a green and black Bedford truck, hunched over a mug of soup, the rain dripping from his waterproofs. Ducane scrambled up beside him.

"Before you say it," the sergeant grumbled, "it isn't! It's been pee-ing down since midday. Poor little sods will get pneumonia!"

Ducane smiled to himself at the unusual sympathy Forbes was showing for his possible new recruits. Obviously he was feeling sorry for himself.

"How long have they been out?"

"Fourteen hours," Forbes said into the mug.

Ducane wiped the condensation from the side window and peered out. No sign. "Four minutes overdue. No one in yet?"

"Just one. Took one look in my eyes and collapsed."

"That I can understand."

"It was exhaustion," Forbes replied darkly. "Kids today haven't got the stamina! Never been the same since they stopped National Health orange juice."

No one in the Special Air Service ever forgot the initial selection trek. A thirteen hour race against time across the Welsh mountains or Brecon Hills in the winter darkness with only a forty-pound pack, a rifle and a compass for company. It was just the first method of whittling down the three hundred yearly applications to join the SAS, always from other army units. It was rare for more than sixty to be accepted.

The half-way point was always popular with the old salts when they weren't away on active service. Because, although it was only half-way, the new recruits were led to believe it was the end of the gruelling cross-country scramble. Just the expressions on their faces brought back the memories of their own agonising days of initial training.

Ducane said: "I'm sorry about that business over the nursing-hostel. I just hope she was worth it."

"I didn't have time to find out, did I?" grumbled Forbes.

"Do I know her?"

"She was at the dance. Sally someone. A third-year nurse. Big brown eyes and big ..."

"And she invited you to ...?"

Forbes glared at him angrily. "What is this, some sort of interrogation? We had this arrangement. Only it seems she forgot about it."

"I remember. I thought she was jokin'."

The sergeant's smile was sour. "It seems you were right."

"So she kicked up a fuss?"

He drained his mug of soup. "Well, wouldn't you if you found a strange man creepin' round your bedroom in the middle of the night?"

"I should be so lucky," Ducane chuckled, imagining the scene. "But why didn't you get out fast?"

Forbes eyed him coldly. "Well, for one I'd had a skinful, hadn't I? And for two I couldn't find my boots."

"Your boots?" Incredulous.

"Yes, my bloody boots, cloth ears! I'd left 'em by the window so I wouldn't make a noise. I wasn't *that* pissed. But when she started screaming I had my trousers off, and by the time I got 'em on again I couldn't find my sodding boots. Now let's drop the subject, shall we?"

"And the sister caught you?"

"I said drop it!"

Ducane shook his head, not trusting himself to speak in case he couldn't suppress the laughter.

"The Old Man gave me a right rollickin'," Forbes continued. "Said he had to do some fast talkin' to stop the girl pressing charges. Silly cow. Threatened to have me court-martialled and this time I had the distinct feeling he meant it."

"Stop boozin' or you're out?"

"Christ! I sometimes wonder if life's worth living, I do really. And after that long chat we had the other week about hitting the Sligo camps. I thought we were gettin' on well."

"That's why I've come up here."

For a moment there was alarm in Forbes' eyes. It wasn't the first time that Ducane had seen fear in the sergeant's eyes; but it was only ever when he thought he might be RTU'd.

Ducane said: "He *was* impressed with your suggestion. I gather it's all in the early stages, but there's just a chance he could get the okay."

"Stop pullin' it, Jacko!"

"It's true. And if it goes ahead, he's as good as promised us first crack. But keep it under your hat."

"Well, I'll be ..."

"Sober," Ducane said.

"Huh?"

"That's his condition. You keep off the liquor, and we get a crack at the job, if it comes off."

The sergeant's moody expression lightened visibly. "You think he meant it? Not just a bit of the old behavioural psychology."

"He meant it, I'm sure. And the fact he mentioned it at all suggests *he* is pretty sure he'll get clearance for the operation."

Forbes wiped the back of his sleeve roughly across his mouth, removing the soup traces from his moustache. He stared at the rain pounding on the windshield, and a large, fat smile began to spread across his face.

The cab door swung open and a bereted corporal looked up, his eyes squinting against the lashing rain, the water streaming down his poncho. "Picked one up, Sarge, hundred yards away! Shall I give him a light?"

Forbes grinned. 'Yep, put the poor devil out of his misery. In this muck he might miss us completely and *we'll* have to go lookin' for *him*."

While the soldier flashed a torch for the new recruit, Forbes and Ducane climbed out into the gushing torrent. The man, a major from one of the infantry regiments, was scrambling up the hillside with difficulty under the weight of his sodden pack, his feet slipping as the loose soil was washed away under the soles of his boots. Progress was laboriously slow as he weaved his way to where the ground was firmer, gradually working towards the torch beam.

Forbes stood erect as he approached, peering down over his barrel chest at the ashen, mud-smeared face as the officer finally crawled onto the trackway.

"Well done, sir," the sergeant said.

"God, am-I-pleased to see you!" The man gasped as he staggered to his feet. "What a night! I lost my bearings round by the stream. It must have added three miles."

"It must have done," returned Forbes, suppressing a sardonic smile.

The man was too exhausted to notice. He just stood there, panting, his legs astride, hands held limply by his side as the rain ran off his smock in rivulets. "Now, sir, I'd like you to turn round and go back over those hills to where you've just come from."

Dark, hate-filled eyes burned up at him from the pale, wet face. "What?"

"You heard right, sir. Go back."

"You must be jokin'! I thought this was the end of the course."

Forbes nodded impassively. "Well, sir, in a way it is. Look at it more as your objective. Your military target. But the colonel's men always have to *return* from their missions. I mean you just can't go to the nearest friendly Russian and say I've just blown up your ball-bearing factory, can you put me up for the night. Now can you, sir?"

"Back?" The major turned and looked back down the slippery slope to where another bedraggled figure was crawling inexorably up the slope, clinging to tufts of grass for support. "No, Sergeant, I've had my lot."

Forbes turned his head and called out to the corporal. "Take the major in, Newton. Give him some dry kit and a big hot mug o' soup!"

As the officer trudged past, Forbes said: "Sorry you couldn't make it, sir."

Ducane nodded towards the second recruit who was reaching the edge of the track. "He's a little one. His pack's as big as he is. Must be from a pigmy regiment."

"Cradle-snatching, now," Forbes muttered out of the side of his mouth.

The young lance-corporal climbed to his weary five feet three and pulled himself to attention. "Perkis, Sarge. Sorry I'm late."

"So am I, boy," Forbes said.

"It was a stream, Sarge; it was swollen so I 'ad to swim it. Current carried me away. I was lost when I got to the other side. Then I sprained me bloody ankle."

"Never mind," consoled Forbes. "You did a good job. Now, I'd like you to turn round and find your way back to where you started."

"Now?"

"Now."

The lance-corporal pulled a resigned grin. "I must be off my head." He turned, heaving the Bergen pack higher on his slim back, and began to retrace his footsteps down the slope.

Ducane said: "Make a note of him, Dave."

CHAPTER 7

He was late.

For the fifth time in as many minutes Roisin McGuire looked at the clock. Harrington had been late many times before, but she thought tonight might have been something special. Perhaps he was just proving a point. After the weeks of her obstinate refusal to see him, she could hardly blame him if he took the opportunity to repay her in kind.

It was not through callous disregard for him that she had refused his calls, both during the two days she had spent in hospital and after her return to the farm. The night that McNally had come had shattered her life, changed everything. Everything had lost its perspective, including the way she felt for Harrington and the way she felt about herself.

Carefully she had weighed the SAS captain's words in her mind, examining them for crumbs of comfort and truth. Sean's death had been a wicked blow and, as many times as she remembered Jacko's assurance that Harrington could have been in no way responsible, her brother's own words kept flooding back to her.

If he had used her to get information about McNally, why not Sean too? Had he wanted her as desperately as he led her to believe, Roisin reasoned, it would be very convenient to have Sean out of the way. Harrington's kind and tolerant words in the car and in the pub could have been a blind. After all, you don't ask a girl to marry you in one breath, and admit you've been responsible for her brother's death in the next.

She stood up from the new sofa and looked around the parlour that had been part of her home for so long. The workmen had done a good job. It was hard to believe how it had looked on that fateful night. Plaster and woodwork had been repaired, the walls papered and the blood-soaked carpet entirely replaced. The Army had advised her to have bullet-proof shutters fitted discreetly to all the downstairs windows, and she saw no reason to ignore their advice. Covered by the new curtains, they did not create the prison-like atmosphere she had feared.

Not that there had ever been the merest hint of danger or reprisals to her. On the contrary her friends and neighbours on nearby farms had been almost too helpful. All had rallied round to do her shopping, bringing gifts to replace damaged household items, and even helping with extra labour. Even her bank manager had offered a loan without security.

No one had actually asked about her involvement. Her injuries had convinced everyone she was in no way in collusion with the Brits who raided the farmhouse. It was 'Lord Charles' who had found his popularity waning sharply, and gossip about his association with Roisin had spread rapidly. The fact that he was no longer seen in her company added fuel to the fire that he was an intelligence agent for the British Army. Even the warmth of Shelagh Brady's welcome when he entered her pub had cooled distinctly.

Everyone had been shocked by the ferocity of the raid. It was said that several bodies had been found, some viciously mutilated with fancy knifework. Jim O'Nions was mourned deeply, although few could tolerate him when he was alive. Two of the others had been locals also. Farmer Dominic pronounced loudly that it was the work of the fiendish SAS, but no one knew for certain. It was a popular theory.

Roisin crossed the kitchen area to where a full length mirror was fixed to the wall. Not bad, she thought. Her previously flawless complexion was distinctly marred now by the angry bootlace scar across her cheek, but the hospital had shown her pictures of worse injuries that had healed over the years. Make-up helped a lot, although it would do nothing for the disfigured ear which still caused her pain. But now that her hair was a little longer, it was hardly noticeable.

She stepped back to admire the new tartan skirt and waistcoat top to which she had treated herself with part of the bank loan. It looked smart over the white sweater, and she wondered if Harrington would like it.

She had eventually agreed to see him after being bombarded with countless letters and a stream of phone-calls. In the end she had been quite rude to him, although she was thankful he did not give up. At first she had been certain that he was the last person in the world she wanted to marry. But as the days drifted by she found she missed his company, her mind wandering more and more frequently to an imaginary cottage on the English mainland. Even dancing had lost much of its joy for her. Although fewer asked her when they saw her face, there were still old boyfriends who were not perturbed. Some used the opportunity to swear vengeance on the Brit pigs in a vain hope they would win her bodily favours.

That was one area where there was no chance of them succeeding. Even now, as she looked back, she could hardly believe that she'd made love with McNally. It was like a horrific nightmare when she remembered, yet at the time she had seemed powerless to resist. Almost as though she was avenging Sean by destroying what she had with Harrington. But she tried not to dwell on the reasons behind it. She told herself to count her blessings. She had had a period since, and there were no outward signs to give her away.

Now she had agreed to see Harrington, she would have to decide whether to keep the secret. It was going to have been easy, just telling him she planned to stay and continue as before. But her desire to see him had intensified in the past twenty-four hours until now she could scarcely wait to be with him again.

She promised herself that, if she agreed to marry, she would tell him about McNally straight away.

The sound of Harrington's car pulling up outside made her jump. Nervously she ran the tip of her tongue over her lips, and straightened her skirt. She was half-way across the floor when the doorbell rang. Something made her stop. It was probably seeing the large plate of steel that had been bolted to the back of the door as another safety measure.

Roisin shrugged, and decided to slip the security-chain into place before opening the door. As it rattled home, the bell rang again.

"Charles?"

"Of course. Who else." The voice was impatient.

When she opened the door it happened. With a wild cry and a crash of metal on metal, the huge steel head of the double-handed axe sliced through the gap, wrenching the security-chain clean out of its mounting with an ear-rending splinter of wood. As Roisin jumped back in horror the door burst open as though a hurricane force wind was behind it. Before she could utter an exclamation the two hooded gunmen were in. They grabbed her arms, jerking them violently up behind her back. Two more masked men pushed their way through the door. Between them a third figure, trussed and bent double in a blood-stained jacket and trousers and a sack over his head, was bundled forward.

A fifth man closed the door. He told two others to search upstairs. There was something familiar about the terse Irish accent, but she couldn't place it.

"What do y-o-u w-ant?" Her voice was no more than a whisper, her throat suddenly parched.

"Shut up, slut," returned the last man as he looked over her shoulder for the gunmen who had gone upstairs. She noticed they were all in black. Black jeans, black leather jerkins and black hoods with sinister white eyeholes. They even wore uniform black leather belts with equipment pouches.

She didn't hear the footsteps of the men returning down the stairs, but they were there when she was roughly turned around and frogmarched across the room.

"Take her to a back bedroom!" the leader snapped. "I don't want no nosey sod noticing anything from the road."

130

Roisin couldn't be sure, but the accent seemed to have a nasal American twang.

Suddenly she remembered Harrington. It wasn't her they were after, it was him. Someone must have listened in at the telephone exchange. Passed a message to someone. He would walk straight into the ambush. Like a rat in a trap. And she was the bait.

She was bundled brutally up the stairs, her arms twisted so far up her back they felt as though they would break free of their sockets.

"Please d-o-n-t," she gasped. "You're hurting me."

Her pleas were ignored and they pushed all the harder, racing her through the door into her own bedroom, so fast and high that her feet didn't touch the floor.

"Get her on the bed," shouted one of them. "And get her sodding tights off, the dirty little Brit fucker!"

The words were like an icy shock. Her belly knotted in a sudden spasm and she felt dizzy. She shut her eyes quickly, her mouth opening to protest as she felt herself being flung backward onto the bed, the two men pinioning her arms above her head.

"No- o-o-o!" Finally she found her voice—it came in a shriek that reverberated around the empty farmhouse. The sound was cut off midway when the fist struck her mouth. She felt the sweetish taste of blood as an angry hand grabbed at the tartan skirt, ripping it roughly from her body. Fingers prodded hastily around her waist, finding a grip. Then she felt the nylon being peeled quickly from her legs.

Oh God, oh God, she pleaded silently, terrified to open her mouth. It wasn't Harrington they wanted. It *was* her.

"Hold her legs open!" More hands grabbed her, fingers hard and hurting. She waited, prostrate and trembling, her legs hooked over the bed, for the pants to be torn from her.

Nothing happened. There was a curious clack of metal and plastic as though someone was fiddling with a gadget. Her chest heaving, Roisin opened her eyes.

Three of the men had removed their hoods. One of them

was patiently fitting a drill bit to a Black and Decker.

The dreaded realisation of what was to happen sank in. She had heard about it happening. Heard of it. But never ... "For God's sake, someone, stop him." Her voice started fading. Her stomach seemed to physically sink as she felt the vomit rising in her throat. But no one made a move to help her.

"Gag the bitch, Reagan! And I don't want those bloody wide eyes staring at me!"

Her world was plunged into breathless darkness as the pillow was stuffed hard into her face. But still she could hear an Irish voice droning on, harsh and bitter. "This is what happens to dirty little sluts who inform on the IRA. A bullet will do it, but we save this trick for the real *bastards*." He spat out the word. "Not only McNally and your own local people, but your own sodding brother. All killed because you blabbed your fuckin' mouth to your soldier boy lover ..."

"Okay, hold yer horses a minute." It was the American voice again. "Bring the jerk in here."

As Roisin gasped to breathe, she heard the noise of two more men entering the small room and the sound of someone resisting. Suddenly she remembered the man with the sack over his head who she had glimpsed as they had rushed in. She had been so shocked and concerned for herself that she had not thought about him.

"Okay, you creep," the man called Reagan said. "You don't care about yourself. Brave, brave stiff upper-lipped Brit bastard. Now let's see how much you care for your little slut."

"Leave her alone!" the voice was choked and unrecognisable as though coming through a mouthful of soap. As she realised that it was Harrington's voice she tried to scream, forcing air into her lungs, but no sound came out.

The sudden high-pitched whine of the power drill filled the room, the sound coming closer.

Strong hands gripped her right leg, forcing the sole of her foot firmly against the floor. The whirring steel bit touched her skin, feeling instantly like a scald, shooting sparks of pain through her nervous system. Then came the agonising grind of indescribable torment as the hard tip bored slowly into her kneecap, spewing a mess of blood and gristle, flecked with chips of white bone. Involuntarily her buttocks clenched and she thrust her pelvis forward in a grotesque imitation of orgasm as the spasms stabbed through her.

It was worse as the whining died and the bit was slowly withdrawn. Her stomach muscles contracted violently as she felt the vomit rising up through her intestines and her bladder empty.

"There," muttered Reagan with satisfaction. "Half-way done. It's all pretty quick. Better'n you deserve." He chuckled. "No Special Air Service boyfriends to rescue you this time, eh, little Brit fucker?"

The American voice was quiet, both soothing and menacing at the same time. "Okay, now we've done the right knee. You know if we do the left the young lady will never get out of a wheelchair again. So, your co-operation is again requested ..."

"Get stuffed!" This time the muffled voice was clearly Harrington's.

There was a slight pause, then the American voice said slowly: "Make sure he watches. Get him close enough so's he can smell the bone burning."

The harrowing sound of the drill began again. Roisin's scream was muffled by the pillow, and this time she couldn't stop the stomach-tearing retch that erupted with the force of a geyser.

It must have been the sound of the single shot that shook her back to consciousness, but she did not realise at the time. She was convinced it had all been a nightmare.

For several seconds she remained inert on her bed, staring at the ceiling, allowing the waves of relief to wash away the cold sweat that bathed her body. As she tried to move her legs the terrible truth dawned on her. Feverishly, she pulled herself up onto her elbows and looked down at the revolting mess on the bedclothes around her shattered

133

knee-caps. It needed no surgeon to tell her that she would never walk again. They had made a very thorough job.

She coughed and spluttered violently, clearing her throat, but found that she was too numb to cry. Movement was agony as she lowered herself to the floor, pulling her lifeless calves behind her across the carpet to the door. It seemed an age as she dragged herself to the top few stairs. Fighting to see through the stinging tears, she peered over the bannisters at the macabre tableau below her.

The five men in black stood in a circle around an empty straight-backed chair. At their feet lay a tall figure curled like a foetus, clutching at his smashed and bloody head. A sheath of hand-written papers lay on the table and a pocket recorder whirred discordantly. It was the end of the tape.

"You stupid bastard, Malone," said the tallest of the figures with the American accent. "What the hell were you thinkin' of?"

Malone held the big revolver limply in his hand. "I told you, sir, he tried to make a grab for me. To kill me."

"For God's sake learn not to panic," came the terse reply. "Besides, how far d'you think he'd have got with five of us?"

"You said yourself to never give the SAS an inch!" Malone retorted defensively.

"Okay, okay. I've told you enough times not to under-estimate your enemy. Anyhow it's done now, I guess. At least you've got fast reactions."

"I said I'm sorry!" Malone said. Angrily, he kicked at the body.

"Okay," said the leader. "Get the papers and the recorder, and let's go."

"What about the body?" asked the man called Reagan.

"It's no good to us now, he can't talk any more," replied the American. "C'mon, move it."

Within seconds they had gone, leaving the body beside the chair where it had fallen. The mantleshelf clock chimed, the noise echoing loudly round the empty farm, ringing in Roisin's head like a church bell.

She pressed her head against the bannisters and began to sob uncontrollably.

Earl Lee McClatcher, with the honorary title of Colonel, Forward Combat Unit of the Provisional Irish Republican Army, stood on the mound of soft turf, and watched the results of the first month's training. The Polaroid glasses he wore against the late September sun gave his face an expression of impassive cruelty as he waited motionless, the chill wind tugging at the collar of his windcheater and the deep peak of the forage cap. His hands remained clasped behind his back, his chest inflated to its full forty-two inches.

The first batch of twenty men who came round the edge of the hill were impressive. They had been the first arrivals: scrawny, unkempt youths from various towns in Ulster, recommended by the Army Council's special selection committee as the most promising candidates for the new crack FCU. Insolent, arrogant and frequently ill-educated, they had presented the two Americans with ideal base material on which to work and mould into the pattern they had in mind. Years of experience at Fort Bragg and the Marine training base at Parris Island had taught McClatcher and Loveday the psychology and the routine —the way to get certain results. McGuiness had sworn that each had a record of 'brave and courageous acts', although the ex-Green Berets had their doubts.

The new recruits received their biggest shock thirty minutes after their arrival at the old friary on a remote peninsula in Galway, when each was wheeled into the temporary barber's shop and shorn like a lamb until just a thin fuzz of hair remained. They were then paraded shirtless before the mound where McClatcher now stood. He had surveyed them in cold silence for a full minute, before he began to speak. Despite the fact that the bitter wind snatched away much of what he was saying, the effect was not lost on the small band of men who looked up at him, as they shivered and shook. There was no doubt what they were in for; no doubt that their lives were about to be changed radically and permanently.

Loveday had brought them to attention. "Right, you fucking jug-ears! Get to attention when I give the word! Not before. Not after, but on the command! And then you won't move a fucking inch until the Colonel has finished with you. As far as I'm concerned you are FINISHED NOW!

"Don't sway in the breeze! Don't fidget! Don't play with yourselves! Just listen! And if your snotty noses run in the cold—LEAVE THEM ALONE! GOT IT!

"Right, then ... HAT-TENTION!!"

McClatcher surveyed the two uneven ranks with thinly disguised disgust as they attempted to obey Loveday's bawling command.

He began: "My name is McClatcher. You will address me as Colonel—but only when spoken to. The master-sergeant is Loveday. But I assure you, you won't love the day you set eyes on his ugly face, because he is going to knock you spineless Micks into something resembling fighting men!

"Personally, I don't think he stands a chance. I think you're a load of FUCKING WANKERS! I've never seen such skinny, gutless morons in my life.

"Now, I've been given the unenviable task of turning you into something called a Forward Combat Unit. That's all very fine 'n' dandy, but from where I stand you stand more chance of killin' British soldiers by makin' 'em die laughin'. That's because Sergeant Loveday and me are Green Berets."

Loveday's voice cracked like a pistol shot: "Take that smirk off your face, turd!" The man in question froze immediately.

McClatcher continued: "Now Green Berets are toughter than any Marines in the US Army, and if you don't think that's significant, you'll soon find out just how wrong you are! Because for the next two months you fuckin' Micks are goin' to become men that the Green Berets might even tolerate in their ranks! GOT IT? Me and the master-sergeant are gonna eat with you, sleep with you, and watch you sweat off your asses until you drop dead or keep runnin'! Here you're A HUNDRED MILES FROM NOWHERE! And your mammas ain't gonna come visitin' you, and you ain't gettin' no postcards or chow from home. You're here on this peninsula until you become what we want you to be—or else you die trying!

"So get it straight! You volunteered for a one-way ticket, and believe me that's *exactly* what you've got. There's only one way out of this camp, and that's in a coffin! Those armed guards aren't to keep people out, they're to keep you civilian shits in until you become soldiers. Not just soldiers, but GREEN BERETS. And Green Berets don't sweat. They don't get cold! They don't get tired! They never stop running! They ain't never scared! They're the best marksmen! They're the best hand-to-hand fighters! And they never say no! You worthless shits are going to be McClatcher's Green Berets. You're going' to be McClatcher's private army. You're goin' to put the fear of Christ up the asses of British soldiers, or me and Loveday will put the fear of the fuckin' Devil up you!"

He paused momentarily, watching the slightly swaying rows of bewildered, frightened faces. "Some of you have got silly titles given you by those jerks in the Army Council. Forget it! You're all just privates from now on. MCCLATCHER'S PRIVATES. The best fighting men in Ireland! GOT IT?"

There was a silence.

"GOT IT?" Loveday bawled.

There was a mumble of incoherent voices.

"LOUDER, YOU FUCKING MICKS!"

Voices rose in a jumble of answers.

"YES, SIR, WE'VE GOT IT, COLONEL!" shrieked Loveday.

"Yes, sir, we've got it, Colonel."

"LOUDER, YOU TURDS!"

Together. "YES, SIR, WE'VE GOT IT, COLONEL!"

McClatcher nodded to Loveday. You will have, my friends, believe me, you will have.

★

That had been four weeks ago, and as McClatcher watched now from his vantage point, he found it hard to believe that they were the same men pounding towards him at the double in perfect time, growling angrily as they ran so that they sounded like a hundred strong.

In those twenty-eight days, the thin ones had added pounds to their weight; the fat ones had experienced the slow tightening of muscles they'd forgotten they possessed. It was a gradual process like the skilful tuning of a guitar string until the perfect note was reached.

A punishing schedule had been vigorously maintained that made no allowance for the worsening weather or minor illness amongst the recruits. Now the breathless had rediscovered their lungs and the weak learned that sheer determination and will-to-win could overcome a body that was already beyond the limits of normal pain and exertion. Loveday was even more hated than McClatcher, his 'TWENTY-FIVE PUSH-UPS!' being issued at the drop of a hat or the careless shuffle of a foot. Just the suspicion of insolence or arrogance, even if it was only in the Negro's imagination, was enough to get the victim on all fours.

Everyone moved 'at the double' wherever they went, from when they were called at 6am to when they fell exhausted into their canvas camp beds at 10pm. The first week had combined hours of drilling and physical exercise with the study of rudimentary infantry techniques and weapons training. Once their bodies had become more accustomed to constant strain and effort, the second week saw even more vigorous bodily demands. Twenty mile cross-country runs and an assault course combined to test stamina, co-ordination and balance to breaking-point.

During the final two weeks, fieldcraft, advanced infantry techniques, weapons training and unarmed combat had come to the fore. It was certainly a crammed course, but it had been more successful than McClatcher had dared dream possible. Three ex-Marine NCOs had been hired for specialist training, and this had eased the management problems as the second twenty-men draft arrived to be put through 'McClatcher's mincing machine'.

There had only been two casualties; one who broke an arm in self-defence training with Loveday, and another who drowned. Driven by desperation, he had attempted to swim the icy waters of the lough, rather than slip through the line of armed pickets who guarded the base of the peninsula. As McClatcher had pointed out, in another two weeks the drowned man would have been good enough to wriggle across the open parade ground in front of Buckingham Palace without being spotted by the sentry.

Three electronics engineers from the first two intakes had been selected for special training on the sensor equipment that was being smuggled in from the United States. Most of it had come from the extensive Igloo White operations in Vietnam in the early seventies, originally purloined by servicemen. They had realised there would be ready money for the equipment on the black market and that a few malfunctioning sensors, out of the thousands in the US Army inventory, would not be missed.

Shortly the men would begin putting their theory into practice by monitoring the recruits' infiltration exercise all over the peninsula. McClatcher was confident that he would soon be able to field an active ten man combat unit, selected from the best of the intake. In another six weeks, he considered he would probably be able to increase that number to nearer thirty. The remainder would be good, but not quite good enough to operate with the necessary impunity. There would, however, be plenty of supporting roles for them to fulfil.

Shortly, McClatcher mused, the Provisional Irish Republican Army would have a group of men worthy of the term. It would be a surprise that the British Army could not easily overcome. McGuiness had meanwhile been working hard at co-ordinating intelligence efforts to build up a complete and reliable picture of Army operations in the border counties. The spasmodic rumours and inspired guesses of the past were gradually being replaced by a steady stream of related facts and figures, which were checked and double-checked before being accepted. From these, patterns were gradually becoming clear. It was now possible to identify foot and vehicle patrols, roadblocks and surveillance operations, the dates when the routes were likely to be changed or modified.

At McClatcher's suggestion, the PIRA's own surveillance was improved and the importance of patience stressed, so that now something was even starting to be known about the movements of the Special Air Service combat teams. The American had suggested the sort of techniques they were likely to use, the sort of ground they preferred. By themselves watching people they *knew* to be involved with the PIRA, the Republicans were more likely to discover clandestine Army surveillance operations. Hints were given at detecting trails: carelessly crushed grass, freshly snapped twigs. How to scan suspected hide-out areas in repeated sweeps rather than the square box method. Many farm dogs were being replaced by similar-looking animals trained to track and sniff out humans. Occasionally a hired aircraft would fly over the border territory in the early morning. Areas usually free from pedestrian traffic, but near to Republican safe-houses, were trampled more frequently by young couples out for romantic walks.

All I need is for this contract to be renewed for another year, thought McClatcher, and I'll have the border country buttoned-up so tightly that even the SAS will think twice before venturing out.

At that moment Loveday called out to him as he came jogging across the turf in long, easy strides from the old friary on the flat-topped hill.

"They're ready," he announced, pounding to a standstill beside McClatcher.

The American nodded at the twenty men now disappearing towards the lough at a steady, rhythmic trot, their angry growl no longer audible above the wind.

"Not bad, eh, Winston?"

The big Negro shrugged. "Not bad for a bunch o' half-baked Micks. Give me a while more, an' I'll let yer have somethin' you can be proud of. Still, I guess that fer four weeks 'tain't too bad."

McClatcher gave Loveday a hard but playful thud in the ribs with his balled fist. "Yer black bastard, I do believe your standards are higher than mine. Now, let's go see these goddamn new arrivals."

Together they strode back up the hill to the old stone building.

"An' how was last night's trip over the border?" Loveday asked.

McClatcher gave a slow smile. "Like clockwork, well almost. I've got an hour-long tape—I'll play it over to you. Packed full of stuff, detailed."

"Reliable?"

"I reckon. We've done some double checks an' it all tallies so far. He sang like a nightingale."

Loveday frowned. "Without the extra persuasion?"

McClatcher said tersely. "No, he wouldn't say a thing until we used the girl. He'd have said more if Malone hadn't panicked when he tried something."

"Shit, man, you shoulda let me come, like I said. Some o' these guys are still trigger-happy."

"No, Malone's shapin' up well really. And that guy Reagan's a mean bastard." He glanced sideways at the Negro. "Besides, you wouldn't have liked what we had to do."

"Don't talk shit, man. I ain't forgotten 'Nam. I know circumstances dictate the actions. Jest don't count me out again, huh?"

As they reached the friary entrance, McClatcher turned. "Listen, Winston, how does this sound—a trip with me to a young lady in ol' London town."

"Pattie Ducane?"

"An' we'll be there tomorrow afternoon."

CHAPTER 8

"Sarah! Don't do that, darling!"

Trish put down the iron and looked across the kitchen to where her daughter was bouncing on the freshly ironed sheets stacked in the plastic laundry basket. Exasperated, she ran a hand through her hair.

"Bouncy, bouncy!" cried Sarah, who was bored at not being able to venture outside—it had been raining relentlessly all day.

"I'll smack your bottom if you do that again." Trish strode over to Sarah and jerked her none too gently from the basket. "Oh, God, look at the time. I've got to be at work in half an hour. I haven't even made the beds yet."

Sarah looked up, wide-eyed, not sure how it was all her fault.

"Well, I'm not going to re-do those sheets. There's not enough time. I'd better change. Come on, we'll get your coat on. I've got to drop you at Mrs Andrews."

"I wanna stay here," pouted Sarah.

Trish scooped her up in her arms and ran up the stairs to the bedroom. Quickly she changed her dress then sat in front of the mirror, running a comb rapidly through her curls while Sarah tried clumsily to cope with the buttons on her red plastic mackintosh. Pat Ducane, she said to herself, you look a wreck. Much more of this and you'll start looking like an old hag.

She had just massaged in some face make-up when the door-bell rang.

"Oh, hell!"

"Who is it, mummy?"

"How should I know. It's probably the milkman. I didn't pay him last week."

She slipped on an off-white, military-style trench coat then pulled the sou'wester over Sarah's head before she led her down the stairs.

Bing-bong, bing-bong.

"All right, I'm coming," she called angrily. She helped her daughter down the last few steps and threw open the door.

"Hi, Pat! Long time no see."

She stared in amazement at the two large men standing on the step, their collars turned up against the rain. For a moment she recognised neither of them, aware only that one was black.

"I'd never have known yer, Pat baby," McClatcher said. "What with yer hair 'n' all. Used t'be straight as an arrow!"

"Real purty though," grinned Loveday. "Wowee! Yessir."

Trish shook her head, bewildered. "I-I'm sorry, I'm afraid I don't think I know you gentlemen ..."

"Honey, how could you ever forget *us*?" McClatcher asked, his voice feigning hurt.

"Who is it, mummy?" demanded Sarah, struggling to look round the door.

"Try Hong Kong, Pat?"

"Huh?"

Loveday began singing. "*I coulda danced all night ...*"

Her hand went to her mouth. "Oh, my goodness, it's Earl! Oh dear, do *forgive* me! I never recognised you. I mean, heavens, it's been so long! And ..."

"Winston, ma'am," prompted the Negro. "At your service."

She laughed. "Oh, of course. Winston. Earl and Winston! Goodness, how did you find us?"

"Courtesy of your wonderful Post Office," McClatcher answered.

"What are you doing here? Are you still in the Army?"

"Hell, no, Pat. Left a few years back now. We're over here on a business trip, y'know. So we thought we'd look up you an' yer husband. Fer ol' times sake."

"I'm afraid Jack's back at the regiment now. If only

you'd called last week. He was home on leave."

McClatcher looked disappointed.

"Never mind, ma'am," Loveday said. "Jest seein' you's a sight fer sore eyes!"

She smiled, her eyes dancing at the compliment. "Look, you mustn't think I'm rude, but I'm late for work. I was just rushing out with Sarah ..."

"Oh, that's okay," McClatcher said.

Loveday was peering over her shoulder into the hallway where Sarah was still struggling to get past her mother. "That must be yer li'le girl!"

Trish turned. "Oh, yes, that's Sarah."

"My, oh my," Loveday crooned, peering into the house. "Ain't she jest a li'le ol' angel. Like a picture of her mom!"

"She's a little devil at times!"

"May I?" Loveday asked.

Trish shrugged, worried about the time. "Oh, of course."

Loveday brushed close to her as he went into the hall. He went down on his haunches.

Addressing himself to Sarah: "Well, hello there, li'le lady. An' how are you?"

Sarah's eyes flashed at him, then to Trish and back again, her hand nervously in her mouth.

"It's all right, Sarah," said her mother. "Winston's an old friend of mummy and daddy."

Sarah stared for a moment, mesmerised by the big dark face a few inches in front of her's and by the gleaming white teeth.

"He's a black man," she said.

"Oh, Sarah ...!"

Loveday chuckled throatily. "That's right, li'le girl. Do you think it would rub off if I scrubbed hard enough?"

"Oh, Winston, don't ..." began Trish, but the question was being given great concentration by Sarah.

"Yes!" she said suddenly, confident she was right.

The two men roared with laughter and Sarah beamed around at them. Loveday reached in his pocket and pulled out a boiled sweet. "Well now, Sarah, let's you 'n' me be friends. How 'bout this candy. All the way from America."

"Cowboy," said Sarah, aiming to please.

He handed her the sweet which she grabbed eagerly, fumbling with the wrapper. "I guess it's okay?" he asked, looking up at Trish.

She shrugged, defeated, smiling. "It won't hurt, I suppose."

The interlude had given McClatcher a chance to weigh things up in his mind. He said: "Look, Pat, why don't you let me 'n' Winston here take you out tonight. For ol' times sake. A nice restaurant in your West End..."

Trish was surprised. "Oh, gosh, Earl, that would be lovely, but I'm afraid with Sarah it's all a bit awkward..."

"No neighbours?"

"Well, not at such short notice. I don't like to impose on people..." She hesitated, wondering whether Mrs Andrews would oblige.

"I tell you what," McClatcher said. "Why don't we bring round a meal to you, huh? Maybe some chicken, or some Chink grub. I've seen plenty o' places round here. And plenty o' hootch, of course!"

Trish suddenly remembered the party in Hong Kong. Her dance. Stark naked. She felt her cheeks flush. The way McClatcher had emphasised the 'hootch' rang a small warning bell at the back of her mind, but nevertheless she suddenly felt happier at the thoughts of a break from the lonely hours watching television.

"Oh, really, Earl, you shouldn't..."

"Nonsense!" he waved aside her protest. "It'll be swell. A nice ol' reunion. Candlelight supper ... You have got some candles, Pat?"

She laughed, the idea appealing. "I can get some."

"Fine, fine. An' you wear a nice pretty dress to go with yer pretty hair!" He smiled expansively. "An' I might even persuade ol' Winston here to scrub up his skin some!"

They all laughed, including Sarah who didn't understand much of the conversation, except that her mother didn't seem in such a bad temper now.

"Eight?" McClatcher asked.

"Fine."

"Right, ciao!" The two men trotted down the steps and set off briskly along the wet pavement, leaving Trish dazed and bewildered. When she followed with Sarah a few moments later, her gait was light, almost a skip, despite the rain that continued to pour.

"So Jacko's goin' back to Ulster?" Earl asked casually.

"Yes, soon now, I expect," Trish replied. It was the third bottle of champagne they'd consumed and her head was feeling distinctly muzzy. She had protested loudly when they had produced them triumphantly from the bag. But McClatcher had ignored her words, insisting that the bottles be put in the refrigerator until they collected the meal an hour later.

Winston had spent half-an-hour telling Sarah, who had lost all desire for sleep, how he'd started life as a white prince and how a wicked witch had put a spell on him, turning him black until he found the right girl to marry. He obviously enjoyed the story, told with passion and in detail, and the inference wasn't lost on Sarah. After promising to wait until she was old enough, he finally managed to get her to drift off to sleep.

Earl had busied himself in the kitchen, preparing the meal they'd brought, Trish being banished to the lounge to listen to records until the work was done. She'd been eased into a big armchair and a large glass of Scotch placed in her hand.

With her feet up on the coffee table, Trish couldn't remember the last time she'd relaxed so much. She felt a welcome feeling of light-headedness at the lifted weight of routine and responsibility, as the men clowned their way through an amusing double-act. Although she had spent some time deciding what to wear, she was pleased she had chosen the long black evening dress with the square neck and buttons down the front. It wasn't revealing but had a slinky, sensuous feel to it which, she thought, was appropriately alluring without being provocative.

She learned that the two men had started up in business

since leaving the US Army, and had set up a firm of military advisors available to governments around the world, particularly emerging third world nations who were prepared to pay good money for advice and experience. They dismissed the idea that they recruited mercenaries with roaring laughter, and explained that their work was restricted to supplying equipment and training instructors. They had had enough of killing and fighting in Vietnam to last them several lifetimes.

Trish was amazed how gentle they had become. At first she had found it difficult to remember the weeks that she and Jack had known them in Hong Kong. But then she recalled their skylarking together in the luxurious hotel swimming pools, the good-natured riots they would cause in the restaurants, and their incessant gambling. The old double-act, she recalled, hadn't changed. But all those years ago there had been something else. A feeling that primeval aggression lay just below the surface. They had both exuded such power and magnetism, that it was not difficult to imagine them in the thick of combat in the vicious jungle war of South-East Asia. They played hard, and she assumed they must have fought even harder. Courageous but ruthless. She remembered how she had experienced a thrill like electricity at the anticipation of danger and excitement when in their company; yet she had always felt safe in their protection. And the wild times they had shared with Jack and Dave did little to convince her that her imagination was playing games.

It was as though domesticity had now permeated into their lives, although neither said they had been married, and the thought seemed incongruous to her, especially as their bawdiness had not diminished over the years.

"I'm surprised old Jacko ain't left the Service yet," Earl said, pouring himself another champagne. "He coulda made himself a killin' in our game. Ain't that so, Winston?"

"Yes, man! I fought with yer husband and he knew his stuff, did ol' Gentleman Jack."

Trish tried to focus on him. "Who?" She pushed the large, gold-rimmed spectacles up to the bridge of her nose.

"Our pet name," Earl explained. "He didn't always agree with some of our methods. But he knew his stuff okay. Yessir, reckon he'd do okay in our business."

She frowned, trying to concentrate on the conversation. "You really think so?"

"Why sure I do. What'ya say, Winston? Could even be a place for Gentleman Jack in our outfit."

Loveday was leaning forward, elbows on the table, fondling the glass in his big hands. "Yeah, I guess we'd have a lots a use for your ol' man, Pat. I mean it could bring in a deal of bread."

She was aware her words were slurred, but the idea was worth the effort to follow. "A lot of money? You mean—er—Jack could work with you and get more'n he'd earn in the Army?"

Earl laughed. "Sure's hell, yes, Pat! More'n a week than he'd earn in a month or two. An', as I said, at the moment business is goin' great for us."

She looked around at the pile of empty plates that had been filled with the most exotic Chinese food she'd ever seen, and nodded slowly, a length of curled hair falling over her face. "It must 'ave cost a fortune, Earl, an absolute fortune. Things must be goin' well."

"Fer you, pretty lady, it was worth it! Every last cent!"

Trish reached across the table and squeezed his hand. It was big and warm, strong under her slender fingers. "Thank you, Earl. It's been a wonderful evening. And you, Winston. You really shouldn't have. I haven't enjoyed myself so much..."

Her eyes focused on the flickering candle flame, mesmerised. "...Oh ... for so long ... I can't remember ... 'Seems like a million years. We don't manage to get ... well, I can't remember the last time we went out ... Jack's always away ... money always short." Trish shook her head suddenly, unsure she was making sense. She realised her hand was still clasping Earl's; she withdrew it quickly. "Oh, Earl ... I'm sorry, what must you think of me ... I think I'm a little tipsy."

"That's okay, sweetheart," he said softly.

"You deserve a li'le relaxation, beautiful baby," Winston added with feeling.

Trish sat upright in her chair, placing her hands on the edge of the table to steady her balance. She said: "I want Jack to get out. Leave ... you know ... out of the Army ... do somethin' else ... I don't know ... he could earn better money ... move from this place."

Winston looked around the room. "Hey, honey, it's no palace. But it sure is homely. Small by US standards but it's homely. Guess it's your touch makes it that."

Trish was looking straight ahead. "Jack won't ... he loves the bloody Army too much ... hasn't got the ... won't try life outside ..."

Earl murmured consolingly: "I can understand that, Pat. As an ex-fightin' man. Life could be hell in the wrong job. That's why he oughta be in our line. Goddamit, it's what he knows. And there's no danger. No more front-line fightin'."

"Plus a big bagful o' bread at the end of the month," added Winston. "'Course it rather depends on what he's bin doin' since we last saw him."

"Yeah," interrupted Earl quickly. "If he's bin doin' active service like you say, well, there's a good possibility we could make room fer him."

Trish shook her head avidly, and more ringlets tumbled over her face. "Oh, he has! He's been doing very well ..."

"I heard some guys from his regiment recently caught an IRA bigwig ...?"

She grinned, sipping more champagne. "Mmm, *that* was Jack! Two of them ... IRA, watchacall 'em ...?" Giggle. "Bigwigs!"

"No!"

"Yes, Jack was very pleased ... thinks it might help his promotion ... it's been a *long* time ..." She stopped abruptly, putting her hand to her mouth. "I'm sorry, I shouldn't say things like that ... It's all very secret ..."

Earl laughed disarmingly, patting her forearm. "Don't you worry, honey! You're talkin' to a couple pros. We keep strictly buttoned, don't we, Winston?"

The Negro nodded. "If we don't know what Jack's bin up to we can't decide whether t' offer him a job wi' us, now can we?"

"I mean," Earl elaborated, "pure soldierin's one thing, but our clients like t' have men with some experience in intelligence. I don't suppose Jack does any of that?"

Her vision was clouding again, the American's words ringing around her head. She couldn't remember if she had already said that Jack was soon going to be doing just that. "Jack did a lot of that ... undercover work ... in Londonderry ... he was after two..." She giggled again. "...two of your bigwigs ... well, not-quite-such-big-wigs..."

"Who was that then ... ?"

Something deep in the back of her brain told her she had said enough; wondered why these old friends needed to know so much. She shrugged.

Earl patted her arm again. "Pat, sweetheart, we'd like to help Jack. Fer ol' times sake. But we must be in the picture, baby. We'd like you to find out all you can about his current operations. Quiet and discreet like, so's we can make a full evaluation."

"I can't ... You must ask Jack..."

"Jack ain't here, sweetheart."

Winston added: "An' we'll be back Stateside before he's on leave again."

"The names, honeychild?"

Trish shut her eyes, feeling Earl's hand stroking her forearm. Too tired, helpless to resist. "I can't remember, Earl ... Honestly. Oh, God, I need some coffee..."

She made a move, stumbling as she climbed from the chair, falling against Winston. She felt the large hands on her buttocks, warm through the material, supporting her. "Careful, honeychild," he said gently. "Let ol' Earl get the coffee. You c'mon sit down. Relax a li'le."

Trish looked down at the concern on the big black face. She watched, fascinated, as the candle-light played across the skin, highlighting its rough texture with a dull sheen, showing up the whiteness of his smile.

She nodded, her head forward, as she felt his arms shift their powerful grip to her waist, as he helped her across to the settee. He sat down, steadying her as she lowered herself next to him. His arm slid around her shoulders, easing her head against his. Gently he kissed the mass of ringlets.

"There, honeychild, ain't that better?" he whispered. "Now you put yer feet up, an' let ol' Earl do some work fer a change. Go'n now, kick yer shoes off."

She murmured quietly, almost to herself, her voice distorted to a muffle by the closeness of his body. "I'm sorry ... didn't mean to collapse ... on you ... not used to all this drink ... I'm sorry ..."

"That's okay, honeychild. You jest hang loose, li'le baby."

"Oh, Winston ..." Half-giggling. "That's an awful expression."

"Mebbe. But ain't that jest how yer feel?" His voice was slow, soothing, masterful. "Lettin' it a-l-l hang l-o-ose ... yeh."

She laughed quietly, let her arm rest around his waist, hardly aware that her finger was drawing small circular patterns against his shirt. "You must think I was ... well, being ... rude ... or ... evasive."

"Huh, honeychild?"

"About Jack ... in Londonderry ... They're all just names to me ... It's difficult ... so many names ..."

"Sure, sure, baby. I know you'd tell us if yer could. You ain't the sorta dame to hold her husband back from a good job."

Her palm was pressing, rubbing against his side, feeling the hardened muscles. She wasn't conscious of the movement. "Is it really ... that important?"

In the kitchen the kettle was beginning its low gurgle as the water began to heat.

Earl motioned silently to Winston from the doorway, nodding vehemently.

"Gee, baby, it's hard to say," Winston said, his lips to her head, his eyes on Earl. "We wouldn't want yer to think we're pryin'. It's jest that we have contacts. We in the military business stick together. What is jest a name to you often means more to us. Gives us an idea of exactly how much the Army values Jacko. I mean *Fred Smith* may jest be some goddamn Mick terrorist to you. To us he may be a company commander. See, it all helps us evaluate ... We gotta evaluate before we shelve out dough ... even on an ol' buddy."

"Oh, course..." she muttered, trying to concentrate. The kisses to her head were lingering, warm. They were distracting. "Does Raymond Duffy mean anything to you?"

"Nope."

"Oh. I think perhaps ... yes, I'm sure that was one..."

"Who, honeychild?" His fingers traced a line down her cheek, scarcely touching the tiny invisible hairs. She closed her eyes.

"I think that's who Jack was after ... in Londonderry that time ... Perhaps Robert ... I'm sure Duffy ... I can't remember the other ... Still, if it means nothing..."

"It does to me, Pat, sweetheart." It was Earl. She didn't open her eyes but heard the gentle rattle of china as he crossed the room and felt the settee dip as he sat by her feet.

"I'll have to check," he continued, "with some of my friends in London. But I'm sure someone called Duffy was important."

Winston frowned at him, questioning. Earl merely shrugged. Obviously the name meant nothing to him.

"How d'ya like yer coffee, sweetheart?"

She opened her eyes, struggling into a half-reclining position. Winston didn't relax his grip, but just let his arm slip from her shoulders to around her waist.

"Black, please."

"Like ol' lover boy here!"

Trish looked into Winston's face, smiling at her, a few inches from her own. She could feel the affection reflected in his dark eyes, and for a moment she felt a sudden urge to kiss the thick, proud mouth. Instead she looked quickly away, accepting the offered cup, drinking quickly, feeling the hot, bitter-sweet liquid burn its way down.

Earl had noticed the framed photograph on the coffee-table for the first time. "Say, how recent is that?"

It was a family shot of Trish, Jack and Sarah with Big Dave taken two years earlier on a beach near Bournemouth. It had only been a long Bank Holiday weekend, but it had been the last holiday they'd had, and they had made the most of it.

"Oh ... Mudeford ... on the south coast ... it's lovely there ... About two years ago ..."

"Jacko ain't aged much," commented Winston. "But with a dame like you, that ain't hardly surprisin'."

"Thank you, you lovely man ... You must come again."

"Feelin' better?" Earl asked.

She nodded. "Not sick now ... Just ... mmm ... oh, deliciously relaxed." Then she became vaguely aware of Winston gently removing her spectacles.

Earl was saying: "Well, Pat, sweetheart, I'm sure we can fix ol' Jacko up from what you say. Maybe pretty damn quick too ..."

"Really? You ... mean that?" She could hardly believe her ears.

"Sure, sweetheart, but don't say anything yet. Many a slip between cup 'n' lip, y'know. He'd be earning ... hell, what's it in English money ... three hundred pounds a week ... as *soon* as he can join us."

Trish felt a glow of contentment sweep through her. She felt sure Jack would be delighted. An opportunity like this, out of the blue, was almost too good to believe. A chance encounter. Fate playing its cards across so many years to give them the perfect break. At last safety and financial security, and a job she felt sure Jack could feel happy in. A chance to give Sarah so many of the things she herself had had to go without.

She said: "It may take a while ... for Jack to get out ... you can't just leave, you know ..."

Earl was reassuring: "We'll make all the necessary money available ... pull some strings ..."

"And he's just going . . . back on a special assignment . . ."

"Oh, yeh?" Winston asked. His large hands were around her waist. She felt his fingertips gently kneading the flesh of her belly through the thin material of her dress. His teeth nibbled persistently at her ear, his tongue flicking around the lobe, tantalising. She felt her muscles contract involuntarily, and a wave of warmth flooded through her body with a suddenness she found alarming.

Another wave of nerve-tingling sensation welled deep inside her, swirling round the tops of her legs.

Dammit, show them your disinterest!

She began talking quickly, her words more coherent, but nervous: "Jack won't be free for a while. A new assignment. Intelligence work. Like you were saying. One of their operators is being pulled out. *Winston*, what *do* you think you're doing!"

He had moved his hand down across her belly and she could feel the pressure of his fingers through her dress.

"Nuthin', honeychild," he replied, but his hand didn't move. Resting still.

Earl said: "Sweetheart, who's being pulled out?"

Trish's eyes were now wide open, trying hard to focus on the white blur at her feet at the end of the settee. She tried to sound matter-of-fact. "One of their people got involved with a local farmgirl. You know, fell for her. Apparently she gave information. So they could catch one of the top Provisionals recently. It's all complicated, but a potential disaster. You can imagine . . ."

Earl nodded. "Sure can." He exchanged glances with Loveday.

Trish said firmly: "Now, I really think we ought to call it a day. I'm very tired and it's getting late."

She could barely make out the smile spread across Earl's face. "Sure, sweetheart. We'll just have one for the road, an' put on a last record. Fair?"

Trish subsided, smiling, feeling the apprehension flow out of her. She was being silly, she told herself. There was no rancour in Earl's voice, no threat. Just gentle reassurance.

"Get comfortable, honeychild." Winston's whisper in her ear was rich and throaty against the background of the soft jazz on the record.

Obediently she slid down, stretching her bare legs, enjoying the cooler air where the hem of her dress had ridden to her knees. The throbbing music filled the room; long, slow and haunting notes that washed her tired mind slowly back and forth like a tide. As she closed her eyes again, she felt Winston's lips brushing the lids, feather-like.

She murmured sleepily: "Just this record, then I must go to bed ... see Sarah's all right..."

A clink of glass as Earl poured a drink, sat down again by her feet. She allowed the music to swallow her thoughts, to sap her concentration and her strength. God, she was so, so tired. Pleasantly, happily tired.

Earl rested his hand on her knee. She jerked in surprise, the softness of his touch and the effect of it reaching through the soporific clouds of her mind. She felt the ebb rising again, a mixture of alarm and sensual pleasure. It rippled up her thighs like a low-tension charge jangling along her nerve-ends until it exploded in a dull ache between her legs.

She opened her mouth to speak. For a second words would not come. Then Winston's mouth came down on hers, muffling her sounds with a deep, penetrating kiss that sent a shock-wave through her body.

Trish knew the signs. Suddenly she saw with clarity that her low-resistance point had been reached. Frantically she tried to move her mouth away from Winston's but already his tongue was probing her mouth, her teeth, seeking her tongue. As Earl's hands traced long, slow movements along her calves, she felt her sudden surge of resistance crumbling. Shame washed over her, wrenching a low animal moan from her throat, as she found herself sucking eagerly at the Negro's tongue.

She forced her eyes open, averting her head, seeing the white blur of Earl's face as he leaned forward to run a trail of kisses over her calves and knees.

"Sweet, sweet honeychild." Winston's voice was almost a moan, close to her ear as he leaned over the ringlets cradled in his lap. "Relax ... my sweet white baby." She felt her pillow stirring, harden.

Trish had scarcely noticed the strong, black hands working with a gentleness and subtlety that did not seem possible for a man of his size, as they plucked the buttons of her dress. It began to open, almost in a bursting effect, in a long vee as the black material parted to reveal the full length of her slender body. The dying traces of a summer tan gave her skin a shade of honey in the candlelight. Her legs shifted languidly.

She clenched her fists, holding them to her mouth which opened soundlessly, her eyes closing against the thrilling tremor that hit her like the note of a tuning fork. Earl's mouth trailed along her upper thighs until he reached the white scrap of her pants.

Her calves started to tremble, the muscles in her buttocks contracting involuntarily in a vulgar motion of eagerness. Winston rolled her nipples in his hand, teasing until they became like hard, tight buttons, puckered in automatic response that caused Trish to groan in humiliation.

As her body began to squirm under the urgent, exploring hands, she felt her last garment pulled away and her knees open in an act of supplication she was unable to resist. Her head dropped violently onto the settee as Winston climbed to his knees above her head. His hands clasped her breasts hard, restraining them as she tossed from side to side.

As Earl entered her, the shock and realisation jolted her, causing her buttocks to thrust forward to meet him. Her stomach contracted in quick, hard movements as the gust of fire burned inside her.

"No, no, no!" she heard her own voice cry, but she knew she did not mean it.

Trish felt sick, disgusted with herself.

Even before she was properly awake, memories of the previous night crowded in on her, adding to the nausea that swilled around the pit of her stomach. She could remember the men coming up to the bedroom, but not clearly. After her first bout of orgasmic delirium, they had gently insisted that she had more drink, talking quietly and persuasively, touching her body. She remembered encouraging them, joining them as they drank straight from the bottle, the flat champagne trickling in streams down her naked body until her skin glistened. Then she'd thrown her arms around them, each in turn, groping them crudely, mouthing giggling obscenities at them she hardly realised she knew.

Then more. Exploding in orgasm after orgasm in a way she had never known before, ever dreamed was possible. She had performed and debased herself like a lust-crazed animal. She had tended their every whim and allowed the excruciating, endless torrent within her to flow and flow until she was like a discarded, sodden rag. Their stamina had been unbelievable. She wouldn't have believed it, but she knew it had happened.

She crawled over the sheets, giddiness sweeping over her as she tried to stand, her knees collapsing under her weight. God, how she ached.

Again she tried to stand, her legs trembling. Slowly she made her way, fumbling, to the dressing-table. Unable to find her spectacles, she tottered naked to the bathroom, half-feeling her way.

"Mummy! Mummy!" Sarah's voice was edged with irritation.

It must be late. "In a minute, darling. Mummy's coming."

Trish hurriedly stepped into the bath, switching on the hand-shower, and let the flow of warm, welcome water wash her clean.

The men had vanished. They must have left much earlier, having first tidied the downstairs room and stacked the dirty crockery neatly on the draining board. An envelope had been left pinned to the cork-tile panel by the telephone. She opened it and squinted at the note:

"With fond memories of Hong Kong
and beyond.
You are great baby!
Love and ... Earl and Winston."

Something else fell from the envelope and fluttered to
the floor. Puzzled, Trish stooped and picked it up. As her
eyes focused on the clear Polaroid photograph fear grabbed
at her stomach like a steel claw. Suddenly she remembered
the series of flashing lights amid the swirling alcoholic haze
of the previous night. Vaguely she recalled posing in her
lovemaking with squeals of drunken laughter.

She frowned, the sudden vision of a hypodermic needle
forming in her mind's eye. Had she dreamt that bit?

"What's that, Mummy?"

"Oh, oh, nothing, darling."

"Has Uncle Winston gone?"

She nodded, hardly thinking. "Yes, they both have.
They're busy men."

Sarah scowled. "Did they have breakfast before they
went?"

"No, darling, I don't think so."

"*I'm* hungry, Mummy."

By the afternoon Trish's aching thighs hurt less and the
taste of bile in her mouth had almost gone. She drifted
through the hours in a curious hypnotic state like an auto-
maton, her memory full of the previous night. Visions of
the Americans kept flashing through her mind, inter-
spersed with pictures of her husband. As soon as she got
home she decided she must phone him.

He was surprised but obviously pleased to receive her
call.

Immediately he remembered Earl Lee McClatcher and
Winston Loveday. Only the slightly hollow ring to his
voice suggested any disapproval.

She wondered whether to mention the prospects of the
job, but decided against it. Her nagging worries about the
Polaroid photograph were growing and she now had severe

doubts about their offer—even if it was genuine. After all, they hadn't even left an address. She blew Ducane a final kiss down the mouthpiece.

As she hung up she noticed for the first time that the family snapshot had gone from its frame. She felt strangely flattered and, again, her thoughts drifted back to the previous night. Despite herself she felt a dull kind of ache begin to throb at her loins.

The sudden shrill call of the telephone jolted her back to reality.

"Pattie?"

"Earl?"

"Hi, honey." There was no mistaking the American's voice.

"Thank God you've phoned," she gasped. "The photograph . . ."

"Sure, honey, I know . . . Now listen, there's no need to worry."

"But . . ."

"But nothin'. You promised last night you'd find out as much as you can about Jacko's operations in Ireland."

"Uh?" She was puzzled. "I did?"

"Yes. D'ya want me to play the tape?"

She was incredulous. "You taped it? Christ, what the hell are you playing at?"

"Insurance, baby. I told you we *need* to know."

Now she was sure. Suddenly her fear gave way to anger. "What the hell d'you take me for? All that rubbish about a job for Jack. God, you filthy bastards."

"Don't call me names, sweetheart," snapped McClatcher. Not after your tricks last night. Now I don't give a shit if you believe what we told you—but I promise you no harm will come t'yer husband."

She shut her eyes and took a deep breath. "Earl, I'm confused . . . Look, whatever you say there's no way I can find out what you want to know . . ."

"Correct, lady," McClatcher hissed. "But you *will* find a way, an' quickly. Two dozen Polaroids and a tape say you will . . ."

"You wouldn't!"

"I don't play games, Pattie." She could feel the steel in his voice. "I want results and I want them fast. And I don't care how you get them. We'll be keepin' an eye on you and as soon as you get an opportunity we'll know about it. An' don't get no ideas about tellin' yer husband—that way *everybody* gets hurt, startin' with him. Just play along an' it'll be our li'le secret. No one gets hurt an' your—er—indiscretions needn't ruin what marriage you'd have left after we've finished with you. Right ... we'll be in touch."

"But..."

"Oh, and by the way," McClatcher added, his voice now sounding mild and over-friendly. "Winston sends his regards to young Sarah. And so do I..."

The strident tone rang in her ear as the American hung up. Very slowly she replaced the receiver.

Part Two

KILLING GROUND

CHAPTER 9

"I'm afraid," said the colonel, "that there have been some unexpected developments."

Although the ancient central heating system was operating to its noisy, maximum efficiency, Ducane felt a distinct chill in the air at the Old Man's words. In fact he had known that something was wrong as soon as he got the message to report. The team had already been briefed the previous day as to the intelligence duties they would be expected to carry out on their return to Ulster, and Ducane had been in the middle of preparing their kit when the orderly arrived. Forbes had been as surprised as he when it was made clear they were both wanted.

The colonel was seated behind his paper-strewn desk, and he was passing his unlit pipe thoughtfully from one hand to the other as he chose his words carefully. "I believe Lieutenant Harrington was a good friend of yours?"

Ducane flinched. Forbes shot him a sideways glance.

"Sir." His voice was hoarse.

The Old Man frowned, studying the bowl of his pipe with intense interest. "I'm afraid he's dead. Murdered by the Provos."

"Where, sir?" Empty.

"At a place known as McGuire's farm. I believe you know the pub run by the Bradys?"

The captain nodded.

"It happened when he was leaving there three nights ago. Apparently to visit his fiancée, Roisin McGuire. They got him in the car-park. It was dark and no one saw what happened. Must have been jumped by a group of them. Judging by damage to nearby cars and the blood-stains found—not his group, you understand—he put up one helluva fight. I think we'd have been proud of him."

"Then they took him to the farm?" Ducane asked, tasting the bile at the back of his mouth.

"Yes, where he was obviously subjected to severe interrogation. He was then shot in the head."

Forbes had said nothing; he just stared grimly towards the window unseeing, his jaw set in a tense, determined line.

The Old Man continued: "I'm afraid the tragedy doesn't end there. Obviously he wouldn't talk so they assaulted his fiancée in front of him."

Ducane shut his eyes momentarily. "Killed too?"

"Knee-capped. Used a power-drill, I'm told ... Crippled for good. She was virtually unconscious for forty-eight hours until her farm hand luckily discovered her."

"Bastards!" spat Forbes, turning his head suddenly to Ducane, his eyes blazing. He snapped his jaw firmly shut in an effort to control his fury.

"Please, Sergeant," said the colonel softly, "let's not make matters worse."

Ducane found his eyes smarting as he remembered the slender young girl in the farmhouse, pale and frightened, but full of self-determination and courage.

"I'm so sorry to have to break this bad news to you both. But bad as it is, I'm afraid it could be the start of something even more serious. More fundamentally dangerous to our operations in Armagh. Let me explain." He opened a pink cardboard wallet on his desk, and glanced over the neatly-typed script. "Over the past week or so we've heard rumours about a new branch of the PIRA being formed. It's been referred to as the FCU or Forward Combat Unit. It was mentioned by a young Provo we picked up in Dungannon. 'Gather the chap was on his way to start training. There was another oblique reference to it in some papers RUC Special Branch intercepted in Newry. One or two stories have also been flying around in the Lazy K."

Ducane asked: "What's so special about this unit, sir?"

The Old Man sat back in his chair. "Bit of a cheek, really.

It appears it's been specifically formed to knock off our chaps ..." He paused, allowing the significance of his words to sink in. As the two soldiers before him exchanged glances, he continued. "... As I say, it sounds a bit ambitious, but rumour has it they've set up a new first-class training camp. Not the usual sites. But somewhere over the border. Looks as though we've really got old Paddy worried lately. Our operations in Armagh have been standing on his windpipe. So he's taking to desperate measures."

"He must be desperate, all right," Forbes said. "I'd like to give these new heroes five minutes on my own. 'Don't care if they bring their training manuals with them!'"

The Old Man stuffed a thumbful of tobacco into his pipe. "That's as maybe, Sergeant, but our information indicates we shouldn't take the threat lightly. They've already had a go at one of our surveillance teams. Two of them badly wounded. And they massacred a VCP patrol, including Major Simmonds of the Royals.

"Apparently they've got hold of some chaps who know our methods. Familiar with the way we work. Procedures, etc. Now they intend to turn it against us. Sort of Chindits of Armagh." He chuckled but without humour.

Ducane said: "I find it hard to believe any of our old Regiment members would do such a thing."

"Probably not. But there have been one or two undesirables we've RTU'd or kicked out of the Army altogether. Anyway, we're having all ex-members checked on by Special Branch, just in case there's a bad apple. It's not impossible."

He made an attempt to light his pipe. "Apparently Paddy's been withdrawing his best men from all over the province. The fit young 'uns mostly, which could explain why things have gone a bit quiet over the last month or so. 'Fraid it won't last, of course. If we're right, the real trouble could have already started."

Ducane frowned. "Not Charlie Harrington?"

The Old Man exhaled a billowing cloud of smoke, watching it rise to the ceiling. "It looks very much like it. For once G1 Intelligence and I are in complete agreement. I gather everything pointed to an operation by this new PIRA cell."

"If they got Charlie," Ducane said, "perhaps they're as good as they say they are."

The colonel leaned forward on his elbows. "*I'm* taking this new unit as a serious threat, Ducane. I can't afford to do otherwise. If half these rumours are true this unit's going to make a right nuisance of itself. And if I get an itch, I scratch it. Hard."

Forbes asked: "Where is this new base, sir?"

"Haven't the foggiest notion. We gather it's not in Sligo or Dundalk, or any of the other known camps, but far away, out of harm's reach. Somewhere where the Irish Government can't or won't touch it. And that's what I need to find out. And fast."

"Any ideas, sir?" Ducane asked.

"I'm making the Bessbrook contingent up to full troop strength. Your team will rejoin Johnny Fraser's and we'll draft in two more of our most experienced Ulster teams. Not sure which, yet, but preferably chaps you've worked with before.

"You'll be in operational command, but I'm sending down an MIO from G1 Intelligence Army HQ—I believe you know Major Bill Harper?—he'll be in overall charge of Int. and liaison for the operation.

"I have in mind that the three teams, operating as individuals if necessary, will stake out or investigate in response to Int. reports. Your team will act as reserve, operating with Harper at a special Ops. centre to maximise security; until we get the lead we need.

"Basically it'll be an anti-anti-guerilla exercise—all damnably confusin', but that's what it amounts to. With any luck we'll actually latch onto some of these Paddies going south. That's where Sergeant Forbes' plans come in."

"Over the border?" Ducane was surprised.

"Let's just say Eire won't necessarily be out of bounds. Nor will Outer Mongolia if that's where they've got it. I'm off to London tomorrow for a spot of lunch. I don't need to tell you who with, but I believe my host may feel as concerned as I do about this new development." His pipe had gone out, and he tapped the contents of the bowl noisily into the old tin ashtray. "It puts a new complexion on your job tidying up Harrington's operation. With Major Harper's help I want you to put everything under the microscope, and turn every stone. Bill will show you the ropes and all that. But your team's personal experience of the people and the area will be invaluable. And you may come up with a clue as to the whereabouts of that base, or the next planned attack by these FCU Paddies."

The colonel's words finished on a high and dramatic note. Ducane never ceased to be fascinated by his ability to instil excitement and get the adrenalin flowing. It was like a call to arms. Every bit as stimulating as a bugle-call or roll of drums, yet spoken in a quiet, matter-of-fact tone that only barely raised its pitch to emphasise that the gloves were coming off.

"When do we leave, sir?"

"You can grab 48 hours leave whilst I get the necessary clearance and while Johnny Fraser starts things rolling at Bessbrook." The Old Man smiled briefly. "Make the most of it, it could be the last leave you have for a spell. That'll be all, gentlemen. Thank you."

As the door shut the colonel sat back in his chair, resting his hands on the edge of the desk, and closed his eyes. This was going to be tricky.

Even if the PM agreed to the proposed operation, the smallest hint of their plan outside of strict DI6, the overseas intelligence agency formerly known as MI6, and SAS Intelligence circles in Northern Ireland could lead to disaster. The old rivalry between DI6 and DI5, previously MI5, which traditionally had responsibility for Northern Ireland, was far from dead, and DI5 retained close contacts with Eire's Garda Special Branch, via Ulster's RUC Special Branch. News of a deep, cross-border penetration raid would be more than political dynamite. It would be a positive thermo-nuclear blast.

The colonel picked up the buff folder marked CHRIS-TOPHER ROBIN. Slowly he flicked through the pages. The dates began in 1973, in his predecessor's time, when it had been recognised that the Ulster conflict was going to drag on for years. It had been decided then to take a very long-term view and plant 'sleepers' in the Republican community. The aim was to achieve really deep penetration. There had been thirteen volunteers, nine of them SAS soldiers and the rest from other regiments. All had genuine Irish ancestry. Three were pulled out after a year when they could no longer take the incessant mental strain; five were withdrawn once it became obvious that the PIRA had become suspicious of their activities; three more were unsuccessful in making any kind of 'contact' with the enemy. In 1974 the last two disappeared, one of them an SAS member.

The project had been cancelled. Then, after a silence of eighteen months, a high-speed Morse message had been picked up by Government Communications Headquarters at Cheltenham. There had just been one transmission lasting under twenty seconds.

The colonel looked at the deciphered transcript: ARRIVED. AM IN WITH A CHANCE. LISTEN OUT. CHRISTOPHER ROBIN.

From that day to this there had been short irregular transmissions, each more intriguing than the last. At first the information had been sketchy, gradually increasing in importance until, in the past six months, it had become clear that Christopher Robin had penetrated the upper echelons of the PIRA.

It was frustrating that, as planned, there was no way to make contact with their man in the field, to ask questions, or to request clarification. But he was in deep and absolutely nothing would be allowed to upset their mole's delicate and deadly position.

The original lead that had enabled Harrington to set up the trap for Cochran. Then a trail to half a dozen major arms caches. And now the *real* source of information about the PIRA's new Forward Combat Unit.

He flicked back the pages and looked again at the faded photograph. *WO2 Michael Coogan. SAS service commenced June 1967. Formerly the Royal Irish Rangers.*

The colonel felt a lump forming at his throat. Quickly he closed the folder. "Good luck, lad, wherever you are."

He knew that Christopher Robin's chances of survival were negligible. Not for the first time he felt himself wish he'd never heard the Regimental motto.

The smell of bacon sizzling in the pan wafted through the small Fulham house, and Ducane was more than ready when the call to breakfast came. It was a scene he dreamed about so much when he was away that, now it was actually happening, it didn't seem real. Breakfast at home in the kitchen, with a plate piled high with egg, bacon and sausages. Trish looking pretty and reassuringly domesticated, and Sarah spreading her meal liberally all over her face.

To Ducane the picture seemed so profound, yet he wondered if most men gave it a second thought. Privation heightened appreciation, and he found that living close to danger always honed a fine edge to his perception. It was the same watching Trish climb from the bed in the morning. The picture of her long, easy strides across to the wardrobe; her slender naked back; the way she tossed her hair; the little self-conscious smile she gave him as she perched the large gold-rimmed spectacles on her nose. All these things were indelibly etched on his mind, stored and remembered for use during the loneliest moments—when home and normality not only seemed, but sometimes were, a thousand miles away.

"I'm sorry it's only streaky bacon," Trish said with a smile. "Times is hard!"

Ducane demolished a large sausage. "But you're managing okay?"

"Scraping by." Trish left her meal to help Sarah in her chair. "It just isn't getting any better."

"Even with the job?"

"Don't know how I managed before at all."

"You must let me know if you need more money," he said.

She looked at him quizzically. "And what would you do?"

He shrugged, concentrating on the remaining sausage with savage intensity. "We'd think of something. There must be some cutbacks possible."

"Mr Andrews started work for a mini-cab firm last month. Mrs Andrews reckons he's coining it in. It was a hundred and fifty pounds last week with tips."

Ducane frowned. "You can't drive."

Trish looked exasperated. "Not for me, Jack. For you. You said you'd leave the Forces if a promotion didn't come through. Or at least revert to the Paras. You could probably go back as major."

He pushed aside his plate. "I said I'd think about it."

Trish studied him over the rim of her spectacles. "Well, I think you ought to think about it some more. We can't go on for ever like this."

Ducane was defensive: "We could always move into married quarters, you know that."

"I don't want Sarah to grow up in a bloody barracks," Trish replied with feeling.

"What's barracks?" Sarah asked with a mouthful of food.

"Never mind," Trish snapped.

"It's not like a barracks," Ducane said. "You know the army estates. They're quite pleasant. And you'd have plenty in common with the other girls." Unlike the rest of the Army the SAS took particular care to break down class barriers between wives.

"No thank you, Jack. I don't want to spend my days gossiping and complaining about my husband's pay and the Army! Look what it did for Dave Forbes and Elaine."

He helped himself to more tea from the pot on the table. "You know Dave and Elaine had other problems. He's always been a bit of a wild lad and she just couldn't cope with it. He was hitting the bottle pretty hard." He used the introduction of the sergeant's name to steer the conversation in a different direction. "Talking of Dave, he may call round this evening to see us."

"Oh, Jack, not this evening! You've only just come home."

Another mistake, Ducane thought grimly. "I thought you'd be pleased to see him."

Trish tossed the curls from her face. She was fond of Dave Forbes, attracted by his animal magnetism and his broad, muscular frame. There was a brooding violence lingering so near to the surface that she found it thrilling and frightening at the same time. His eyes sometimes burned with a passionate fierceness as he looked at her. Somehow you could look at Dave Forbes and sense the rogue in him immediately. He could so easily have been an Elizabethan pirate or a highwayman; it was as though he'd been born in the wrong age, when the world had grown too small to hold him.

She had once felt that same strange spark of excitement with Ducane. The electricity she felt at being close to him, absorbing the scent of violence that always simmered just below the quiet surface. Time had changed that. Time and responsibility had mellowed Jack, she thought. Particularly since Sarah had been born. But Dave Forbes remained untamed, a wild beast at large in a civilised society, not prepared to be chained for any reason or, as Elaine had found to her cost, for any woman.

But since the visit by McClatcher and Loveday, even her instinctive interest at the mention of his name caused a rising disgust with herself.

She said: "You know I like Dave, but I thought we might be alone again tonight. That's one thing I like about hardly ever seeing you—we have some great reunions."

He laughed. "I'll make sure he leaves early. Tonight could be the last time for a while, and I want to enjoy it too. But we need to talk over our plans for the operation."

"What operation?" She almost blurted the words. McClatcher's insistent voice seemed to be ringing in her ear.

*

After lunch they went to the park, kicking their way through the carpet of brown leaves towards the lake where Sarah threw bread at the ducks.

Trish said: "It's so quiet. Not like at weekends."

"Sarah's creating enough noise to make up for it," he laughed.

Trish tightened the knot of her headscarf. "Funny to think it's in the middle of London."

He nodded, then stooped to help Sarah break up the bread.

She glanced down at her husband, choosing her moment. "Don't you miss all this? Sarah. Me. Walks in the park like this."

"Yes. I must be getting old. When I'm home with you and the little monkey it seems like a different world."

It was a long shot, but if she could persuade him to quit now, there was a chance McClatcher would leave her alone.

She said quietly: "Give it up, Jack. Forget about the Army. You'll never get any thanks for what you're doing. Sarah and I would like you home."

He squinted at the far side of the lake. "It's all I know, Trish. Without the Army I'd be lost. I don't think I could ever be a mini-cab driver."

"There are other jobs."

He breathed in a deep lungful of air. It was rich, damp. How could he explain to her? How could he make her understand that the smell and colours of the park didn't compare with County Armagh? Or with the superb hues of the Dhofar desert at dusk. Or the vivid greens and yellows of the Brunei jungle. Or even the frosty blue-white wilderness of northern Norway.

How could he tell her how it felt to be called into the Old Man's office at Bradbury Lines? The sense of anticipation and challenge as you waited for him to get to the point of the assignment. Anything, anywhere. At the drop of a hat. A short hop by helicopter to the airfield. The old Hercules waiting, its engines turning, ready to go. Anywhere within its four thousand miles range. The other side of the world before, at home, Trish had even begun to stir from her sleep. As the inscription at the headquarters read:

> *"We are the pilgrims, Master, we shall go*
> *Always a little further. It may be*
> *Beyond that last blue mountain barr'd with snow,*
> *Across that angry or glimmering sea."*

How did you explain to a woman as loving and sensual as Trish that this peaceful, domestic interlude was just one small part of your life? One day it would be more, but only when you were past your prime. The day when you knew the killer instinct had left you. The day you hung up the sand-coloured beret with the winged dagger emblem for the last time.

And how did you explain the animal fear and elation as you chased the most difficult quarry of all? A beast with more cunning and audacity than any animal. When you pitted your wits and instincts against his, moving and counter-moving until one of you cracked. When you went beyond the point that any training could prepare you for. The moment of frightening realisation that it was your will against the enemy's. The ultimate personal confrontation and challenge. Your life or his.

No, it was not something he could even attempt to tell Trish without the words sounding hollow and clumsy. Thankless and self-indulgent.

"I could make major this year."

"With that Royals CO in Ireland making a complaint about you to Hereford?"

He half-smiled. "That's the Army way. Your chaps are using too much muscle. Must toe the line, old boy. Don't let it happen again. Back at Hereford, our colonel congratulates us. It's just the Army way."

"If you Returned to Unit, at least it woudn't be so dangerous."

Ducane grimaced. "I'm not so sure. Simmonds is dead. A Provo ambush."

Trish looked shocked. She went to say something, then stopped.

He looked at Trish, smiling. She was trying hard. "I'll think about it, love. Really. And if I don't get a crown up this year, I'll think seriously about mini-cabbing, or something."

"Promise?"

He kissed her forehead lightly. But she knew it would be no solution to the immediate problem that was closing round her like a steel trap. McClatcher's voice whispered in her ear like an evil psalm.

Dave Forbes arrived just after dark in the late afternoon. He received his normal rapturous welcome from Sarah, but he instinctively noticed Trish's coolness to his usual flirtatious approach. He quickly decided that there'd been a row and he'd do his best to keep well clear of it.

He settled down with Ducane to a bottle of Scotch and to discuss the details he had been thinking over at his brother's home in North London.

Forbes had refined the initial plan they had developed on the train to London. As usual, nothing committed to paper would leave Bradbury Lines. Like the habitual re-folding of a map, so that it was impossible to tell which page had been studied, it had become second nature. Mentally the sergeant had turned the list of equipment and methods needed for the cross-border operation over and over in his mind.

He had largely ignored the preliminary organisation of the operation, preferring Ducane to sort out the aspects of intelligence-gathering and collation, and deployment. Final details would be confirmed in the 'Quiet Room' back at Hereford, where intricate planning would be plotted and written up.

Ducane asked Forbes several penetrating questions and quickly pin-pointed the shortcomings which were then thoroughly discussed and amended. Two minds were better than one, and the captain appreciated his friend's ferocious enthusiasm and ingenious way of solving seemingly insuperable practical problems. They came to the end of the planning at the same time as they reached the bottom of the whiskey bottle.

As Trish opened the kitchen hatch and slid in a tray of coffee, cheese and biscuits, Ducane said: "Dave certainly believes in taking the battle to the enemy."

"So does the Old Man," Forbes returned. "Recommended my proposed course of action." He turned round and took the tray from the hatch.

Ducane laughed. "Suitably modified, of course."

"Of course."

Trish came through the door. "Well, if it goes ahead, I just hope Jack keeps well clear of any trouble. If his promotion doesn't come through, I want him in one piece for Civvy Street."

Forbes was surprised. "You're not telling me old Jacko's pulling out of the service? Not hanging up his bayonet?"

Ducane drank his coffee. "It's a possibility."

"But he's one of the best. He's got more experience and skill than the rest of the troop put together. You're not serious?"

Trish looked sideways at her husband. "I don't know how serious he is. But he's also married with a daughter."

Forbes looked decidedly astounded, staring first at Trish and then at the captain for confirmation or denial.

Ducane said: "Things have changed, Dave. I'm not getting any younger and my promotion prospects haven't looked too rosy recently. If I am going to leave the Forces, the sooner I start a new career, the better." He inclined his head towards Trish. "Civvy Street's got a lot going for it, you know."

That was something Forbes could not deny. In similar circumstances Trish Ducane might conceivably persuade him to step out of his uniform for good. He wasn't sure he would ever be happy about it, but at least Ducane seemed to enjoy a domesticated bliss he had never been able to share with Elaine. And you needed something worthwhile to persuade you to go back to Civvy Street.

He said: "But we've all had good times in the Army, Trish. Remember when we were based in Hong Kong, before going to the Jungle Training School in Singapore. We had a ball." He shook his head, recalling. "And those

174

Yanks we met up with ... The ones Jacko said called the other day."

"Oh, God!" She'd missed the cup as she poured another coffee.

The men smiled at her in sympathy and then continued their conversation.

Half an hour later, when Ducane saw the sergeant to the door, Trish stacked the used coffee cups onto the tray, which she then took through to the kitchen, placing it on the worktop by the serving hatch to the lounge. She listened for a moment until she was sure she could hear the men still talking.

She opened the biscuit tin and took out the small battery-operated Hanimex tape-recorder. Quickly she extracted the cassette and slipped it into the pocket of her apron.

CHAPTER 10

When Ducane's team arrived back at Tac HQ Bessbrook they found that a small and cheerless operations room had already been commandeered for them. It was the first sign they had that the resourceful MIO, Bill Harper, a stocky Welsh major, had preceded them and was already in control.

With a mind like a laser-beam, a persuasive charm and an infuriating constant chuckle, Harper had already organised a bank of telephones, complete with scramblers, which had been patched into direct links with the G1 Intelligence Army HQ in Belfast, SAS Bradbury Lines and the Regiment's Liaison Officer at the Ministry of Defence in Whitehall. Several large-scale maps of the area were pinned to the yellowing walls and covered with perspex sheets to take the markings of chinagraph pencils; an old wooden filing cabinet had been loaned from the Royals' CO, and a large blackboard and easel stood in one corner. His prime acquisition was the installation of their own Int. cell VDU terminal and printer to the Army's central computer that kept details of everyone ever suspected or detained over the past five years, all cross-referenced with car registration numbers, addresses, known associates, and much more besides.

"I hope you'll forgive me for making a start, Captain," chuckled the major as the four men trudged in. "We've nearly got everything ready. An electric kettle's on its way with a positive mountain of coffee tins. So no need to wait for the char wallah. And I've got my eye on a very pretty little WRAC to come and do our typing for us." He held up two pudgy hands. "I'm afraid I've a two-finger handicap when it comes to secretarial work!"

Ducane glanced around the room. It looked like a scene from an operations centre at New Scotland Yard.

The wisdom of the Old Man in selecting Harper from G1 was self-evident—he had spent most of his time in the SAS Intelligence unit known colloquially as 'The Kremlin'.

"I couldn't have done better myself, Major."

The Welshman laughed, his thick neck quivering. "Pleased to hear it, Captain. I don't like to let the grass grow, you know." His eyes looked suddenly cold. "Especially when we're after little rats like the lot we're chasing. I've managed to persuade the Royals' CO to get every available man out at VCPs, screening as many cars as possible, and making house-to-house searches. We've also got a direct line with the RUC, but of course we're keeping them in the dark about this particular op. The results of all interviews will be fed straight to us here, as soon as they're available. Either typed or phoned in and taped. That's why I want our own little WRAC. To type them out immediately." He jabbed a thumb in the direction of the easel. "That's the first batch of Int. Summaries. We can go through them as soon as you've had a cuppa and some chow."

Ducane said: "Fine, fine." Amazed by the complexity of the operation the little Welshman had established so speedily.

"I'm just co-ordinating Lieutenant Harrington's files. Matching up ID reports and photographs. It won't be long, but like so many of us, his book-keeping was a little lax!"

By the time the wintry dawn light had begun to rise the initial report was already completed in long-hand, written out laboriously by Young Tom who, it was decided unanimously and conveniently, had the only decipherable style. The room was stale and airless, clouded with layers of tobacco smoke, and the table piled high with cups. Despite the weariness of the men, Bill Harper had kept them going at a cracking pace throughout the night apart from a hastily-snatched meal at the 24-hour cookhouse. The major involved everyone in discussions over each point of interest and detail of every report, fiercely promoting ideas and theories, however outlandish, for examination.

A statement attributed to Roisin McGuire had made particularly nauseating reading, but it contained the first mention of two names. One was Reagan, the other Malone —who was thought to have been over the border since the farmhouse raid. Bill Harper had spent hours on the telephone, badgering and bullying every Int. unit in Ulster he knew, for a grain of information on the men. He spared the unlucky recipients no quarter, not hesitating to call two colonels out of bed, and insisting that office-staff be recalled in the small hours to answer his questions. He was relentless and determined, asking about one related subject after another, until Ducane's team felt sure they would succeed at nothing but causing fury at Harper's countless probings, many of which seemed decidedly trivial.

At 0400 hours an interesting break had come. A man called Malone, answering the description of the man known to Roisin McGuire, had appeared in a routine RUC Special Branch report 18 months previously, after he had been seen in the company of ex-Lazy K prisoners under surveillance. The central computer revealed that he had previously emigrated to Australia in 1965, several years before the latest troubles had started. There was no official record of him returning to Ulster.

However he had quickly disappeared, this time before he could be brought in for questioning. No further police or intelligence service contact had been made with him, although the name did crop up from time to time in reports from informers.

Surprisingly there was absolutely nothing at all on Reagan. A thorough checking of the late Lieutenant Harrington's private papers revealed a renewed contact with Malone just a few days previously, although any enquiries he may have made were not official. Certainly nothing was recorded in writing.

"Looks like both of them were late starters," commented Bill Harper. "But they've certainly made up for lost time. This Int. Sum reports Malone being seen in regular company with none other than Martin McGuiness."

"You mean a sort of bodyguard?" Young Tom suggested.

The Welshman shrugged. "Could well be. When you get to the top of the PIRA you can't help but make a few enemies. Stands to reason."

"Makes sense," Forbes agreed, half to himself. "But doesn't that suggest that McGuiness himself is taking a pretty keen interest in the McGuire business?"

Harper sucked his cheeks thoughtfully. "It would, wouldn't it? But then with two VIPs snatched on this patch recently, it's hardly surprising. He's been very much the blue-eyed boy from what we can gather. Bit of a trouble-shooter."

"Perhaps," Young Tom said, "this whole FCU idea is his brainchild."

Harper nodded. "It's a daring enough idea. And if Harrington's murder and the business with the girl was one of the operations, it looks fairly well co-ordinated. Professional. The McGuiness touch."

Forbes climbed to his feet. "Well, I'll leave you intellectuals an' ol' boyo here to discuss your fancy notions. I'm goin' to get some kip. If we get into a fire fight later, one of us ought to be awake!"

As he ambled towards the door, Young Tom stood up. "Okay if I turn in, boss?"

Ducane nodded. He was feeling the strain himself and there was nothing more they could do until the latest reports came in from the night patrols and checkpoints.

Young Tom hesitated at the door, his Bergen pack slung casually over one shoulder. "Er, does anyone happen to know which hospital Roisin McGuire's in?"

The captain frowned. "Royal Victoria, I think. Why? You planning on sending a get-well-soon card?"

The soldier paled, his lips pinched with anger. "I don't think she will *get well*, sir."

"Of course not. I'm sorry."

"I was thinking more of a visit. If that would be all right, sir?"

Ducane rubbed his eyes. They were red and sore and his mouth tasted dry and bitter. There was no denying it would be a nice gesture; he was not unaware that their involvement had contributed to her predicament. But they were also on instant standby. "I'd like to let you go, Tom. But I can't justify it under the circumstances."

"I see, sir."

Bill Harper glanced across at both men, weighing the problem quickly in his mind. "Look, Captain, I know you can't justify the lad going. But if it would help, I can. I'm quite justified in having the young lady interviewed again and I'm sure this soldier would be as good as anyone in the team."

"I'm sure he would," Turnbull mumbled in disgust.

The Welshman looked at his watch. "I'll wangle a chopper ride for you. Be to Belfast and back before lunch. 'Course, means you'll be dead on your feet. Still, how does that sound?"

Ducane reluctantly agreed. "Okay, Tom, get ready and report back here in fifteen minutes. But remember I want a full statement from her." Then he added quietly: "And don't go getting involved. The kid's got enough problems without some lovesick private mooning over her."

Young Tom nodded, saluted hastily and left the room, whilst Turnbull shook his head in disbelief.

After a quick telephone call, Bill Harper managed to delay the next helicopter shuttle for twenty minutes. Ducane noticed that his manner had become less jovial. Perhaps it was just the strain of the long night.

"What's up, Bill?"

The major shook his head, hesitating. "I don't know, Jacko, something doesn't seem right. Nothing concrete, y'know. A feeling in the water. Wish I could put my finger on it."

*

He waited two hours before the sister came to tell him he could see her.

"She's still under sedation," she said. "So I doubt you'll find her talkative. Just a few minutes will be enough, anyway."

The bunch of flowers in Perrot's hand had wilted visibly during the long wait, and he felt foolish as he followed the sister down the corridor, to the obvious amusement of other uniformed soldiers on guard duty. He held the posy behind his back as he was shown into the small private room. Immediately he detected the all-pervading smell of disinfectant.

As they entered a nurse was adjusting the pillows behind Roisin's head, but she left quickly when she saw them.

"We have a visitor for you, Miss McGuire," the sister announced. Then quietly to Young Tom: "Remember, five minutes only. And try not to cause her any distress."

The door closed and Perrot found himself standing awkwardly at the foot of the bed, watching the small ashen face fringed with short black hair. It wasn't the face he remembered. The was a mass of blue and yellow bruising, so extensive that the bootlace scar on her cheek was scarcely noticeable. Her lips were puffed and cut, and as she opened her mouth to speak he noticed one of her front teeth was missing.

"Who is it?" The voice was no more than a whisper, apprehensive. She screwed up her eyes to focus, but the flesh around the sockets was red and swollen. Whether by tears or bruising was hard to tell.

He took a hesitant step forward. "It's Trooper Perrot, miss ... Tom Perrot."

She closed her eyes in an expression of resignation.

"Do you mind if I sit down?"

Roisin shook her head, turning it to the pillow.

He pulled out the chair, knocking it clumsily against the paraphernalia of the drip-feed trolley. He said: "I've brought you these. They've drooped a bit, I'm afraid. It's very hot in here."

She made no effort to turn her head towards him.

"Won't you look?"

Slowly her head turned, until she faced him. "What do you want with me?"

He flushed. Damn Ducane, how in God's name could he take down a statement? "Don't you remember me? I sat with you that night at the farm."

Her head hurt and her mind was clouded with the effect of the injections. Vaguely she could recollect the slim young soldier who had tried to comfort her. She remembered he was more shy than she was; but he had shown concern.

Her silence embarrassed him. Making an effort he said suddenly: "We can't keep meeting like this."

For a moment he caught the hint of a smile in her eyes. Her voice had a slight lisp and a whistle to it, caused by the damage to her mouth. "You seem to make a habit of turning up when I'm not at my best."

"I was very sorry to hear ... about what happened. We all were. All the lads, that is. They send their love. Well, you know."

She remembered the four soldiers. Remembered how they'd stood in the bedroom, staring, mesmerised by her nakedness. It seemed like an age before they'd been able to take their eyes off her. She wondered if they would find it so difficult now.

"That's good of them."

Encouraged, Young Tom said: "And we want you to know that we'll get them. The bl ... the men who did this to you."

Abruptly she turned her head away again. He strained to catch her words. "What good will it do? Adding to the killing, that's all. Enough people have been hurt. How many more ... How many more?"

"It's only justice."

He saw her shoulders shake and guessed she was crying. He said: "I'm sorry. I didn't mean to upset you. But I thought you'd be pleased to know we intend to sort them out."

Her voice was barely discernible. "You fool, you don't

182

understand ... Only Charlie knew ... He knew it was all pointless."

"It has to be done, miss. Whatever the rights and wrongs," Young Tom insisted.

Suddenly she turned back to face him. Her eyes were filled with tears. "And what if they got you and your friends first?" she demanded. "Then where would you be? Just another statistic. Just another tragic little news story ... Why are you all so blind? I'm beginning to think that Sean was right about all this. My brother. It was all right until you all came with your guns and your big Army boots!"

He reddened. "Look, miss, we didn't start all this. We're just doing a job. Trying to stop people getting hurt. Innocent people like you."

She forced herself to calm down, taking a deep intake of breath. "I suppose that's the way you see it. To me it seems you're just adding to the trouble. If it hadn't been for your people I wouldn't be like this ..."

"But ..."

She looked at him directly. "I'm afraid it's true. If I hadn't got involved with Charlie it wouldn't have happened ... Or if my brother hadn't been involved, I suppose. Anyway, if you catch the gang or if they catch you, it won't help me walk again."

. Without thinking he reached out to hold her hand. It felt cool in his grasp. "You will. Given time."

She shook her head, looking sympathetically at the conviction in his clear eyes. "That's not what the doctors say."

He held her stare. "They can do wonders nowadays. With determination and effort ..." He searched for words. "Who dares wins!"

"What?"

"Our regimental motto. If you try hard enough, anything is possible."

For the first time the clefts at the corner of her mouth dimpled into a smile. "You are funny."

"Am I?"

"You have a very blind faith ..."

183

"I do in you," he said earnestly.

She averted her eyes. "Please don't say that." She tried to remove her hand from his grip, but he held it tighter.

"I believe you can get better ... Perhaps not completely ... I mean nothing very energetic ... running or the like. You'll just need perseverance."

"Don't I know it!"

"And when you're out of here," he added, looking down at her hand, "I'd like to take you out."

Roisin gave a small, bitter laugh. "In my wheelchair?"

He looked back into her eyes. "I'm not trying to be kind. I mean it. I've always found you attractive. And nothing that's happened has changed how I feel."

She swallowed hard, stifling the lump of emotion in her throat. Her teeth were clenched as she spoke for fear that the flood of sobs would not stop once they began. "Leave ... me ... Please go now ... I don't want to see you again ..."

Young Tom went to speak, but stopped himself. He took a deep breath and got to his feet, carefully tugging on his beret. He looked down at the discarded posy she'd hardly noticed.

Finally he said: "Please remember me. I'll tell the sister how I can be contacted if you change your mind." He paused before shutting the door. "Good luck, Roisin."

Outside, the sister was coming back.

"Did you get the report you needed?"

"Oh, stuff the damn report," he said quietly and set off briskly down the corridor.

Five minutes later, when the sister entered the room, she found that Roisin McGuire had drifted back into a drugged sleep. She eased the bunch of wilting forget-me-nots from the young girl's hands and, smiling to herself, placed them in the empty vase at the bedside.

"'Name Duffy mean anything to you?" Bill Harper asked. "Richard Duffy?" He had just been speaking to the colonel at Bradbury Lines.

Ducane and Forbes looked up from the table where they

were finishing a brunch of friend bacon sandwiches, and exchanged glances. The Welshman was relaxing in a chair, his stubby legs up on the table in front of him. It was now 1400 hours and, when the captain and sergeant had entered the operations room a few minutes earlier after an exhausted sleep, they had found the major already hard at work, freshly shaven, and showing no signs of strain. They, in contrast, had eaten their meal in broody silence, Forbes concentrating on the plump bottom of the blonde WRAC called Sally, as she pounded furiously at the ancient typewriter.

Hearing the major speak, she had discreetly stopped and begun filing the mass of memos and papers on her desk.

"She's a little poppet," Forbes commented appreciatively, quickly distracted.

"Duffy's a fella, Sergeant," chuckled Harper.

Ducane stood up. "I think you could say we know Duffy. We spent three months in Londonderry trying to corner him. Really tricky lad. One of their best, I'd say. They pulled us off the case in the end; brought in some new blood."

"Just as well," Forbes sneered. "I'd had enough of waitin' to catch the sly bugger red-handed. I was all for us handing him a bomb in a carrier bag and shooting him as soon as he looked inside."

Harper scratched his head. "Doesn't look like your successors had better luck either. He's still loose, and there's still no evidence for a conviction."

Forbes raised his eyebrows in despair. "God preserve us from politicians!"

Ducane looked over the major's shoulder at the notepad in his hand. "What's he up to now, anyway?"

"Well, can't be sure, but it looks as though he's a potential recruit to this new FCU lot. It appears that a couple of years ago The Kremlin back at Hereford fielded some secret squirrels of their own. I don't remember much about it as I was working on Dhofar section then, but it appears one of those squirrels is still loose under the code name of Christopher Robin." He looked up and grinned.

"Nice touch of class that, as the operation name is Pooh Corner."

"Jesus," Forbes muttered in disgust.

Harper scowled at the sergeant's irreverence. "Well he managed to get a message through to Hereford, tipping The Kremlin off about Duffy being recruited into the FCU. As a result we've managed to put an SAS tail on him. And up to an hour ago they hadn't been shaken off. 'Last reported driving south in a pick-up truck at Omagh, heading towards Dungannon."

Ducane wandered over to one of the large maps on the wall, studied it for a moment, then added a circle in red chinagraph on Omagh. He also added 1400 hours.

Forbes wiped his moustache with a handkerchief. "Looks like he's coming our way."

"Convenient," Ducane observed. "But how reliable is this Christopher Robin character? If that information is wrong and we show our hand, they'll change tactics and we may never find the FCU base."

"The Kremlin reckons he's got a hundred per cent record," Harper replied.

"Can we ask for confirmation?"

The major shook his head. "He's in deep, Jacko, and on one-way transmission—same as you'll be once you go over the border. And The Kremlin's giving nothing away, the whole business is so sensitive. In fact the Old Man and head of Int. section are the only ones who know about it."

Forbes studied the WRAC carefully as she leaned over her desk, still busy. "I wouldn't like to be in his shoes. But neither do I fancy going off half-cocked if your secret squirrel's got it wrong."

"Even if he doesn't lead you to the FCU base, he's got to lead you somewhere," Harper said. "Whatever happens it's unlikely to be a complete waste of time."

"That's not the point, Bill," Ducane answered. "The FCU's got top priority. With the success they've been having lately we can't afford a wild goose chase *and* the chance of blowing the fact that we're on to them."

The major smiled. "But we may never get such a positive lead again. It could take months. The Royals have come up with nothing despite an extensive operation."

Suddenly everyone seemed aware of Sally rustling her papers. Ducane nodded soberly.

"Up the sharp-end again?" Forbes asked, grinning.

The major said: "Shall I push the button? It's your decision."

At that moment the telephone rang. Quickly Harper picked up the receiver and listened for several minutes to the voice at the other end, interrupting only with gruff monosyllabic questions. Finally he asked the caller to hold and, clamping his hand over the mouthpiece, addressed Ducane: "It's the latest report on Duffy. He's approaching Drumsallan on his way to Armagh. Do you want full alert and continuous reports?"

Ducane nodded. "Let's go."

Within twenty minutes each of the three patrols in the troop had been deployed for surveillance and tracking duties should Duffy abandon his vehicle and proceed on foot. All regular VCPs on approved border routes at Middletown, Carnagh, Cullaville, Tullydonnell and Killeen, in a wide sweep around the border of County Armagh where it bit into Eire, were instructed not to apprehend the pick-up truck for any reason. Regular Army units carrying out spot-checks were similarly informed. In case he stuck to the roads, a souped-up Ford Escort was on standby for Ducane's patrol.

Every few minutes messages were exchanged with The Kremlin at Hereford, informing them of every move. At 1800 hours the Old Man came on the telephone for a first-hand account. He sounded cheerful. Obviously he felt no need to restrict the operation, so his visit to London must have proved fruitful. He was still talking to Ducane when Sally handed him a new report. Duffy had turned off the main road near Silver Bridge and had left the truck in a deserted layby, no more than four miles from the border. He was proceeding southward through the rugged hill country between Tullydonnell and the town of Forkill.

"Don't let him slip through your fingers now, Ducane."

"I won't, sir. One patrol's already been dropped by chopper, and more are being dropped ahead of him, covering all possible routes. We're leaving now, sir. We'll take up the trail as soon as he crosses the border."

"That's the ticket, Ducane. Good luck." The colonel hung up and stared blindly out of the window onto the darkened drill square. This was more like the old days, he thought, stuffing tobacco into his pipe. Ducane could almost have been a replica of himself twenty years ago. What he wouldn't give to be out there with him. Have to make sure his promotion went through this time, he decided, and scribbled a note to remind himself.

Young Tom had made himself scarce since his return in the mid-afternoon. He hadn't wanted to risk being bawled out for failing to get the written report, so he had phoned the temporary operations centre and told Sally that Roisin McGuire had been heavily sedated, and her mumblings incoherent. He had then tried to sleep, but had only managed three hours of disturbed slumber before Forbes called him to get ready to go.

Once dressed he sat on his pack, scribbled two hasty notes, stuffed the envelopes in his pocket, and made his way to join the others.

The atmosphere in the operations room was electric. As he handed the envelopes to Sally and asked her to send them for him, telephones were trilling from all corners. Additional SAS support staff, who had been called in to assist, rushed from one set to another taking notes and passing them to Major Harper who stood before a giant wall-map. Only the comparatively diminutive form of Turnbull was distinguishable in the three-man team, each figure covered by bulky non-standard issue anoraks, smocks and waterproofs and woollen hats, their faces blackened with cream as they prodded fingers at the markers on the map.

"No doubt about it," Bill Harper said. "That's him.

God, thought he'd slipped through then. You can pick him up from Remick's patrol on that hill overlooking the border. Chopper can land down-wind. Safe as houses."

"Let's get going," Ducane said.

"Mind if I join the official waving party?" the Welshman asked.

"'Course not."

As the five men turned to go, Sally confronted them. Big blue eyes looked up at Ducane and Forbes from below a neatly-trimmed fringe of blonde hair.

"I've never been involved in an op. like this before," she said quickly. "And I just want you to know I'll be thinking of you. Please take care."

Forbes kissed her quickly on the nose, leaving a smear of camouflage cream on its upturned tip. "Sunbeam," he said, "when we get back you and me's gotta date!"

"C'mon," Turnbull said and pushed him roughly towards the door.

It was a crisp, clear December night. At five hundred feet the rolling woodlands were quite distinct as the Wessex 2 helicopter swept along the winding valley between the hills. The slipstream was icy as it whipped into the open hatchway where Ducane and Bill Harper peered down, identifying landmarks to one another.

Against the appalling clatter of the overhead blades, Ducane yelled: "ANY MOMENT NOW! TO THE RIGHT!"

"YES! LOOK!"

Sure enough the pin-prick of red light flashed briefly in the surrounding black mass of trees. Almost immediately the helicopter peeled off to the west as the pilot spotted the signal. They slowed quickly to a hover as, below them, the vegetation began to take on the distinguishable shape of individual trees and bushes.

Strips of fluorescent orange plastic had been laid out to form a letter T to identify the landing spot. The winchman in his white helmet shouted: "DOWN THE LINE, I'M AFRAID! CLEARING IS TOO SMALL!" His meaning rather than the words were understandable.

Ducane merely shrugged, but Bill Harper looked petrified, watching in amazement as Young Tom calmly took up the rope in both hands.

"CHANGED Y'MIND, BOYO?" It was Forbes. His teeth a mocking white in the blackened face.

Harper shook his head, unable to hear above the din.

"WATCH TOM!" the sergeant yelled in his ear. "HAND OVER HAND! AND GRIP WITH YOUR FEET! USE 'EM AS A BRAKE!"

Harper watched with his mouth open as Ducane slapped Young Tom's shoulder and the soldier stepped out into the void, slipping expertly down the rope in a series of short, controlled movements.

As he hit the ground, Forbes nodded to the major. "AFTER YOU, BOYO!"

Taking a deep breath, Bill Harper grasped the rope and flung himself out. For a moment his stocky body hung, the short legs threshing the air, before he suddenly plummeted out of sight with a squeal. Shaking his head Forbes made his exit, quickly followed by Turnbull and Ducane.

After the deafening roar of the helicopter fuselage and the swift fifty-foot descent to the clearing, the new world seemed quiet and eerie. The group had already joined the two shadowy figures Ducane knew to be from Remick's patrol. Bill Harper was standing slightly apart, rubbing his palms together in an effort to quell the pain of the friction burns. Few words were exchanged as the two men from the SAS surveillance patrol led the way up the stone-scattered hillside under the high canopy of rustling leaves.

Ten minutes laborious uphill struggle brought them to a small circle of gorse bushes that looked over the vast panoramic sweep of the border strip. Far in the distance pin-pricks of light marked isolated farmhouses and villages of Eire.

Captain Peter Remick was on his haunches, talking into a radio handset. His companion, a chunky corporal called Anderson, sat studying the display unit of the Tobias alarm system, which could be linked up to as many as twenty buried geophones on each of the four channels. Each geophone sensor would record man-made seismic activity up to three hundred yards away.

"Welcome," Anderson said without looking up from the screen. He had been monitoring their progress ever since they had come within two hundred yards of the temporary lair.

Remick said: "We've got our three suspects in view." He jabbed a finger at the blobs on the screen. "They're getting towards the limit of our coverage. We'll lose them in about twenty minutes, so you'd better get under way."

Anderson showed Ducane the position of Duffy and his two companions in relation to the map and, after a quick check over the terrain with a long-range IWS 'Twiggy' night-sight, the four-man team set off. Using a radio link, Remick guided Ducane's men to a safe intercepting position so that they were able to fall in some hundred yards behind the party of Provisionals.

At last the tell-tale indicators disappeared off the top of the screen. Corporal Anderson snapped off the machine with a flourish. It was a gesture of finality.

"Well, we have lift-off," he mused. "They're out of our range now."

"And on their own," Bill Harper said. He was standing, legs astride like the captain of a ship-of-the-line, the Starlight scope to his eye.

"Lucky beggars," Remick muttered. "Give a month's pay to be in their shoes."

Harper had long lost sight of both groups and reluctantly handed back the device to Remick. "It's a tough assignment. Could be nasty."

"All the better," replied Remick.

The major shook his head. He could never understand these men. Tell them their chances of survival were nil and they'd queue up to volunteer. Mad, the lot of them.

Remick's call-sign came up on the radio. Absently he replied and listened intently to the message from Bessbrook. He shook his head slowly. "Negative. Repeat, negative. The mission has left and they are beyond recall. Over." He paused. "I read you. Out."

Major Harper's face was etched with concern. "A recall? For Christsake, what's happened?"

Remick shook his head in disbelief. "It's an order relayed direct from Hereford. Codeword Christopher Robin. Apparently a message received advises abort mission. Enemy have prior knowledge of plans ..."

Major Harper paled visibly. Because of the sensitive nature of the mission Ducane's Sabre team had no transmission of any kind; its discovery by the Irish authorities would cause diplomatic and political scandal beyond imagination.

There was absolutely nothing he could do.

CHAPTER 11

Before crossing the border, Sergeant Dave Forbes had concealed their radio behind the loose stones of a roadside wall, having first informed Captain Remick's team of its location. It would be collected at first light the next morning, along with the geophones that had been secreted in the area.

Without the radio all communication with the outside world was severed. The feeling of isolation pressed in on the small group, heightening their sense of danger and anticipation, as they continued after Duffy and his companions.

Only Young Tom was unsure whether he enjoyed this new thrill. As soon as he knew that they had crossed the frontier into Eire his sense of perception had increased as though an unseen hand had twisted a tuning dial deep inside his brain. His eyes seemed to focus in the gloom with a clarity almost as vivid as the Starlight scope; the muffled snapping of a twig underfoot sounded like cracking china to his ears. Even sounds he had not noticed since their arrival by helicopter took on a new, individual significance: an owl-hoot in the mid-distance, a rodent rustling in the undergrowth nearby, the faraway rumble of a lorry.

To the others the feeling was familiar. It was always *after* their early assignments that they had been able to analyse their feelings and realise that life had reached a new peak only when the adrenalin was flowing freely. Only during later periods of inactivity did they start to yearn for that sense of danger and excitement. And somehow it was never stronger than when crossing a frontier. Danger, it seemed, had its degrees. But only over the border of a hostile land did it reach such a tingling zenith. After an illegal border crossing everything else seemed second rate.

None of the three older men considered Eire to hold many fears. They held little respect for the Irish border patrols, believing that no accidental encounter would hold the same stark horror as East German frontier guards or the trigger-happy Russians north of Norway.

Ducane and Forbes took it in turns to maintain visual contact with Duffy, the remaining three men in the team dropping back still farther. By this method, if the leading soldier was unlucky or careless enough to be discovered, the others would have time to disperse and counter-strike before the enemy realised what had hit them.

But this night the quarry gave no sign that it suspected it was being followed. Their movements were cautious, with heads frequently turning to scan the surrounding countryside, though the action was instinctive rather than deliberate.

Progress was rapid as they moved south between the rivers of Cully Water and Kilcurry, keeping to open country. They had skirted around the populated Dungooly Cross Roads and proceeded towards Lurgankeel, their passage sheltered by low hills on both sides. After half a mile they had veered suddenly westward through the low-lying swampy ground. Here the going was arduous with mud squelching in hungry sucks as each foot was wrenched from its persistant grip and placed laboriously after the other. Feet became tender and chaffed as cold water found its way into the boots that were never quite water-tight.

Silently Duffy's men had crossed the main road that led to the Ulster border in the north and Lurgankeel a mile farther south. This was the area where the Provisionals were most at risk. The road was subject to frequent patrols by the Irish Army and Garda, but tonight there was no traffic of any description.

The ground began to slope away rapidly to the gurgling flow of Cully Water. It was swift, but shallow here, easily fordable by deep-wading at several points. Beyond this point the river widened, the torrent increasing, controlled by weirs around the grounds of Falmore Hall and Balregan Castle where it merged with the Kilcurry River.

The men grimaced good-humouredly at each other before plunging into the shock of icy water that threatened to pull their feet from the precarious grip on the loose stones beneath the surface.

From then on the journey became decidedly unpleasant. For another hour they trudged over the undulating terrain in cold discomfort, anxious for the chance to change into dry clothes and to eat something hot.

The first perceptible glow of dawn was beginning to lighten the eastern sky in a dim aurora when they came to the outskirts of the village.

Young Tom was suddenly aware of birds chirping, busily waking their feathered neighbours. He was scarcely conscious of the increasing visibility until he saw Ducane waving for the main party to join him.

Turnbull was first away, breaking into long, easy strides over the rough, sloping pasture; Forbes was next with surprising speed and power for a man his size; Young Tom followed.

They dropped down beside Ducane on the roadside embankment.

"I think they've come to roost," the captain said, pointing to where the narrow road circled out of sight between the first houses of the village.

"I should bloody well hope so," Forbes said irritably. "So damned cold my balls have shrunk like dried peas."

"Lucky you didn't get your head wet," Turnbull quipped.

"Where they goin', boss?" asked Young Tom, peering out of the fringe of grass to get a better view.

The large hand of the sergeant landed firmly on his head, pushing it down. "Didn't I teach you nothin' at camp, Perrot?"

"Sorry, Sarge, but I haven't seen the buggers all night."

"And they haven't seen us!" Forbes replied. "Let's keep it that way."

Ducane said: "Dave, you take the other side of the road.

I'll take this side. Once we're sure they're staying put, one of us will come back for you two." He turned to Turnbull and Young Tom. "Meanwhile you can change into some dry civvies. And grab some chow if there's time."

Turnbull nodded silently as the two men sped off at a running crouch in different directions. There they go again, he thought bitterly, the bloody dynamic duo.

He found the teamwork of Ducane and the sergeant irritating. They always assumed the lead-roles; forever in their element up the sharp-end, seeming to read each other's mind without exchanging a word. As a cold shiver rippled through him, he was nevertheless pleased at the opportunity to change into something warm. He was never at his best when he was cold; it seemed to numb his thinking process, slowing it down to an unacceptable speed. He had always disliked Arctic warfare, but at least in the dry, crisp Scandinavian snow you had the proper kit, and you weren't troubled by gnawing damp.

Forbes returned half an hour later, changed quickly into jeans and sweater, and led the others back to Ducane's temporary hide. It was in a copse of trees overlooking a picturesque old brick schoolhouse with a neat playground lined with iron railings.

While Ducane changed into a dark leather jacket and brown corduroy trousers, Forbes explained the situation. "Duffy and friends have parked themselves in the annexe building behind the school."

Now that the sky was lightening rapidly, Turnbull and Young Tom could see the long one one-storey slab of pre-fabricated concrete that ran the full length of the rear wall of the school, destroying the building's overall quaintness.

Turnbull slitted his eyes, trying to determine some sign of life. "'They parallel bars on the walls?"

Forbes nodded. "I think it's a gym. Obviously one of the staff or the caretaker is in with the Provos, because they just walked in the back door. Used a key."

"Perhaps it was the builders?" Young Tom suggested.

Forbes scowled. "Eh?"

Perrot nodded towards the railings. "There's a sign hanging up. Some decorators. *Douglas and Sons*, or something like that."

"*Douglas and Douglas*," Turnbull corrected quickly.

There he goes again, thought Forbes. Brainy bastard doesn't miss a trick.

Ducane finished dressing and packed away his anorak and waterproof trousers in the collapsible holdall with his empty back-pack, boots and equipment. He pulled a neat, cellophane-wrapped chicken drumstick from the bag and began munching eagerly.

Between mouthfuls he said: "I think Tom's right. A building firm provides good cover. Lots of blokes to-ing and fro-ing. Often covered in dust and paint. Always different faces."

"And transport," Turnbull pointed out stiffly.

Ducane smiled, gulping the last of the meat from the drumstick. "I hadn't overlooked that one." Mild rebuke.

He jabbed the bone towards the road that ran in front of the school. Opposite was a second-hand car showroom. The conventional narrow shopfront had been ripped out and a plate-glass door installed. Inside two cars had been squeezed side by side. The remaining vehicles had been backed onto the wide pavement; others appeared to be parked down the narrow side alley.

"Convenient," Forbes murmured.

"Anything take your fancy?" Ducane asked.

The sergeant rubbed his chin thoughtfully. "Better not be too small for us lot. Hopefully a bit of poke in it. Inconspicuous."

"That old blue Zephyr looks nice," Young Tom commented, appreciatively.

Forbes looked at him disapprovingly. "Looks nice, does it, Perrot? Fancy that one do you?"

Young Tom looked apprehensive. "Well, yes. Nice condition."

The sergeant looked to the heavens. "Want an AA inspection, do you?" He gave the soldier a hard but friendly shove. "C'mon then. If it's pretty enough for you, it's pretty enough for me too. You can keep your eyes peeled whilst I do the dirty work."

Crouching low, the two set off towards the road and the showroom. The Zephyr that Young Tom had selected was down the side alley which was still in shadow. Once at the roadside, the younger man strolled openly across to the parked cars, peering through the windows, idly kicking the tyres, and making appreciative nods for the benefit of any passers-by. Meanwhile Forbes crossed the road, out-of-sight of the school building, and made his way down the narrow service road that ran behind the showroom, until he could approach it unseen.

Already there were signs of life as the community stirred itself at the start of a new day. Somewhere along the road a housewife put out empty milk bottles, looked up at the sombre sky, grimaced and retreated indoors. Two agricultural workers in flat caps sauntered along the pavement together, each clutching a lunchbox. A delivery van trundled past, seeming very noisy in the early morning quietness. Cycling lazily, with a short ladder over his shoulder, a window cleaner zig-zagged his way down the centre of the road.

"Peaceful," Turnbull commented, struggling to get the remains of the camouflage cream from his face with a wad tissues. "Makes you wonder why there're so many violent buggers in the world."

Ducane laughed. "Does, doesn't it. But I don't think we'll ever be out of a job."

Turnbull shrugged. "No, I'm afraid you're right. It's just when you see a village like this. So quiet. Friendly . . . It all seems such a bloody shame." He ran a hand over his chin. "Is it all off yet? This cream sticks like glue!"

"Your cheek. The left one, below your eye."

Turnbull found it. "I feel positively naked without this lot!"

You don't look it, thought Ducane. As usual Turnbull had managed to look immaculate in a light suede jacket and beige mohair slacks.

At that moment the serenity of the village was shattered

by the rumble of a lorry as it approached from the far end of the high street, changing gear noisily, spewing out a cloud of blue exhaust. Once the paintwork had been white, but now it was pitted and stained with sand and cement so that the black legend along its side was only just legible: *Douglas & Douglas—Builders and Decorators*.

Instinctively Ducane and Turnbull moved forward for a better view. Across the road, Young Tom took care to avert his face as he wandered to the end of the alley, hands thrust casually into his trouser pockets. Ducane guessed he was whistling 'Colonel Bogey' to warn Forbes of danger as the lorry bounced its heavy nearside wheels onto the pavement and jolted to a stop outside the school entrance.

Two young workmen in stained white overalls climbed down from the cab, laughing as they shared a joke together. They were joined on the pavement by the driver, an overweight, florid-faced man in his fifties. Casually they proceeded to the school gates, inserted a heavy key in the old-fashioned lock, and let themselves into the playground. They didn't look round but continued joking amongst themselves as they disappeared into the annexe.

"Are you thinking what I'm thinking?" Turnbull asked quietly.

Ducane nodded. "Do you think you can get a bug on that truck?"

"I'll have a shot."

The captain rummaged in his holdall and extracted a sealed aluminium container. Inside was a small receiver set and half-a-dozen miniature radio transmitters, no larger than a half-pence piece. Powered by a small mercury battery, they would transmit a continuous signal up to a range of three miles.

Quickly Ducane activated two of them by inserting the batteries, and handed them to Turnbull, who pocketed them swiftly and made his way through the bushes to join a gravel path that ran alongside the school to the road. Once there he stepped off the pavement, walking behind the vehicle, using it to screen himself from any watchful eyes in the school. Seconds later he emerged from behind the vehicle, walking towards the village centre. No one would suspect he had stopped to slap the magnetic grips against the lorry's metalwork as he passed.

Ducane switched on the receiver, thumbing the small dial until he picked up the first bleep, repeating rapidly due to the nearness of the transmitting bug. He twisted the dial again. There was no sign of the signal from the second transmitter. Carefully he repeated the process. Still nothing. Either there was a malfunction or else it had dropped off and been damaged.

Just as he began to curse, there was a movement from the annexe and the three workmen emerged, still laughing amongst themselves as they carried lengths of timber and toolbags back towards the school gate. The fat man had lost some weight, and the younger man had aged considerably.

Ducane glanced across to the car showroom. There was no sign of Perrot. God, he thought, I just hope Dave isn't having trouble. It would be unusual for him not to bring the most stubborn engine to life in a matter of seconds. But it was just possible that the cars tucked in the alleyway were awaiting servicing, or were generally not up to the standard of those prominently on display. It wouldn't take long for the lorry to cover the three miles that would take it out of transmitter range.

Working rapidly, Ducane gathered the four bulky items of luggage together and, picking up two in each hand, stumbled towards the main road.

He had only just begun his agonising walk when the builder's lorry jerked noisily into life. With a crunching of gears and a clumsy over-use of the accelerator, the big vehicle got underway, making a wide U-turn and gathering speed back towards the centre of the village.

As he dumped the last item by the roadside, Ducane heard the spluttering cough of a car from the alleyway opposite. It faded and died. Again the metallic bronchial stutter, followed this time by a sudden throaty roar as the engine caught.

After a moment the big Zephyr edged out of the alley and swung onto the road. Young Tom was at the wheel. As

Ducane staggered across the road, the young soldier climbed out and opened the boot for the luggage.

"Where the hell's Dave?" Ducane demanded.

In answer, Forbes' bulky frame emerged from the alley hunched astride a roaring Triumph Bonneville motorcycle. His moustache protruded each side of the battered white crash helmet as he grinned broadly.

"Thought we could do with extra wheels. Your escort, boss!"

Ducane returned the grin. Bloody maniac. He said: "Okay. But keep behind us until we need you."

He slammed the door shut as Young Tom accelerated towards the village centre. They picked up Turnbull at the village crossroads and continued, keeping the monotonous signal of the receiver at a regular beat, indicating that Duffy's truck was about a mile ahead.

In the mirror the large be-goggled figure maintained its distance some two hundred yards behind.

There was only one route to the friary which could be used by vehicles, but it wasn't designed for the low-slung Rover 2000.

It was half an hour's bumpy ride since they had left the main road and Billy McKee felt bilious and irritable. The front wheels hit another pot-hole, and the chassis bottomed again with a teeth tingling grind. He swallowed hard, glancing at his companions for an indication that they shared his discomfort. He felt annoyed that Doherty next to him and Martin McGuiness beside the driver saw no reason to curtail their heated discussions, despite the fact that their heads were frequently jarred against the roof as the car climbed the pitted track.

McGuiness was explaining: "You can see why they chose this spot. Even in the height of summer the tourists are few and far between. And they rarely leave their cars."

Eamon Doherty nodded appreciatively, his eyes scanning the bleak Galway countryside. "Hikers could be a problem come June."

"No. McClatcher reckons we'll be fully operational by

then. We're closin' it anyway in a few days and going onto a new site. I've suggested we start a gymnasium somewhere during the summer. At least it'll keep the lads fit when they're not operational."

The Rover hit another rut and McKee bounced violently in his seat. "How much farther?" he demanded, feeling the acid aftertaste of the cheese and stout lunch they'd eaten earlier. "This road isn't fit for a mule, let alone a car."

"We could have walked, sir," Doherty reminded pointedly.

McKee grunted. "Don't tell me we can't run to a jeep?"

Doherty replied: "McClatcher's group have got three, but they're all in use. He refused to send one to meet us."

Again McKee grunted. "'Bout time he knew who's running this show."

Doherty just managed to restrain a grin. "I think he knows."

"We're nearly there," consoled McGuiness.

Even as he spoke the Rover reached the peak of the track and started the gentle downhill run to the old friary. As they approached, the flat gleam of Lough Corrib shone through the mist that drifted across the small peninsula. A glimmer of sunlight shed an etching line of shadow around the undulations in the turf, highlighting the weather-worn stone walls in bold relief.

Here and there the rolling shades of green were broken by jutting outcrops of rock, like balding brown skulls amid the turf and gorse.

As the driver applied the brakes, McKee sighed with relief, thankful for the opportunity to get out into the surprisingly mild air. He frowned as he scanned the deserted landscape. The only sign of movement was a hawk drifting on an outstretched span of wing, circling lazily above the range of boulder-strewn hills in the distance. Nearby a flock of sheep appeared almost stationary, nibbling contentedly. A lone bleat reverberated forlornly across the quiet waters of the lough.

Suddenly McKee said: "You sure this is the right place, Chief? 'Countryside round here all looks much of a sameness. That friary hasn't been inhabited for years by the look of things."

McGuiness and Doherty exchanged glances. The ex-paratrooper had been let in on the secret. He couldn't conceal his admiration for the cheek and style of the Chief of Northern Command.

"I just hope our Brit friends think the same way," McGuiness replied. He extracted a whistle from the pocket of his raincoat and put it to his lips. Twice the shrill whistle blasted, its vibrant echo lingering in the air, fading slowly.

McKee glanced around, suddenly alarmed. "If this is some sort of ..."

The words died on his lips in disbelief. Even as he watched figures materialised out of open countryside, growing slowly like trees or shrubs. He gasped audibly as he realised that every clump of grass and bush had concealed a man, each expertly camouflaged with material and sprigs of vegetation. It was only possible to distinguish them when they moved.

Panic seized McKee. He never carried a 'short' and for once he cursed the empty pocket of his overcoat. It was an ambush. By the Army. An Army—but British or Irish? The thoughts raced through his mind.

His mouth fell open as a section of the bare, flinty track just a few feet in front of the car yawned open and two hooded figures peered out, each pointing an Armalite rifle.

He let his shoulders relax. They were completely surrounded. He would never have believed it possible. There were forty men if there was one.

His head turned quickly as he heard McGuiness laugh. "Don't worry, sir. These are *our* lads. Just a little dem-onstration for your benefit."

McKee felt the anger rising, replacing the numbing fear that had paralysed his thoughts and actions. "You'd better have a good explanation for this!"

The younger man was ignoring him, still smiling, as he looked towards the old friary and the two large figures who had emerged from the rough stone archway. Both wore military-cut green shirts and trousers. Only as they approached the car, saluting casually, did McKee recognise Earl Lee McClatcher and Winston Loveday.

"Thanks, Colonel," McGuiness said, anxious to prevent McKee from launching into his usual battery of verbal broadsides. "I think we all appreciated that display. Didn't we, sir?"

McKee grunted, turning up his coat-collar. Now his sense of priorities had returned, he was anxious that none of the armed men surrounding him should be able to identify him at some future date. He indicated to McGuiness and Doherty to do the same.

McClatcher said brightly: "I'm glad you liked the show of force, Mr McKee. An' believe me, them bastards is as mean as they look. They kin handle anything the British can throw at 'em. Later we'll show you. But first if you'd come up to the old monastery we'll give you some chow and some good news." He turned to Loveday. "Okay, Sergeant, get the men dispersed. We'll give a combat demo in about an hour. Okay?"

"Yessir!" The Negro snapped to attention, threw a sharp salute, and strode off calling the men into line.

McGuiness found his bemusement replaced with a profound sense of surprise. He was impressed.

He could sense, too, that McKee and Doherty found it hard to comprehend that the obedient, quick-moving group of armed men around them were just a rag-tag collection of Provisional gunmen and bombers a few weeks previously. They could almost have been watching an exercise on Salisbury Plain, as the men fell into line and marched off in a perfect column, with Loveday at their head.

Twenty minutes later the Army Council members had been shown around the crumbling friary that served as a headquarters. One cell had been stuffed with electronic gadgetry, and the bank of monitor screens, which plotted movement throughout the peninsula, had suitably impressed everyone.

McClatcher explained that they had installed a mix of remote control television cameras, seismic sensors and listening devices over much of the five square miles, from the edges of the lough to where the base of the promontory reached the mainland road.

"I guess we've all main approaches covered," McClatcher conceded confidently. "We were monitoring yer movements all the way up the track. I'll show you a video tape later if we've time."

McGuiness said: "I think we ought to break the latest news."

The American allowed himself a slow smile. Without rushing he lit a cigar butt and blew a ring of smoke. He wasn't displeased when the draught from the makeshift tarpaulin roof drifted the pungent cloud directly at McKee.

Stuff you, he thought. This is McClatcher's moment. This is the moment when you choke on your own cynicism. When you realise McClatcher's not as good as his word. He's better.

As McKee's nose wrinkled, the American said: "I'm able to report our first successful strikes against your buddies of the Special Air Service! In the past fortnight three SAS patrols have come under fire. Severe casualties have been inflicted. Our teams have also killed or injured fifteen regular troopers."

He waited for the words to sink in. McKee frowned. "I heard that report. Casualties are not even confirmed."

"Shit!" McClatcher snapped. He was angry. This was not the reaction he wanted. "Complete crap! Listen, man, you'd better start believin' what I tell you, or you 'n' me are goin' to fall OUT!" McKee's cheeks coloured visibly with indignation. Before he could retort, the American continued: "Do you want my sergeant to present you with scalps?"

Quickly McGuiness intervened: "I can verify the colonel's claim, sir. During the past weeks our own intelligence network in the area has improved dramatically with his help."

"I can also tell you that yer own security ain't nuthin' to write home about," McClatcher grated. "Our intelligence tells us the SAS already know too much about the FCU and are mountin' an operation to locate us." He jerked his cigar end in the direction of a large map on the wall. "At this moment four SAS men are happily crossing Eire in hot pursuit of Mr Duffy. They'll be here by nightfall."

The Council members exchanged glances.

Tersely McKee asked: "What happens now, Colonel?"

The American stamped a heavy boot on the cigar butt he dropped on the flagged floor. "As we were anticipatin' such action, we've had our men watchin' fer SAS groups tailin' our new recruits on border crossings. At this moment two of our people are keepin' an eye on them. When the moment is right, they will be eliminated. And you can actually have your scalps."

McKee nodded. Carefully he eyed the bank of monitor screens, watching the driver of the Rover smoking surreptitiously, unaware he was under surveillance. "I hand it to you, McClatcher. You've done well. I had my doubts, but you've proven McGuiness's confidence in you was well justified." Praise indeed.

The young Provo commander felt pleased. This operation promised to be the highlight of his career. Once the story spread, his name would become even more of a legend than it already was. Only from now on the Brit bastards would tread more warily when dealing with his men. Treat his name with a little more reverence and respect. And within the organisation his word would be sacrosanct. Amongst the rank and file his followers would be legion— with the loyalty normally earned only by martyrs.

This was only the beginning. Twenty-four hours after its next victims were caught, the friary campsite would disperse, all signs of its very existence gone. Then, in a month or so, things would start to happen in Armagh, in Belfast, in Newry, in Londonderry. His squad would go on the offensive, quiet and deadly, fired by their early successes.

Even now he had laid plans with McClatcher and the big Negro. Some in embryo; some quite detailed. The American was a genius.

In the past many brilliant plans had gone wrong. So many 'own goals' had been scored, the term laughingly given when a bomber shot his bolt. So many well-conceived campaigns had backfired. And always because of the calibre of his men. Now it would be different.

Sabotage on an unprecedented scale. Army surveillance teams dropping like nine-pins. The FCU would strike like phantoms out of the darkness. Set-up after set-up. It would be a blood-bath.

The Brits would have to draft in the whole Rhine Army. And even then they wouldn't cope. Not with two hundred of McClatcher's privates to deal with!

Then, inevitably, the Brit withdrawal.

Martin McGuiness stepped out into the mid-afternoon sunlight that bathed the loughside in a subdued light from the shredding cloud cover. McKee was impressed and he followed the small party to the mound of high ground from where they were to watch the display of armed and un-armed combat.

But his mind was thinking beyond the present leaders of the Army Council. To the inevitable time of the Brit withdrawal. No doubt the final act would be heavily disguised with artificial objectives and official pronounce-ments. Just like President Nixon's 'Vietnamisation' before the Yanks finally threw in the towel. Hand the power and military punch back to the people. Get just enough prom-ises to justify the abdication of responsibility. Then get out fast as hell while the going is good.

If it goes wrong then, too bad. Once the Brits left they'd not come back. Not this time.

McKee found it difficult to believe they'd ever get a political settlement, despite his earlier optimism. Now he steered the Army Council with an air of resignation. The attitude of a man who knew what had to be done, but no longer knew how long it would take or if it would ever succeed. His blind faith had gone unquestioned. It was the blindness of one who did not want to see.

But McGuiness knew different.

He knew things would change. History proved it. A solution would be found and he intended to be ready when it did. He had seen McKee age, seen the hatred and bitterness of failure gnaw away at him. When the time came, freshness of approach and a fist of steel would be required. Maybe the fiery Communist, Gerry Adams.

McGuiness knew that the strange forged friendships between the hardliners of the Provisional and Protestant gangs in the prison of Long Kesh had sparked a new hope. A new aim. A new symbol of unity.

Not of a united Ireland. Not now. But of an independent Ulster. This was the ever-growing battlecry of all the hardline socialist factions. United by a common enemy: the Brits.

McGuiness knew it would come, because it was the only option the Brits hadn't tried. It was the only one that had support from extremists on both sides. A small following now, but growing with the speed of bindweed. And giving off a heady fragrance.

Unknown to many, the Catholic population of Ulster was no longer significantly smaller than the Protestant. As job discrimination had been removed, Irish Catholics no longer emigrated in vast numbers to seek a living wage across the water. But more Protestants did, uncertain and concerned at what the future held. In the schools now there were more Roman Catholic children than Protestant. Strange that, but true. In thirty years, or even less, the tide would be completely reversed.

McGuiness watched the group of men running steadily up from the shore-line of the lough, pounding along in powerful, united strides as they prepared for their display.

Tomorrow it would be the real thing.

McGuiness felt suddenly cold. When Independent Ulster came he would be ready. Ready with the most ruthless, best-trained private army the British Isles had ever witnessed. Ready to seize power and control from any other group in the political running.

High above the hawk still circled, silent, watchful and menacing. Waiting its moment.

He turned his head, looking north-east across the flat waters of the lough to where he knew his latest prey was moving inexorably into his web.

Somewhere out there. Four men in a car.

Dave Forbes was enjoying himself.

It had been some years since he had owned a motor-cycle and, as he relaxed astride the powerful machine, he recalled the leaves he had spent with Elaine touring Europe. They were pleasant memories, warm and sunny with the carefree joy of youth. It was strange, he reflected, how the bad moments were shut out by an invisible barrier in the mind. Only with effort did you look beyond it; too painful.

He throttled back, allowing the Zephyr to edge ahead beyond the next bend.

There was little traffic on the road. So unlike Ulster or the mainland; here life ran at its own easy pace. Always time to pass the day; no rush, no urgent needs, no over-bearing demands. Even the people here seemed friendly. Curious to see a British visitor, but rarely hostile. It was the air. It slowed you down, its soporific effect seeping into your bloodstream like alcohol. Drowsy, lazy. Every-thing can be done tomorrow. Have another Guinness—you've time to wait for it to be slowly poured; time to savour it. Today's too good a day for cares and worries.

He glanced down at his watch. 1500 hours.

It was two hours since the truck had pulled into the roadside cafe. Tom Perrot had turned the Zephyr into a layby where the rest of the team had stopped and attacked their rations eagerly. After the night of hard activity appetites were not easily satisfied. Certainly not with K-rations.

Forbes had gone onto the cafe, parked near to the truck, and strolled in to order roast lamb, potatoes and cabbage. The oily gravy wasn't extra. The customers were mostly lorry-drivers and local workmen. Some ate quietly, reading papers or magazines. Others chatted in small groups, laughing between mouthfuls of food. Two men worked silently and without humour at the fruit-machine.

Dumping the crash-helmet on a spare chair, he had seated himself at a table opposite Duffy.

It was the nearest he had ever been to the man he had hunted years before. He was hardly recognisable as the face in the flat, over-lit mug shots he had seen that time in the operations room at Ebrington. It was hard to imagine that the sandy-haired man with the freckles who was laughing with his mates just ten feet away was really 'Big Dick'. The long, lanky frame, awkwardly sprawled in the chair, seemed too clumsy; the face too young.

Difficult to believe, thought Forbes, this was the bomber who had eluded them for so long, the smart-arse who had wreaked so much havoc in Derry and always managed to get away with it. Even the raid on the Smugglers' Inn, the notorious Provo meeting place at Cladby. He had even got out of that. Through the lavatory window and a three hundred yard sprint to the border. Some berk had spent so much time calling out the Yellow Card routine that 'Big Dick' got over the frontier. Untouchable.

And after all those months of effort. Forbes stabbed at the meat on his plate, finding it hard to keep his angry gaze from the man opposite.

This time, bastard, you've had it. The pilgrims are after you. Sitting opposite. It was a nice try though, the school-house and the builders' truck. Typical 'Big Dick' Duffy. Slippery.

By rights you should be dead now. If this was Aden or Malaya ... Not to worry. This pilgrim's got his finger on you. You've blown your last bang.

Duffy's companions, two men in their late thirties, were looking anxiously at their watches, but the other man waved aside their words. He ordered more tea.

What makes you tick, bastard?

What makes someone like you blow up a factory or a shop? Do you care if the warning comes too late and people get killed and maimed? Do you ever think what it's like to see your whole life stretched out before you and know you've got to finish the course with a limb missing? Sometimes all four.

Do you know what it's like to make love to a woman with no legs? Can you share her shame, her humility? Or what it feels like to know there's so much shrapnel in you the doctors will never find it all?

Do you feel remorse? Go to the confessional and beg forgiveness, then brag about it in the Smugglers'?

You nearly got me once too, 'Big Dick', didn't you?

Forbes drained his tea, remembering the patrol at company strength that nearly caught the Provo bomber two years before. He had been attached to Three Platoon, B Company of the Queen's operating with the big Scottish Colour Sergeant, guiding and advising.

Forbes had seen it coming, but only just. Too late to save the Scotsman as he passed the freshly-painted, white house front. From the alleyway opposite Duffy would have had to be blind to miss the silhouette.

Colour was back in England now, in some home or other. Forbes had visited him once, but there had been no point. The fearsome head wound had left the man without the powers of coherent speech and without control of his body. But Forbes knew from the sad, alert eyes that the Scotsman understood every word he said. Try as he might, Forbes couldn't even recall the Colour's name.

He was pleased when Duffy left the cafe, because his anger had risen to boiling point and it was difficult to contain. The Irishman had stopped for a few minutes at the coinbox in the entrance hall before joining his impatient companions. Outside the air was fresh and cool. It seemed to blow away the filth, ease the fury.

Now Perrot was ahead again, in the Zephyr with Ducane and Turnbull, keeping a safe mile behind Duffy's truck. Leaving Forbes alone with his thoughts, free to enjoy the rolling farmland.

The sharp blast from the hooter made him swerve.

Stupid sod! Forbes veered back into the kerb as the powerful black Triumph sped past, a copper-haired woman passenger mouthing silent obscenities at him like a goldfish through the glass.

He held the machine steady, avoiding the drain-grating that threatened to topple him. The car disappeared fast around the next bend.

Forbes cursed himself, glancing in the stalk-mirror on the handlebars to inspect the clear road behind him. They must have been going a fair lick for him to have missed them. Still, they should have been in his rear view for some seconds before they passed; he should have seen them. A stupid road accident would have been an ignominious way to go!

He was still chiding himself as he rounded the bend to find the black Triumph saloon in front of him. It had slowed to a mere crawl. He jammed hard on the brakes. Ahead, just disappearing over the brow of a hill, he could see the boot of Ducane's Zephyr.

He swore loudly at himself for not having realised earlier. Everyone in Eire drove in a lazy, easy-going way, frequently on the wrong side of the narrow roads, especially during drinking hours. But an angry motorist was a rarity.

He allowed himself to drop a comfortable distance behind, his mind racing to establish the significance of the couple in the Triumph.

Forbes didn't like the answers he got. He remembered Duffy's phone-call from the cafe.

There was little doubt in his mind that the newcomers, having raced to catch the Zephyr, were deliberately hanging back.

His mind went back to the discussions with the Welsh major. Was someone just taking precautions, or was it possible they knew about this mission? He recalled Harper's instinctive feeling of unease. Even a few minutes ago, he would have dismissed the idea. It was crazy, impossible.

But the couple in the Triumph were no figment of the imagination. A smart move. Typical Duffy. Observing the observers. Hunting the hunters.

Shit! Wasn't that supposed to be the whole idea of the stupid Provo plan they'd heard so much about? The whole purpose—to give his regiment some stick.

With a terrifying clarity he realised that the whole scheme could just work. He had not accepted the concept, and he doubted that Ducane had really worked out the possibilities.

The contempt with which the SAS generally treated the hooligans and bullyboys of the Provos and hard-line Proddies could be turned against them. If it was just possible to train a handful. Really train them.

If, and it was a very big *if*. How many men would be killed before GHQ Northern Ireland realised exactly what they were up against?

The thought made him shudder. They could be marked down to be the first. Ducane, Turnbull, Perrot and Big Dave Forbes.

He remembered having seen the county border sign of Galway many miles back. Already they were fully committed. Another thirty miles or so and they would reach the west coast. The Atlantic.

So it had to be soon.

Hardly had this thought entered his mind when he crossed the brow of a hill that fell away to the loughside miles beyond. He could see both the Triumph and Ducane's Zephyr on the ribbon of road that stretched across the rolling heathland. Both looked like toys in the distance, the Triumph slowing as it approached the small collection of houses that strung along both sides of the road.

Nearing the isolated community at low-level the buildings seemed different to those Forbes had glimpsed from his vantage point on the hill. From tiny model dwellings on a diorama they had developed a life-size character of their own.

The buildings looked tired and weather-worn from the constant Atlantic breezes that blew across Galway, gathering strength over the lough. The total lack of pedestrians added to the sense of desolation and weariness, faded and forgotten by the outside world.

The black Triumph had pulled into the side of the road outside a dilapidated garage forecourt beneath a row of ancient, overhead davit pumps.

Farther down the street, the Zephyr had pulled into the shallow parking recess outside a confectioners-cum-guest house which boasted the inevitable bar. From a concealed spot in a layby at the edge of the village, Forbes narrowed his eyes as he sought a sign of the builders' lorry. He could see nothing. Someone climbed out of the Zephyr. He thought it was Ducane, but at that distance it was impossible to be sure.

He sniffed the air. It smelt very fresh with just a trace of seasalt. To the south he knew Galway Bay couldn't be far away. High above a seagull cried plaintively, the sound rippling in a mocking echo across the lough. In the far distance a large bird of prey hovered menacingly over a rocky peninsula of land.

He shivered involuntarily and returned his gaze to the deserted village. The passengers of the Triumph had made no attempt to leave their vehicle; still no one had approached to see if they required service.

Perhaps this was the end of the journey? Somewhere around this barren and rocky heathland? Or in the steep hills flexed like hard granite muscle amongst the undulating grey-green flesh? Somewhere, half-hidden in the veil of mist, their target must lie. Unnoticed by the world at large.

There could be worse places to site it, he reasoned. And if Ducane had halted because Duffy's truck had stopped, then he must quickly satisfy himself that he was right about the Triumph.

He kicked the motor-cycle into life and moved down the road. He pulled in across the front of the parked Triumph. Slowly he dismounted and flicked down the prop-stand with his heel. Then he strolled across to the driver's door of the car. The man inside looked irritated. His eyes were bright and blue, fierce almost, an effect heightened by the ruddy complexion and wild ginger beard and whiskers. His thick matching eyebrows were half-hidden by a soft chequered fishing hat.

In Gaelic, Forbes said: "Good day to you, friend. 'Nearly had me off my bike back there."

Not bad, he thought to himself. Pity I don't find Russian this easy.

Unable to hear, the man wound down his window angrily. The woman passenger, her long copper hair restrained by a floral scarf, ignored him completely, raising herself in the seat to see over the motorcycle that now blotted her view of Ducane's Zephyr. She was probably in her late thirties and had been pretty once, thought Forbes, and fiery. But, like her companion, she'd grown bitter. It was hard to imagine that those thin, compressed lips had ever smiled; her eyes were a shade of pale green, lacklustre. Forbes guessed she drank heavily. That would explain the rolls of fat that were beginning to disfigure a once-good shape. In a few years she would be a hag. Twisted with hatred. Frustrated and useless to everyone.

The man's ginger whiskers twitched in annoyance as he spoke. "What?"

Forbes beamed at him. "Good day to you friend." Again in Gaelic.

The man sighed impatiently. "Can't you speak English?" he demanded.

Christ, Forbes thought, I'm more bloody Irish than he is and you could cut his accent with a chain-saw it was so thick.

"I was sayin'. You nearly had me off my bike back there. But it was my fault. Wandering all over the shop. 'Sorry if I gave you a shock—drivin' in front of you like that . . ."

The man looked irritable. The tiny veins on his ruddy face became more noticeable. "Think nothin' of it, mister."

Forbes leaned across to the woman, who continued to look straight ahead at Ducane's Zephyr.

She said tightly out of the corner of her mouth. "For God's sake, Bill, get *rid* of him!"

"Now, look here . .!" began the man.

Forbes beamed again. "Just bein' friendly, m'am. 'You here on business? It's a bit quiet here for business." He

215

paused. " 'You travellers? You know, reps."

"We're on holiday," replied the man impatiently.

Forbes said quickly: "Coincidence. I'm on holiday too. You stopped to find a place t'stay? Let's try that guest house."

He could almost hear the woman's teeth grating. She exchanged glances with her companion. He shrugged.

Forbes smiled. He had seen Young Tom and Turnbull start to take the luggage out of the Zephyr's boot, and in through the front door. Something was up.

He restarted his motor-cycle and allowed the Triumph to follow him across the narrow street, careful not to give the vehicle passing space until he had stopped alongside the Zephyr.

As the couple climbed out, Forbes said: "Let me buy you a drink, seein' as how we seem to be fellow travellers."

The woman smiled unconvincingly. "I'm *very* tired."

"Later maybe," grunted the man, extracting a small overnight case from the back seat.

Young Tom clattered out of the front door to the Zephyr. The sergeant saw his eyes flicker in surprise. But it was only a fleeting sign of recognition. He whistled softly as he retrieved the fourth holdall.

He then appeared to notice the three of them for the first time. "Hello, folks," he said brightly. "If you're planning on stopping, I think you're in luck. Only six rooms, but it's out-of-season."

Forbes sighed in silent relief. He was pleased Perrot hadn't attempted the Irish accent. Languages weren't his strong point.

"English?" asked the woman. Her voice sounded like crushed glass. Although she spoke with a smile you could detect the hatred without difficulty.

Young Tom inclined his head. "Yes. I'm on a trip with a friend and my old Irish uncle!"

Don't overdo it, lad, cringed Forbes. Ducane was the other linguist in the team, and he didn't seem to fit the role.

"Let's go inside," Forbes suggested.

★

"Have they started the holiday season early this year?"

The young girl laughed at her own joke, as she served out the drinks in the spartan bar. Her hair was auburn, framing a cheerful freckled face, making her look younger than her twenty-five years.

As she pulled a pint of bitter for Forbes he noticed her muscular arms, white and with a rash of freckles to match her face. Well-rounded, even plumpish. Nice, thought Forbes appreciatively, as he wetted his lips at the sight of the frothing glass.

"No, my beauty, we've come for some ski-ing on the Galway mountains!" He chuckled loudly, turning to the Irish couple who had reluctantly succumbed to his insistence that he should make amends for his careless driving. The man was in no mood to share the humour, but the woman allowed herself an ingratiating smirk.

"You're in luck," the girl said, lifting the guest-book from under the bar. "Are you all together?"

"No," the woman said sharply.

"I see," the girl said, unsure of the sudden hostility. "We've just let two of our doubles. There's only one left. A bit small. And a single ..."

"The double will do," the woman said quickly.

"What's the single like?" Forbes asked, smirking.

"Small enough for *one*," the girl replied mischievously. She twisted the guest-book around for the couple to sign.

Forbes glanced carelessly over the man's shoulder. *Mr & Mrs William Kelly*. As he laboriously wrote out the address, the sergeant glanced around the bleak, yellow walls, broken only by cheap prints of the Galway landscape. Turnbull and Young Tom were seated together at a plastic-topped table over a couple of drinks.

Two elderly men, one in a flat cap and collarless shirt, sat in the corner. Obviously they were companions, but neither spoke, both content to idly watch. Ruminate. They thought they'd seen the last of the foreigners coming to trample over their farmland this year.

There was no sign of Ducane.

"Is there a telephone we can use?" the woman asked the girl.

"On the landing upstairs. A public phone."

The woman looked at her husband and inclined her head towards the stairway at the back of the bar. He picked up the room-key and followed her obediently.

As they disappeared, Forbes crossed quickly over to his companions. "What's happening?" he demanded in a low voice.

Turnbull said: "The truck driver dumped Duffy and another one. They set off on foot. The boss is following. Don't get too comfortable, we may have to move quickly."

Forbes nodded, turning over the facts in his mind. They were in a remote spot suitable for the rumoured camp. It would make sense if it was inaccessible by road.

"Who're your two friends?" Young Tom asked.

The sergeant glanced quickly around the bar to check that no one was within earshot. One of the old boys was staring blankly at him. He smiled back with a wave of his hand.

Lowering his voice still further, he said: "We've got ourselves a tail."

"Those two upstairs?" Young Tom asked.

Forbes nodded.

"Christ!" Turnbull hissed. "This could mean we've been set-up. Are you certain about them?"

"I wouldn't stake my life on it," Forbes replied. "But I'd stake yours ... Yes, I'm sure.

"Those two jokers are goin' to make a call. I'd feel happier in my bed tonight if no one knew where we were." He looked at Turnbull. "You come up with me. Perrot, you stay here and make sure we don't get disturbed for five minutes."

Young Tom looked alarmed. "How can I stop anyone? What if the barmaid wants to go up?"

Forbes looked at the ceiling. "Use your initiative. Chat her up. You'll think of something."

Without further delay the sergeant mounted the steps, Turnbull close behind with one of the holdalls.

Upstairs the door of the first room on the left was ajar, and the man in the fishing-hat could be seen attending to the small travelling case. At the end of the landing the copper-haired woman was busy thumbing through a notebook, her handbag open on the table by the wall-mounted telephone.

Forbes indicated the door. Turnbull nodded.

The woman was cursing low under her breath as she attempted to dial whilst juggling with the notebook. Her struggle was made more difficult as Forbes' large hand closed over hers, forcing the handset onto its rest.

"Hello, my beauty," he said.

"What the ..."

As she gaped at him in surprise with her hands full, Forbes quickly dabbed a handkerchief into her open mouth. She fell back against the wall, choking in a muffled cough. Her notepad dropped to the floor.

Roughly the sergeant spun her round, jerked her hands up behind her back and snapped on a pair of Plasticuffs. He pushed her across the hall and into the open door, stooping to pick up the notebook as he followed her.

"One squeak out of you, darling, and it'll be your last."

The bearded man had lost his fishing hat. He was sprawled face-down on the bed and insisted on kicking his legs violently as Turnbull attempted to bind them with pyjama cord, despite the fact he, too, was handcuffed.

"You're too nice," Forbes muttered disapprovingly, and hit the man over the back of the neck with a bunched fist. There was a painful gasp.

Turnbull looked up at the sergeant. "Clever sod, now he's gone and coughed out his gag!"

But the man had lost his will to fight. After a few moments the two Provisionals were sitting side by side on the end of the bed: the man moaning at his headache; the woman eyeing them malevolently.

"Okay," Forbes said quietly. "Let's have your name, rank and number and no one will get hurt."

He removed the lipstick-covered handkerchief from the woman's mouth.

The abuse came out in a violent tirade. "You fucking Brit pig! 'Might have known, you pissing, sodding shit . . !"

The crack of Forbes' knuckles across her mouth made Turnbull wince. The sudden silence was absolute.

"Listen, you stupid hag," Forbes spat. "I've been in West Belfast and I've heard all that filth before from hard-bitten bags even worse than you. So stow it!"

He stood up, his cheeks white with anger. Forbes had a simple affection for women of all shapes and sizes, but one thing he could not stand was women debasing themselves with gutter language. His ideals were simple. Women should be clean and pure in mind and body. It didn't matter how stupid they were, or often how ugly. He could overlook these things if they were ready and willing.

He said patiently: "Let's try again, sweetheart."

"Fuck off!" she said with feeling. "I don't know what you're talking about."

Turnbull said: "You and your gentleman friend here were both carrying guns. Not the usual practice for law-abiding citizens in Eire, is it? So cut the innocence and let's have your names for starters."

The man was looking wildly at the woman, his bright blue eyes bulging with effort as he tried to gurgle words through his gag.

"Ah," Forbes said. "Looks like your boyfriend has something to say."

He pulled the gag from the man's mouth. "Don't say a word! We'll be dead if you do!"

Forbes snorted. "You'll be dead if you don't!" He looked down at the man, then recalling their signatures in the register, added: "Now, c'mon, Mr Kelly, tell us a bit about yourself . . ."

The face went a deeper shade of red. "How d'you know my name?" he demanded.

"Oh, we know a lot about you, Mr Kelly. Like your lady friend here . . ."

"My wife!" Kelly snapped.

Turnbull shook his head sadly. "Try again." He was

leafing through the woman's notebook. "It says here, this book belongs to Clare Flynn ..."

"You stupid cow!"

"Tut-tut," Forbes said. "That's no way to talk to your wife."

At that moment Young Tom came in. "Finished?"

Turnbull said: "Shut the door. Any sign of the boss?"

The young soldier shook his head.

The corporal said: "Tom, I want you to go downstairs and find out from that barmaid if there are any other hotels or guesthouses in the area. Get the name of one of them, right?"

Young Tom looked puzzled.

"What you thinkin'?"

Turnbull waved the notebook at him. "We'd better finish that phone-call for Miss Flynn here, before someone starts getting worried. We'll tell them we're staying somewhere else. You know, just in case."

Forbes frowned. "There's probably a codeword."

Turnbull waved the book in triumph. "There is: *Orange Disorder* by the look of it ..."

"Stupid bloody cow!" Kelly growled again.

The woman looked white, her lips beginning to swell.

Forbes laughed. "I guess that's what you call the Paddy Factor."

As he went out of the door, Young Tom was smiling to himself.

"Reckon you can impersonate Clare Flynn's voice?" Turnbull asked.

Forbes leered at her. "I wouldn't insult the lady. But I can manage him."

He stooped to pick up the square of white card that had slipped from the notebook as Turnbull waved it.

"What is it, Sarge?"

For a moment he didn't answer. He was staring closely at a poor print of a photograph he recognised. The furrows deepened on his forehead.

"A snapshot," he said slowly. "From the boss's family album."

CHAPTER 12

Winston Loveday strolled into McClatcher's flag-stoned cell, grinning broadly. "Looks like they've come home t'roost, Earl."

The other man looked up from the bunk where he sprawled untidily with a half-empty whiskey bottle. His eyes were sunken and red-rimmed with tiredness, his face drawn with the tension of waiting. Failure to locate the SAS hit team would mean the certain loss of the contract from the PIRA Army Council.

As the Negro's words sunk in, the gaze in the deep blue eyes sharpened, and his teeth gleamed white against his tanned, unshaven face.

"Thank Christ fer that," he breathed.

Loveday sat himself on the edge of the bunk, recoiling as he caught the odour of stale whiskey. "Dammit, Earl, it's a bit early to celebrate, ain't it?"

Earl eyed him coldly for a moment, then dismissed the rebuke he was about to mouth. Things were looking up. In a sudden violent movement he sat up, swinging his legs over the edge of the bed.

He plucked a fresh cigar from his tunic and lit it quickly. His voice was hoarse when he spoke. "I wasn't celebratin' nothin', Winston. Just gettin', morose and itchy. It's bin a long wait—with at least half a million bucks restin' on the outcome."

He offered the bottle to Loveday who declined with a shake of his head. "Well, rest easy. I've just had a report from Kelly. Phoned in to confirm they've arrived and the message got to me by RT not five minutes ago."

McClatcher frowned. "Codewords?"

222

Loveday nodded, waving his hand. "No sweat. All AOK."

"Took his bloody time."

The Negro grinned at the other's impatience. McClatcher was a goer all right. Determined to make it to the top no matter what the cost. While he was content with a beer and a broad and a pocketful of bread, McClatcher wouldn't be satisfied until he had a private estate in Florida, an ocean yacht and his personal Learjet.

"He had to be sure they'd holed up for the night. Didn't wanna raise any false hopes."

"Where are they?"

"Dalmeny Farm. 'Bout fifteen miles down the road from the village. Seems they're posin' as tourists. The place does bed 'n' breakfast."

McClatcher climbed to his feet and moved across to the map pinned on the wall. He peered at it closely.

"That's a long way from where Duffy was dropped by the lorry. 'You had Kelly's story checked out?"

"I got Malone an' Reagan to go down in one of the jeeps to confirm Ducane's car is there. We've had reports that someone is followin' Duffy up here to the camp. If that's so, we should pick something up on the camera shortly."

McClatcher rubbed his chin thoughtfully. "Okay, Winston, gimme five minutes to freshen up an' I'll join you in the surveillance room."

"Yessir," the Negro said and made quickly for the door.

Alone again McClatcher took a final gulp of whiskey and poured some fresh cold water into a bucket in the corner. He began to feel better as he quickly drew the razor through the tough stubble on his face.

He was reasonably satisfied that everything was going to plan. Ever since his lucky break when he had telephoned Pattie Ducane a couple of days earlier, and she had tried to buy him off with information she had overheard, he had been expecting some of his new recruits to be tailed over the border. The news had not surprised him, as the FCU had been making its presence felt in Ulster. But the speed of the SAS reaction did. So did the good fortune of Ducane's unexpected leave and the fact that Pattie had been able to gather so much detail on how the operation would be mounted. The fact that Ducane and Forbes would be on the mission was another unexpected bonus. Having worked with them in 'Nam he knew their strengths—and that would be their biggest weakness.

McClatcher had been harbouring only one private fear, although that danger seemed to have passed.

The lush Clare Flynn and her boyfriend Kelly were dedicated Republicans, but were blinded by hate and irrational behaviour. They weren't the ideal choice to pick up anyone tailing Duffy, but they were the only experienced people the PIRA had in the area of the border crossing.

McClatcher was relying on picking up Ducane's team before they had a chance of locating the camp site and relaying the position back to GHQ in Ulster. If Flynn and Kelly gave the game away, Ducane would be on his guard, could go to ground, complete his surveillance, and have a large-scale deep-penetration raid organised by a full SAS squadron.

In its capacity as the strike-arm of the intelligence services, McClatcher had no doubts that the Special Air Service was quite capable of mounting such a deadly large-scale operation at very short notice. In fact he knew from Pattie that the necessary contingency plans had already been laid.

He felt pleased as he slid the fresh tunic over his shoulders. He would personally ensure that Ducane's team got no closer, and the thoughts of action again gave him a dull thrill deep in his gut. Afterwards he'd present the Army Council with the SAS men's ears.

As he buttoned his tunic he felt the familiar stiffness in the fingers of his right hand. Over the years he had become so used to it that it caused him no more concern than a mild irritation, but now he recalled vividly the moment in the Vietnamese village when Ducane's foot had crushed his fingers into the ground, breaking the small bones in a dozen places.

Ever since the SAS man, then a Second Lieutenant, had been seconded to the Green Berets at Fort Bragg there had been no love lost between them. Forbes had been all right, he remembered, accepting the punishment McClatcher had dealt out to suspected VC sympathisers without a word. Ducane had been insensed on many occasions and had finally acted in the quiet riverside hamlet.

McClatcher and three cronies had a girl in one of the huts. She was about fifteen. Perhaps younger, it was hard to tell with Gooks. The American had been convinced she had deliberately led two Berets into a booby-trap ambush, which had cost one his life and the other both his legs. They had the girl stripped naked, and McClatcher was going to be the first to rape her.

Speaking in a low voice, Ducane had calmly told the four men to leave her alone. They had ignored him, until his foot had shot like a bolt into the side of McClatcher's head, sending him sprawling into the array of clay kitchen-pots. The American, staggering under the blow, had reached for the combat knife which lay by his discarded clothes. It was then that Ducane had lunged with his booted foot, grinding McClatcher's fingers into the hard, cracked earth.

The other soldiers had pounced swiftly, two of them holding the Englishman back while a third pummeled his stomach with hard right-handed jabs. Then Forbes had burst in, his rifle held low and steady. He had undoubtedly saved Ducane's life.

Afterwards they'd all tried to make light of it, but things had never been the same. And McClatcher had never brought himself to forgive the Englishman for the weeks of pain that followed.

He finished securing the buttons and stood upright before the mirror. Slowly he grimaced. He had not forgotten the incident and as he got older, the increasing rheumatic soreness in his right hand served as an almost constant reminder.

When he had been released from the military hospital in Saigon he had heard about the girl. Later she had proudly and defiantly told her captors that she had deliberately lured the two soldiers into the booby-trapped clearing.

No one knew what had become of her.

"It's there all right," Ducane said, lighting a cigarette.

He and Forbes were sitting in the small, single bedroom the sergeant had booked, whilst Young Tom and Turnbull guarded William Kelly and the woman.

"What happened?" Forbes asked.

Ducane exhaled a stream of smoke. "I sauntered up this cart track, doing my best to look like a tourist on a walking holiday. Obviously I couldn't go prancing around hiding behind bushes, and when Duffy began running I just had to let him go." He lifted the curtain and looked out at the lough. It was almost dark and a strong wind had whipped up small frothy crests of the wavelets that rushed into the shingle shore. "Duffy sprinted through a screen of trees, and when I got there I was confronted by some fella in plus-fours with a loaded shotgun."

"A farmer?"

"That was the idea." Ducane smiled. "I was told politely but firmly that there had been an outbreak of foot-and-mouth disease, and the entire peninsula had been sealed off until the agricultural ministry gave clearance."

Forbes nodded. "That's what the lassie in the bar told me, too. They've been putting about the story for the benefit of inquisitive locals. Anyway, what did you do then?"

Ducane shrugged. "There wasn't much I could do. I took a stroll across the base of the peninsula. About three miles altogether. And the one time I tried to cross the boundary again, another farm-hand popped out of the bushes and waved me away."

"They've done a pretty thorough job then?"

"They have. Not only manpower, but I reckon they've got some sort of surveillance system operating. There's no way they could have had me in view on the second occasion without one."

"Tricky," Forbes said, joining Ducane by the window. Dusk was settling around the outcrop of rock far out on the lough. It began to blur, melting into a purple murk. Suddenly it looked very menacing.

Ducane turned away. "Shut the curtains, Dave, that place is starting to give me the creeps." He sat down in the small armchair and stubbed out the half-smoked cigarette in the ashtray. "And tell me what's been happening this end?"

Quickly Forbes explained that they had found telephone numbers and code-words in Clare Flynn's diary and that he had phoned in, assuming William Kelly's voice. The person at the other end of the line had given no indication that he doubted the message when he was informed that the SAS team had booked into a farm down the road. Young Tom had already taken the Zephyr down there and left it at the side of the road. Short of actually visiting the farm and questioning the occupants, the story could not be disproved.

"Round one to us," Ducane murmured thoughtfully.

"I'm not so sure, Jacko."

Ducane looked puzzled as he saw the expression on Forbes' face. "We found this on the Flynn woman."

Ducane said nothing as he was handed the photograph. The furrows deepened on his brow as he studied it, mesmerised by the blurred images of his family. Slowly he shook his head, scarcely aware that Forbes was still talking.

". . . I wanted to talk to you alone about this. I don't think the others quite appreciate what it means. I don't know that I do myself."

Ducane's knuckles showed white. Still he stared at it in disbelief.

"I don't know how many copies there are," Forbes

continued. "But I've only ever seen one. In your lounge at home. Unless, of course, someone got hold of the negative . . ."

"Save yourself the effort, Dave. I can tell you where it came from." Ducane was aware of his own words, but they sounded strangely distant. "Someone's been to my home."

"That can't be true, Jacko. There must be another explanation . . ."

Ducane climbed slowly to his feet, staring vaguely in the direction of the bed. "Someone's got at Trish . . ."

"Oh, for Christ's sake . . . !"

Forbes stopped as he saw the look in the captain's eyes. He had known him for a long time. Too long perhaps. Had known him since he was a tough and ruthless new recruit to the Special Air Service, before he had become mellowed by the experience and wisdom learned on countless combat missions. He had not seen that look for many years. And it frightened him.

Slowly Ducane said: "I never gave it a second thought. But you remember who called on Trish the other day?" He pulled out another cigarette and lit it. "A certain Earl Lee McClatcher. Retired US Army Special Forces."

Forbes frowned, uncomprehending. "Yes. Those Yanks we ran across in 'Nam?"

Ducane nodded.

"You don't think he's behind this . . . this . . ."

"I gather he's in the arms business on his own account now."

"McClatcher! Working for the Provos! He'd throw a thousand fits!"

"Even if the money was good enough?"

Forbes sat down heavily on the edge of the bed. He said nothing as his mind pieced together the odd events of the past few days.

At last he said: "Trish would never have told him anything. I'm sure of that."

"Not knowingly. But if he made it sound casual, or . . ." He hesitated. "Gave her a few drinks."

Forbes' eyes flashed. They both knew what he was implying. Forbes could recount several occasions when Trish had become over-amorous with strangers at parties over the years. And he recalled that she had been obviously attracted to the big American all those years before.

"I expect he just got a few snippets of info from her in conversation," Forbes suggested. "And helped himself to the photograph."

"And what else, I wonder?" Ducane's voice was scarcely audible. "Something that could have led to blackmail?"

He moved back to the curtains and thrust them angrily aside. It was now completely dark, only the faint glimmer of starlight giving the surface of the lough a dull satin sheen.

"Do you want to phone her?"

Ducane shook his head. "No. I can't accuse her of anything, without evidence. She mentioned they had drinks in. Maybe she just let a few things slip."

Christ, thought Forbes savagely, I just bet they did.

"Besides being strictly against orders, they've got this place so well buttoned up, they could have the phones tapped."

Forbes said: "Look, Jacko, from what you say, there's no way we're going to get near that peninsula without those bastards knowing. And if we get in they'll just close the doors behind us. Sodding rats in a trap. The Flynn woman says she understands there's up to a hundred of the buggers up there. Let's pull out quick. Tonight. The Old Man will have the boys in within twenty-four hours."

Ducane said quietly: "In twenty-four hours, McClatcher could be a thousand miles from here! Besides the photograph combined with the fact that we've been tailed suggests to me they know all about this mission. If Trish overheard our plans the other night ... If she was scared for Sarah's safety she might have tried to buy them off with information ..."

"Three of us could make sure McClatcher goes nowhere, while you catch the next plane to England."

"Don't be daft Dave. There's no way three of you can

229

prevent McClatcher getting out. The territory's too bloody big. Besides he's as much a pro as you or me. And if you follow that to its logical conclusion, they're already out looking for us. So we don't have long."

"The bastard," Forbes growled, annoyed at his own naive optimism.

Ducane wiped the condensation that was gathering on the window. "Do you remember, Dave, that time in 'Nam?"

Forbes looked up, a half-grin on his face. "'Course I do. You should have stepped on both his sodding hands!"

"I never thought we'd meet again."

"You haven't—yet."

Ducane allowed himself a faint smile.

Suddenly Forbes knew what was going to happen. Despite himself he was aware of the quickening of his pulse, and the dim glow in his belly. He looked up at his companion.

"You're mad, Jacko," he said quietly.

"I'll forget you said that."

"You know damned well we'd never get near the place."

"Since when has that been a deterrent?"

Forbes shook his head slowly.

Ducane said: "Call in the boys. We'll put it to the vote."

Dear Roisin,

I'm not too good at letter writing, but I really felt I had to say that I meant what I said when I last saw you. I'm sure you'll get over your injuries—even though it may take a while. And, however long it takes, you can count on my help. If, of course, you want it.

Shortly I'll be taking R and R back in England and I'd be pleased for you to come and stay for a holiday with my family in Dorset. I'm sure my mother would be delighted to meet you. A real break away from all your problems will help you get well, I'm convinced. And please don't think that this is some sort of act of charity. My motives are very selfish.

You laughed when I tried to cheer you up and give you

the courage to fight back by having faith in our regimental motto 'Who Dares Wins'. Well, I must tell you, the lads have their own reply to that—'Who cares who wins!'

And I don't care who wins, either. So long as you win through. You're the only thing I never want to forget about Ulster. I mean that.

Please drop me a note via the sister and say you'll come.

Yours,

Tom.

P.S. Writing to you is better than writing reports any day.

She read it through for the fifth time and shook her head slowly.

Why, in God's name, couldn't he leave her alone. She was a physical and mental wreck. She would probably never be able to lead a normal life again. It would take years to adjust. She just *had* to be alone.

Her eyes trailed across to the withered bunch of forget-me-nots in the bedside vase.

She would need help though. Understanding, but without probing questions. Her mind went slowly through the list of relatives she could stay with. It was hopeless.

Again she picked up the letter. Dorset. DAR-SET. She smiled imagining Tom Perrot in a farmer's straw hat and dungarees.

The door opened.

"Well, hello there," the man in the white coat said. "You must be Roisin McGuire. My name's O'Rourke. Dental surgeon extraordinaire." He extended a long, pale hand.

She hesitated.

"It's okay, Roisin. The most artistic hands in the hospital." He was in his early fifties with iron grey hair and a long, crinkled face. His eyes were kindly. "You look surprised."

"I didn't think teeth rated that highly. Sure, I've plenty other things need fixing."

He grinned at her. "Well now, that's true." The dentist

parked himself on the edge of her bed. "But apparently sister's had a note from a young admirer of yours. A soldier boy who visited you recently."

"Oh?"

"He was quite insistent that here was one young lady who wanted ..." He paused. "Now how does the song go ..? *All she wants for Christmas is her two front teeth.*"

Roisin's jaw dropped in surprise.

"Ah," O'Rourke said. "I see he was right! Very kissable lips but the ol' front tooth would be a distinct improvement."

She blushed.

"We should manage temporary choppers before Christmas, if we try. And some super Hollywood ones soon after." He held her hand. "Your young admirer seems to be a bit of a psychologist."

"Yes."

"To tell the truth, I think sister's taken a bit of a shine to your young man."

"So that's the situation," Ducane concluded. He was still standing by the window overlooking the lough.

Young Tom sat in the small armchair and Turnbull on the edge of the bed. Both had listened in silence while the captain told them as much as he knew. As neither had met Trish, they were in no position to jump to any conclusions other than the fact that she had been tricked into saying too much by an alleged old friend.

"This McClatcher must be a right bastard." It was Young Tom who spoke.

"I've met nicer," Ducane murmured.

"I still can't believe it," Tom said, half to himself.

Turnbull stood up and paced across the room, his head bowed as he turned over the various implications in his mind. At last he said: "Look, boss, you've given us the *situation* as you put it. It's them over there." He nodded towards the window. "On what is, in all probability, a highly-defended peninsula. And us here on the lakeside. As I see it, we've accomplished most of our mission by locating the camp site. I agree we can handle a lot, but sixty bloody Provos might be pushing it a bit far." He grinned without humour, before adding: "Even for us."

Ducane nodded in agreement. "So you're for pulling out? Even though McClatcher and these Provos will probably get away."

"'Goes against the grain," Young Tom admitted.

Turnbull looked down at him sadly. "As I see it, boss, what I think is neither here nor there. You make the decisions around here. You say go and we go."

"That's right," Ducane answered, his voice very quiet. "And I wouldn't hesitate to call off the mission in other circumstances. To take a chance the Old Man can organise a strike fast enough. But as I've just explained, the situation has got a bit personal."

"For you," Turnbull said evenly. "Not for the rest of us."

"Hey, steady on, Corp!" began Young Tom.

Turnbull ignored him. "It's your wife who's been blabbing. Not our mothers, girlfriends or whoever. And she's been blabbing stuff she shouldn't even *know*. Information she could have only got from one source. You!"

Ducane said coldly: "That's right, John. I can't deny that. And I apologise for any danger that it's put you in. But if you ever cared for anyone but yourself, you might find that you too said more than you meant to on some occasions. That sort of thing can happen when you get really close to people and trust them."

Turnbull's cheeks reddened. "I don't have to take that from you! If you're that close to someone you don't tell 'em anything—for their own bloody good."

Young Tom said: "I don't think you understand, Corp."

Turnbull snorted. "I understand all right. Our commanding officer has dropped us in the shit, thanks to his own unprofessional conduct. And now he's appealing to our better nature by having a heart-to-bloody-heart! So he can get himself off the hook. Not only that, but he's adding to the felony, by trying to persuade us to fight his own personal vendetta for him!"

Ducane said quietly: "That's enough, John. I can make no excuses for myself. Nor for my wife. It's a million to one chance that things have worked out this way, but coincidences have a nasty way of happening when you least expect them." He paused. "What I'm saying to you now is that we either go on or turn back. One course is obviously more risky than the other. Either fulfils our orders. But it is a choice that, under the circumstances, I feel I must ask each of you to make individually."

"What did the Sarge say?" Young Tom asked.

"He'll go on."

The young soldier nodded. "I thought so."

"Typical!" Turnbull murmured.

"Then count me in, too."

A silence followed until Ducane asked: "Well, John, if you're turning back, you'd better start now. The sooner you alert the Old Man the better."

Turnbull had dropped down again onto the edge of the bed. He looked up, his eyes squinting at the tall figure by the window. "I never said I was turning back. I don't want this Yankee bastard to get away with it anymore than the rest of you. At least if I come along, there's a chance we won't *all* get killed."

Tom smiled broadly. "Attaboy, Corp."

Turnbull added: "But so help me God, when we get out of here I'm going to make an official complaint at the highest level! Perhaps Perrot and Sergeant Forbes won't mention your wife's involvement—or yours—but I'll make damn sure they know about it. Because I don't think you're fit to be an officer in this regiment."

Ducane said: "Obviously you are perfectly within your rights to do what you think fit, John ..."

"Bloody creep ..!" interjected Young Tom.

"... But," the captain continued, "since you have now decided to bless us with your company, you will keep your mouth firmly *shut*. Especially when it comes to your *personal* opinion about me or how I run this unit. Understood?"

The corporal opened his mouth and shut it again quickly. He shrugged resignedly. "Okay, boss, you've let me make my point. I'll save my complaints for when the mission's over." He stood up suddenly. "Now how are we going to crack this impregnable fortress?"

The rain was falling heavier now, driven inland across the lough, beating hard against the side of the Land Rover which was parked outside the short lane leading to the farmhouse.

McClatcher and Loveday were alone in the vehicle, sitting in the back seats and leaning forward to peer anxiously through the monotonous swipe of the wipers. Opposite they could see the Zephyr pulled up on the grass verge.

"Taking his bloody time," McClatcher muttered irritably.

The Negro shot him a sideways glance. He shared the other man's growing sense of apprehension. There was something about the car that gave it an abandoned look. Surely, Loveday reasoned, if Ducane's men were staying there, they'd have taken it up the drive and parked right outside the farmhouse. Malone had only been gone for a few minutes, but it seemed like a lifetime.

Again McClatcher looked at his watch. "Why Reagan or Malone didn't think to check with the farmer when you first sent them, I don't know."

Loveday chuckled. "I think it's what the Brits call the Paddy Factor."

McClatcher wasn't in the mood to appreciate the joke. "Whatever the reason, Ducane could be a hundred miles from here by now. You'd've thought that stupid bastard would've reasoned there was something odd. Parking on the road when there's plenty of space in the farmyard."

Loveday shrugged. "'Don't necessarily mean nuthin'. After all, we got the coded message from Kelly. So no sweat, man."

The big American grunted. In his own mind he was already fully convinced that the Irish couple had been jumped and that the message was a hoax.

"At last!" breathed McClatcher, as the raincoated figure of Malone trudged along the churned-up drive.

The Irishman opened the door and climbed in, his dark eyes burning like coals beneath the beetle eyebrows.

"The ol' gaffer's not seen anyone," Malone said tersely. "He saw the car parked earlier, but don't know who it belongs to."

"I knew it!" McClatcher pounded a clenched fist into his open palm.

"Slippery motherfuckers," Loveday growled.

"But I think I know where they are," Malone added quickly. "There's a bar down at the village where we turn off for the camp. The ol' boy was down there earlier tonight, and said there were some strangers stayin'. 'E said they sounded like they could be the ones I was lookin' for ..."

McClatcher looked at his watch. "Eleven."

Loveday prodded Malone in the back. "Step on it, Private. Don't sit on yer fanny like a fart in a trance. We gotta go places!"

The Irishman hurriedly put the Land Rover into gear, and, with its wheels spinning over the wet, mud-splattered road, roared off in the direction of the village.

It was an uncomfortable fifteen minute drive to the bar, with the rain-laden wind buffeting the canvas sides as the Land Rover sped on its way. Malone drove nervously and badly, cornering too fast as he heard McClatcher cursing at him from the rear seat. He pulled into the narrow parking space at the bar and thudded to a halt with the assistance of the crumbling brickwork.

"We're getting warm," Loveday observed. "There's Kelly's car."

Hurriedly the three men pushed their way inside, pausing for a moment in the doorway of the empty bar, the rain dripping from their overcoats. The draught scattered the mess from unemptied ashtrays.

"I am sorry, gentlemen. We're just closing down for the night."

McClatcher saw the girl behind the bar and grinned broadly, touching his hat as he strode across to her.

"I'm sorry too, ma'am. It's an inconsiderate time to call. But me an' my friends here just heard you got some visitors. Old friends of ours."

"Oh!" The girl looked bewildered, glancing at Loveday and Malone uneasily. "Oh, I see. Well, we do have some people staying. What's the name of your friends?"

McClatcher forced the grin to stay on his face as his impatience grew. "Ah, well, they're more acquaintances than friends, see. Only met 'em yesterday. Farther north. Only know their Christian names, see. Now there's a Jack and a Dave. David, y'know?"

The girl fumbled at the register. "They've just put initials. No J or D."

"Say, miss," Loveday interrupted quickly. "Just tell us what they look like, huh. We ain't no good on names. Four fellas, huh? Together."

The girl frowned. "Only three together. Two fair-haired and one dark. English. One quite young."

"They split up," Loveday muttered.

"Oh, I don't think so," the girl replied. "There was another man. Irish. But they weren't together ..."

"Which room, miss?" McClatcher asked.

She glanced at the clock behind the bar. "Oh, you can't go up. It's much too late and ..."

Loveday swivelled the registration book round on the bar top. "Five."

"But you mustn't," the girl began, as they started towards the stairs at the back of the bar.

"It's okay, li'le miss," Loveday said lightly, "they won't mind."

Quickly the girl moved parallel with them behind the bar, not sure whether to be alarmed or just annoyed at their arrogant persistence. McClatcher was already on the stairs as she reached out for Malone. As her hand grasped his arm he spun round, pushing her heavily so that she crashed into a stack of bottle crates. With a resounding smashing of glass she sprawled out, helplessly winded.

Loveday eyed Malone coldly. "You gettin' a taste for thrashin' women, Private? You'll wake the whole bloody village."

Malone stared down at the inelegant splay of legs, and wiped his forearm roughly across his mouth. "Her own fault, stupid bloody bitch!"

"Never mind about that!" McClatcher snapped. Quickly he pulled something from his pocket and Malone saw the glint of gun-metal. "Look, Winston, we can't afford no chances. We'll just have to take 'em now while we can—*if* they haven't already heard us. And get that fuckin' jackass out of our way before he gets us all shot!"

Loveday pulled the Beretta automatic pistol from his overcoat pocket. He motioned to Malone. "Get that kid outa sight. Anyone passin' can see her. An' stay here 'til we fetchya."

So saying, he spun on his heel and scrambled up the stairs after McClatcher.

On the upper level the corridor was deserted, their quick footsteps muted by the expanse of threadbare carpet as they crossed to the door of Room 5.

They stood one each side, guns held upright with safety catches off, moving in unison like a well-oiled machine as they had done so many times before.

McClatcher nodded. He raised his foot and stamped hard at the handle of the door. It burst open as Loveday dropped to his knees in the opening, his pistol held straight and level in a double-handed grasp. The crack of gunfire shattered the silence as the shells tore into the bodies on the bed as they struggled to sit up.

The stink of cordite filled the air and McClatcher waved aside the smoke as Loveday climbed to his feet and cautiously approached the bed.

As he saw the blood-stains seeping through the eider-down he relaxed. A grin spread across his face. "Two down and two to go!"

McClatcher rasped: "The other two must be in the

other room! They must have heard that racket!"

"Number Six!" the Negro shouted, but the big American was already moving. He leapt down the short corridor to reach the room before the occupants could realise what had happened.

There was no time to wait for Loveday. A second's delay could be fatal if the men inside realised the danger. After years of experience, a sixth sense could wake a true professional, even on a silent night. And the gunfire had been loud enough to wake the dead.

McClatcher twisted the door knob and drew back, allowing the door to swing open under its own weight. Quickly he slid to the floor, his automatic aimed, so that the occupants would look first at face-level where they would expect to see the intruder.

The steel pip of his gunsight traversed a room shed in the light from the corridor. Nothing stirred. The single bed was empty.

Cautiously he climbed to his feet. "Nothing," he thought aloud.

"Earl!" It was Loveday.

He turned, surprised that the Negro wasn't right behind him, covering his rapid entry. He moved fast back to the first bedroom, where Loveday stood by the bed.

He was holding up the eiderdown to reveal a cascade of flowing copper hair. Beneath it a white and stricken face stared up at him, the eyes fixed and glassy like a stuffed fish, the bright red mouth opened around a gag of coloured cloth like an obscene and offered kiss.

Momentarily McClatcher shut his eyes. It was like a nightmare. "Stupid fucking bitch!" he mouthed beneath his breath.

"And Kelly," Loveday confirmed. "Both bound and gagged." He nodded towards the window where a length of rope stretched to the bedleg jammed beneath it. "They're already on their way ..."

"Just a *minute!*"

McClatcher spun at the sudden sound of the angry voice. He was aware only of the bulky frame silhouetted in the doorway for a fleeting second as the automatic in his hand pumped into action. The sudden crash of shells was deafening.

He heaved a heavy sigh as the disembowelled figure fell back against the corridor wall, the red-sodden pyjamas leaving a smear of sickening graffiti down the wallpaper.

It was the barmaid's father.

"I thought you were supposed to be the bloody locksmith of this outfit!" Forbes hissed.

"Piss off," Turnbull replied as he inserted the thin wire again.

"My old granny could do better."

His words were whipped away by the wind that whistled off the lough and down the wind-tunnel formed by the two adjacent boat-houses. At least it provided some shelter from the rain which caught on the corrugated roofs and dripped in a steady curtain on the four huddled figures.

"Gotchya!" Turnbull said with delight as he felt the lock tumblers turn and the wooden door begin to shake in the wind. Climbing to his feet he slid quietly in, holding open the door for the others to follow.

The four soldiers had changed back into anoraks, waterproofs and non-standard webbing. If found discarded there would be nothing to suggest that the clothing hadn't been purchased from a civilian camping or surplus store.

Ducane turned on the flashlight and ran it quickly around the upturned dinghies. They lay in various states of repair as the owners began the long process of scraping and revarnishing in readiness for the next season and the steady trickle of holiday fishermen.

"Christ," Young Tom said. "I just hope one of them is seaworthy."

"It'll be a rough crossing all right," Forbes added, peering out at the rain-lashed shoreline.

"If there's nothing here," Ducane said, "we'll try the other boathouse. Ideally we want a rubber dinghy. Low-profile. And a powerful outboard."

They were to find neither. They discussed the possibility

of swimming across using the large black polythene bags, carried by each man as a buoyancy tank, in which weapons and equipment would also be stored. But the real risk of hypothermia in the icy water, and the possible need for a fast getaway across the lough recommended the use of transport. The appalling visibility would be in their favour.

After an exhaustive search they settled for a small fibreglass dinghy painted dark blue and two battered outboard motors, one to be used as a spare. Between the four of them it weighed very little and was no effort to carry across the shale to the water's edge. There they loaded the spare weapons, grenades and ammunition.

It was impossible to see more than thirty yards across the choppy surface before the lough was enveloped in an inky blackness. Only with the starlight scope did the dark smudge of the peninsula become visible on the far horizon, murky behind the sheets of driving rain.

Young Tom and Turnbull rowed the boat slowly away from the shoreline using makeshift muffles of clothing tied around the oars. Forbes planned a roundabout course that would take him far around the outermost rocks of the peninsula and into the exposed northern flank. There, Ducane reckoned, a landing would be least expected.

Once the shoreline had been swallowed up, Forbes began swinging the lanyard toggle on the outboard. At first it gave no sign of life. Two hopeful croaks followed, then nothing.

"Sodding useless lump of metal!" he cursed, attempting to maintain his balance in the heavy swell.

"I suppose there's fuel in it?" Turnbull suggested.

"Sod off!" Forbes snarled. "And keep rowing."

He swung again, almost stumbling over the side. A wave slapped heavily against the transom, splashing heavy dollops of cold water over the men in the stern.

"Pull up, Tom," Ducane snapped. "Keep her into the wind."

Young Tom looked down at his wet hands. "I'm getting blisters," he observed.

"If you don't get rowing, Perrot," Forbes roared above the wind, "you'll get blisters on your bleedin' arse!"

Turnbull said: "Try puttin' your hand over the air intake."

"You try . . ."

Ducane nudged him. Forbes shrugged and swung the lanyard for the tenth time, using his palm to cut off all the air. This time the little outboard coughed and spluttered, coughed again, and roared throatily to life as Forbes opened up the throttle.

Young Tom and Turnbull needed no bidding to ship the oars after the strenuous rowing of the past ten minutes.

Forbes grinned widely, the spray glistening on his face as he peered into the gloom, clutching the tiller arm lightly. "Ah, this is the life!"

Ducane smiled. "It may be the life, Dave, but it's the wrong direction. You're headin' back."

"Bloody good idea," Young Tom muttered.

"Typical ex-RCT," Turnbull snorted, relaxing on the thwart.

"Sod off, the lot of you!"

For twenty more minutes the little boat struggled on against the racing waves, their tops frothed and flattened by the wind. It was like being at sea, with no sign of land in any direction through the filthy murk. Eventually Ducane picked up the jagged outcrop of the peninsula through the Starlight scope, sticking upright out of the heaving water like a broken black tooth. As he scanned back and forth along the shoreline he could see no sign of life. No indication of the reception committee that might be waiting. In this weather, he thought grimly, you could hide a whole infantry battalion in the vegetation by the water's edge.

Idly he switched the gaze of the nightsight right across the expanse of the lough, fascinated by the relentless motion of the waves as they tumbled after each other in a frantic race for the shore.

"Cut the engine!" he yelled suddenly. "Down!"

The other three sprang to life, scrambling to get down

in the boat, Forbes fumbling to cut out the throttle. As the throaty roar died, they were suddenly aware of the low, monotonous howl of the wind.

"What was it?" Forbes asked between curses. He was kneeling in the swill of bilge water.

"A boat out there." Ducane peered over the gunwhale, resting the nightsight on the edge as he tried to pick out the ominous black shape and the tell-tale cream of her wake.

"What sort?" Turnbull's whisper was hoarse.

Ducane stared into the rubber eyepiece. "There she is. An old fishing boat. About twenty foot at a guess."

"Local fishermen?" Young Tom suggested.

The captain shook his head. "No lights. And something nasty on the bow. Looks like an old RP-46 machine gun. Drum magazine."

"Range about 1,000 metres," Turnbull added.

"If I can see him," Ducane said, "then we're well within shot."

Forbes wriggled across the deck-boards to his pack. He plucked out a couple of smooth tinplate frag grenades and tossed one down to Turnbull.

The sergeant then passed the Sterlings down to Ducane and Young Tom.

The dark shape was now taking on distinctly recognisable lines as it slowed, wallowing slowly across their path, some thirty yards ahead, beam on.

"Looks like they've spotted us," Young Tom said. His mouth felt suddenly dry. Instinctively he thumbed off the safety. A metallic rasp and click followed as he pulled the bolt back with the cocking handle.

Quickly Ducane said: "We'll put any searchlights out first, then abandon the boat. Take your arms and we'll each make for their stern. Each man for himself."

"We'll take the bastards with us, that's for sure," Forbes said, squinting his eyes against the stinging rain.

"Did you see that?" Turnbull asked suddenly.

Again the light flashed from the shoreline of the peninsula.

"The boat's answering," Forbes observed. "Shit, my Morse is rusty."

"Like your Russian," Turnbull quipped.

"Routine check, I think," Ducane said. He couldn't read the ship's Aldis in reply.

"Never listen to half a conversation," Forbes mused.

"The shore-party just told 'em to keep an extra sharp look out," Ducane continued. "Looks like they've been to the guest-house."

"I just hope that couple didn't give them anything useful," Young Tom said.

Forbes shook his head. "No, we didn't discuss anything in earshot. They've only got our descriptions to go on."

"That's bad enough," Turnbull replied.

The urgent throb of the heavy-duty inboard diesels began as the boat suddenly gathered speed, moving away to concentrate its patrol on the south coast of the peninsula.

"Round one to us," Forbes commented.

"By default," Turnbull added.

Ducane said: "Let's get on."

CHAPTER 13

Thirty minutes later, through the rain that was now slanting down like steel rods, they at last heard the water breaking over the boulder-strewn shoreline. The dinghy was responding sluggishly, wallowing like a clumsy toy in each trough as the waves urged her towards the slippery rocks. Turnbull and Young Tom were baling as fast as they could, but it was not fast enough as each passing wave slopped in another bucketful of cold water.

Even with the little engine racing at full revs, their headway was slow, denying them the ability to steer safely through the maze of granite teeth that were appearing all around them in a welter of spray.

A violent shuddering shook the boat as its fibreglass hull scraped across a submerged outcrop.

"MORE POWER!" Ducane yelled above the howling wind.

"THERE ISN'T ANY!" Forbes bawled, although his words were scarcely audible to the captain next to him. Another wave smashed against the boat in an explosion of foam, pushing the hull back against the outcrop. A grating crackle of fibreglass followed, and a hairline split suddenly appeared below the centre thwart.

Turnbull put a leg over the side and jammed his boot hard against the granite obstruction, pushing firmly. More waves buffeted the tiny vessel, forcing against the soldier as he heaved with all his strength.

A sudden gust hit the side of the boat, contemptuously throwing the hull farther onto the outcrop, half-crushing the man's boot as the rubber sole slid from the slimy rock.

"FUCKING HELL!" Turnbull shouted. "Nearly lost my bloody foot."

"SIT DOWN, YOU SODDING HERO!" Forbes yelled. In

245

support of his words another wave hit the transom, rocking the craft with a violence that almost toppled Turnbull.

The fracture in the fibreglass spread as the hull was forced over the outcrop, finally breaking free with a crunch of steel as the propeller pin sheared and the safety cut-out killed the engine. Helpless in the sudden rush, the boat began to gyrate towards the ragged shoreline some thirty feet away. Turnbull and Young Tom needed no instruction as they scrambled to get the oars out.

"Oh, fuck auntie!" Young Tom exclaimed. "The bloody rowlocks gone!"

"How deep you reckon it is, Dave?" Ducane asked.

"Maybe six feet," Forbes replied, still clutching the tiller arm in the vain hope it would provide some steerage. "Maybe more."

Ducane slitted his eyes against the rain and murk. "I'm going to try and get a line ashore. Maybe we can beach her on that strip of shingle."

"Maybe you can drown yourself, too."

Another resounding crack. The boat jolted as it hit another rock, the engine being torn from its mounting before Forbes could raise the propeller shaft. The fracture in the hull was beginning to weep.

"Four men in a sieve," Turnbull muttered.

Hurriedly Ducane began to undo his boots, cursing the laces as he raced against time, his fingers clumsy and numb with cold. He stumbled painfully forward, taking the painter rope coiled in the bow.

As he lowered himself over the side, Young Tom said anxiously: "Careful boss."

Ducane released his grip on the gunwhales. Immediately he vanished from view to emerge, spluttering and coughing in a ring of foam some feet away.

"Christ! It's freezing ..." he was seen mouthing.

Turning awkwardly, he struck out for the shore. His sodden anorak dragged him down, making movement sluggish and exhausting. Twice he was hurled with bone-crushing force against partly submerged rocks, until he finally gained a foot hold on the shale bottom.

The numbing cold acted like an anaesthetic to his skin so he was unaware of the livid bruises beginning to swell along his legs and back. Rapidly he hauled the rope taut, dragging in the water-logged boat that stubbornly refused to co-operate, bucking heavily in each swell.

At last it was close enough for Turnbull and Young Tom to plunge waist-high into the icy water and join the efforts to guide it in.

Forbes waded straight ashore with his Sterling and scrambled over the shingle, up through the strewn rocks and stunted bushes, to the upper ledge of the shoreline.

After a few moments Ducane arrived, dropping exhausted down beside him. Breathlessly he asked: "Anything Dave?"

"Not a bugger in sight. But it's hard to tell without the 'scope."

Ducane handed over the nightsight and watched as Forbes scanned the barren landscape that climbed gently into the darkness before them.

After grunting a couple of times, Forbes shook his head. "It's not much better with this in these conditions. Anyway, they'd have to be pretty determined to be out in this."

"They are determined," Ducane replied testily. He flicked the strands of wet hair from his forehead. "According to the map there should be an inlet a quarter mile along this shore. Probably be a bit more natural camouflage there for the boat."

"As well we brought that spare engine," Forbes conceded.

"Let's just hope we don't have to start it in a hurry. After your last attempt."

Forbes pulled a face and grinned.

After twenty minutes they were ready to proceed and, following the route they had memorised from the large-scale map at the guest-house, they moved deeper into the peninsula in pairs.

As they started east across the width of the promontory, the ground rose sharply in a series of low, rocky hills. Vegetation was sparse and stunted. The men took their time, content to use the natural contours of the land for cover as they progressed, carefully studying each possible hiding place as they went. Although the rain eased off at about three-thirty in the morning, it was still uncomfortable going, their wet clothes chaffing tender skin and a dull aching cold they knew would not go until a warm meal had been eaten and daylight arrived.

On their route, both Forbes and Ducane were beginning to get an uneasy feeling. They had found no sign of life after an hour of patient searching. They took it in turns to survey the landscape with the nightsight, while the other stood as rearguard, always standing with the back to something solid to prevent being surprised by a sneak attack from behind.

Already they were at the foot of the low hills where the ground was more sheltered. There were encouraging signs of vegetation and even the occasional clump of thin trees. Ahead of them the ground began another gentle incline to a high ridge where, with the improving visibility, they could distinguish the outline shape of a ruined building.

Forbes dropped down beside Ducane in a shallow depression surrounded by thickets of gorse, forming a rough circle like a fairy-ring.

"That must be the friary," the sergeant observed.

Ducane nodded. "According to the map, it's the only goddamn building around here."

"You still reckon that's their base?"

"Unless they've got a camp site for sixty-odd blokes, I don't see the alternative."

Forbes scratched his chin. "Well, they certainly haven't pitched any tents on our route. Unless, of course, they're scattered through the entire peninsula, and camouflaged."

"It's possible." He looked around at the desolate landscape, now dimly discernible. "But I don't like it at all. Not a sign of life ..."

Forbes shrugged. "Perhaps we've been wrong about the whole thing."

"That fishing boat was real enough."

"True. Still perhaps reports about the size of the

operation were exaggerated. A bit of Paddy optimism."
He peered towards the dark outline of the friary. "Christ,
I could do with a smoke."

"Shut up, Dave," Ducane said good-humouredly.
"Have a bar of chocolate."

"Good idea."

"Hey!"

"What?"

Ducane pointed the nightsight towards the friary.
"We've got company after all."

"Thank God for that. I was beginning to feel lonely.
What 'you seen? Man Friday's footprint?"

"I think it's an OP, just below the old building." He
concentrated in silence for a full two minutes, conscious
of Forbes' heavy breathing beside him. At last he said:
"Christ! It's well-hidden. 'Have done our lads proud."

"McClatcher's influence?"

Ducane handed across the nightsight. "He learned a lot
about camouflage in 'Nam. I looked straight at it and
couldn't see a damned bean until something bright
glinted."

Forbes squinted into the eyepiece. "You're right. It's
bloody good. It makes you wonder what the hell we've
passed on the way here."

Ducane felt an involuntary ripple pass up his spine. He
glanced quickly around the protective ring of gorse. Suddenly it seemed very exposed.

"Do you want to risk going any closer?" Forbes asked.
"I think we could do a sketch of the layout of the place
from here."

Ducane nodded. "If Turnbull's been able to get round
the other side, we'll have a full picture."

"Old 'Action Man' will get there all right. You can stake
your life on it."

"Now we've some idea what we're up against, I don't
want to get nearer until we've developed a full plan of
action." Ducane glanced up at the sky, his eyes narrowed.
It wouldn't be dawn for a good two hours, but there was
a faint lightening as the storm clouds thinned and the

occasional star tried to brazen its way through. "Let's get back whilst the going's good."

Hastily Forbes began scrawling the layout of the ridge and the old friary on a notepad, careful to include the solitary wizen tree to the north and the apparent size of the space inside the building. It was easy to recognise the main hall, and then the lower southern section which housed the smaller cells of the monks' quarters, probably running off a central corridor. He pencilled in the observation hide and the other likely OP sites. Finally he snapped the plastic-covered wallet pad closed.

"Done," he said.

Ducane nodded and began to wriggle carefully out of the shallow saucer of land, between the gorse. A sudden clatter of metal came from behind him. He turned quickly, his hand nervously fingering the trigger of the Sterling he held at the ready.

"What the hell ... ?" Forbes was saying as he prodded at something in the thicket.

Ducane crouched by his side, puzzled at the grey metal box and the blue-black fish eye that glinted up at them from the undergrowth.

Forbes said: "It's a bloody camera."

"Jesus ... I was right!"

"Huh?"

"I said I thought I must be under observation yesterday. After that guy with the shot-gun warned me off."

"TV cameras?" Forbes asked incredulously.

"Low-level. Remote control. This bastard must have had our whole approach covered."

"Shit!"

As if in response to his words, the camera twitched suddenly like a living thing, beginning a sweep.

Forbes stared at it. "You mean it's watching us now ... ? Fucking hell!" He stood up quickly and stamped hard on the metal shell with his boot, distorting the heavy-duty casing and shattering the lens. As if in a death spasm, the crushed object tried to obey its command to rotate, whirring like a giant insect. Forbes kicked it again.

At that moment a stream of machine-gun fire burst from the direction of the low hills they had descended earlier. The violent, explosive stutter was accompanied by a stream of tracer shells that ripped apart the gorse by their feet, spinning branches and clods of earth skyward in a sudden fountain.

The Sterling leapt in Ducane's hand as it spat out returning fire. Forbes jumped back into the depression, rolling over in the grass as he went. Ducane gave a second short burst and went after him in a crouching run.

Together they peered over the rim, through the shattered patch of gorse, Ducane pulling at the straps of the nightsight case. "No wonder we didn't see anyone," he panted. "If they've got cameras all over the place, they can watch it all at home like bloody *Coronation Street*!"

He scanned through the viewer. "Dave, can you see that tree at one o'clock?"

"What do you think I am? A bleedin' cat?"

"Well, take my word for it. The bastards have got themselves a nest up there. We must have walked right under the damn thing."

Forbes grimaced. "I'm beginning to feel like a bloody amateur."

Ducane said thoughtfully: "I just hope they haven't got the whole place covered."

"If they have," Forbes said, "*I* just hope they ain't got no mortars. Otherwise they could be zero-ing in on us right now."

Ducane shook his head. "The locals would hear it."

Forbes grabbed his arm. "You sure you want to take that chance?"

Ducane smiled. "No. Let's go. You lob a couple of flashbangs as near the tree as you can. I'll do the shootin'. Right?"

"Okay, Jacko."

Hurriedly they extracted the anti-dazzle goggles from their smocks as another burst of machine-gun fire streamed overhead. The tracers appeared curiously slow, like lazy fireflies, disappearing a split second before they thundered into the centre of the depression in a furore of earth and smoke.

"Careful," Ducane warned. "They've probably got 'scopes."

Forbes nodded.

Together they sprinted forward towards the tree, crouching low. Immediately the machine-gun opened up again with a noise like ripping calico, the rate of fire so rapid that it was almost like one continuous sound. The tracer shells hit the turf in a ragged zig-zag pattern, wildly inaccurate as the gunner tried to pinpoint the dark running figures.

The prolonged burst was an extravagance he couldn't afford. When the two soldiers were some fifty yards from the tree, taking their time to run in an indirect and weaving course to throw off the gunner's aim, the firing ceased abruptly. Both Ducane and Forbes recognised the familiar clink of the firing-pin biting hungrily at an empty ammunition belt. They could imagine the curses as fumbling fingers tried to feed in the new belt too quickly. However good they were, it would take seven seconds before they could resume accurate fire. And that would be seven seconds too long.

In one fluid, practised movement, Forbes hurled the tubular cardboard stun-grenade and threw himself forward into a clump of tall grass, hurriedly levelling his Sterling to cover Ducane's advance.

Even in the open air the effect of the small device was impressive. A blinding white sheet of dazzling light tore through the inky black night, so bright that it paralysed the senses. The noise was even worse, pitching fractionally below the decibel level that could result in permanent deafness.

There was no explosion as such, but the shock on the nervous system was sufficient to send one man toppling from the tree-nest in sheer fright. Forbes' gun barked a short burst, several shells finding their target before the man hit the ground, with one leg badly ripped at the knee.

The sudden crack of Ducane's gun joined the mounting crescendo as he fired from less than twenty yards, blasting away the makeshift wooden platform, tearing away some of the lighter branches.

Two more shattered bodies joined the first on the ground with a double thud.

Suddenly it was over, and all was quiet but for the low whimper of a dying man.

Cautiously Ducane and Forbes approached the tree, the sergeant putting his back to the scarred and punctured trunk, scanning the surrounding bushes for a sign of movement.

Ducane stood up from examining the bodies, having made a neat pile of the considerable arsenal. Apart from the machine-gun they had all been armed with Kalashnikovs and half-a-dozen old pineapple hand-grenades.

The man who had been moaning carried a radio set in his back pack. Evidently it had broken his spine when he fell. Now he stared up at the soldiers in stark horror, his body paralysed and helpless.

"What we going to do about him?" Forbes asked.

Ducane grunted. "Homicide goes against the grain. Better leave him. He can't tell 'em anything they don't already know."

"I reckon you'd be doing him a favour."

"This isn't 'Nam, Dave! Just because McClatcher's a bloody butcher doesn't mean we have to do the same." He turned and looked up the slope to where he knew the friary stood. "They'll be down soon enough to investigate. They've probably got some tame doctor in a nearby village."

"If I remember old Earl, he's more likely to put a bullet in his brain. The ultimate discipline he used to call it."

Ducane's voice was hoarse. "That's his problem." He stooped beside the man and said gently: "Sorry, old lad, I want that pack off your back. It might hurt."

If he felt pain the Provo said nothing. Numb fear gazed back into Ducane's eyes as he manhandled the body out of the harness. The radio was still hissing and chirping.

"Step on it, Jacko," Forbes urged. "I can hear a car engine."

Ducane finally tugged the radio free, slinging it over his shoulder, then picked up his Sterling.

Forbes had made sure that the machine-gun would not fire again and, hanging the spare ammunition belts around his neck, he set off hurriedly towards the nearest cover.

They were scarcely over a shallow rise when they clearly recognised the familiar sound of a Land Rover. There followed an excited jabber of voices, the exact words lost in the distance.

At the first opportunity they left the footpath that was almost certainly covered by a camera. They moved across country until they reached the narrow bed of a stream that gabbled noisily after the heavy rains. They moved along it towards higher ground before they sank, exhausted, behind a large clump of gorse.

Forbes peered back down the valley with the nightsight. "No sign of the bastards!"

Ducane nodded. "No point in them taking risks. Someone could get hurt chasing after us in the dark."

"You reckon they'll wait till dawn?"

"Wouldn't you?"

Forbes nodded. "If I'd got the place covered in TV cameras, I'd bide my time."

"Especially if you knew we couldn't get off the peninsula."

"You reckon they've got the boat?"

Ducane unscrewed the cap of the water-flask. "It's not beyond the bounds of possibility. Especially if they've got a number of those cameras." He took a draught of water, wiping his lips with his sleeve. He offered it to Forbes who shook his head slowly as he considered the possibility that their entire approach had been monitored.

"This peninsula's pretty exposed, Jacko, so it wouldn't take much equipment to cover all the lines of approach. That wooded inlet where we hid the boat was the only bit of cover for miles." He scratched at the stubble on his chin. "You wouldn't have to be a bloody genius to guess we might have used it."

Ducane took a final swig from the flask. The cool water helped to clear his head. "We daren't stay in one spot for too long, Dave. Call up Turnbull and tell him what we've found. We'll meet at RV One and take a discreet look at the inlet."

"I just hope they've kept plugged in," Forbes muttered. He switched on the Pye Pocketfone and said crisply: 'Sabre Two this is Sabre One. Have engaged. All okay. Under TV surveillance. Caution. Make RV One 0500 hours. Out." Almost immediately he heard two answering clicks in his earpiece. Message received and understood.

They approached RV One across country, ten minutes ahead of time, and settled down in a clearing in a dense patch of scrub overlooking the junction of two paths. To the unaccustomed eye it would have still been pitch black but, after an entire night in the open, they would have been able to pick up a careless movement at a hundred yards or more. It was to Sabre Two's credit that Forbes didn't spot them until they were virtually at the junction. Evidently heeding the warning about cameras, they too had come overland, making their final approach along a drainage ditch that was operating at maximum capacity to cope with the water still flooding from the hills.

Turnbull, wet and cursing, was first to scramble up into the clearing where Ducane and Forbes waited. Tom followed close behind, looking even more dishevelled and uncomfortable.

"I'll get those sods for this!" Turnbull hissed and spat out a mouthful of ditch-water and sodden leaves. "It's bad enough being out on a night like this without having to bellycrawl everywhere."

"Sorry about that—but they really have got cameras."

Turnbull forced a smile. "Yeah, I believe you. They've got more than that, too."

"What?" Forbes demanded.

Young Tom's eyes brightened. 'Seismic sensors! They must be able to hear everywhere we go."

"Do belt up, Perrot!" Turnbull snapped irritably. "Let

255

the senior ranker report first. You can add your four pennyworth later." He turned back to Ducane. "After we got your message, we thought we'd see what we could find over our side. It's quite open and they'd obviously have to use high ground to cover all the approach routes economically. So we had a look-see. Not only bloody cameras, but a PSID unit with a lead going down to a spiked geophone buried at the side of a path."

"Christ!" Forbes said. "Are we sure the bleedin' US Army hasn't invaded Ireland and someone forgot to mention it?"

Ducane ignored the outburst. "How close to target did you get?"

"A hundred metres or so. Close enough to get a decent diagram. Apart from a friary, there's a fuel tank and generator. And three Land Rovers. Everything's under camo. Good job they've made."

"OPs?"

"A couple. Gave themselves away when some fireworks went off the other side of the friary. Your party, was it?"

Forbes chuckled. "Let's say three of 'em will remember our visit. The boss got a present, too."

Ducane swung across the radio, which Turnbull grabbed avidly. "American. I think the sarge might be right in his US Army invasion theory." He inspected it with disdain. "What you been doing with it?"

"Got a bit dented when some Mick sat on it from a great height," Ducane explained. "If you can get it working, we could do a little eavesdropping. Probably still tuned in."

"May be possible," Turnbull agreed.

"It could make life easier if we know what they're up to," Ducane returned. "But with it working or not, we've got to make plans on the assumption they've got this whole area well-sewn up. That means that they've been monitoring our progress since we landed ..."

"The boat!" Young Tom began.

Turnbull nudged him hard in the ribs. Ducane continued. "As our brilliant recruit here has pointed out, if the roles were reversed we wouldn't bother chasing around in the dark, we'd corner them where we knew they had to go." He paused and watched each face as it nodded in agreement. "That inlet would be ideal for an ambush. I think we ought to pay 'em a visit and see if they're doing it properly."

"Attaboy," encouraged Forbes.

"That's all very well," Turnbull said, "but even if we bushwhack some of them, they're hardly likely to have left the boat in a seaworthy condition. And it's a long swim."

"The corp's right, boss," Forbes said. "We've still got the problem of four of us versus God knows how many Micks with the most sophisticated electronic gadgets going. In fact they're probably listening to us discussing our plans right now!"

That brought forth a spontaneous laugh from all four of the dirty, bedraggled soldiers, and it took a few moments for the mirth to subside enough for Ducane to finish. "Look, lads, I've got a few ideas that are beginning to form. That recce has proved invaluable, because at least we know what we're up against. And that's half the battle. Now we'll all give it some thought over a hot meal. This clearing's quite secure. I'll draw up some plans while Turnbull plays with that radio. Dave, you and Tom go to RV Two and bring back the kit and spare smudges we stored. We'll all think better when we're warm and got some chow inside us."

Forbes was already on his feet. He kicked Young Tom playfully. "C'mon, lad, back into ditch. Show me how fast you can crawl."

Tom Perrot shrugged. "And to think I joined the Army to see the world."

Turnbull was unmoved by the sudden wave of jocularity. "Dry kit and grub won't solve our problems, Sarge. I think we've got ourselves into a bloody jam."

Forbes leaned down until his face was almost touching Turnbull's. "Listen, Corporal, if you don't like the heat in the fuckin' kitchen you should've joined the bloody Marines. Me 'n' the captain have fought the Vietcong, the

Russians, and the bloody Yemini bandits and we sure as hell ain't going to give a gaggle of thick Provos the privilege of burying us."

He turned abruptly and disappeared into the ditch with the agility of a teenager.

Winston Loveday treated himself to one of McClatcher's plump cigars. He allowed the smooth smoke to escape his teeth with a long low hiss of satisfaction. From his seat in the Land Rover he could observe virtually the entire expanse of the inlet. Forty feet up on the west bank, the vehicle had been expertly covered in brush and camouflage nets under his personal supervision. Some twenty feet below him ten of McClatcher's privates were concealed, overlooking the bushes where the dinghy had been hidden. These men formed the main group of the ambush, armed with automatic weapons and hand-grenades. He had decided against using one of the two French Hotchkiss-Brandt 60mm mortars they had in their arsenal. The ranging shots may have alerted the SAS group, and he wasn't convinced that his men had yet mastered their use. Already there had been an unfortunate incident which had cost him an instructor.

The opposite bank, about seventy-five yards away, was unoccupied to avoid accidents with cross-fire and rico-chets, although he had taken the precaution of blocking access routes up the embankment using trip-wires fixed to grenades. If anyone attempted to escape that way when his trap snapped shut, they'd get a nasty headache.

He leaned forward and peered south to the apex of the inlet. It was the direction from which Ducane's men were expected to come. They would be allowed to pass the first stop-group—three men with a heavy machine-gun. He smiled slowly. He knew he was looking directly at the clump of undergrowth where his men were concealed, but he could distinguish nothing to give away its existence.

In the opposite direction, where the mouth of the inlet widened into the lough, the second stop-group was hidden, with two more heavy machine-guns. Beyond them, hidden in the pre-dawn murk, the motor fishing boat waited at anchor. The final insurance policy in case any of Ducane's men escaped the ambush.

There was a sudden movement outside the Land Rover as one of the Provos looked in through the open window. "The rear group's in position, sir."

Loveday allowed the man a brief smile. "Well done, soldier." He reached for the radio, pleased he had decided to take the precaution of covering his own rear. Ducane was no fool and, if he expected an ambush had been sprung, Loveday was convinced he might try and turn the tables on them. If he tried, now he would come face to face with a concealed machine-gun nest.

The sudden crackle of static filled the Land Rover. Loveday picked up the handset: "Ratcatcher to Bishop ... Ratcatcher to Bishop ... Over."

"Hi, Winston, how goes it?" Despite the distortion of transmission, the cheerfulness in McClatcher's voice was unmistakable.

"We're all set, Earl. I've put out a rear guard, after all ... Better to be safe than sorry. If that ain't enough, then a whole battalion won't do it."

"Okay, if you're happy. You usin' a trip-flare? Over."

"Yep. Right in front of us. I reckon there's another hour before it gets light. Any sign of 'em? Over."

This time the edge of optimism was missing from McClatcher's voice. *"Nothin' for the last two hours, I'm afraid. I guess they know about the cameras. Over."*

Loveday frowned. "Nothin' on the ground sensors? Over."

"Not yet, Winston. I guess they're steering clear of the paths. At least we know they ain't anywhere near the friary and they ain't got no other place t'go except their boat. I'll contact you if anything breaks. Over."

"Okay, Bishop. Out." He hung up the handset and fell back against the seat. The cigar stump clamped between his teeth, he stared blankly at the windscreen. The elation he had been experiencing a few minutes earlier had dissipated under the weight of a nagging concern.

Nothing on the television screen. Nothing on the sensors. And, of course, the missing radio set.

Angrily he mashed out the cigar butt with his boot on the floor. He just prayed that he was being unduly pessimistic.

The faint whine of the nightsight died away as Forbes switched it off and replaced it in the stout leather case.

For almost an hour they had studied the inlet from the last of the high ground before it flattened out to the edge of the lough, now discernible as a sheet of dull metal in the glimmer of pre-dawn light.

Ducane's booted foot kicked away the last traces of the three-dimensional model of the inlet he had constructed in the mud. As he felt the excitement of anticipated action increase he craved for a cigarette. But they all knew it was their ability to resist such temptation and suffer hardship that gave them the edge over other lesser mortals.

"Any questions?" he asked. He looked steadily at each man in turn. The expression of every face was set firm and humourless. Only Forbes' eyes gave away his enthusiasm to get started.

It was an audacious plan. Anyone who didn't understand the SAS training philosophy would have called it foolhardy. There was certainly much that could go wrong; but coping with and anticipating the unexpected was the name of the game. The odds *had* to be improved.

Ducane climbed to his feet. "Okay. Twenty minutes until the fireworks go off. 0700 hours." He buckled on his belt and picked up his Sterling. "It's not the easiest operation we've had, lads, but it's one we won't forget."

Turnbull stepped forward. "Look, boss, you know I haven't been happy with a lot of aspects of this ..."

"... Not now, John," Ducane returned coldly.

The man shook his head. "No, let me finish. I want you to know that now we're in, I'm with you all the way. I think we might even pull it off." He half-smiled. "And I was all for pulling out. I can see that if we did, McClatcher's mob would go to ground before we could do anything. They're too well-equipped and well-organised for us to allow them to get established in the north. Our next chance would be in Armagh ... and by that time they'd be even better."

"We haven't beaten 'em yet, Corp," Forbes said. "Let's not count our chickens."

Turnbull looked sheepish. "I just wanted you all to know ..." His voice trailed off.

Ducane nodded. "If the plan even half-works, John, it'll be largely due to you. You've thought things out well. It's a valuable asset."

Forbes sounded disgusted. "What's this? Bloody mutual admiration society?"

"Piss off, Sarge," Turnbull returned amiably.

Ducane moved off and Young Tom silently shouldered his Sterling and fell in quickly behind him.

As they watched them go Forbes said to Turnbull: "Poor little bugger. He's sheet white. Scared out of his bleedin' wits."

Turnbull laughed as he began burying the spare weapons and equipment. "Guess that makes four of us."

CHAPTER 14

Ex-US Marines Sergeant Carl Bristow sat at the edge of the machine-gun nest that formed Winston Loveday's first stop-group. Chewing morosely on a wad of stale gum, he watched the shallow valley from which the SAS team was expected to approach. Beside him a young Provo sat, crouched over a ·30 Browning, his finger playing nervously on the trigger. Another recruit lay by his side, ready to keep the weapon fed as its insatiable appetite devoured cartridge belts at a rate of 120 rounds per minute.

All three were dressed in waterproof trousers and combat jackets, stained by hand to blend with the mellow shades of winter foliage, so that even from a few feet away they would be indistinguishable from the dead bracken and sparse shrubbery.

"Finger off, Muldoon," the American muttered laconically. "With your itchy digit yer likely to scare the bastards off as soon as they show."

The Irishman's hand jerked instantly as he obeyed, and Bristow felt the hot flush of anticipation sweep over him. Christ, he thought, these guys are so keyed up they're likely to let fire if someone yells *"Boo!"* Darn near opened up when I spoke to him then.

Bristow didn't look much like a veteran. But his long unruly hair which curled over his collar had been grown in an attempt to hide the effects of his two years in Vietnam. Even his old buddies in the leathernecks wouldn't recognise this scruffy hippy as the close-shorn Sergeant Bristow who won the Purple Heart when he routed an entire company of VC almost single-handed outside Khe Sahn. But when he'd been invalided out, the length of his

262

hair and faded denims couldn't disguise the hard glint in his eyes. The mischievous sparkle of the fun-loving college boy he'd been 24 months earlier would never return. He had seen too much, and done too much.

As he sat waiting for the first fingers of dawn to reach across the Irish sky, he could not accept this was really happening. That somewhere, out there in the brooding, mean landscape, four men were waiting who had a reputation for cunning and fighting prowess in excess of anyone he had met in the Far East. Not here in Eire, the lethargic backwater of Europe, where the mild-mannered, generous people spent their time in endless conversations and gossip over countless glasses of Guinness. Unthinkable.

The radio earpiece crackled. *"Bishop to Pawn One. Bishop to Pawn One. Over."*

He found his pulse quickening as he flicked the switch. It was difficult to maintain his usual easy drawl as he replied: "Receiving. Over."

"Geophones got someone comin' your way. Three minutes. Over."

"Pawn One ready, Bishop. Out."

He cringed inwardly as he gave their call-sign. Pawn One. It was all right if you were Bishop or Knight or some-such. The connotations of Pawn gave one an uneasy feeling in the gut. Especially when it was just you and a couple of greenhorns.

He forced a grin. "We got visitors, it seems." He kept his voice low, little more than a murmur. "Keep off the trigger until they've passed right into the inlet an' I give the word."

The two men nodded and glanced at each other nervously. Bristow closed his eyes briefly. Give me strength, he thought.

As his lids opened again, his eyes focused directly on a slight movement a hundred yards away, down the shallow incline that ran to the apex of the inlet. The stark arms of a long-dead shrub swayed slightly beside the track that led into the peninsula.

He put the Zeiss binoculars that hung around his neck

to his eyes and adjusted the focus as he zeroed in on the shrub.

Bristow grunted to himself. There was someone there all right. A few minutes earlier the shrub had been thin and spindly; now it seemed thicker around the base. More substance. More colour, too. But, however hard he tried, he could not distinguish the shape.

He shifted the gaze of the glasses inland, along the path. Again he grunted. Whoever it was down there, they must have passed right along the edge of the path without him seeing, using just the short turf and natural undulations of the ground for cover.

They were good, he decided. Or else he was very out of touch. After all it had been five years since he'd last played cat-and-mouse in the rain forests. He felt a sudden thrill. His mouth was quite dry.

He swept the penetrating gaze of the Zeiss farther inland, towards the rise that overlooked the inlet and his machine-gun nest. Much earlier he had thought he had seen movement, but had discounted it after studying the spot for almost half-an-hour. Now, once again, he wondered if he had been right. Whoever it was below him could have been on that rise an hour earlier, presumably watching the inlet.

Instinctively he glanced behind him. The ground couldn't be seen as it rose gently away behind the nest because it had a thick covering of bracken and brush. Dead leaves crackled as the wind moaned mournfully. There was no other sound. He shivered.

Bristow's was the first stop-group of the ambush. It was perched on a spur of land on the west bank of the inlet, commanding a view of the approach from inland. Directly below was a blind-spot created by taller bushes and trees, and then, if the machine-gun was traversed, it had a wide field of fire straight down to the inlet itself towards the lough.

Once the intruders were at the water's edge in the inlet, the main party on the west bank, where Loveday had his Land Rover, would open up with automatic weapons and grenades. Pawn One would then slam shut the door of the trap, opening up down the inlet with a withering fire of ·30inch shells, cutting off any chance of retreat.

Bristow pressed the switch. "Pawn One to Bishop and Ratcatcher. Someone wants to come in. Reckon one. Maybe two. Over."

Loveday's voice sounded cautious. *"Okay, Pawn One. There's four of d'bastards. Ratcatcher to all groups: Watch yer ass! Take special care 'til all four are identified. Out."*

The silence seemed oppressive after the sudden raucous crackle of the radio. The loader began shuffling his legs uneasily. Bristow ignored him and again concentrated the Zeiss on the shrub below them at the pathside.

This time he thought he could make out a definite shape. He leaned forward, screwing up his eyes and willing the lens to give a little added magnification. Was that a gun barrel? It had obviously been threaded with twine and grass stalks, but the general shape was too rigid to be natural.

A long, slow smile began to spread across Bristow's face. It looked as though the quarry was getting ready to move deeper into the inlet ...

Something was wrong. He suddenly knew that he faced danger. That old familiar instinct was nagging at his mind. Quickly Bristow checked his senses. It wasn't vision; there was nothing out of place. He could hear nothing distinct above the monotony of wind and rustling bracken. His nostrils were filled with the pungence of peat and rotting leaves and a hint of oil from the machine-gun.

Then he knew it was touch. Not his hands, but the crawling skin on the back of his neck. The exposed flesh had been cold and numb, and suddenly there was just the slightest warmth. Like someone's breath.

Bristow's thought process had taken a mere millisecond. But that had been too long. And he knew it.

Even as the hot ebb of fear rushed through him and he braced himself for the pain, the padded forearm snapped over his face like a steel mask.

The breath exploded through his teeth with the force of a steam turbine as the knee drove into his pelvis, hauling him backwards into the carpet of leaves. Involuntarily his arms spread to protect himself from the fall. He could only hear the gasping exertions of an unknown human and the urgent shuffle of heavy boots amongst the bracken and cartridge belts.

Acting on trained reflexes Bristow forced himself to ignore the excruciating pain at the base of his spine and the iron-hard knuckles that were trying to force his torn lips and teeth down his throat. Instinctively, he realised that his attacker had botched it. He should have been dead, but he wasn't, He should have already felt the lethal prick of the knife-point in his jugular. But it hadn't happened.

Bristow drew a deep breath with the sound of an animal snort through his half-smothered nose, and wriggled with the strength and agility of a python.

He heard the muffled cursing sound hard in his ear. He felt the grip around his mouth begin to slip until his teeth came in contact with bony flesh. He bit hard into the pink skin, tasting salt and blood on his tongue.

There was no air left in his lungs to make a sound as he tried to yell, but the exertion prised him free of the bleeding hand.

He forced himself forward, turning awkwardly as he did so to face his assailant.

A quick visual impression of chaos was left imprinted in his mind as his head turned. The machine-gunner was sprawled prostrate across his weapon which had collapsed under his weight; a length of garrotte wire hung from the man's throat like an absurd necktie. The loader was engaged in a furious wrestle with a big man in a camouflage smock. He caught a glimpse of fair hair before he completed his turn to come face to face with his own attacker.

The man was sitting on his knees, clutching a bleeding hand. He looked up in surprise and anger, as if not believing his victim had escaped his deadly grasp.

It seemed an age while the two men faced each other, both breathing heavily as they weighed up their adversaries, although it could have only been seconds.

Bristow was surprised how young the man was. Despite

the smears of blacking on his face the American was certain he was hardly out of his 'teens. The eyes had been smarting with tears of pain, and the face was pale with fear.

The younger man's glance fell to the glinting metal blade that lay between them in the leaves.

That's why I'm not dead, thought Bristow. The youngster had dropped it in his haste and inexperience.

Both men leapt for it simultaneously. Bristow's fingers got there first, quickly grasping the haft, before the young soldier's hands clasped his wrist.

Their posture seemed ridiculous: both bodies flung fully forward with hands grasped at arm's length, neither able to press home an advantage. Each staring into the other's eyes, as they strained muscle for muscle and will for will.

Bristow raised his left arm and swung it at the youngster's face, as his feet scrabbled madly to gain a grip in the slippery leaf mould. But the other's reflexes showed the difference between their ages. Deftly the soldier rolled to one side, so that the American's knuckles just grazed his cheek before they thudded uselessly against the turf. The sudden jolt caused Bristow to flinch and his grip on the knife slipped a fraction.

Gauging exactly his split-second of advantage, the youngster swung his legs round until he could twist himself onto his knees, while the American remained prostrate.

Still grasping Bristow's clenched fist with both hands, the soldier used the grip to pull himself to his feet. He followed it up with the full force of his boot to the American's throat.

Bristow's teeth snapped together hard over his tongue as he felt the toecap punch into his Adam's apple. His senses reeled as he toppled backwards and the knife span into the undergrowth.

Red mist clouded into his vision as he tried to focus on the youngster, who fell exhausted on top of him. The breath had left the American's body and the lump in his throat seemed to have swollen to the size of a brick, cutting off the air supply to his lungs. As he tried to stifle the involuntary cough it triggered off a spasm of choking sobs. His windpipe had constricted to the size of a drinking straw. The burning sensation glowed in his throat like a red hot coal. There was nothing he could do to stop the rising vomit. As it forced its way through his oesophagus his whole chest and head seemed to disintegrate into pain. Finally, with the heavy weight of the soldier sprawled over him, he gave way to the dizzy waves of unconsciousness . . .

Young Tom, trembling with exhaustion, panted for breath as he raised his head from the chest of the dead American. He saw Ducane dusting the leaves and twigs from his smock and let his head fall back onto the still body beneath him. He shut his eyes and forced his mind to relax.

Perrot, you stupid bastard, he told himself, that was nearly the last mistake you ever made.

A hand touched his shoulder. Again he raised his head, forcing his eyes open. Ducane was crouched by his side, the deadly knife that had dispensed with the machine-gun loader already back in its sheath.

"Okay, Tom?"

Perrot nodded, not trusting himself to speak in case his voice betrayed the fear and utter fatigue he felt.

"Well done," Ducane said, glancing casually at the corpse. "He was a big bastard. Tough, too, from what I saw. Gave you a hard time?"

Young Tom muttered between clenched teeth, angry with himself.

"What was that?" Ducane asked.

The young soldier forced himself up into a half-crouch, still not trusting his legs to hold his weight if he stood up. He looked down at the mess of blood and vomit on his smock. "I dropped the bloody knife when I went for him. Sorry. Just careless. He nearly got it and carved me . . ."

He looked down at the ground.

"You're here. He isn't." The voice was without emotion.

Ducane half-sat in the bracken. The weathered, grease-smeared face suddenly cracked into a white grin.

Young Tom half-smiled, self-disgust giving way to a

sheepish embarrassment. "I didn't even stick him. He must have choked himself to death."

Ducane stood up. "Then it must be your lucky day." He looked down the slope to the path where Forbes and Turnbull should be waiting. "I'd better get moving now. You clear on everything?"

Young Tom nodded. "Guess so, boss."

Ducane nodded reassuringly and returned to the edge of the bracken where he had been lying in wait. He hauled out the canvas bag that carried an Army-issue battle smock and threw it down at the other's feet. "Okay, Tom, get weaving. You've got exactly twenty minutes before you make the transmission." He went to turn away, then paused. "And good luck."

Picking up the machine-gun and an ammunition case, Ducane melted silently into the brush. Within seconds Tom could hear only the rustling of the wind in the sea of waving ferns.

Sitting down beside the body of Bristow, he extracted a frag grenade from the deep pocket of his smock and placed it carefully on the ground. Then, glancing quickly around him, began to unbuckle his belt pack.

From his concealed position at the base of the tree by the pathside, Turnbull could see halfway down the inlet, until the gorse-covered embankments kinked to the right, obscuring the mouth of the stream where it opened into the lough. Only some twenty feet in front of him the stream broke noisily from the undergrowth, crossed the footpath, and gabbled over the shale. Swollen by the earlier rain, it had widened to some twelve feet by the time it reached the kink and disappeared. Turnbull reckoned it was probably up to knee-height at its deepest point.

Ducane followed the direction of the corporal's pointing finger to the thicket on the left bank, where they had stowed the boat. It showed no signs of having been disturbed.

"If you look above the hide," Turnbull said, "that's where they are."

Ducane squinted but could see nothing. "Any idea how many?"

Turnbull shook his head. "No, boss. They're being good boys and keeping their heads down. At a guess, anything up to twenty."

"What about the other bank?"

Forbes interrupted. "If you hope they're going to shoot each other, Jacko, you're out of luck. I've been watching for twenty minutes, but there's not a twitch."

Ducane rubbed his chin thoughtfully. "There's bound to be another stop-group at the mouth of the inlet. In case any of us escape their initial burst."

Turnbull nodded. "We've managed to pick up some of their transmissions. They'd taped the frequencies they were using to that set you found. Call-sign Bishop appears to be the main group. He's been communicating with Pawn One and Pawn Two, and with Ratcatcher, which appears to be your friend McClatcher. Back at the friary I should think."

"Winston Loveday's in charge of the ambush," Forbes interjected.

Ducane frowned. "Bit careless of them to use names."

Forbes said: "That's what happens when you get too confident. The Yanks always were a slovenly loada shits."

"Don't *you* get too complacent either, Dave," Ducane returned. "They may be sloppy but they're also pretty good. Some of them."

Turnbull said: "If you've disposed of Pawn One, then Pawn Two is probably the stop-group at the mouth of the inlet. There's also a call-sign called Neptune."

Ducane chuckled. "Original."

"That fishing boat we met last night?" Forbes suggested.

The captain shrugged. "Probably. They're determined we don't get off this peninsula in one piece."

Suddenly the radio crackled into life. *"Bishop to Pawn One, over."*

The three men exchanged worried glances. "I hope Tom answers," Forbes said.

270

"I just hope the radio's still working," Ducane added. "What's Tom's American accent like?"

Forbes shook his head. "Sounds like a bloody Australian!"

"Bishop to Pawn One. Come in!" The static accentuated the irritability in Winston Loveday's voice.

The three men watched the set, willing something to happen. After what seemed an age Tom's voice could be heard amidst a sudden flurry of interference. *"Pawn One to Bishop. Transmission trouble. Over."*

Forbes laughed. "Crafty little sod!"

Winston's voice came over again. Loud and demanding. *"Any movement on your contact? Over."*

Amidst more static Tom's voice sounded feeble and distorted. *"Hardly hear you, Bishop. Fading. Contact still under cover. Will advise if there is advance to inlet. Over."*

"Do you want replacement transmitter? Over."

Tom's reply sounded almost too insistent. *"No, Bishop. Am in direct line of fire. Cannot risk contact. Reception seems to be improving. Out."*

Ducane breathed a sigh of relief. "Right, lads, let's get going before Loveday's patience runs out and he sends a runner to Pawn One." He turned to Turnbull. "You happy with your role?"

Turnbull's small, humourless face flickered briefly with a smile. "Drawing enemy fire's never my idea of fun, boss. Just make sure you fire first. I don't want the first incoming shot to be hostile." He shrugged and looked up the inlet. "I'll use the stream-bed for cover. It's not much but ..." His voice trailed off.

Ducane gave the corporal's shoulder a reassuring shake as he stood up in a half-crouch. "Come on, Dave," he said to Forbes. "We've got ten minutes to cover 150 metres. Let's move."

Ducane threw himself at the path, rolling rapidly across the exposed ground, and climbed onto one knee in the cover of a bush on the other side. Forbes threw across the machine-gun and the ammunition canister they had taken from Bristow before rolling across the pathway himself.

The crawl up the slope to the right hand bank, opposite Loveday's ambush group, took five minutes. It seemed like five hours. It was a strenuous, excruciating task, edging through the foliage on elbows and knees that became grazed and raw with the constant friction against hard shale and rock. Ducane led the way, making quick but careful progress. Forbes lumbered breathlessly behind on his elbows, with the machine-gun balanced across his crooked forearms. Sweat was rolling so profusely from his forehead into his eyes that he almost collided with Ducane's feet when the SAS captain stopped.

Forbes squeezed his eyes hard shut to stop them smarting and clear his vision. Ducane was indicating the thin strand of nylon wire that ran across the path.

In explanation Ducane mouthed the word "Grenade". It seemed obvious that the right-hand bank, although clear of the enemy, had been sown with booby-traps. If Ducane's group had attempted to escape from the ambush, by running up the opposite slope, they would have tripped the wires.

Tracing the grenade and securing the pin in place whilst the wire was cut was a quick task. But, had they been running under fire, it could have been a very different matter.

The grenade was added to their armoury along with two other booby-traps they found. They had also come across a hurriedly placed seismic sensor which they swiftly covered with a sheath of field-dressing wadding to muffle any giveaway sounds. Finally Ducane was satisfied that they were opposite Loveday's main group.

Forbes glanced at his watch as he feverishly opened the ammunition container to thread the belt into the machine-gun's cartridge port. They were overdue.

"Pawn One to Bishop. Over." Winston Loveday had been waiting so intently for the message that, when it came, he physically jumped. He snatched up the handset. "Go ahead, Pawn One."

"Contact advancing. One man going point. Another 100

metres behind. Two others advancing towards our position here. Over."

"Jesus!" Loveday spat, his mind racing at the likely result of his first stop-group having been spotted. Controlling his excitement he said calmly: "Okay, Bristow. Watch yer ass and try not to fire till we've caught the two over here. Out."

One of Loveday's men had crawled out of the vegetation overlooking the inlet and raced across to the camouflaged Land Rover bent double.

The Negro climbed out of the seat to meet him.

"One of the bastards come out the treeline," the young Irishman's words came out in a gabble of thick brogue that Loveday found hard to understand.

"Okay, soldier," the Negro snapped. "Get back in line and hold till the second man's in the open and I give the word."

As the man scrambled back down the slope, Loveday leaned against the wing of the Land Rover and peered down at the stream-bed. At first he found it difficult to see the man standing motionless in the water, his battle fatigues blending perfectly with the bleak winter countryside, a Sterling held at the port.

Winston froze. It seemed as though the man was staring directly at him, but at that distance he couldn't be certain. It was uncanny. He cursed himself for leaving the safety of the disguised Land Rover. And he cursed the Provo gunman for having left his position.

Through clenched teeth he hissed as loud as he dare. "Hold your fire till the other one appears!" He wished to God he could move and grab a weapon, or at least his binoculars. His eyes were transfixed by the lone figure. A single, small offered target. So insignificant in the grey-brown sweep of the inlet, yet full of menace and danger. If only he'd move ... just to indicate he didn't really expect anything.

Winston's mouth moved imperceptibly. "Come on, little bastard, a few more steps into my web." A pause, his throat going dry. "C'mon now." Coaxing.

The head with the woollen skull cap flicked suddenly, as though checking an unexpected movement.

"Fer Chrissakes," Loveday growled, his coaxing tone giving way to anger at the man's caution. He was afraid his own men would not be able to resist the offered target much longer, but the range was far enough to make a hit unlikely.

As the Negro blinked the man had begun to move forward. Very slowly, with the gurgling waters swirling around his knees, the soldier advanced three paces before pausing again.

Loveday bared his teeth. "You don't suspect, baby. There ain't nothin' here but the birds and insects. C'mon now." He was willing him on, convinced, as the figure advanced again, that he must be feeling more secure.

As he kept on moving slowly forward Loveday was able to study him more closely. He was too small for Ducane or Forbes. This man was a stranger; an unknown quantity.

Fifty yards and another stop.

Loveday frowned. The soldier, his body kept at an oblique angle to where the Land Rover was hidden, looked only at the bank where the boat had been left. Never once did he look to the right-hand bank. Why?

Just as Loveday's eyes swung towards the opposite side of the inlet, he heard one of his men shout out a warning.

The stillness of the inlet was torn apart with the violent stutter of machine-gun fire. Glass splintered behind him as a burst of shells studded the Land Rover.

Loveday hurled himself down instinctively, his eyes seeing the vivid wink of muzzle flashes from the opposite slope. Pain, fierce and excruciating, exploded in his thigh as he pressed himself hard against the turf.

"Fire, you stupid fucking bastards!" he yelled.

Suddenly the silence from his startled men was broken by the ragged report of returning firepower.

He squeezed his eyes tight to force the flooding red tide from his vision, and reached down to the sodden mess of his leg. Again he flinched. "Shit, man," he

274

muttered to himself, "I'm gettin' too old for this sorta caper."

The trouser leg was ripped and the flesh hung in ribbons, exposing white bone scorched where the cartridge had deflected. A fraction of an inch nearer the centre of the femur and his leg would have come clean off.

He decided it would have to wait for a few more minutes. Summoning all his strength and determination, he pulled himself over to the Land Rover. He reached in and hauled himself up into the seat. Peering down into the inlet, the lone soldier, who had been advancing, had disappeared. A sudden crackle of fire from the shale sides of the stream and a wisp of blue smoke told Loveday where. At least he was pinned down by the returning fire from the Provos. He quickly scanned his own position, and his heart sank. Five of his men lay motionless; whether dead or injured it was impossible to tell. The others were more concerned at hiding from the withering rain of lead from the opposite bank, than returning it.

Loveday made a quick decision and snatched up the handset, half-expecting it to have been hit. To his surprise it was operating. "Bishop to Ratcatcher. Bishop of Ratcatcher. Over!"

Instantly McClatcher's voice came over the air in a hiss of static. *"Okay, Bishop. What gives?"*

"We found 'em, Earl. Or to be more precise they found us." He went on quickly before McClatcher had a chance to explode. "They're on the opposite bank and giving fire. I've had fifty per cent casualties." He looked soulfully down at the stream of blood pumping from his mangled leg. "Including me."

There was a brief pause at the other end. *"Seems like Ducane's learned a few tricks in the past few years ... Don't worry. I've a back-up squad standing by. I'll bring 'em up behind the bank opposite you. Hold tight, black boy! Out."*

Loveday replaced the handset and fell back against the seat, fighting back the waves of giddiness and nausea.

His eyes opened suddenly at the sound of a new noise. The distant muffled crump of grenades. He turned his

275

head wearily in the direction of Bristow's stop-group on the spur. Pawn One was under attack.

The big Negro grabbed the Medic kit and eased himself out of the Land Rover's cab and onto the ground, out of the firing line.

The return of fire from the Provos had finally died away to an occasional crackle. Across the flat river-bed there was no sign of movement from the undergrowth on the bank. Ducane counted three bodies lying in the grass but he guessed there were more. If not, at least the men were sufficiently pinned-down to consider shooting back to be too dangerous.

He nudged Forbes who lay with his shoulders hunched over the machine-gun stock. From their position they could see around the dogleg kink of the inlet to the mouth of the stream, where it merged with the sluggish grey swell of the lough. "Dave, I think they've recalled the other stop-group. Look."

Forbes swung the machine-gun muzzle to the right, following Ducane's directions. Three men were making their way awkwardly through the thick cover of the other bank, evidently struggling with heavy equipment.

"Three hundred metres," Forbes decided. "I could give 'em a burst to keep their heads down."

Ducane nodded. "I think we'd better. 'Looks like they've got some heavy stuff."

"Machine-gun?"

"Or a mortar even." He glanced down at the ammunition belt in Forbes' machine-gun. "Is that the lot?"

"Yep. Just a couple of bursts."

Ducane nodded. "Well, Dave, next comes the tricky bit."

The sergeant chuckled. "Your plan sounded fine in theory." He squeezed the trigger and the machine-gun jumped into life, spitting flame in the direction of Loveday's re-inforcements from the lough mouth. It was difficult to see exactly what the effect was, except for the flurry of dead leaves and branches. The three men had disappeared from view. It was unlikely that they'd been hit.

As the sound of the automatic fire echoed flatly across the landscape and dwindled away, a new sound could be heard. A four-wheel drive vehicle being gunned hard across rough terrain.

Ducane turned his head and peered behind them, through the copse of thin trees. "We got visitors, Dave."

"How many?"

"Can't see 'em yet. Sounded like a Land Rover. It won't take 'em long to come through the trees. We'd better act quick before some silly bastard panics and shoots us. The middle of a firefight isn't the wisest time to surrender." Ducane switched on the Pocketfone. "This is Group Leader. We have enemy closing in from our rear. Time for you to clear out, Corporal. Acknowledge. Over."

Sporadic fire from the west bank was beginning to gain momentum. The enemy's confidence was returning while Forbes conserved his ammunition.

From their position they could see Turnbull some hundred yards from the treeline, still lying prone at the edge of the stream, where he had been using the gentle shale slope for cover. There was a slight movement as he answered the signal.

"*I read you, Group Leader. I'm on my way. Can you cover me? Over.*"

Ducane flicked the switch. "Will do. Good luck. Out."

Forbes eyed him carefully. "Shall we wind up?"

A burst of bullets punched into the ground a few inches away in a shower of earth and torn grass.

Ducane spat the grit from his mouth. "Let 'em have it, Dave."

The machine-gun stuttered noisily into action, the hail of shells scything through the vegetation on the opposite bank, subduing the Provos' fire. In the cover of the wafting gunsmoke Ducane sprang to one knee and hurled three frag grenades, one after another.

The first blew at the foot of the embankment opposite, exploding in a deadly spray of tiny steel fragments and slivers of broken shale. The second and third burst farther up the slope, the force of the blast softened by the thick vegetation, the sound muffled to a dull thud. As the smoke and flying debris subsided, the full scene of devastation was revealed. Three small, scorched craters smouldered amid the winter foliage like ugly sores, each strewn with scarcely recognisable human shapes.

Forbes grimaced. "That should shut the bastards up."

A brittle crackle of fire opened up from the top of the opposing bank. Ducane dived for the ground as the magazine of shells hammered into the tree behind him.

"Christ!" Ducane hissed, "that was close!"

Forbes squeezed the trigger again. There was a forlorn metallic click as the firing pin snapped on an empty chamber. He threw the machine-gun angrily aside, and picked up the Sterling. "It's Winston Loveday. I swear to God it is!"

"He fired?" Ducane demanded.

"Up by the Land Rover. He was a nigger all right and I ain't seen no cotton plantations 'round here."

Ducane forced a grin. "Don't hit him, Dave. I'd rather us give ourselves up to him than a bloody Provo."

As the captain hurriedly tied a tattered white handkerchief around the barrel of his Sterling, voices were heard behind them. The sound of feet crashed through the undergrowth. Both men pulled out the Pocketfones and smashed them with the butts of the Sterlings.

Ducane raised the white rag. "HOLD YOUR FIRE, LOVEDAY! WE'RE COMING OUT!"

It suddenly seemed frighteningly quiet. The air was charged with tension like electricity. In the copse behind them the sound of the approaching re-inforcements grew louder. Voices were raised. Angry, excitable.

"Shift it, Dave!" Ducane snapped. "Before those trigger-happy sods decide to use us for target practice."

"HOLD YOUR FIRE, LOVEDAY!" Ducane stood up, hands raised. "D'YOU HEAR ME? CALL OFF YOUR DOGS!"

At last the sound of the Negro's voice came across the gap. It sounded strangely weak and feeble. "Come on down, Mr Ducane! Nice'n'easy!'' The captain started down the slope.

"Throw down the gun! You don' need no flagpole fer a white flag.''

Ducane tossed the weapon down and Forbes, a few yards behind, did the same.

The Negro appeared at the top of the bank, a broad smirk cracking his face. He leaned against the wing of the battered Land Rover with a sub-machine gun held loosely in one hand. The other clutched at a blood-sodden bandage around his thigh.

"An' if it ain't my old friend, Dave Forbes. Whooo-ee! Fancy meetin' you here!''

The two soldiers paused in the centre of the stream, hands raised.

There was a sudden burst of activity behind them as half-a-dozen heavily armed men burst noisily out of the copse, shouting and waving their weapons.

"HOLD FIRE, MEN!'' Loveday bawled. "I DROP THE FIRST MAN WHO SHOOTS!''

They fell into a bewildered silence, as more movement indicated the arrival of other re-inforcements from the apex of the inlet. To the north the fishing boat had also pulled in close to the mouth of the stream and an outboard dinghy, weighed down with more gunmen, was weaving shoreward.

From the corner of his mouth Forbes said: "I think this is what is called Check Mate.''

Ducane attempted to smile; it wouldn't come. He looked around him as the ring of men closed in. There was no sign of Turnbull.

CHAPTER 15

The Land Rover slewed to a halt in the mud outside the friary. There followed a noisy clatter, as the men clinging to the framework jumped off, thankful to stretch their aching muscles after the cross-country ride. Standing in a ragged semi-circle, they watched with expressions of hatred and curiosity as the two captives were hauled roughly from the back by two armed Provos.

A heavy metallic click caused heads to turn in the direction of one of the watching men. Reagan was only of medium build, but the camouflaged jacket and makeshift webbing added pounds to his stature. The whites of his eyes seemed to gleam in the dirt-smeared face, accentuating the bright irises like hard, black diamonds. The barrel of the sub-machine gun in his grip wavered between the two men who stood between the guards.

"We oughta kill the focken bastards now!" he said angrily, his voice encrusted in a thick Irish accent.

His companions glanced nervously at him, then back at the two prisoners. They seemed harmless enough now, heads hung low, unable to straighten up after the stomach-pounding they'd been given on the ride. The biggest one with the moustache had lost a front tooth and looked almost comical. Hardly the invincible warriors of the SAS. It was difficult to believe it had been necessary to train so hard and use so many men to corner them. And the end, when it had come, had been so quick that the men who had been in the thick of the firefight could scarcely believe it. Believe the carnage and destruction these two had wreaked on their companions. After enduring the weeks of merciless training by McClatcher and Loveday—only to be torn apart by grenades and vicious automatic fire. Just from these two men.

The Provo's finger tightened on the trigger. His eyes looked wild. "Let's kill the fockers now!" His voice was hoarse with anger as he glanced around at the weary look on the faces of the others. "They've rubbed out between fifteen and twenty of us since last night. Harry, Sean, Pat, Paul and the O'Casey brothers! Are we going to let them go unpunished?"

One of the guards, the Provo called Malone, raised his weapon in readiness. "Shut up, Reagan, you stupid bugger. They aren't going nowhere. If anyone touches them, McClatcher will take someone apart."

"Sod McClatcher!" Reagan spat contemptuously. "What the hell does he know about the Republican cause?"

The man beside him, with a shock of ginger hair that looked odd sprouting above the blackened face, said wearily, "Perhaps *he* knows how to make it work. We've been at it since '69. It's about time we started getting results."

The fair-haired prisoner raised his head and held Reagan in a hard gaze. "What's the matter, boy? Need your mother to pull the trigger for you? Or would you feel more comfortable if we turned our backs on you?"

One of the Provos laughed, stopping suddenly. The guards tightened their grip.

Reagan froze, the gun trembling with rage in his grip. He stepped quickly forward, his eyes flashing. "No one asked your opinion, you Brit bastard." He raised the barrel to swipe it across the captain's unprotected face.

"*Enough!*" There was no mistaking Loveday's voice. The second bullet-ridden Land Rover lumbered to a halt behind the first, in a cloud of steam that billowed from the shattered radiator.

Loveday hobbled out, supported by two men. He straightened himself up to his full height and viewed the bedraggled collection of men. Instantly he could tell those who had been in the ambush party. They were dirtier than the others, and their eyes held the resigned, lack-lustre look of men who had survived their first close action.

He knew they'd had enough; wanted only sleep. It was strange how just a few moments of vicious, nerve-shattering combat, after hours of waiting and rising tension, could have such an effect. Even on the best-trained.

His anger towards Reagan subsided. After all, they'd done it. This ragtag army of fanatical misfits had completed their mission. Even more successfully than he'd thought. And Malone was proving himself to be reliable and professional. He allowed himself a slow grin, forcing himself to forget the painful throb in his leg. McClatcher's Privates had done even better than his two prisoners knew. But he would break that surprise to them later. When it suited.

He addressed himself to the guards. "You know where to take 'em, so get on with it." As they jerked the prisoners away, he turned to Reagan. "If you've got all this energy left, soldier, you'd better come along and see if you can't work it out on our new arrivals."

Reagan's angry expression turned to one of bewilderment and then a smirk of satisfaction.

Loveday began struggling towards the friary entrance. Then he noticed Malone and stopped, beckoning him over.

"Sir?"

"I was pleased with yer sense of responsibility back there, soldier." The Negro looked at the Irishman approvingly. "Yer a mean son-of-a-bitch an' a wild 'un. But y've learned pretty fast. Now I'm agoin' t' give you the chance to earn yer spurs. A mission into enemy territory, so to speak. The mainland."

"Sir?"

The American drew an envelope from his pocket and handed it over. "It's a vital mission an' must be carried out t' the letter. Savvy, man?" Malone nodded. "Go to the address on the envelope. It's a pub in Fulham where we have a permanent room booked under the name o' Adrian Brown. When you get our telephone call, yer to open the sealed instructions an' follow 'em to the letter. Okay?"

"When do I leave, sir?"

"Immediately, man, immediately." Loveday smiled reassuringly. "Pack a few personal things an' get the hell goin'. Grab yerself a driver to take yer to Shannon. Then the first goddamn flight you can t' Heathrow."

Malone smirked with pleasure. "What about me weapons?"

"You'll find all y'want under the floor behind the door in the room at the pub. That's all, soldier."

Still smiling, Malone saluted smartly and marched off to find a driver.

Loveday turned and hobbled into the friary helped by Reagan. Outside the brightness of the new dawn was subsiding, giving way to the promise of another bleak, colourless day.

Against the stark, crumbling interior of the damp, flag-stoned cell, McClatcher looked clean and immaculate. The trousers and military-cut shirt were pressed and his stance emphasised his barrel chest. He was clean-shaven and his brown, weathered face disguised the red rings around the sharp, blue-grey eyes.

When it came the smile appeared genuine, as he looked down at the two men on the spread of straw in the corner.

"It's been a long time, Jacko," he said amiably.

"Not long enough, McClatcher."

The American grinned and his teeth glistened menacingly in the shaft of light from the narrow window. "Not a friendly greeting."

"Piss off," Forbes offered.

McClatcher relaxed his shoulders and leaned against the rough stone wall. As he plucked a cigar from his top pocket and set about lighting it, Reagan watched curiously from the doorless arch where a blanket had been fixed as a screen. He fingered his sub-machine gun fondly.

Ducane said mockingly: "I hear you've made full colonel. Not bad going for a captain who was kicked out of the US Army."

McClatcher exhaled a long stream of smoke. It curled

283

and hung in the still air like a thin, blue snake. "My efforts are appreciated here," he replied evenly.

"This bunch of monkeys would appreciate Ghengis Khan," Ducane snapped.

"Or Adolf Hitler," Forbes added.

The American smiled slowly. "You English underestimate the Irish. Always have. These men might not be much, but they're improvin' daily." In the corner Reagan stiffened. "They might not be up to our standard yet, but *you're* the ones sitting under guard."

"That could have something to do with numbers," Ducane replied.

McClatcher's smile broadened. "You always were a smart-ass, Jacko." There was no humour in his voice this time. "We've known every move you've made in an attempt to locate us. We set you up and you took the bait. Hook, line and sinker—as they say. Now, that ain't so smart."

Ducane shuffled uncomfortably on the floor. The hands tied behind his back were bent awkwardly and the lack of circulation was numbing his fingers. "All right, McClatcher, you're a clever boy. But this location is known to the authorities. You're living on borrowed time."

The laugh was harsh. "That's a pretty feeble line, Jacko! I'd have expected something better from you."

"The captain's right," Forbes confirmed.

McClatcher held up three fingers. "You carried short-range radios." He tapped the first. "Second, there was no communication equipment in the luggage you left at the guest house. And, lastly, since you could have located us, there have been no phone calls made by you, except that attempt to dupe us." He closed his fist, massaging the stiffness in his fingers that Ducane had caused all those years before. "In case you wondered, before we chose this place, we made sure—sure as hell—we had a Republican girl on the local switchboard."

Slowly he crossed the room to the bare wooden table in the far corner. "So, my limey friends, I deduce that you're on a *sensitive* mission. On your own with no back-up."

"For Chrissake, McClatcher," Forbes said. "D'you think this yellow-backed government of ours would do anything to upset the Irish Republic? Jesus, you must be as thick as these Micks you call soldiers!"

It was a good try and a fleeting expression of doubt flickered in the American's eyes. Quietly he said: "I don't need to play guessing games, Dave. The facts speak for themselves. During the night this camp will be vacated and there'll be nothing to prove anything or anyone was ever here. And, quite frankly, I don't give a monkey's toss if the whole bloody Irish Army arrived. We've got mortars and anti-tank missiles. Even a couple of RPG-7 anti-aircraft jobs so we'd give 'em such a warm reception ..." He stopped suddenly and smiled again, slowly. "But then that is hardly likely now, is it?"

Ducane asked: "And where are we moving onto?"

McClatcher sat on the edge of the table and, stretching out his legs, crossed them casually at the ankles. "Where *we're* going is nothing to do with you. Where *you're* going— ah!" He dropped the butt of his cigar on the floor and left it to smoulder. "That, my limey friends, is very much in your hands.

"You see, there's a lot you can tell me about what's going on over the border. Operations in Armagh, names and addresses, safe-houses, IRA suspects. No chickenshit— the works. I want that information and I'm prepared to get it by any means possible. Remember what happened to your friend, Harrington." He waved his hands expansively. "Voluntarily or under persuasion. Make it easy on yourselves and there could even be a job in it for you."

"Go fuck yourself," Forbes snarled.

Ducane watched the American in silence. If he really planned to set himself up against the Army in Ulster he was now in the position to extract enough information to endanger hundreds of British soldiers. Not just SAS and undercover operations, but ordinary squaddies as well. Christmas was only a couple of days away, and by the New Year McClatcher's men would certainly be well enough trained to see that it was welcomed in with a maelstrom of destruction and carnage.

If they offered information, true or false, without resistance McClatcher would be suspicious. That alone might extend their time alive, but it was unlikely to be a pleasant existence. If they were caught out at deceit, he was sure McClatcher would not hesitate to use the same physical excesses he'd used on the VC in Vietnam.

By resisting in the earlier stages, now, they could relent before the punishment got progressively worse. It would also allow them to play for time.

McClatcher's words shocked him: "I imagine you're both working out how long you can spin this out before your colleagues arrive!"

Ducane's heart pounded like a trip-hammer.

The American turned to Reagan. "You'll find a couple of packages in the back of Sergeant Loveday's jeep, soldier. Go bring 'em in pronto. An' be sure you keep someone on this door."

For a moment the man hesitated, then he pushed aside the blanket and disappeared.

Forbes glanced nervously at Ducane. The captain shrugged.

A few moments later there was a scuffle of clumping boots outside and a sound of heavy breathing as Reagan and another dragged in the two bodies.

The men dropped them to the floor. There was a sickening squelch as the shattered skull of one corpse hit the stone. Half the face was missing, as though it had been chopped cleanly with a giant meat cleaver, and a thick mucus of flesh and grey brain matter spilled onto the stone. An eyeball floated in the mess like an egg.

The other corpse had no skull at all. Just a brittle white stalk of neckbone protruded from the top of the torso where the head had been snapped off like that of a doll.

There was no mistaking the blood-soaked camouflage smocks. They had been drawn from the quartermaster at Hereford barracks before the team left.

Ducane swallowed hard and breathed deeply to check

the vomit rising from his stomach. Forbes wasn't quick enough.

He spat the stuff from his mouth. "I'll bloody stick you, McClatcher!" he choked, fighting hard to regain his breath. "So bloody help me, I will."

The American nodded at Reagan. "Okay, soldier, get these stiffs outa here. Organise a burial detail an' dig it real deep. Then get back in here."

Reagan gave the two pitiful bodies by his feet a bilious glance and promptly called in two men to take them away.

McClatcher turned to Ducane. "I'm sorry about yer friends. I'd've preferred 'em alive, too." He smiled, but this time there was scarcely a pretence of humour. "Now that your plans have been circumvented, yer needn't waste my time hoping for something to turn up. Are you goin' to co-operate?" He lit another cigar. "An' none of that name, rank and number crap."

Ducane said evenly: "The sergeant spoke for both of us." He smiled slowly. "Go fuck yourself."

He didn't see it coming, the steel-capped boot moved so fast. It slammed into his cheek like a demolition ball and he heard the bone crack as his head exploded in brightly-coloured stars. He slipped heavily against Forbes as he felt the pain swell up in his face until he thought it would burst.

Through the thudding noise in his head, Ducane heard McClatcher's voice. It was menacingly quiet and restrained. "I've no compunction, Ducane, in taking you and your buddy apart piece by piece. We've a chainsaw here and I'm quite prepared to take off a limb at a time ..." He waited for the significance of his words to sink in. "Like me you are trained to resist interrogation, so I'm not goin' to sod about pulling out fingernails."

Ducane's vision gradually started clearing and he watched the American's blurred shape move until it was standing over Forbes. "Or I could start with you, Sergeant. I've no compunction 'bout taking yer balls off with a bread knife."

Forbes' chuckle was dry and lacking humour. "I've been

meaning to get 'round to a vasectomy for years . . ."

McClatcher ignored him and returned to sit casually on the edge of the table. "It strikes me, however, that this overt violence might be unnecessary." His voice sounded confident. "You no doubt found the happy family snapshot of the Ducane family. It was missing from Kelly's body . . ."

The silence became brittle. A slow grin of satisfaction spread across McClatcher's face, his teeth gleaming demonically against his tanned skin. "Ah, looks like we hit a raw spot. That's good, real good. Because it'd be more fun roughin' up a lady like your Patricia than it would you two ugly motherfuckers."

Ducane studied the American with fresh contempt. He didn't trust himself to speak. Earlier it had crossed his mind that McClatcher might use such a threat, but he'd dismissed the idea. Unless she'd been kidnapped and brought to Ireland, the idea seemed preposterous. But, as McClatcher continued speaking, he realised that it was far from an idle threat.

"Our guy Malone is now leaving for the mainland. By this evening he'll be stationed near your home—just waiting for a telephone call. You remember him, don't you, Jacko. You met at the McGuire farm. He'll have no compunction in obeying orders. He may even add a few ideas of his own."

"You're a fucking liar, McClatcher!" accused Forbes.

The American smiled and pulled out a sealed envelope from his pocket. He proceeded to open it slowly.

He scanned his eyes over the sheet, smiling to himself. "This is a copy of the sealed orders Malone is carrying with him. On receipt of our call he's to open 'em and carry out the instructions. He'll contact one of our sleepin' cells an' proceed immediately to your home an' hold your wife 'n' daughter." He paused, raising his eyes to look directly at the SAS captain.

Ducane shook his head.

McClatcher continued. "Their instructions are to abuse your wife on a prolonged basis, takin' care not to let her become unconscious or to die. Your daughter will be made to watch ... I won't bore you with the details ..."

Miraculously Ducane was on his feet in one swift movement, swaying precariously to keep his balance as he strode forward. His foot was already driving towards McClatcher's groin as Reagan stepped between them, swinging the butt of his sub-machine gun over the soldier's neck. A heavier build, Forbes tried in vain to follow-up with the same speed. He half-stumbled over Ducane's collapsed body and came face-to-face with the muzzle of the Irishman's gun. He fell back against the wall.

Reagan hooked his booted foot under Ducane's shoulder and rolled the unresisting body back into the corner.

The American was well-pleased with the effect of his plan and lit a fresh cigar as he waited for Ducane to regain consciousness. It did not take long before the captain was struggling into a sitting position.

McClatcher sounded relaxed and confident, his drawl becoming more pronounced. "Well, Ducane, do I send the message or not? Your little ol' lady has a sweet little ass an' I'd hate t' see it harmed. But I'm sure you don't doubt what I'm prepared to have done. After all, you saw what we did to those Gook women in 'Nam."

"Christ," Forbes said. "You're the biggest yellow creep I've ever come across."

"Shut your mouth, Sergeant," McClatcher replied. "She ain't your ol' lady. It's yer tight-lipped captain who has to decide."

Ducane had difficulty in speaking, his lip was split and bleeding, one side of his mouth paralysed with pain. He spat out blood as he cleared his throat. "You go ahead, McClatcher. I'll remind you the IRA doesn't hold with molesting women and children. When the news gets round what you've done—if you can carry it out—your life won't be worth a shit."

McClatcher grinned. "Ain't gonna help your little wife 'n' kid none, whether the Micks approve or not." He blew a long spiral of smoke at the two men on the floor.

"Besides, I think they'll *forgive* me, when I achieve what I promised 'em."

Forbes said suddenly: "Jacko, you're putting Trish and Sarah in the front-line. You can't do it. And the boys in the regiment wouldn't want you to. Or expect you to."

Ducane stared blankly at the stone wall. His voice was low. "We all know the risks, Dave. Every now and again someone has to pay the price. The regiment has a damned strict rule about telling wives too much. Both Trish and I know it. You know it. We broke that rule. She'll understand. She'll have to."

Forbes' eyes burned fiercely. "And Sarah? Will she understand?"

Ducane shut his eyes. He tried to speak, but couldn't find the words.

The sergeant looked up. "McClatcher, you're the worst kind of prick ever turned out by the military. You're a perfect example of what happens when the system goes wrong. But I can't let Jack make this decision." He paused, glancing sideways at Ducane. "I maybe don't know as much as him, but I know enough. I'll tell you what you want."

McClatcher raised his eyebrows cynically. "Uncorroborated testimony, Forbes? What's that worth?"

Forbes shrugged, his eyes pleading. "Give us a few minutes alone. I'll try and persuade him."

McClatcher chewed uncertainly on his cigar. He looked at Reagan but got no inspiration. "Okay. Three minutes. But I warn you, I'll keep a full guard mounted with orders to kill if you try so much as breathin' too fast." He strode towards the door.

"I said alone," Forbes reminded, indicating Reagan.

Reluctantly the Irishman shuffled out after McClatcher.

Forbes let out a low whistle of relief, then rolled over until his face was only a few inches from Ducane. "Christ, Jacko, you deserve a bleedin' Oscar for that."

Ducane rubbed his shoulder against his swollen cheek. "What makes you think I was acting? I didn't really think he'd ever threaten Trish and Sarah."

290

"That fucker would carve-up his own grandmother if it suited him. 'Pity we didn't frag him and Loveday when we had the chance in 'Nam."

"But we didn't. Threatening Trish has rather un-balanced the odds ..."

Forbes said: "Okay, it's not the game we wanted, but we're still in with a chance if we can keep going long enough."

Ducane's eyes looked very blue and very cold. "And how long is enough? If we can't keep to the story we discussed, they'll have us in no time."

Forbes bit his lower lip. "If we've any doubt we'll just have to go for the truth."

Ducane shook his head. "No, we'll just have to give the most likely-sounding story ..."

With a sudden rush Reagan burst through the curtain, gun at the ready, as McClatcher re-entered.

"Well, my friends, have you decided to be sensible?"

Forbes said: "I think I've just persuaded Captain Ducane to commit treason."

CHAPTER 16

For three hours the questions had been coming hard and fast. Ducane had no time to relax and scarcely less to think out his replies. He had been taken to another flag-stoned cell in the old friary, while Forbes remained in the first.

He had been stripped naked and tied with thick steel wire to an upright wooden beam that had once held the roof in place. Winston Loveday had done the interrogating. He seemed remarkably fit and awake, despite the leg wound, and sat up in a camp bed whilst Reagan and another Provo prompted the prisoner every time he paused to think or tried to slow the pace of the questioning.

Ducane's groin had become one prolonged, throbbing ache from Reagan's vicious attentions with a gun butt. Raw patches of cigar burns spotted his torso. The method was as effective as it was cruel. Working from a prepared sheet, Loveday ran down the list of questions at a rattling pace, demanding instantaneous replies and punishing hesitations with increasing degrees of pain. He darted from one question to another, then returned, re-questioning and asking additional related questions. It was clear, almost from the outset, that there would be no chance to confine answers to those subjects Ducane had pre-prepared with Forbes. From the start the questions were probing and far-reaching, touching areas of military sensitivity. Codes and code-words; current operations; details of personnel, safe-houses, observation posts and operational timetables; levels of penetration and manning; betrayals and informers, suspects ... names, occupations, ages, weaknesses ...

Almost immediately Ducane had been forced into half-truths and distorted replies, trying desperately to remember what he'd said fifteen minutes previously. A fourth man stood in the corner with a portable tape-recorder. Every twenty minutes he would put on a new cassette and take the old one outside to some other part of the ancient building.

"Harrington," Loveday snapped. "What was his rank?"

"I told you five minutes ago ... Aaaagh!"

"Wrong answer, Ducane! Think! Your balls can't take much more."

"Lieutenant."

"In what?"

"Artillery."

"You said seconded to the SAS."

"Well, yes! Oh, Chr-i-i-st!"

"Then say so." A fleeting pause. "What was the name of the operation at the farmhouse?"

"Trunk Junction."

"How many men in the operation?"

"Eight SAS. About thirty regulars."

"Tell me the names and duties of the SAS men?"

"Again?"

"AGAIN!"

"Let me have some water."

"Shit! Dammit, man! Ain't you got no STAMINA!"

Reagan punched at Ducane's testicles viciously with his rifle butt.

As the cry echoed around the tiny cell, there came a sudden commotion from outside. McClatcher's voice was heard long before he entered with half-a-dozen of his men.

He stood between Ducane and Loveday's cot, legs astride and his face distinctly red with anger.

"Ducane, what sort of stupid ass d'you an' your sergeant take me for!" His eyes blazed as they swung from the captain to the Negro and back again. "We've been cross-checking your replies with your sergeant's! Goddammit, how many names does one soldier have in your outfit? 'Cos I got five different versions for each one. Timetables would do credit to your goddamn British railway system! An' these operation details you gave are a loada bullshit!"

Ducane said: "Dave doesn't know as much as I do. He's bound to get confused. Got things wrong."

McClatcher stepped around until his mouth was within inches of Ducane's battered face. "Well, you both got things wrong, Ducane. Very wrong! Now I ain't got time to fart about and be made a fool of. I'm goin' to give you a quick, sharp example." He turned to Loveday. "Put some clothes on this fuckin' limey and get him outside pronto!"

He spun on his heel and pushed his way through the small crowd that had gathered.

Five minutes later Ducane, his hands bound tightly behind his back, was thrust out into the open. After the dimness of the friary the dull afternoon light was dazzling. He squinted at the scene around him, fighting the burning in his eyes.

An early twilight mist was beginning to form on high ground and across the flat grey expanse of the lough. Visibility was restricted to barely half-a-mile. Where the ground sloped away in front of him, towards the water's edge, the men of McClatcher's private army had gathered in a large semi-circle around a shallow depression. Behind them stores and equipment were spread out neatly over the rough turf. Evidently they were ready to be loaded aboard large covered trucks, which had been parked under the copse of spindle trees and covered with camouflage netting.

Fear formed like a steel barb in Ducane's stomach. It was as though he suddenly realised the enormity of McClatcher's intentions and the sheer professionalism with which his operation was organised. The American's driving force and vast military know-how would have little difficulty in turning the PIRA Army Council's aspirations into numbing reality. But the bustle of activity, the air of strict discipline, and the array of military hardware didn't hit Ducane as hard as the sight of forty uniformed men waiting, patient and grim-faced, for their next order.

They were ready to move out, to disperse without

trace—only to reform later at a succession of pre-determined points throughout Ulster. Ready to embark on the bloodiest campaign ever mounted against the British Army in Northern Ireland. And there was no doubt that the campaign would be thoroughly planned, researched and executed.

As he stood, wearing just boots, trousers and a combat smock that flapped open in the wind, Ducane realised that the American would spare nothing to extract the information he wanted. That knowledge would provide McClatcher with the final key to unlock the bloodbath. The ferocity and surprise with which the attacks would undoubtedly be mounted would leave the security forces winded and running around like headless chickens. During the interrogation he had realised the depth and extent of his own knowledge, and the countless numbers of lives that would be imperilled before new measures could be introduced. Within a month an organisation like McClatcher's, armed with the information he possessed, could be easily responsible for the deaths of a hundred British soldiers. Two hundred even. Under the American's professional leadership, the province would be under attack from within, by a force the like of which had never before been available to any terrorist group in the world. The PLO, the Japanese Red Army and Bader Meinhoff would be like amateurs in comparison.

The outcry on the mainland at the carnage could be imagined. Demands for the withdrawal of British troops would rise to a deafening pitch.

Ducane was jerked forward by his escorts and led roughly to the high ground, overlooking the depression and the gathering of Provos. In the middle of the semi-circle Forbes lay sprawled on his back on the turf, his hands tied behind him. To one side stood the man called Reagan, both hands clasping the handle-grip of a chain-saw like a medieval double-handed sword.

His escorts stopped Ducane next to McClatcher, who was standing on the high ground, patiently observing the ranks of his men and the prone British soldier. He stood erect, impervious to the chill of the winter afternoon, deliberately ignoring Ducane. The men below him waited for his announcement, the excitement they felt given away only by the flicker of interest on their faces.

McClatcher waited until Winston Loveday had reached his side, helped by a stick and a medical orderly.

As he spoke his voice was brisk and clipped. "I don't need to tell you guys how pleased I am with what you have achieved today. You were put against the enemy you've been training to fight. And yer won." He glanced quickly around at the faces of the young Irishmen. There were a lot of half-smiles and an underlying sense of achievement could be seen on their faces. "Casualties were high, but we were fighting the best and without the benefit of surprise. An' surprise is what our planning will give us in the campaign to come. Strike—HARD—then melt away." He allowed himself a wry grin. "Only to strike minutes later, a hundred miles away ... The enemy won't know his ass from his elbow. An' all the time reinforcements will be trainin' in new secret camps like this one set up here in Eire, the States and in Libya.

"As soon as night falls you will all disperse. Orders will be given to you individually when I've finished talking to you. Unknown to each other you'll be sent to separate addresses in Ulster, close to other members of the fire-teams we have selected. That is three or four man teams—best qualified for the tasks you will be set. Targets will be members of the British Forces, particularly the SAS, transport and communications. Some of you will be asked to form sub-teams of your untrained colleagues in the North. They will be sent out against known informers. From our preliminary investigations and research we already have a list of three hundred names ..."

A ripple of disbelief ran through the gathering. Ducane was incredulous. Even without his knowledge, McClatcher had obviously been hard at work with his Special Forces techniques.

"Our first priority is to re-establish our control of Armagh. Over the past year it's been heisted from us by the SAS, backed up by regular units adoptin' similar techniques. This'll open up safe lines of supply to Eire and, believe me, we're goin' t'have one helluva lot of supplies for you guys!"

The cheer and catcalls were instantaneous. McClatcher had carefully worked them to a pitch where they believed in their own invincibility. As well they might, thought Ducane bitterly.

McClatcher raised a hand and immediately silence returned to the ranks of the men. "After the Armagh clean-up, which—make no mistake—will be damn tough, success will gather momentum. But the success in Armagh will be helped one great deal by the information provided by the men you guys got this mornin', who you now see in front of you." He glanced sideways at Ducane and smiled, his white even teeth glistening against his tan.

"But our SAS friends, true to their reputation, are playin' at bein' smart-asses. They've bin givin' us bullshit —pages of it—all day long! So we're wonderin' whether we should ask 'em again, nicely, to co-operate, or have some fun with Sergeant Forbes down there, an' tickle him a little with the chain-saw ...?"

Several of the men shouted up angrily. Ducane heard the words: "Cut the Brit bastard down the middle!" Other suggestions were hidden in the sudden surge of angry voices demanding vengeance.

McClatcher turned to Ducane. His voice was very quiet. "You see, Jacko, this is true democracy at work."

"One day you'll pay dear for this, you sod." Scarcely audible.

McClatcher's smile remained on his lips, but his eyes were humourless. "One day, Jacko, but not today, eh? Today your friend is goin' to pay dear. A leg first. Then an arm. On opposite sides of his body. We have medical people to ensure he'll stay alive ... At least long enough for us to remove the other arm and leg if you still refuse to co-operate." He looked down at Forbes sprawled help-lessly on the ground. "And should you still resist, that phone-call to the mainland ..."

Ducane could scarcely believe his ears. It was never planned to be like this.

"What makes it all worthwhile, McClatcher? What does it take to make a man sell his soul?"

McClatcher's smile cracked into a wide grin. "In my case, man, a million bucks. An' in your case, your buddy's right leg and the chance to save your wife's pretty little ass!" The American turned sharply back to his audience.

Ducane heard the sudden urgent shriek of the chainsaw as it whined into life.

His knees felt suddenly weak and the barb in his stomach twisted, getting bigger and harder. He shook his head, trying to clear his brain. He *must* think of something. But exhaustion and lack of food and sleep dulled his mind like a drug. None of this should have happened. He'd had every chance to do things differently.

Even now he could hear Turnbull's voice, clear and incisive, back at the hotel. He had made it plain enough that the odds weren't on, but it had been Ducane himself who used the regiment's tradition and training to get his own way. No one else would benefit. Just the satisfaction of a personal challenge against a man he had disliked since he'd first met him. And he knew it wasn't just McClatcher's callous method of operation in Vietnam and the atrocities over which he had smugly presided. The fact that he so obviously attracted Trish had touched some raw spot. He had quietly hidden the jealousy and anger he felt, and had buried it deep in his mind in the intervening years. With the birth of Sarah, a new life had opened up. He had mellowed and had accepted his wife's physical needs. He had never suspected her of being unfaithful, but then he had taken care not to look too hard. But McClatcher had been at the start of it, and now, in recent weeks—in fact ever since she had phoned him about the American's visit—it had been gnawing at the back of his mind like a cancer.

He said quietly: "Tell me, how much did my wife tell you?"

McClatcher jumped at the chance to twist the knife.

"Once Trish has her legs open, she'll tell you anythin' yer wanna know."

"An' believe me," it was Loveday's voice in his ear, "we poked dat little pussy from dusk t' dawn. Yessir, an' she jest loved it ... Whowee!"

"FOR CHRIST'S SAKE!" Forbes' voice yelled as Reagan dropped the spinning blade until it hovered just above the left thigh.

McClatcher twisted round. "Reagan. Take his leg off!"

"NO!" Forbes cried out involuntarily.

Suddenly his shout was drowned by another noise that seemed to come from the very bowels of the earth.

Even as the violent shockwave of the debris showered over them, Ducane found himself reasoning that a blast of such ferocity couldn't have been caused by grenades alone. Ammunition must have already been loaded on one of the covered trucks.

His sideways roll was involuntary as the broadside of displaced air hit him. At the same time the gathered men in the depression were also scattered like ninepins, some stumbling, falling over each other. The few who could catch their breath screamed with shock and fear.

Amid the flying debris Ducane forced himself to look around. Whether caught off balance or by sheer reflex reaction it was impossible to tell, but both McClatcher and Loveday were lying prone, as turf and scraps of metal flew all around them. For a moment he had the crazy thought of leaping on one of them and trying to grab a weapon. But he held himself in check. Trussed like a chicken, the chances of success were virtually nil.

Instead he turned his attention to Forbes, who had used the diversionary explosion to roll sideways into a patch of scrub at the side of the depression. This quick action had left Reagan momentarily stunned. He was standing in a dazed half-crouch, gazing in bewilderment at the charred framework of the burning vehicles. Another series of dull explosions boomed from inside the wreckage, sending livid sparks and clouds of smoke into the air.

It took only a fraction of a second for Ducane to weigh

up the situation. Although he reasoned that he wasn't exactly in a position to be of any help to Forbes, he felt a compelling need to be at his side. Even tied with hands behind their backs, their chances of survival together must be better than if they remained separated. Hastily he struggled onto his knees and pitched himself forward down the slope. Visions of a grey, smoke-smudged sky spun before his eyes as he rolled. The force with which he hit the bottom knocked the breath from his body. The momentum of the slope kept him moving. He crashed through the dry scrub until he came to rest a few feet from Forbes' grinning face.

"Nice of you to drop in, Jacko."

Ducane twisted round until he was able to get onto his knees. "Quick, Dave!" he panted. "Back-to-back. My ropes have loosened a bit."

Forbes had obviously been given some rough treatment and it took an age for him to climb onto his knees and shuffle nearer. The initial pandemonium had subsided, but now McClatcher's men were still suppressed by an accurate and vicious hail of machine-gun fire. It came from somewhere beyond the burning vehicles. Now that the heavy tyres were ablaze, it was impossible to make out anything beyond the thick columns of stinking smoke.

Ducane felt the sergeant's fingers working at the bonds on his wrists.

"An' what d'hell d'you think you're doin'!" There was no mistaking the menace in Reagan's voice. Or the shrill whirr of the chain-saw as the figure approached through wafts of smoke.

Forbes' fingers plucked feverishly at the ropes, blindly trying to unravel the puzzle.

Ducane glanced around desperately. If he was hoping for some salvation, he was disappointed. As the palls of black fog blotted out the landscape, the only person he could see was another of McClatcher's men, in beret and camouflage jacket, jogging forward to assist Reagan. Ducane's heart sank.

Reagan lifted the spinning chain-saw above his head with both hands and ran the last few feet towards the struggling SAS men.

Ducane thrust backwards, hard, toppling Forbes onto the ground. He felt the cold displacement of air as the rotating blade slashed past his cheek. His face hit the turf with a thud. Again the awful noise. Twisting onto his back, he looked up. The Irishman suddenly seemed enormous, towering above him, filling his whole vision. Then a glint of light as the thrashing blade came down.

For a moment the sudden stammer of fire meant nothing. It was just part of the background turmoil. Ducane heard the blade hit the earth, inches from his head, and watched with stupefied curiosity as Reagan froze, a look of total surprise on his face. Slowly he began to twist at the knees, his entire body pivoting and he collapsed over them. Reagan's glazed eyes stared into his, only inches away.

Ducane felt the warm, sticky wetness on his face as he struggled to free himself from the weight of Reagan's body. Then it was lifted and the bereted man, who he had seen running towards them a few seconds earlier, was crouching by his side. The sub-machine gun, resting carelessly across his knee, was still smoking. Even through the thick smudges of camouflage cream, Ducane could recognise the boyish grin.

From the helpless position on his back where he had been thrown, Forbes scowled. "What the hell kept you, Perrot?"

Young Tom laughed. "Thought we'd like to see how y'got yourself outa this one, Sarge."

"Cheekly little bastard ..."

Turning Ducane over, the soldier slid his knife easily through the ropes. As he sat up and worked the circulation back into his hands, another figure came scrambling through the smoke behind them.

Corporal John Turnbull seemed so weighed down with weaponry that it was hard to imagine how his small frame could have carried it all. His face looked pinched, white and drawn; more doll-like than ever. Thankfully he dropped the heavy load of ammunition pouches and spare grenades.

"Sorry, it took longer than I thought." He smiled broadly, quickly unstrapping the guns from both shoulders. "I was planning to get you from the friary. Rather messed things up when they brought you out here. I had to think fast. Thank God those lorries were parked there!" He handed Ducane one of the sub-machine guns.

"For Chrissakes," Forbes said. "When you old women have finished gossiping, will *some* bastard undo these fucking ropes!"

Ducane's hands worked automatically over the Sterling as he looked out across the depression. The coils of obnoxious, thick rubber smoke were gradually clearing, but still clung reluctantly to the contours, despite the tugging of the breeze. Ducane smiled to himself as the far side of the depression became visible. Some thirty of McClatcher's men had thrown themselves on the embankment to avoid the earlier hail of fire from Turnbull. Now one or two were feeling braver and more inquisitive. They peered over the rim of the depression at the skeletons of the trucks that were now burning fitfully. It had not even occurred to them that the elusive enemy they feared were now sitting fifty feet behind them, quietly checking an array of automatic weapons and hand-grenades.

As Ducane's team prepared to assault the men opposite, McClatcher and Loveday appeared at the top of the slope. For a fleeting second the faces of the Americans registered total surprise, immediately recognising that they had been duped into believing two of Ducane's team had been killed.

McClatcher's reaction came first. There was a quick burst of fire, directed straight from the hip. The shower of lead was returned by Turnbull and Young Tom. McClatcher dived for cover.

Loveday needed no second warning. Firing a quick, inaccurate burst he, too, dropped behind the crest.

At the sound of the commotion behind them, some of

the FCU men on the opposite bank of the depression looked round. Expressions of curiosity turned first to utter shock, then panic . . . Figures started jumping involuntarily as Forbes and Ducane opened up, methodically hosing the opposite bank with automatic fire. As the stream of shells laced across the confused and stumbling men, hurled grenades added their own dull, vicious *crump* to the increasing rattle of fire. Hot steel fragments sliced across the embankment, followed by more automatic fire. Additional bodies fell motionless, some twitching in their death throes.

It was a massacre, ferocious, quick and bloody. It lasted scarcely forty-five seconds, but it was enough. The scene, viewed through the wreathing gunsmoke in the dying afternoon light, went suddenly quiet and motionless. Like a macabre painting. Only half a dozen men near the top of the depression had decided to risk the unknown and had rushed towards the burning lorries. The others, fumbling in terror to bring their weapons to bear on the enemy at their backs, had been consumed by the murderous outburst of gunfire and grenades.

As the air cleared of the acrid scent of cordite, one of the figures twitched involuntarily. Forbes' Sterling gave a quick, harsh cough. The body fell still. The smoke wafted slowly away. Far out over the lough, a hawk circled, its presence eerie and mournful.

Already Ducane was worming his way up the embankment, sliding expertly over the rough ground. Turnbull followed.

They peered over the crest together, only to be greeted by a splatter of fire from the building some hundred and fifty yards away. A small group of men were giving covering fire to the survivors who were trying to reach the protection of the friary stonework. There was no mistaking Loveday as he limped awkwardly after the running men. McClatcher was helping him with one hand and waving furiously with the other. He was attempting to get his bewildered men to form a defensive perimeter. His bawling seemed to be falling on deaf ears.

Ducane gestured down to Forbes and Young Tom to join him.

As they reached his side, he indicated the three jeeps parked in a neat row, sideways on to the friary. Already the vehicles had been stripped of their camouflage in readiness for the civilian roads. Two were attached to the generator trailers that had been supplying power to McClatcher's headquarters.

"Dave, come with me," he snapped. "John, you and Tom give us covering fire. If anything happens to us, put those Rovers out of commission ... I don't want any of those bastards getting off this peninsula."

Turnbull palmed a fresh magazine clip into his Sterling. "Don't worry, boss, they ain't going nowhere."

"When Dave and I get to the Rovers," Ducane continued, "give us fifteen seconds, then open up with everything you've got. Stop when the grenades go off, because then we're goin' in. Right?"

"Gotcha," returned Turnbull. His eyes flashed in his darkened face. "Good luck, boss. Keep your head down."

Ducane elbowed Forbes. "Let's move it!"

Two Sterlings crashed into life beside him, the shells arcing almost lazily through the void between the crest and the ruin. The returning blink of muzzle flashes was diffused as brick dust, debris and sparks showered around the old walls.

Crouching low, Ducane and Forbes sprang towards the parked Land Rovers. Immediately a vicious hail of shells ripped at the turf by their feet. But the covering fire from Turnbull and Young Tom, combined with the curtain of dust, had deprived McClatcher's men of a clear target.

Ducane dived the last few feet into the shelter of the first vehicle. Forbes followed, stumbling awkwardly on top of him. The next volley of opposing fire was closer in, finding its accuracy. It tore up the ground where the sergeant would have been, had he not jumped.

His heart pounding after the sudden exertion, Ducane fumbled in his ammunition-belt pouches. He laid half-a-dozen grenades on the ground. There were two stun-grenades, two white canister smoke-grenades and two live green L2 frags.

Half kneeling with his back against the side of the Land Rover, Forbes poured two two-second bursts into the empty windows of the friary.

The covering gunfire from the embankment eased while one of the two SAS men changed over magazines. Someone in the old building—it was impossible to determine who—took the opportunity to send a withering return of fire at Forbes. To the sound of ripping canvas the jeep's soft top fell apart in shreds. Shells hammered into the far side of the bodywork. With a sudden, spitting hiss of air the heavy-duty wheel by Forbes' feet deflated. The vehicle lurched suddenly, half-poised above him, swaying threateningly under the impetus of the onslaught.

"Hurry, for Christ's sake!" he yelled at Ducane. "Before I get this lot on top of me!"

The captain jumped to his feet and hurled the two stun-grenades, overarm, at the stone window arches.

Nothing, silence.

He tossed two spare grenades across to Forbes. They nodded to each other and threw.

SSshreeeee!

In the confines of the small building the effect of the exploding flash-bangs must have been mind-blowing. Even with their eyes closed both men could see the murky outlines of the building through their eyelids, so dazzling was the sudden flood of light.

Ten seconds the manual recommended. *One.* Releasing the fly-off levers, the smoke-grenades were tossed to cause confusion when McClatcher's men recovered from the paralysing shock. *Two, three.* Firing two precious bursts in the direction of the window arches, as they sprinted into the billowing clouds of smoke. *Four, five, six.* Fighting against the choking fumes, eyes smarting as they tried to determine the way in. Aware, vaguely, of Turnbull and Young Tom rushing in to join the assault.

Seven, eight, nine, ten. Into the smoke-filled room. Nothing but murky figures in the coiling, white fog.

Shouts of panic and spluttering coughs as panting lungs were burned by the phosphorous smoke. Men falling back from the windows. The clatter as a weapon fell to the uneven flagged floor.

Movement.

"Far wall!" Ducane.

"Watch it!" Forbes.

A stutter from the Sterling. The bright wink of muzzle flashes and the sergeant's gun finds its target. A man drops in a bloody mess against the far wall.

A sudden rush as three men fall over themselves to get away from it all, through a door designed for one.

Ducane's barrel lowers and jerks involuntarily as it spits out one second's worth of low velocity parabellum rounds. The mass of men collapse.

Now the smoke is clearing.

"Loveday!" Forbes shouts in warning.

Ducane spins round.

"Fuck!" Forbes yelled. Sterling jammed.

The big, black face grinned broadly as the giant hand closed on the trigger.

Ducane saw death. There was no way his body could pivot the final three inches needed to bring his weapon to bear. Suddenly there was no option but to accept the sickening thud of exploding lead into frail human flesh. Suddenly it was pointless to resist, to go on. No contortions this time; no death defying leaps to safety. No reprieve.

Loveday's M16 thundered into action, gobbling up the magazine. A full clip of cartridges that went on and on. It filled the small building with its crescendo of noise and the wail of ricochetting shells spinning round the stone walls.

Ducane sank to the floor, deafened by the torrent of fire, his eyes blinded by the powder flashes at point-blank range.

The noise stopped. He could feel no pain, but knew that didn't necessarily mean anything. Immediately he attempted to pull the Sterling into a firing position. Without difficulty he shifted his leg to release the steel stock. Although there was a tell-tale rip in his smock, there was no sign that he'd been hit.

It had taken only a fraction of a second to bring the weapon to the ready. But even in that time he had questioned how Loveday had managed to miss him at such close range.

The answer stared him in the face.

Loveday was staring curiously at him, his eyes wide and disbelieving. He sat, his legs sprawled, with his back propped against the far wall. The blast that had disembowelled him had thrown him there. In the poor light the spreading pool of blood in which he sat looked like black varnish. In his hand the M16 rifle still smoked.

The miracle of his reprieve hit Ducane like a shockwave. His intestines seemed to knot and paralyse his nervous system. It took supreme effort to command his legs to takes his weight as he climbed to his feet.

All other firing had come to a stop. Soft moans and coughing drifted through the wreaths of gunsmoke and phosphorous.

Turnbull got to Loveday first, quickly wrenching the weapon from his grip and tossing it aside.

"Thanks, John," Ducane muttered. "I thought I'd had it."

The corporal grimaced. "Luck. He was the first one I saw."

Loveday spoke, his words sounding breathless. "Yeah, Jacko, I guess you kin thank yer guardian angel. No one deserves that kinda luck ..." He broke off into a fit of coughing. He clutched his stomach in a vain attempt to stop his guts from oozing through his fingers.

While Forbes and Young Tom moved cautiously around the building, examining each of the bodies in turn, Ducane crouched down by Loveday and examined his wound. Turnbull remained standing, his Sterling trained on the Negro and a look of disdain on his face.

"Not too good, eh?" Loveday asked.

Ducane glanced at him. "No worse'n you deserve."

The Negro gave a snort of laughter. It hurt. "Same pious prig you always were."

The captain's jaw stiffened. "Time you learned a little humility Winston. From the look of this, you've bust. Your time on this planet's running out."

A look of alarm flickered in Loveday's eyes momentarily, then he gave a resigned chuckle. "Open up dem Pearly Gates ..."

"Not where you're goin', nigger," Turnbull snarled.

Loveday frowned, as though the thought of what lay ahead of him had crossed his mind for the first time. A wave of pain crashed through him and his eyes shut. When he spoke, the power had left his voice. "Don't hang around here, Jacko ... Get back to your wife ... before ..." He winced as another bolt of pain shot through the remains of his stomach.

Ducane was puzzled. Gently he shook the other's arm. "Before *what*?"

Loveday forced his eyes open, but it was difficult to focus. "McClatcher's raving mad at you ... screwed his plans ... screwed his chance of a fortune ... Man, he's mad ...!"

"He's dead," Ducane returned coldly, but doubt suddenly started nagging at him.

The Negro's chuckle broke into a wracking cough. A trickle of blood escaped his mouth. The stench from the stomach wound was starting to become nauseous. Finally he managed to get out his words. "I hope you's right fer yer wife's sake ... he threatened t'give you a lesson you'd never ... forget." Agony contorted his face.

At that moment Forbes came into the room from searching the rest of the building, Young Tom following behind with both arms cradling a collection of weaponry.

"Hey, boss, McClatcher's not here."

"Shit," Ducane murmured under his breath. He shook Loveday roughly. "That line you were shooting about a man in England? Is it true?"

The Negro clenched his teeth. "Christ, man, I dunno ... I can't think straight ... I've got some bellyache."

Ducane gripped the man's chin in his fingers and twisted his head around to face him. "Well, you'd better start thinkin', black-boy!" he hissed. "Otherwise your last minutes on earth are goin' to be worse than *anything* you'll meet hereafter!"

More coughing, the pool of black varnish spreading wide and thick. "I tell you ... McClatcher's mad at you ... An' he ain't goin' to risk no Provos t'do the job." He forced himself to go on. "It's personal now ... I *know* him ... He'll crucify you ... one way or another ..." A slow smile grew over his face. "That Pattie is okay ... don't let that butcher get to her ..."

Turnbull said: "He can't get far, boss. All the transport's outside."

Ducane stood up slowly. "Good point. Get the Rovers covered, John."

"Right," he answered, moving towards the entrance.

Forbes said: "It's a long way back to England."

Ducane nodded. "I know, Dave, but he's got friends here; we haven't. And I can't believe he hasn't got some escape route planned ... Give this bastard a shot of morphine ..."

The sudden sound like a whipcrack was hardly discernible. Muted by the wind outside it sounded as harmless as a firecracker. But the small gathering of men knew better.

Instinctively they ducked below the level of the stone window sills as the air hummed with ricocheting shells. Turnbull, who had been approaching the doorway, on his way to check the Land Rovers, was tossed contemptuously backwards by an unseen force.

Ducane scrambled across the flagstones towards him. Outside the urgent noise of a vehicle being gunned into life smothered the sound of fire.

Forbes leapt over Turnbull's body and flew at the doorway. His Sterling crashed violently into action.

"McClatcher's making a break!" he yelled. The firing ceased abruptly as the magazine emptied.

Young Tom joined him at the entrance. Two of the Land

Rovers lay at crazy angles, the tyres ripped to shreds. Their bodywork was distorted with bullet-holes like frenzied, blackened teethmarks. The third vehicle was disappearing fast over a rise that led to the main road.

"Quick, Dave!" Ducane yelled. "Give me a hand, John's copped it."

Forbes spun round. There was a look of horror and amazement on his face. He had the idea that Turnbull had thrown himself to the ground to escape the stream of automatic fire. The thought that the indestructible 'Action Man' had been hit, had simply never occurred to him.

"Keep guard, Tom," he said hoarsely and stepped back inside the ruin.

Ducane was cradling Turnbull's shoulders in his arms, looking down at the shattered skull that was almost beyond recognition. Forbes crouched over him in disbelief. The high-velocity round had hit him directly in the left eye, gouging out a hole the size of a fist. The bullet had exited somewhere behind the ear, causing the entire cranium to fracture as though hit by an axe, so that the whole left side of his face had collapsed into an ugly pulp.

"He's still alive?" Forbes whispered.

Ducane nodded. "Get some morphine, quick, Dave. Fill him up with it."

"'That you ... boss?" The words, breathed more than spoken, seemed to emanate from deep inside the emaciated flesh. He opened an unseeing right eye, but it swivelled uncontrollably in its socket.

"Okay, John," Ducane said softly. "Dave's getting you a quick shot. Ease the pain, eh?'

"'*Should have seen it ... coming.*" Ducane gritted his teeth. Ever the perfectionist. The super-professional even now.

"You couldn't have known, John." Ducane looked down at the strange, monstrous thing in his arms. It wasn't Corporal John Turnbull. He was just going through the reflex words of comfort and consolation.

"*I can't ... see.*" The whispered words sounded frothy now. "*It's bad, isn't it?*"

Forbes unscrewed the cap of the 30mgs Min-i-jet syringe. He burst the diaphragm with the pin, squeezed the tube to expel the air, and then emptied the contents rapidly into Turnbull.

"It looks worse'n it is, old lad," Ducane lied. He was surprised how easy it was.

After a few minutes the effect hit the corporal; his body relaxed and his shattered head lolled against Ducane's chest. Slowly Ducane laid him on the flagstones using a makeshift pillow. Wearily he climbed to his feet and wiped the mess from his smock.

He exchanged glances with Forbes and shook his head.

When he spoke, Forbes' voice was thick with emotion. "I can't imagine John as a blind cripple ... disfigured like that."

Ducane looked down again at the man who had saved his own life on a number of occasions. However much that analytical mind had found fault with Ducane's plans, he had never shirked his responsibilities. And, regardless of personal risk, had made sure that he was always seen to act to the highest professional standards. If he couldn't beat the army system by rank, he had made sure that he had never been the weak link in the chain in any scheme that went wrong. Cool and critical, he had always won the personal battle with his own conscience. Until now.

Suddenly Ducane made a decision. "Dave," he said quietly. "We've got some more morphine tubes. I'm going to give him another 30mgs."

Forbes nodded soberly. "Old Johnny would have come to that conclusion three minutes ago ... He wouldn't want to be a cabbage ..."

"Shut up, Dave," Ducane snapped, suddenly angry. He didn't want to talk about his decision. The time of analysis and discussion was past. "See if you can do something for that bastard Loveday. And make it quick, we've a lot to do."

*

They buried Corporal John Turnbull on the rise overlooking the lough.

He had been stripped of all identifying clothing and papers, and the grave was left unmarked. It was that which hurt the remnants of Ducane's Sabre team most. Although Turnbull had been an intensely private man, he was above all a man who valued the pride and traditions of the young regiment. Perhaps he even took them too seriously, depriving himself of friends by setting standards that no one else could maintain. But then, Ducane reasoned, because of that he would have anticipated and understood the unmarked grave. In a regiment that maintained anonymity in action, so anonymity in death was only to be expected. And accepted.

Without the facilities for a blood transfusion, there had been little they could do for Loveday. He had died only minutes after the SAS corporal. In his last moments he had made a determined attempt to shake Ducane by the hand. A last, desperate plea for clemency? A gesture of friendship or repentance to carry him through the valley of death? It was rejected.

As darkness crept fast over the forlorn landscape, the three men had put all the usable tyres onto one of the Land Rovers and had plugged the holes in the fuel tank and radiator.

While Forbes drove out across the peninsula to recover the equipment they had left at their various temporary RVs, Ducane and Young Tom sifted through the crates of documents and equipment that had been stored in the friary ready for loading.

Although they had no time to study the piles of typewritten material they found, a cursory glance was enough to confirm that McClatcher had made plans—sometimes in draft, sometimes in detail—for a full campaign operation in the months ahead. Lists of recruits and of targets, death lists and novel ways of disrupting Ulster were found within the cardboard folders. Many were only in carbon copy form, directed to the PIRA Army Council, indicating that they had already been dispatched. Others comprised carbons and top copies. No doubt they were to be offered one by one in return for increased fees as the operations progressed satisfactorily.

Hastily the most important papers were locked in a couple of suitcases that had contained the personal effects of two members of McClatcher's private army. Ducane knew that they would be a God-send to the Int. boys. No doubt all or some of them would gradually be filtered back to the PIRA, many suitably doctored or amended, serving as jokers in the pack as the Int. boys played their deadly game of bluff and counter-bluff.

There was no time to do anything about the bodies, including the corpses of the two machine-gunners who had been decapitated by Tom Perrot's carefully-placed grenades. No one would ever know how successful the ruse had been now they had served their purpose. Ducane had guessed correctly that only once McClatcher thought all the SAS team had been eliminated, would he feel safe to recall his men. Only then the overwhelming enemy force would be together in one place. Vulnerable. It had been the only way.

A can of red paint had been found, and Ducane had ordered Forbes to scrawl NOWHERE IS SAFE FROM UDF AVENGERS. KNOW IT! on the inner wall of the friary. This, together with a few other pieces of evidence, would direct investigations neatly towards the outlawed Protestant Ulster Defence Force in Northern Ireland, an outfit the SAS were happy to keep the pressure on anyway.

All the remaining American electronic equipment was put in one cell of the friary while Forbes set a PE 808 charge.

"That's about it, Jacko," the sergeant reported. He sniffed at the smell of the plastic explosive with disdain.

It was approaching dawn before Ducane took a final look around the ruins. As far as they could tell no incriminating evidence remained. If there was anything, it was too bad. He had been pushing the nagging fear for Trish to the back of his mind. But now it kept forcing itself to the forefront of his imagination.

Forbes seemed to read his mind. "McClatcher's going to be too concerned about his own hide to wage a vendetta on you, Jacko. I'm quite sure Trish is safe. McClatcher'll be on the first plane to New York."

Ducane nodded. "I agree with you, Dave, but Loveday seemed adamant."

"Just trying to give you a final kick in the crutch before he pegged out. That's all."

The captain smiled, uncertainly. "It hurt."

Forbes put a hand to his shoulder. "Well, we're ready to clear out now, so we can both put our minds at rest." He grinned. "I'm pretty fond of your ol' lady too, you know."

Ducane laughed with a strained humour. "I get the distinct feeling my missus is too popular for her own good, Dave."

"Most guys fall instantly in love with her," the sergeant said quickly. "I guess that's a pretty precious gift. But from your point of view it must be hard to take sometimes."

Ducane bit his lip. "I wouldn't trade her . . . you know." He turned as Young Tom approached. Absently he added: "We'll head for Shannon Airport and grab the first available flight."

Tom said: "I've topped up the tank, so that's no problem. It's around eighty mile drive."

"On these roads," Ducane said, "it'll take a good two hours. And I don't know how late there'll be flights to London." He pointed at the two suitcases ready to be loaded. "I don't want to risk taking this material through Customs. So we'll go to Shannon then, Tom, you can go on alone to the British Embassy in Dublin. It'll be a long haul and, frankly, I doubt if you'll get there before midday. Insist only on speaking to the Military Attache."

Young Tom was enthusiastic. "I'll get there, boss, in no time."

Ducane nodded. "That means getting there in *one piece*, Tom. Right, now let's get going."

Putting the luggage aboard, the three men set off into the darkness towards the main road. Five minutes later a glow lit the sky briefly as the time-fuse ignited the plastic explosive packed around the electronic equipment and other incriminating evidence.

The men exchanged silent glances. Young Tom smiled to himself as it dawned on him that he'd just completed his first deep penetration mission. Forbes knew how he was feeling, but with the death of Turnbull weighing heavily on his mind, he found it difficult to share the youngster's satisfaction. Instead he shrugged matter-of-factly and settled down to study the road ahead.

Ducane, his face set in an expressionless mask, swung the Land Rover onto the main road to Shannon.

EPILOGUE

Martin McGuiness replaced the receiver and turned, grim-faced, towards the handful of PIRA Army Council members who had been hastily called to the Christmas Eve meeting in Cork. Although they didn't know the details, the young Irishman's expression left them in no doubt as to the magnitude of the disaster.

McGuiness stared down at his feet, as he tried to control the emotions of anger and frustration that threatened to choke him.

"For God's sake spit it out, Martin," snapped Gerry Adams, the twenty-eight year old barman, who had recently been promoted from a Belfast commander to the PIRA General Headquarters Staff. He had made his support of McClatcher's methods loudly known. His gaunt features looked macabre in the poorly lit room, the light glinting on the wide lenses of his spectacles to give him a blank, owl-like expression.

McGuiness cleared his throat. "That was a message from McClatcher."

"He's alive then," said Chief of Staff Seamus Twomey brightly. It was the first optimistic news snippet he had heard since the rumours had begun spreading.

"Be quiet," Billy McKee ordered softly. "Let him finish."

All eyes watched as McGuiness resumed his seat and clasped his hands carefully on the table in front of him.

"Yes," he said quietly, "McClatcher's alive. Together with about fifteen others. But they've scattered and some of them are badly cut up."

"Fifteen?" Gerry Adams gasped incredulously.

"Holy Mother!" Seamus Twomey muttered as the facts sunk in.

For once Billy McKee overlooked the profanity. It was more than understandable.

"It was a Brit hit-squad apparently, despite the fact that they've daubed UDF slogans everywhere."

"So McClatcher wasn't so damned smart," Twomey said flatly.

"For God's sake ...!" McGuiness snapped. Exasperated.

"All right, Martin," McKee said, "try and keep calm. We've had worse setbacks. Where is he now?"

"England, I gather," McGuiness replied evenly. "He's had a get-away route planned from the start—several, in fact. He took a private aircraft to England. He's got friends and can lose himself there completely—and no connection with our cells. It was safest."

"The least he could do, would be to have reported to us first," muttered Twomey.

McGuiness shook his head. "I agreed with him that England was best. If anyone was looking for him, it would be at Shannon and airports on the East Coast of the States." He smiled gently. "Besides, he said he had something to do that the SAS hit-squad wouldn't forget."

"What do you mean?" Adams demanded.

"He wasn't specific," McGuiness lied. "But I trust his judgement."

A murmur of approval went around the table. Most of them, the young Irishman mused, would have considered any move ethical in order to slake their thirst for vengeance. Only McKee's steadying influence kept the group from baying for blood like starved wolves.

Seamus Twomey shook his head slowly, his eyes seeming grotesquely large and moist behind his spectacle lenses. "I just don't believe it. Some forty-five of our best men slaughtered like pigs. Thousands of pounds of equipment lost ... and all for what!"

At the far end of the table Gerry Adams slapped a document down noisily on the beige cloth. "It was the price to be paid for this!" he said angrily, his voice thick with emotion. "And it was the price we had to pay to recognise our own stupidity. Even when we hired McClatcher, most of you didn't want to know. We needed a bloody Yank to show us how to beat the Brits."

Roughly he opened the document in front of him. "But have you even begun to read this, any of you?" he challenged, his Ulster accent deepening with his anger.

"The ideas are impractical," McKee began. "Blowing up the members of the Royal Family, MPs, hitting targets in Europe, co-operating with international terrorist organisations, it will get us no sympathy. Like the Birmingham pub bombings it'll get us no support from across the water."

"Fuck their support!" Adams snarled, ignoring McKee's obvious displeasure. "We'll blast the buggers into submission—and McClatcher knows how to do it."

"So what do you suggest?" McKee demanded. His patience was wearing thin.

Adams closed his eyes in disbelief. "*Do* what McClatcher says," he hissed. "A tight-knit cell formation. No more than four or five men per unit, and no one cell knows the other."

"But our popular support?" Twomey interjected. "What about our traditional power base in the Catholic community?"

"And what fucken support are you goin' to get at this rate? All our supporters'll be dead or interned ... Well, they won't because they'll revolt first. Already there's talk of splinter groups ...'

"Not that Irish National Liberation Army rubbish ..."

"Rubbish?" Adams demanded incredulously, as though his hearing had failed. "Is that what you think?" He shook his head in slow exasperation. "Are you really *that* in touch ...? Do you really keep your ear to the ground? God Almighty, haven't you heard the jokes about the Army Council going the rounds ..."

"There's always dissension amongst the ranks," muttered Twomey. "'Always has been. The lads always think they could do better."

"Have you ever thought they may be right?" Adams replied angrily. "A bunch of fucken monkeys could do better. And, as far as I'm concerned, this business with McClatcher's the final shame. Our younger leaders are sick to death of working for this Mickey Mouse organisation. If the INLA comes to nothin', then it'll be another offshoot ... unless the Army Council can pull its fucken socks up. You're a bunch of ol' men fightin' for a lost cause ..."

"Watch your tongue!" McKee hissed pure venom.

McGuiness smiled quietly to himself. He had been right about Adams. His controlled anger, reasoned logic and natural flair for oratory marked him out as a future leader. He shared his own convictions about the futility of their current tactics, and acceptance that they were a spent and shattered force. The difference between them was that Gerry Adams would come out into the open and say so. He was fearless of reprisals, perhaps certain that the Army Council must know in its heart and head that what he said was right.

It would take a while yet, but, eventually, McGuiness was sure, Gerry Adams would control the Army Council. Whilst he controlled the real power, the FCU.

Tension evaporated around the table as Gerry Adams moderated his voice. "I'm sure that we must restructure on the lines that McClatcher suggests. We must also recognise that we are losing our grip on many younger members. Indeed, the very objectives our younger brothers believe in."

"By feeding them with your Communist clap-trap about a Socialist Ulster?" Twomey provoked.

"It appeals to a lot of our younger fighters who want to see true social justice," Adams replied calmly. "And it's also a concept that many young Proddies sympathise with.

"You cannot divorce politics from the military option. Socialism puts fire in the bellies of the kids, our only source of recruitment nowadays. They hate capitalism as much as you hate imperialism. And it joins us in a common bond with every freedom fighter in the world today. We have powerful allies willing to give us everything we want ...

"That means we'll get all the money and equipment we so desperately need, and the biggest fucken propaganda and disinformation organisation in the world behind our cause. The new political platform will renew our power-base with deprived young Irishmen everywhere—an' allow us to forge useful links with sister organisations in Europe and the Middle East. With a renewed socialist political concept and McClatcher's military plan, we have an un-beatable combination!"

Gerry Adams' words hung in the air. The silent room seemed charged with static electricity. All eyes turned to Billy McKee.

He looked drawn and tired. Like a man who knew he had lost a fight against a terminal disease. To him it seemed that the old cause had somehow lost its direction over the years. Values had changed. Ideals too. And he knew in his heart that everything Adams had said was true. The Provisional Irish Republican Army was slipping into the hands of the Communists from its bruised young roots up to the very top branches. Nothing he or his old and trusted colleagues could do would be able to change the inevitable course of history.

When he spoke his voice was hoarse. He didn't look up as he addressed himself to McGuiness. "Martin, do you feel you are in a position to recommend a course of action to the Council?"

The answer was crisp. "Yes, sir, I do."

"Then proceed with your recommendation."

Martin McGuiness looked at the faces around the table before beginning. "I recommend that we reconvene in about four weeks time. By then Mr Adams and I will have been able to consult more fully with Colonel McClatcher. Subject to those consultations, we shall commence the re-establishment of the Forward Combat Unit under my overall control, and put a new team into training. They should then be deployed in the way recommended in McClatcher's reports to us."

"How long will all this take?" McKee asked.

McGuiness frowned. "A year. To do it thoroughly. Maybe a little longer."

"We've got McClatcher's reports," Seamus Twomey said. "Couldn't all this be done without the man?"

"I would say, it's possible. But it would be much more difficult and would take much longer. And I doubt if it would ever be so effective without his expertise."

Billy McKee grunted. "So we will have to renew his contract?"

"I would say it is absolutely *vital* if we are to be certain of success."

By the time the 737 of Aer Lingus Flight EI 144 touched down at Heathrow a tense, brooding silence had developed between the two men. They had exhausted all the possibilities of locating Malone and disarming him. The chances were that he would be waiting on a corner or, because of the declining weather, in a parked car. If his whereabouts were not immediately obvious, they would rush to the house. They would keep Trish and Sarah there until the police could be alerted to seal off the area and conduct a house-to-house search to establish that the place was no longer under surveillance.

Neither had wanted to call in the police and risk a shoot-out. There should be no chance that the gunman could get to the house and hold Trish or Sarah as hostage. Working together, they reasoned they had a better chance.

The afternoon traffic was heavy on the way back to London down the M4, and came to a virtual standstill as the taxi worked its way down through Hammersmith towards Fulham. The pavements were crowded with late Christmas shoppers, heads bowed against the bitter north-easterly wind. Neither SAS man had realised that it was actually 24th December.

Ducane pulled across the glass partition to speak to the driver. "Next one on the left."

"Okay, guv," the East Ender replied, slowing down. "Hey, looks like there's bin a motor shunt. 'Lot of coppers and rubbernecks on the corner."

Ducane and Forbes exchanged glances. The captain leaned forward for a better view of the crowd on the pavement. As the taxi slowed, a white-helmeted police motor-cyclist approached them.

The cabbie wound down his window. "What's up, mate?"

"Sorry, sir, this road's sealed off. 'Fraid there's been a shooting." He peered into the back. "'Your passengers live in this street?"

Ducane and Forbes were already on their feet.

"What house number, officer?" Ducane demanded. "Number Three?"

The policeman looked alarmed. "'You got relatives there?"

"I live there," Ducane replied impatiently. "Has anyone been hurt?"

The policeman was still suspicious. Years of experience had taught him to recognise men of violence at fifty paces. "I don't know exactly, sir. You'd best come with me and talk to the Super."

Stunned by the sudden turn of events, the cabbie sat gaping after the three men, forgetting to ask for the fare.

Half a dozen uniformed constables stood at the end of the street, surrounded by an inquisitive group of neighbours and passers-by. Outside Number Three the driver of the parked ambulance stood talking to a gathering of plain clothes detectives.

"'Scuse me, sir, these gentlemen live here."

The tallest of the detectives, a florid-faced man with a shock of thick white hair and penetrating grey eyes, looked round.

"My name's Jack Ducane. Captain in the British Army. Can you tell me what's happened?"

"Detective Superintendent Miles," the policeman introduced himself. His eyes narrowed. "Where were you last night?"

"I've just flown in from Ireland with my colleague, Sergeant Dave Forbes." His patience was running out. A feeling of nausea was twisting in his gut. "Now what the hell's happened? Are my wife and daughter all right?"

From the expression on his face, it was evident that Superintendent Miles had just eliminated the two men from his immediate list of suspects. "Your little girl is fine, Captain Ducane. But ..." he paused, always hating this moment.

Ducane and Forbes knew what was coming next.

"I'm afraid your wife, Mrs Patricia Ducane, is dead." Again a slight pause. "It appears that she's been murdered."

The knotted fist in Ducane's stomach twisted a few more turns. A sickening numbness crawled inside him, like a paralysis.

His voice sounded strangely disembodied, as though someone else was speaking the badly-scripted words. "I must see her."

"I don't think that's wise, sir ..." he began. Then he saw the look in Ducane's eyes. "Of course, if you insist ... Come with me."

As they turned, Forbes asked hoarsely: "When did it happen?"

Probably no more than twenty minutes ago now," Miles replied. "'Neighbours heard gunshots. I've only been here myself less than ten minutes."

Together they walked down the hallway towards the solemn mumble of voices coming from upstairs. Somehow it was no longer the same building they had known for so many years. The corridor was narrow and seemingly endless. In the eerie glow from a feeble 40 watt bulb it seemed sinister and claustrophobic.

Ducane was close behind Miles. "Have you got the man who did it?"

Miles mounted the stairs. "No, sir, we must have just

missed the killer. My men are questioning anyone who might have seen someone acting suspiciously. I'm sure he won't get far."

He pushed open the bedroom door. The bright blink of flashlights blinded him. The dark-suited men gathered around the bed stopped their conversation abruptly. Bland faces turned in the direction of the newcomers.

Miles coughed delicately. "Gentlemen, this is the lady's husband. He'd like to see her. We'll only be a minute."

A young detective stepped forward. "Sir, do you think it's ..."

"Just a minute, Pearson." Insistent.

In silence the group of men stepped back from the bed. Ducane swallowed hard. Trish's body lay spread in supplication on the white bedspread, her dressing-gown thrown open in frozen abandon to reveal her pale, naked body. The thick mane of curls splayed on the pillow seemed unnaturally bright.

Her eyes were open, looking glazed and questioning. Her lips were parted in a cry. A cry she probably never made, because the wire garrotte had embedded itself deep in the flesh around her throat and vocal chords. A thin trickle of blood had run down onto the bedclothes, where it had congealed in a small pool.

"Jesus," breathed Forbes.

Ducane bit his lip and nodded. Enough. Miles looked across at his men and indicated with his hand. They gathered round the bed again to continue their work.

"For God's sake, do they have to stand around gawking?"

"Sorry, Captain, they've got a job to do. They don't like it any more than you do." A sincere smile.

"Then cover her up. She's still my wife." *And my God I still love her*, he added fiercely under his breath.

His heart had begun to thud painfully and he felt faint. He breathed deeply and tried to put the mental picture of the last time they'd been together out of his mind.

He steadied himself on the door. "Was she ... was she assaulted ... you know ..?"

"Sexually? No, sir, it doesn't seem so."

"And Sarah. What about Sarah?"

"Your daughter? She didn't see anything. She was in her room." He nodded in the direction of the other door. "There's a WPC with her now, just until we found a neighbour. Or until we could locate you."

"Thank God she's okay. 'You *sure* she didn't see anything?"

Miles smiled. "No, your daughter saw nothing. She's confused and knows something's wrong, of course. I'm afraid it's your decision what to tell her."

Ducane shook his head. "Tell her that a fuckin' demented Mick strangled her mother because of her Dad's job? Christ, some decision!"

Miles' eyes narrowed. "You have an idea who did this? Something to do with your work?"

Forbes proffered a cigarette. Ducane took it thankfully. His hands were trembling as he lit it.

He said: "Yes, Superintendent, there's an Irish dimension to this. It's a reprisal killing. The sergeant and I have been on special duties."

"Oh, I see ..."

"The man you want is an Irishman called Malone. About five-seven and ten stone. He's got black hair and thick eyebrows. 'Meet in the middle."

Miles' eyes flashed. "That's more like it ..." He turned to call one of his men.

Ducane restrained the detective. "Before you launch a full-scale manhunt, you'd better contact Special Branch and get them to call my regiment in Hereford." He paused. "It may be stating the obvious, but Malone is very dangerous."

"I'll do that, Captain."

"Now I'd like to see Sarah."

Forbes put a hand on his shoulder. "'Want me to come with you, mate?"

Ducane nodded.

The WPC was embarrassed. She couldn't have been more than nineteen. She obviously didn't know what to say to either of the men or to Sarah, who looked frightened and bewildered.

"Daddy! Daddy!"

"Hello, sugar." He scooped her up in his arms.

"What's the matter, daddy?" She pouted.

"Nothing sweetheart."

"You're crying. Your eyes are wet."

Quickly Forbes stepped forward and tousled her hair. "How's my little girlfriend, then?"

The WPC looked on, ill at ease.

Despite Forbes' grin, Sarah knew something was wrong. She frowned. "Where's mummy?"

The smile fell from Forbes' face.

Ducane said hoarsely: "Mummy's had an accident. She's going away for a while." He looked at Forbes as though to ask if he was saying the right thing. The big man shrugged helplessly.

"For long?" Sarah asked.

He bit his lip. "Yes, darling, for a long time."

The WPC stepped forward. Her eyes were wide, bright and moist, he noticed. It wasn't easy for her.

"Look, sir, do you have a neighbour or relative we can take Sarah to for tonight?" She hesitated. "You might find it easier on your own. I mean, to sort things out."

Ducane forced a smile. He looked down at Sarah, "How'd you like to stay with Auntie Rena, sweetheart?"

Sarah's eyes lit up. "Now? Will mummy come?"

Ducane nearly choked.

"Later, baby, later," Forbes said quickly. "Okay?"

Sarah nodded vigorously.

"You'll find Rena's number on the list by the telephone downstairs. It's Chiswick."

The WPC smiled sheepishly and took Sarah gently from him.

Ducane said: "The sooner you get her out of here the better. And break it to Rena gently. Just say an accident. I'll contact her later today."

The door closed leaving the two men together.

Forbes moved over to the window and lifted the net

curtain. There was not much daylight left, but enough to see the rows of tiny, pocket handkerchief gardens backing onto one another, and the houses opposite. There were some lights on already.

Apart from one old boy tending his winter cabbages, there was no one about. It was bleak and bare, the patchwork of worn grass and vegetable plots unbroken except for the shed at the bottom of the garden opposite. The door swung gently in the wind. Immediately below, two uniformed policemen talked together in Ducane's garden.

At last Forbes spoke. "I'm sorry, Jacko. I loved her too, y'know."

Ducane lit another cigarette. "I know, Dave. She's ... she was ..." His voice cracked.

"Fantastic?"

Ducane nodded. "I just can't ... can't believe it."

The sergeant rubbed his nose roughly on his sleeve.

Suddenly the door opened. It was Miles.

"I'm sorry to disturb you both." His voice was excited. "My officers have just found someone. Upstairs in the attic room. He's been shot. If it's not that man Malone, there's the damnedest likeness to your description."

Ducane and Forbes exchanged puzzled glances.

As they started to the door, Ducane asked, "Has someone contacted Hereford?"

"Yes," Miles replied, leading the way up to the second floor, "they're sending someone down by chopper to Battersea Heliport. A Major Harper."

"Good ol' boyo," Forbes said, pleased to hear some good news.

Miles opened the door of the spare bedroom that led to the attic cupboard under the eaves.

Malone was lying on the floor, propped up against the foot of the bed. An ambulance man knelt by his side preparing a morphine jab, helped by a young, uniformed constable.

The Irishman didn't look too well. In fact Ducane and Forbes had seen enough dying men to know that his time could be measured in minutes. There were two holes in his chest the size of a fist.

Miles said quietly: "He can't be moved. The medics are going to bring up equipment, but it's a lost cause, I'm afraid. The question is who shot *him*?"

Forbes said: "Not Trish, that's for sure."

"Someone strong enough to drag him up here and stuff him in the cupboard," Miles said.

"But not Trish's body?" Forbes turned to Ducane apologetically. "Sorry, Jacko."

The captain ignored him. "Perhaps he was interrupted ..."

Miles said: "He's been trying to tell me something, but I can't make head nor tail of it. I thought you might understand as you know what this is about."

"The medic?" Forbes asked.

Miles shook his head. "He doesn't mind. He knows there's nothing we can do. He should be dead now by rights."

Ducane and Forbes knelt down beside him.

"Malone?" The captain's voice was sharp.

Slowly, painfully slowly against the light, the Irishman cranked open one eye. He was having difficulty in focusing.

"'That you, Ducane?" His words were little more than heavy breathing.

"Yes, it's me. What's been going on?"

"Your wife." He tried to speak louder, but it just caused a burbling sound in his chest. "You know ... about your wife?"

"I know."

"I'm sorry ... God, believe me ... I'm sorry."

Ducane frowned. "What the hell d'you mean?"

"I did my best, mate ... My best ... But McClatcher is good." He coughed suddenly, a trickle of blood escaping from the corner of his mouth.

"McClatcher?"

Malone nodded. "He killed her ... your wife. I reckon I was goin' to be next ... Witness ... Anyone who knew him ... and ... revenge ... God, he hates you ..."

Ducane was stunned. Forbes shook his head in disbelief.

Malone's voice was fading. "I tried to ... to stop him ..."

"Why should you?" Forbes was puzzled.

The Irishman's lips twisted into a wry smile. "I reasoned my cover had to stop ... somewhere. I already had to kill Harrington ..."

"You did?" Forbes couldn't grasp what was being said.

"... That was bad enough ... I couldn't do anything else ... he was talking ... Blown everything for nothing ..."

"Blown what?" Ducane demanded.

But Malone didn't seem to hear. "I had to watch what they did ... to that McGuire girl ... Innocent ... just a child ... So I couldn't let your wife die ... I was so surprised when McClatcher turned up ... A private plane from Shannon ..."

"And we assumed he'd hightail to America," Ducane recalled, angry at his own stupidity.

"He guessed we'd have him buttoned up in New York by the time he arrived," Forbes suggested.

Malone's eyes were closing. Ducane shook him vigorously; it was only a matter of minutes. "Are you saying that McClatcher got the drop on you?"

No answer.

"Tell me!" Ducane hissed fiercely in his ear. "What you're saying doesn't make sense!"

Suddenly Malone's eyes opened wide. With effort he said: "Christopher Robin."

His body stiffened and began to topple slowly towards the ambulance man. His eyes stared blankly ahead.

Ducane and Forbes looked at one another and climbed to their feet.

The Superintendent seemed impatient. "Well, did it make any sense to you?"

Ducane said slowly, "I find it hard to believe, but he just mentioned Christopher Robin."

Miles looked blank.

Forbes said: "It's the codename for one of our men

who'd supposedly infiltrated the Provos at the top."

Ducane looked down at the dead man. "Looks like he succeeded."

"And tried to save your wife," Miles murmured. He sniffed heavily. Life was getting too complex. "Let's get downstairs and see what we can sort out."

Ducane followed the detective through the door. Forbes glanced down at the ambulance man as he prepared a stretcher. He started to follow the others, then stopped.

Slowly he walked across to the window and peered down at the back gardens. The light was fading fast now under the leaden sky, but he could still see the outline of the fences and the garden shed opposite.

He reasoned that McClatcher had been interrupted after the sound of gunfire had caused an inquisitive neighbour to raise the alarm. And the police had called before the American could dispose of Trish's body. Panic. Controlled perhaps, but panic nevertheless.

Forbes' eyes narrowed. Out of the back door into the garden. Overlooked on all sides. No cover and an old boy pottering.

In the garden opposite, the shed door still hung open.

Slowly Forbes' hand reached down to his ankle. His fingers closed firmly around the haft of the fighting knife.

This he would do alone. For Trish.

Night would soon bring the cover that McClatcher was waiting for. But he would never see daylight again.